"I am going to show you what a gentleman expects of his affianced bride," announced Shannon, whose patience was at an end. He drew Jynx closer and kissed her most thoroughly, during which process he so forgot his sworn restraint as to dishevel her considerably. "Will you now berate me and demand apology?"

It came to his notice that Jynx's shoulders were shaking in the most odd fashion, and that she was biting her lower lip. "Good God, Jynx, I'm sorry! There's no need to cry about it!"

But Miss Lennox was not weeping; Miss Lennox was in the midst of a fit of hysterical merriment....

LADY BLISS

MAGGIE MACKEEVER

FAWCETT CREST • NEW YORK

"*Marry* you?" Had Viscount Roxbury not been so excellent a horseman, he would have lost his seat. "Good God, Jynx!"

"Don't refuse me, Shannon!" his companion protested quickly. "At least not before you've listened to what I have to say! Consider it from the practical point of view—unless your affections have become fixed elsewhere?"

Lord Roxbury gazed down upon her with a fascinated expression, and admitted himself heart-whole.

"Excellent!" said Jynx, and edged her mount closer. No easy matter, this arrangement of matters matrimonial whilst riding on horseback in Hyde Park. "Or—the idea is not repugnant to your feelings, Shannon? I am shockingly forward, I suppose. But you won't mind that!"

The viscount did not. The viscount explained that, having known his companion for the past twenty-two years, which constituted the grand total of her time on this mortal sphere, he didn't find her brashness the least off-putting. Nor was he prey to any revulsion of feeling, though he did admit to considerable surprise. He begged that she continue.

"Well, as long as you haven't taken me in dislike!" Jynx nodded to Lady Jersey, and bowed to the Princess Lieven. "They say that one may meet the large portion of one's acquaintance in Hyde Park at this fashionable hour, which is why I do not make a point of appearing here at this time of day. It is such dull stuff! Since I've gone to all the trouble of putting on this ridiculous habit, the least I might be allowed is a gallop! But no, we must dawdle along at this tedious pace."

Lord Roxbury cast a practiced eye over his companion's severely cut habit, molded to her figure—and though there were many who claimed that Jynx was plain, none could deny that her figure was nothing short of remarkable—and came to rest with some bemusement upon the curled ostrich plume that adorned her small hat. He opened his mouth.

"I know!" sighed Jynx. "One does not gallop in the park. To do so would be the utmost impropriety. Nor does one share a residence with my Aunt Eulalia without being *very* well versed in propriety." She took a deep breath. "To say the truth, Shannon, my Aunt Eulalia is one of the reasons that I have decided to broach this matter to you."

The viscount elevated his appreciative gaze from his companion's lush figure to her piquant face. She was looking most uncharacteristically glum. "That old prattle-box!" he remarked inelegantly. "What's she said to you now?"

"It's not what she *says*." Jynx wrinkled her nose. "Although she claims I've frittered away my chances, and that I puff up my own consequence, and—oh! all sorts of similar things. Eulalia cannot like my die-away airs."

"Fustian!" interrupted the viscount, rather violently.

"So it is!" agreed Jynx. "I do not take her seriously. But Aunt Eulalia seems determined to cut up my peace. And she dislikes what she calls my 'unbecoming levity.' I tell you, Shannon, I am quite worn to the bone. So I have decided that I must contract a marriage. Eulalia will not be able to pester me once I have settled in matrimony. And if she tries to do so, I shall deny her entrance to my home!"

"That's all well and good," interrupted the viscount, who was long familiar with his companion's unique methods of reasoning, "but why choose *me?* It's not as if you had a dearth of suitors, Jynx! At last count, you'd rejected two baronets, three earls, and a royal duke, and you'd left a marquess waiting at the altar. I never did understand *that!*"

"He was a great deal too ardent," Jynx replied simply. "The man positively exhausted me. And I didn't leave him at the altar, precisely. I withdrew from our engagement with the utmost propriety."

On Lord Roxbury's handsome face—and Lord Roxbury was uncommonly handsome, being blessed with reddish gold curls, green eyes, and features of an ascetic yet sensual cast— was an expression of the utmost fascination. "You would not expect ardor from me, then?"

"Certainly not!" Jynx looked horrified. "I do not expect to marry for love. I consider a reciprocation of passion both absurd and tiresome. I have decided that the best marriage is one based on mutual esteem. Certainly we esteem one another, Shannon! I even admit to a certain affection for you."

"You honor me!" murmured Lord Roxbury when she paused for breath.

"Pshaw!" Jynx said rudely. "You are a gentleman who possesses not one known vice, who has never been heard to utter a licentious word; I am a lady whose conduct has ever been irreproachable."

"What a pair of dull dogs we sound," interrupted the viscount. "I feel obliged to point out that my greatest virtue is discretion, and that your exemplary conduct is due to nothing more worthy than an innate laziness. In short, my poppet, dissipation would require of you too much energy."

Jynx acknowledged the truth of this frank observation with a rueful and dimpled grin. "You own large properties in Hertfordshire, Suffolk, Berkshire and Norfolk, and are heir apparent to a great duchy and its vast estates beside; I am heiress to the vast Lennox fortune. You are society's spoilt darling; I am very much à *la mode*." She shrugged. "There you have it! A match that is in every way unexceptionable."

"And since I do not love you," observed the shrewd Lord Roxbury, "I will not enact you any tiresome emotional scenes. Still, you haven't convinced me why *I* should be eager to marry."

"I shouldn't have to! First of all, you need to get an heir." Jynx's tone was severe. "The rest should be apparent even to you." The viscount's bewildered expression indicated, however, that it was not. "I will be blunt! You are the most eligible bachelor in all of London, the natural cynosure of all women's eyes. Matchmaking mamas set traps for you; young ladies expire at your feet. It must all be very wearisome! Too, you stand in grave danger of gaining an exaggerated opinion of your own importance."

"I had not thought of the matter in that light." The viscount appeared to be gravely stricken. "Clearly, it is incumbent upon me to wed."

"I've taken you by surprise," Jynx said kindly. "You will wish to consider the matter." Generously allowing him an opportunity to do so, she urged her horse forward and paused to talk to this and that dignitary.

Hyde Park was thick with superbly mounted gentlemen, and ladies in elegantly appointed carriages, as well as a large representation of the Fashionably Impure. One did not move quickly through such a crush; one certainly did not proceed with any anonymity. Already Miss Jessamyn Lennox's prolonged conversation with Lord Roxbury had been noted, and commented upon; it had long been thought odd that Lord Roxbury, who might have been on the most intimate terms with any young lady—or for that matter any lady aged anywhere between the cradle and the grave—should enjoy such camaraderie with the phlegmatic Jessamyn. Miss Lennox was no *belle idéale*, for all her vast wealth; she lacked animation; she was of a disposition that her many friends called *fainéante*, and her enemies stolid.

Yet Jessamyn had not exaggerated when she claimed she was *à la mode*. Her debut had caused her Aunt Eulalia a hideous embarrassment, and Viscount Roxbury exquisite glee: when presented with gratifying attentions, Miss Lennox had reacted in an apathetic manner that left no doubt of rapidly approaching ennui; when offered profuse compliments, she had smiled and yawned. Only on such unsuitable topics as the shocking living conditions of the lower classes, and the even more shocking topic of emancipation for females, could Miss Lennox be roused to enthusiasm, and she had not been the least reluctant to make *those* opinions known. Eulalia had evidenced on several occasions a wish to sink through the floor; she had expressed, even more frequently, a conviction that Jessamyn would be pronounced a vulgarly outspoken bluestocking, and thereafter shunned.

Despite her aunt's dire prophecies, Jessamyn had not been branded an outcast, a fact amply attested to by her leisurely progress through the park—and a fact, suspected Lord Roxbury, that caused the detestable Eulalia considerable chagrin. Ladies called out to Jynx, gentlemen saluted her, and the regent himself was seen to pinch her cheek. Jynx was greatly sought after by fashionable hostesses who trusted the languorous Miss Lennox to enliven with her lazy and irreverent remarks *fêtes* and *soirées* that promised to be flat; and Jynx had yet to disappoint any one of them.

Shannon followed, indifferent to the furor that accompanied his own progress; Shannon's progress had been accompanied by great tumult since the day he was breeched. "Too, our interests march together," Jynx remarked, as he came up alongside of her. "Did I not accompany you to view the factories in Manchester, and the exhibition of the steam locomotives in Tyneside, even the atrocious trial last year of Leigh Hunt? Poor man! But he should have known better than to traduce Prinny. Ours would be a *mariage de convenance*, but I think we might deal well together. After all, we always have!"

Lord Roxbury did not point out that there was a vast difference between friendship and marriage; instead, he studied Miss Lennox. Even a lifelong acquaintance who possessed a great fondness for Jynx could not call her a beauty, or claim that she would ever be one. Her hazel eyes were much too large for the rest of her face, as was her mouth, on either side of which a dimple danced each time she smiled, which was frequent. Additionally, she possessed the Lennox nose in all its long and haughty arrogance, a forceful chin, and strongly marked brows. These latter attributes, in combination with her slumbrous eyes and generous mouth and masses of chestnut curls—which were worn habitually in an untidy chignon because their owner professed herself incapable of expending the effort to dress them properly—gave an effect both contradictory and whimsical. Then, mused the viscount, there was the rest of Jynx. But the sleepy eyes were, currently, fixed on his face.

"Too," she said, "you are used to having women throw themselves at you. The ladies fawn and the gentlemen are jealous. Poor Shannon! If you do not take care, you will earn a reputation as a philanderer—unjustified, naturally."

"Naturally," agreed the viscount, who was perfectly aware, as many people were not, that beneath his companion's placid exterior lay an extremely strong will. In some inexplicable manner, and with every outward evidence of complaisance, Junx invariably succeeded in doing precisely as she pleased. "You honor me, poppet."

"Ah! Next you will tell me you're very much obliged." Gloomily, Jynx surveyed her friend, who was looking even more peerless than usual in a riding coat of green superfine, an exquisite waistcoat, leather breeches, and a pristine cravat. In fact, she decided, Lord Roxbury was, from his high-crowned hat to his gleaming top-boots, the epitome of manly pulchritude. "It is no more than I expected, I'll admit, that you should shatter my hopes. I suppose you don't wish to be tied up."

"Did I say so?" Lord Roxbury coolly acknowledged the presence of a lady who had been for some time trying to gain his attention. She wriggled her fingers at him and colored most becomingly. "Indeed, I have had a similar proposal in mind."

"But you did not plan to make it to me, I'll wager!" Jynx remarked shrewdly, regarding the simpering lady with some curiosity. The lady returned her interest with a look of keen dislike. "It occurs to me that your friendship has made me a great many enemies! I don't regard it, of course, any more than I regard the fact that, in the matter of looks, you cast me quite into the shade. You're a trifle too serious, and I'm a trifle too apathetic—but there! Obviously it won't answer the purpose, and I shall say no more of it!" She chuckled. "Still, I'll warrant you'll remember this day, for it can't be in the ordinary way for ladies to make you offers whilst riding in the park!"

"Not more than once a week," agreed Lord Roxbury.

"Coxcomb!" said Miss Lennox, appreciatively. And then she saw a young lady waving rather frantically, not at the handsome viscount, but at her. "The deuce!" she ejaculated, and touched her heel to her horse's flank. "Cristin!"

Lord Roxbury was rather astonished by her abrupt departure; young ladies, in Lord Roxbury's experience, were far more likely to attach themselves like limpets to his side. He gazed upon the phaeton toward which Miss Lennox advanced, with her usual serene forthrightness. In that phaeton sat a blondhaired and blue-eyed damsel, with a fetching little elf-shaped face; and beside her was an older woman, of thirty-five, with black hair and lovely clear skin. Accompanying the phaeton was a dark-haired gentleman.

"The devil!" muttered Lord Roxbury, and in his turn set forth. His progress was a great deal less leisurely than that of Miss Lennox; it caused various pedestrians to scramble hastily for safety, and horses to take umbrage, and every person within earshot to breathlessly await the explosion that, judging by Lord Roxbury's irate expression, was soon to come.

Miss Lennox, happily unaware of the pursuit, smiled upon the young lady who had so violently beckoned her. "Cristin!" she said. "How nice to see you again! It has been a long time, has it not, since Mrs. Maybury's Academy?"

"Oh, it has!" breathed Cristin, in her pretty way. "How happy I am to have come upon you, Jynx! I have particularly wished to speak with you. But I must introduce you to my uncle and my aunt!"

"You must not, I think," said Lord Roxbury, who at that moment had caught up with his quarry and halted her progress by the simple expedient of grasping her reins. Jynx stared at him in astonishment. "Miss Lennox is engaged elsewhere." Without heed of Cristin's cry of distress, or the dark-haired lady's obvious indignation, or their companion's even more apparent amusement, he led Miss Lennox away.

"Heavens, Shannon!" said Jynx, who was possessed of a considerable fund of good humor and good nature. "What prompted that?" It was not an unreasonable query; Lord Roxbury was admittedly disdainful and superior, but she had never before known him to be deliberately rude.

"*That*," retorted Shannon, in the grip of strong emotion, "was none other than Adorée Blissington, and her rakehell brother, and I do not intend to have your acquaintance with them on *my* conscience. Believe me, Jynx, they are not at all the thing."

"Lady Bliss?" echoed Miss Lennox, craning her head to look back at the phaeton. An altercation appeared to be in progress: the black-haired lady was expostulating at some length to the gentleman, and the young lady appeared to be on the verge of tears.

"None other." Lord Roxbury attempted to regain his composure, a feat that was in no way aided by his companion's unladylike posture, which displayed to extremely effective advantage the perfect fit of her riding habit. "Do stop gawking, Jynx!"

Even this crude stricture she accepted with equanimity. "I wonder what Cristin does with them," she murmured, twisting her head from atop her shoulder to look thoughtfully at Shannon. "We were at school together, and Cristin is a good sort of girl. As silly as she is lovely, of course, but unexceptionable—if, that is, any Ashley can be considered unexceptionable, with their twin vices of gaming and improvidence." She looked wistful. "I might have found out, if you had not interfered."

"Interfered!" All things considered, Lord Roxbury was having a most trying afternoon. "I fancy the chit is the daughter of the oldest Ashley brother, who ran up a staggering number of debts and then—in true Ashley tradition—sat down and shot himself. We will speak no more of it, if you please! As much as mention Lady Bliss to your aunt, and Eulalia will demand my head on a platter. And so she should!"

"In a pig's whisker." Miss Lennox wore an unusual expression of intent and abstracted meditation. "Since when are *you* afraid of Aunt Eulalia?"

Never before had Lord Roxbury seen that look on his companion's tranquil face, and he did not care for it. "I'm not," he said brusquely. "But in this case Eulalia would have the right of it." Jynx shot him a glance that was almost quarrelsome. "Too," he added, in softer tones, "I would not care to have my wife associate with a lady who is a great deal less prudent than she should be."

Even Miss Lennox's legendary pose was not proof against this sally. Her sleepy eyes opened wide; her placidity was replaced by a look of sheer astonishment. "Your *what?*" said she.

"You expressed a wish to gallop," countered Lord Roxbury, uncomfortably aware of the speculative gazes that were fixed on them. "Since we have already disgraced ourselves, we might as well treat our audience to an exciting finale." And, he added silently, divert that audience's attention from the shocking fact that his dear friend Miss Lennox had come disastrously close to making the acquaintance of his current flirt.

"There may be hope for you yet, Shannon!" remarked Miss Lennox, rather enigmatically, and gathered up her reins.

Gallop they did, to the startled consternation of all who witnessed this reckless feat, and the *on-dits* flew after them like a swarm of angry bees. Some claimed that Lord Roxbury was responsible for the scandalous act, for it was well known that Miss Lennox was not one to willingly bestir herself to any arduous exercise; others averred that Miss Lennox herself had been the instigator, but declared that Lord Roxbury was at fault, for he had clearly ripped up at her, and his thundercloud demeanor had been sufficient to rouse the most somnolent of young ladies to flight. On one point only did all agree, that the pair had patently taken leave of their senses.

If so, the miscreants had derived great enjoyment from their temporary insanity. Lord Roxbury drew rein, and led Miss Lennox into a leafy copse. She adjusted her hat, which had slid so far forward that the ostrich plume tickled her nose, and regarded him. Lord Roxbury gazed upon her flushed countenance and heaving breast and smiled.

"If you meant to distract me," remarked Miss Lennox, who had long professed herself immune to the most glorious of masculine smiles, another attribute which Lord Roxbury undoubtedly possessed, "it did not serve."

"You did not enjoy your gallop?" interrupted the viscount, as he placed his hands around her little waist and helped her to dismount. "I made sure you would."

"It was glorious." Jynx did not remark upon the fact that his hands still grasped her waist. "Aunt Eulalia will have recourse to her vinaigrette when she learns of it. I wish that she might have a spasm."

"You need not," offered Lord Roxbury, noting the delightful way in which her lovely hair escaped from beneath her hat, "give further consideration to your Aunt Eulalia."

"Oh?" Jynx raised her sleepy eyes to his face. "Shannon, you can't *truly* wish to marry me?"

"That's a damned silly question," retorted the viscount, roughly. He had just, upon such close inspection, been visited by a sudden suspicion that though Miss Lennox might be no great beauty, she was possibly a great deal more. "I shall marry you with the greatest pleasure on earth, poppet."

"Oh," said Miss Lennox, rather doubtfully.

Barely in the nick of time, Lord Roxbury recalled the fate of a former suitor who had courted this young lady too ardently, and released her hastily. "As you so concisely pointed out, we may expect to rub along together very comfortably."

"So I did," Jynx uttered serenely. "I suppose I exhibited a shocking lack of conduct. Aunt Eulalia is forever saying that I have no delicacy of feeling. You will be accustomed to ladies who are a great deal more skilled in the casting out of lures."

"True." The viscount thought of the notorious Lady Bliss. "You may have noted that I didn't offer any of *them* marriage. What's this, poppet? Have you already repented of your choice? If you mean to cry off, do it now. *I* don't mean to be left waiting at the altar!" He squelched an impulse to sweep his newly acquired fiancée summarily into a passionate embrace. "Have you decided that we *shouldn't* be comfortable?"

"Not at all," protested Jynx, with every evidence of sincerity. "I have no wish to cry off. Nor would I leave *you* at the altar, Shannon! It would be a very shabby way in which to treat a friend."

Lord Roxbury was greatly moved by this declaration, but he contented himself with dropping a chaste salute on the tip of the haughty Lennox nose. "Then the next thing is for me to speak to Sir Malcolm," he said cheerfully. "I suppose he'll consider my suit."

"I know he will." Miss Lennox toyed idly with her riding whip. "Papa professed himself very agreeable when I broached the matter to him."

"He did?" There was a distinctly abstracted expression in Lord Roxbury's green eyes. "*You* did?"

"Naturally." Jynx was intent on her own train of thought. "You don't think I'd marry without papa's consent? Tell me, Shannon, *why* did you decide to marry me?"

"There is," the viscount pointed out, apologetically and with no little curiosity, "the matter of an heir."

"Ah!" To complete his bewitchment, she blushed. "There is one more matter that remains to be discussed."

Thus ended his hopes. No reason, now, to wonder how he was to arouse warmer affections in a young lady who had professed herself so adverse to romance. "Do you know, poppet," Lord Roxbury remarked ruefully, "I rather thought that there might be?"

Miss Lennox grimaced, flicked her riding crop against her booted leg, then raised her lazy eyes once more to the viscount's handsome face. "Dear, *dear* Shannon," she murmured. "I trust you will not insist on tight-lacing?"

"Tight-lacing?" echoed the befuddled viscount.

"Corsets," explained Miss Lennox, succinctly. "I abhor the things."

Chapter Two

Having been assured by Lord Roxbury—after he had recovered from the paroxysms of mirth into which her remarks had cast him—that he hadn't the least objection if his viscountess looked a great deal more like an opera dancer than a female of frail fragility, Miss Lennox was able to greet the following day with her usual aplomb.

It was ten o'clock of a Wednesday morn, and the Lennox family was assembled in the dining room of their grand old Jacobean house in London's Lennox Square. Three people were seated around the Grecian table of semicircular design, its supports ornamented with lion masks and rings: Sir Malcolm Lennox, who owned this munificence and a great deal more besides; Sir Malcolm's sister-in-law, Eulalia Wimple, who had taken over household matters upon the death of his wife, five years previous; and Sir Malcolm's sole offspring, and heiress to all he owned, Jessamyn. Of the three, Jynx alone appeared to enjoy her meal. But then, Jynx had the rare ability to enjoy herself even in the midst of a dreadful storm.

And a storm was in truth raging, as it did every morning in the Lennox household. This day's turbulence was of such awesome proportions that Sir Malcolm had taken refuge behind that morning's edition of the *Times*. Jynx regarded him with some amusement, spread a lavish amount of marmalade on a muffin, and then turned her attention to her aunt.

Eulalia was a tall and stately woman, in her fifth decade, a *très grande dame* with elegantly coiffed—if improbably colored—yellow hair, sharp black eyes, and an air of perpetual discontent. Currently, her features were screwed up in an expression of the utmost disapproval, and the black eyes were fixed relentlessly on her niece. "Well, miss?" she snapped. "What have you to say for yourself? Galloping in Hyde Park! Never have I heard of such a thing."

Obviously Eulalia *had* heard of it, in grand and glorious detail, but Jynx was so amiable a young lady that she did not point out this fact. Actually, so amiable was Jynx that she had never in all her twenty-two years been known to utter a cross word. Nor did she do so now, but gazed serenely on her aunt. " 'Tis naught but a tempest in a teapot, Eulalia. I wished to gallop, and Shannon obliged me." She bit into her muffin, then licked marmalade from her fingers in a very vulgar way.

"Roxbury," offered Sir Malcolm, from behind the *Times*. Had Sidney Smith ever been privileged to break his fast in Lennox Square, he would have described hell not as an eternity of family dinners, but as a Lennox *petit déjeuner*. "Well, Jynx?"

"Well indeed, Papa." Jynx surveyed the array of cold meats, game, broiled fish, sausages, eggs, kidneys and bacon, and helped herself to generous portions of each. "By-the-bye, what do you know of Adorée Blissington?"

This innocent query, which had been prompted merely by a vague curiosity about why Lady Blissington's presence in the park should have inspired Lord Roxbury to such desperate diversionary measures as a frantic flight, brought Sir Malcolm out from behind his newspaper. His daughter raised a weary eyebrow, and his sister-in-law erupted into scandalized observations on the young lady's shocking want of delicacy.

"Oh, do hush, Eulalia!" said Sir Malcolm, rather irritably. Eulalia, who owed her position in the Lennox household entirely to Sir Malcolm's forebearance, did so. A pretty pair were Sir Malcolm and his daughter, she thought in disgruntlement, both lazy as the day was long, with no awareness of their consequence, and a reprehensible tendency to find humor in the most unsuitable things. They even resembled one another, Eulalia decided, as she stared at the provoking duo. Sir Malcolm's hair had long ago turned white, but he as well as his daughter possessed the large hazel Lennox eyes, the arrogant nose and forceful chin.

"Lady Bliss," repeated Sir Malcolm, having determined from his daughter's ingenuous expression that she was unaware of the lady's association with Viscount Roxbury, and of his own futile pursuit. "She's a charming scatterbrain who lives by her wits, which are not considerable, and the nonexistent proceeds of the discreet card parties she holds nightly

16

in her home. Entrance by invitation only—you know the sort of thing."

"Illegal, ain't it?" interrupted Eulalia. "Arrest the jade!"

Sir Malcolm looked pained. Certainly he was a man of the law, a magistrate; equally certainly it was no part of his many duties to imprison a lady to whose favor he had once aspired. "Adorée Blissington is a widow," he continued, rather hastily. "Her husband, a scapegrace baronet, was killed in a duel over a lady's honor—not hers. He left his widow penniless."

"I saw her yesterday in the park," Jynx remarked, around a mouthful of eggs. "There was a dark-haired gentleman with her. He may have been a relative, from the resemblance."

"Innis Ashley." Sir Malcolm's reply was prompt, and delivered in tones of the utmost distaste. "The youngest Ashley. Adorée's brother. A thoroughly bad lot."

"I thought he might be." Miss Lennox speared a sausage. "One more question, Papa, and you may return to your newspaper. Why is she called Lady Bliss, rather than Blissington?"

Sir Malcolm surveyed his inexcitable daughter, and his all-too-volatile sister-in-law, and grinned. A close observer might have noted that Sir Malcolm also shared with Jessamyn the Lennox dimples. "Because, m'dear, the lady is intoxicating. Bliss is supposedly the state achieved by her admirers, who by this time have reached awesome numbers—or so rumor has it."

"Rumor, Papa?" Jynx's sleepy eyes were fixed on her sire's face.

"Magistrates," replied Sir Malcolm, with a profound vagueness, "learn all sorts of things."

"I'll warrant!" retorted the impenitent Miss Lennox.

"Jessamyn!" Eulalia was patently scandalized. "This conversation is not at all the thing! How can you speak so to your father, you unnatural girl? You should not even admit the existence of such creatures as Adorée Blissington. I am thoroughly shocked that Lord Roxbury pointed her out to you—for so he must have done, since you were with him in the park, and if he had *not* pointed her out, you wouldn't have known who she was! I shall have several words to say to him on this matter, you may be sure!"

"Poor Shannon," remarked Jynx, rather ambiguously. "He told me she was not at all the thing." She turned once more to her father. "Shannon has engaged himself to speak to you this morning, Papa."

"Very proper." Sir Malcolm cast a keen glance at his lethargic offspring.

"Yes, isn't it? I told him it wasn't necessary, but Shannon is a great one for the *form* of things." Replete, Jynx dropped her fork and leaned back in her chair. "He said that since I've persuaded him to take the fateful step, he means to see that it's executed properly. Which I will admit is generous of him."

Eulalia was not attending wholeheartedly to these remarks, but pondering the uncooperative attitude of her deceased sister's family. Eulalia had done the best she could for the Lennoxes, had attempted to divert Sir Malcolm from his pursuit of matters legal to an appreciation of his social position, had tried to instill in the unenthusiastic Jessamyn an allegiance to ladylike behavior. Her efforts, unfortunately, had been only partially successful. Though Sir Malcolm refused to neglect his magisterial duties, he had taken time to ensure that his daughter stood in highest favor with the *ton*; and though Jynx was in all appearances—save for her *most* regrettable figure—ladylike, and behaved always—or almost always—with decorous affability, she was utterly and unalterably unfashionable.

Eulalia stared at that young lady, who was dressed in a morning dress of white French lawn. The gown itself was unexceptionable, as Eulalia well knew, having herself selected it. However, Jynx's indecent proportions transformed even the primmest gown into something suitable only for a demirep. Furthermore, the girl hadn't bothered to do anything at all with her hair, so it was tumbling down her back in a most hoydenish way. Clearly, Eulalia's efforts had been futile, and unappreciated beside. It was scant wonder that she could think of nothing but the wrongs done her by the insouciant Lennoxes.

Sir Malcolm and his daughter had taken advantage of Eulalia's abstraction to pursue their conversation. "Good girl!" Sir Malcolm uttered then. "I knew you'd take the field."

"Did you, Papa?" Miss Lennox looked wry. "I confess I haven't your faith in my persuasive abilities."

"What's this?" inquired Eulalia, brought back to the present by a conviction that if Sir Malcolm approved of his daughter's conduct in some instance, Eulalia herself was certain to disagree. "Just who have you persuaded to do what?"

"Shannon." Jynx was of too kindly a nature to allow

18

anyone to suffer needless confusion. "I made him an offer, and he accepted me."

"You did *what?*" shrieked Eulalia, so shrilly that the chocolate cups rattled in their saucers. "I cannot credit it! How *could* you behave so brazenly? But I see, this is merely another of your tasteless jests. At least, Jessamyn, you might be serious on the subject of your marriage!"

Jessamyn squelched an ignoble impulse to remark that, on the subject of marriage, her aunt possessed sufficient seriousness for ten. Eulalia was forever pointing out dire examples of young ladies who had succumbed to the blandishments of polished gentlemen, only to discover too late that their adoring bridegrooms were the greatest beasts in nature—if not worse. "You misunderstand," Jynx said calmly. "I am perfectly serious about marrying Shannon. We shall suit each other very well."

Eulalia was stricken dumb with horror. She might not understand her niece's popularity with the gentlemen—as evidenced by two baronets, three earls, a royal duke and an unhappy marquess—but she had taken steps to counter it. Eulalia had warned her niece at great length against fortune hunters, had stressed that it was not Jynx herself but the Lennox wealth which held great allure, and for good measure had waxed graphic about the horrors of the marriage bed. It had been with great satisfaction that she'd seen Jynx treat her suitors in a most cavalier manner, had heard Jynx express herself fatigued by persistent avowals of devotion. "The deuce!" Eulalia ejaculated, recovering her powers of speech. "I hope you may not have to repent of your choice, my girl! Lord Roxbury will make you toe the line; *he* ain't one to put up with your odd humors and your air-dreaming and your megrims!"

"I don't see why not," replied Miss Lennox. "He's been putting up with them for years."

Sir Malcolm, upon this renewal of strife, exchanged the *Times* for the *Morning Post*, and withdrew once more. Sir Malcolm was very fond of his daughter, who had never in her entire life caused him a moment's unease. Furthermore, he understood her, as Eulalia did not. Jynx disliked fuss and bother; she refused to have demands made of her; she was expert at removing herself from unpleasantness.

The current unpleasantness from which Jynx sought to divorce herself appeared, to Sir Malcolm's shrewd eye, to be

Eulalia. It was as good a reason as any to marry, and so he did not interfere. Left to herself, Jynx would doubtless have drifted into a dilatory spinsterhood, and Sir Malcolm had a strong wish to view at least one grandchild before he expired of old age. He listened with irritation to his sister-in-law's unlovely voice. Sir Malcolm had an even stronger wish to rid himself of Eulalia and he would do so promptly, once Jynx was safely wed.

This Eulalia did understand. Since she had no intention of departing the comfortable opulence of Sir Malcolm's residence in Lennox Square, it was clearly incumbent upon her to see that Jessamyn did *not* wed. Thus she proceeded to paint a harrowing picture of married life, during which Jessamyn slumped even more dreadfully in her chair. How the *devil*, wondered Eulalia, who had not been made privy to Jynx's own opinion that the viscount had agreed to marry her out of sheer self-defense, had her niece managed to lure London's most sought-after and elusive bachelor to the altar? Doubtless by the practice of wicked art and depraved contrivances! It passed human bearing. The girl should have been at her last prayers, safely considered on the shelf.

"You'll have to change your ways," Eulalia continued craftily. "Believe me, Jessamyn, what a gentleman accepts casually in a friend, he will not tolerate in a wife. There'll be no more highty-tighty behavior, and the viscount will not permit his wife to play off airs. *He*'ll see that you take your rightful place in society."

Jynx, to her aunt's disappointment, took these dire predictions in good part. "I do not enjoy frivolity," she replied equably. "I do not care to be racketing myself to pieces or exhausting myself with the trivialities of life. Shannon understands perfectly."

"Almacks!" cried Eulalia, horrified. "The opera!"

"Tedious," retorted Jynx. "Unutterably and intolerably insipid."

Aghast as she may have been at these blasphemous announcements, they suited Eulalia very well. "You will be well-served," she remarked slyly, "when your indifference drives your husband to seek consolation from Paphian girls, and takes all sorts of vulgar mistresses. It ain't like you're making a love match! He may even form a connection of a more particular nature, and *then* where will you be, miss?"

"Why, then," remarked Miss Lennox, with every evidence of unabated good humor, "I shall be smack in the midst of a *ménage à trois*. I confess to a certain curiosity as to how that particular relationship is accomplished."

"Serves you right, Eulalia!" The unpaternal Sir Malcolm roared with laughter as his sister-in-law spluttered indignantly. Jynx, meanwhile, had glanced at the doorway.

"Good morning, Shannon!" said she. "You will have heard me telling Aunt Eulalia that I've no objection should you become enamored of a *fille de joie*."

Lord Roxbury, who had spent an informative few moments in the Lennox hallway, had heard a great deal more than that, as a result of which he was possessed of a fervent desire to wring Eulalia's scrawny neck. "You've no objection to anything, my poppet," he responded, and ruffled his fiancée's hair. "It is no small part of your charm. Good day, Eulalia. Sir Malcolm, how goes the war?"

This matter of her niece's betrothal, decided Eulalia, would require considerable thought. She did not like Lord Roxbury, who had all the instinctive aloofness of one born to wealth the most enormous; but even Eulalia had to concede that he was sardonically elegant, if a trifle cold in his manner; and that he was undeniably handsome and a fine catch for any girl. Sir Malcolm approved the match, as was obvious from the enthusiastic manner in which he addressed his prospective son-in-law. Having been acquainted with the viscount for so many years, neither Sir Malcolm nor Jynx were likely to credit any attempts to blacken his character. Eulalia sank into a rather sullen meditation.

"I almost forgot." Lord Roxbury handed Jynx a note. "It was delivered by a grubby urchin while I was still at the front door." With exquisite tact he turned back to Sir Malcolm, and thus did not see Jynx glance at the missive, then tuck it hastily into her sleeve. "What think you of Napoleon's chances of success now, sir? His *Grande Armée* is in inglorious retreat, forced out of Moscow, and harried incessantly by Wellington in Spain."

"Napoleon has made two fatal errors," offered Jynx, propping an elbow on the table, and resting her chin in her hand. "He attempted to annex Spain against the wish of the Spanish people, and he tried to invade Russia. Now his defeats in Russia and Germany constantly reduce the number of French troops in Spain. The Corsican has spread himself a great deal too thin, I think."

Young ladies should not, of course, have dared to thusly ruminate, and Eulalia said so. "If you don't like the conversation, Eulalia," retorted Sir Malcolm, "you may leave!" Lord Roxbury, thereby relieved of the necessity of defending his fiancée's right to think anything she wished, smiled upon Jynx and removed a dangling chestnut curl from the marmalade.

"I have it on good information," continued Sir Malcolm, pleased to have silenced—if only temporarily—the annoying Eulalia, "that what we hope will be Wellington's final advance through Spain has begun."

"And the Russians, assisted by the Hohenzollers, are sweeping the French from Northern Germany," offered Jynx, as she licked the marmalade from her hair. "Napoleon's star is on the wane, poor little man. But Shannon will have other appointments today, Papa, as you do yourself! Perhaps you might wish to speak privately."

Sir Malcolm, unaware of the import of the note his daughter had received, considered this unusual impatience on her part an indication of prospective marital felicity. Lord Roxbury, who did not similarly flatter himself, regarded her rather warily. Jynx raised limpid eyes to his face.

"Come, Jessamyn!" Eulalia saw an opportunity in which to further spread her poison. "The gentlemen will not require your presence."

"Ah!" said the viscount, who made a formidable opponent. "But the gentlemen do." Jynx regarded rather wistfully the tanned fingers that clasped her wrist. This rare melancholy was not prompted by such physical intimacy—Lord Roxbury had, during the years of their association, clasped this and various other portions of Miss Lennox with fair regularity—but by a regret that she had ever received the wearisome note that rested with all the potential threat of explosive gunpowder in her sleeve.

Eulalia goggled. The viscount, she decided, was a very great bit of an oddity. "But marriage portions!" she protested. "And settlements! You don't want Jessamyn to hear about such things."

"Why not?" Lord Roxbury raised the gold-handled quizzing glass that hung on a black ribbon around his handsome neck, and utilized it to good effect. "Since it is Jessamyn who is being thusly disposed of, I think she might find the proceeding of interest." He dropped the glass—having reduced Eulalia to glaring speechlessness—and studied his fiancée. "Would you, poppet?"

"Rather!" Jynx would have welcomed any opportunity to

22

delay a perusal of her letter. That illegible handwriting could have been scrawled only by one pen; and involvement with Cristin Ashley, in Jynx's experience, invariably led her to strenuous exertions indeed.

In high dudgeon, Eulalia swept from the room. Wonderfully strange, the affectionate manner in which the high-and-mighty Lord Roxbury regarded a mere dab of a girl. Strange, but to Eulalia's advantage. Unaware that her phlegmatic niece was by her own, albeit unwilling, efforts about to land herself in a peck of trouble, Eulalia had conceived of a brilliant scheme.

Chapter Three

Eulalia Wimple was not the only person to bewail the betrothal of Lord Roxbury to Miss Lennox; a positive dirge was underway within the walls of a certain red brick house in Portland Place.

Adorée Blissington was in her drawing room, a rectangular chamber with an elegant coved ceiling, doorways of Italian Renaissance design, and walls hung with rich damask. The furnishings were of cane, boasted clever lattice work, and were painted with classical subjects and floral designs.

Lady Bliss lounged upon a two-back settee, with medallions painted in the Kauffman style. She was *en déshabillé* in a froth of ruffles and lace. Her hair was in artful disarray; her gray eyes were red-rimmed; and her elegant nose was buried in a lace-edged handkerchief.

"Come, do not take on so!" said her gentleman companion, who was sprawled in a decidedly uncomfortable chair. "It's not as if you didn't expect to be given your *congé.*"

"But one *should* weep on such occasions!" Lady Bliss briskly blew her nose. One should love with utter abandon, and utter indifference to what people think and say. And it is very lowering to be cast aside like—like an old shoe!"

"More fool you," retorted the unappreciative gentleman. "Had you heeded my advice, you wouldn't be in this fix. The next thing you know we'll have an execution in the house, and Jews at the door filling up their carts, and the place overrun with bailiffs."

"Oh, don't say so!" wailed Lady Bliss, regarding her brother with dismay. "You know very well that my creditors have begun to hound me in earnest—and I'm sure I'm not entirely to blame, even if I *am* a trifle careless about paying my bills. Nor should you scold me for it, Innis! You are very expensive, and I haven't noticed that *you*'ve made the least attempt to economize!"

Innis Ashley put forth no argument; in justice, he could not. Innis was, according to his detractors, the number of whom were considerable, a gentleman totally devoid of sentiment or shame, a gentleman who was committed to a continued routine of dissipation, and who possessed not one estimable or redeemable quality. He had, at thirty-two, earned no little notoriety as a philanderer; he had, it was said, already possessed one-third of the female population of the town. This may have been slight exaggeration—and again, it may not—but those who knew Innis accorded him the epithet of *très amoureux* but *très inconstant*.

Lady Bliss continued to bemoan her perennial financial crises, waving her handkerchief for emphasis. "And to run a polite gaming house was *your* idea, Innis! You said that if we issued discreet cards of invitation, and set out faro tables and handsome suppers and good wine, and let it be known that the play was fair, we would speedily become rich. But we haven't! And I'm sure I don't wonder at it, since champagne costs seventy shillings the dozen, to say nothing of spring chickens and salmon and green peas. I shall end up in debtors' prison, I know it, and *then* you'll regret your treatment of me."

"Pax!" Innis interrupted, and crossed his legs at the knee. "Considering that you have enslaved half the government, I doubt not that you'd be rescued from Newgate gaol by some admirer who wouldn't wish to suffer the embarrassment attendant upon your presence there. But you worry needlessly, Adorée. It won't come to that. I fancy I've found the perfect way out of our difficulties."

Lady Bliss did not respond enthusiastically to the ray of hope thus proffered; Lady Bliss had what might be charitably called a one-track mind. "I will admit," she said stiffly, "that I have had my share—perhaps even *more* than my share—of amorous intrigues."

"What you've had," remarked Innis, who wasn't one to coddle any lady, "is a series of highly publicized and scandalous flirtations. And not one of them did you turn to advantage! Never did I think to see an Ashley whistle a fortune down the wind! Yet here we are, suffering from a run of the most damnably persistent ill luck, with one disastrous occurrence following hard on another, and you allow one of the richest men in England to escape your net."

Lady Bliss surveyed her brother, whose blue coat and fawn pantaloons and Hessian boots displayed his magnificent figure to a nicety. His countenance was honest and open and cheerful, his manner disarming, and his dark locks tumbled in an engaging and careless manner over his noble brow. Lady Bliss evinced little appreciation at the handsome picture he made. "You would have me act the tart," she pronounced awfully. "I have told you before, Innis, that I refuse to capitalize on my, er, *affaires de cœur*."

So she had, and Innis considered it further proof—not that further proof was needed—that his sister was a skitterwitted slow-top. She was his meal-ticket, however, and he did not wish to argue with her. "So you have," Innis replied cheerfully. "So be it! I shan't say another word about Roxbury."

"Oh, Innis!" Lady Bliss was immediately distracted, as her brother had intended she should be. "He has behaved *so* handsomely!"

"He has?" Accustomed as he was to his sister's limited powers of intellect, her utterances sometimes caused Innis a certain confusion. "Dash it, Adorée, the man gave you your ticket-of-leave!"

"Yes, he did." Lady Bliss again had recourse to her handkerchief. "And the sapphire set he gave me as a parting gift was *very* handsome! And he has a sincere regard for the girl, which is *so* affecting, and I think it's all marvelous!"

"It'd be a great deal *more* marvelous," retorted Innis, "if Roxbury had a sincere regard for *you!* Will you wear the willow for him, then? I thought you didn't care for the man."

"Wretch!" Had not Lady Bliss so adored her younger brother, she would have been all out of charity with him. It was only fair that a female who had just received a terrible blow—albeit for the hundredth time—should be permitted to indulge in a slight display of wounded sensibility. "I care for *all* of them!" She sniffled. "Of course, no one can ever compare with my dear——"

"Courtney! I know, I know!" Innis was in no mood to hear again a catalogue of his happily deceased brother-in-law's nonexistent virtues. Sir Courtney Blissington had been of a disposition and character that made the feckless Ashleys appear models of virtue in comparison. "Sometimes, Adorée, I think you have windmills in your head. Roxbury was the plumpest pigeon that's ever come our way, but you had to turn squeamish and refuse to feather your nest! Ah well, what's done is done, and can be *und*one, I always say! Where *is* this fine sapphire set?"

"Innis!" Lady Bliss quite forgot the loss of her latest swain in the face of this new threat. "You don't mean to take them from me?"

"May I recall to you the bailiffs and the moneylenders, the champagne and spring chickens and green peas?" Innis held out his hand. Adorée sighed and reluctantly placed in it a jeweller's box. "That's my girl!" applauded Innis, and inspected the gems. "Very fine, in truth! Never mind, sister, you'll have even finer, and before long."

Nor did Lady Bliss respond to this tantalizing promise; Lady Bliss was contemplating the patent absence of her guardian angel on this miserable day. Not only had she lost Lord Roxbury, who had been generous if a trifle dilatory in his attentions; but even worse, she had been deprived of the splendid jewels with which she might have consoled herself. Life, decided Lady Bliss, was most extraordinarily unfair.

Innis had a fair comprehension of the reflections that passed through his sister's lovely, if empty, head: Innis was the only Ashley to have ever possessed any degree of native wit. He was shrewd, and canny, and had a remarkable flair for recognizing and using to his own good advantage the foibles of his fellow men. "Young Cristin," he remarked, seemingly at random, "has gone with Eleazar to Gunther's. It is an excellent time, Adorée, to discuss the future of our niece."

"Eleazar! At Gunther's!" echoed Lady Bliss, then giggled most delightfully as she envisioned that aged *roué* in a confectioner's store. Her merriment was replaced by a sudden suspicion. "*What* plans?"

"Don't you trust me, sister?" Innis prudently allowed her no opportunity to reply. "Believe me, I have everything very well in hand."

"Poor little Cristin!" Lady Bliss looked woebegone. "She should be able to enjoy her stay in London, instead of hiding herself of an evening in the upper story of the house. And no, Innis!" she added, for he had moved as if to speak. "I have told you before that I will not have Cristin in the gaming rooms."

So she had, to Innis's grave disappointment, and it was furthermore a point on which she had proven unusually

27

adamant. "I don't see," Adorée continued, "why you had to bring her *here*. Surely Niall's affairs weren't in such bad train that she couldn't have been placed elsewhere?" Innis's crude rejoinder recalled to her the ne'er-do-well nature of their elder brother. "Oh, curses! The thing's done, but understand this, Innis! I will not have Cristin bothered with our little problems."

Innis stretched out his long legs before him and contemplated his sister's mentality, or lack thereof. If being harried half to death by creditors was a small problem, he hated to think what Adorée would consider extreme. "You have not grasped the situation," he remarked. "It was the greatest stroke of good fortune that brought Cristin to us. And I think I may safely wager that our niece's London sojourn will not be without, ah, happy consequence."

Adorée Blissington may not have been the most nimble-witted of ladies, but this observation caused even Adorée to stare. She sincerely doubted that Cristin would consider joining her aunt in debtors' prison a happy consequence; and she hardly thought that Niall's death, by his own hand, after amassing a staggering amount of gambling debts, could be considered fortunate. "Innis," she said sternly, "something must be done!"

"And so it shall be." As if, reflected Innis, he hadn't been trying to explain that very thing for the past half-hour. "Think, sister—if you can! Our beloved niece became acquainted with a number of well-heeled young ladies while at that select academy. How Niall would swear if he knew *I* was to reap the advantages." Lady Bliss looked confused by her brother's enthusiasm. "This is a perfect moment, Adorée, for our niece to renew those friendships."

Niall would indeed have sworn, had he been aware that he was to be posthumously bested by his younger brother in their eternal game of one-upmanship, but Lady Bliss didn't understand precisely how Innis meant to see the thing done. "But, Innis!" she protested. "No young lady of good family will be permitted to associate with Cristin, because of Cristin's relationship to *us*. Oh, what a dreadful state of affairs!"

"Don't fly into the boughs!" Innis said hastily, before his sister could again succumb to hysterics, an act which she performed frequently, if with considerable grace. "There is one young lady, at least, who will be happy to renew her friendship with our niece. Or have you already forgotten the episode in Hyde Park?" It was clear from Lady Bliss's blank

28

expression that she had, and Innis stifled irritation. His sister was easily led, once she comprehended a situation. Unfortunately, the dawning of that comprehension was all too often depressingly difficult to bring about. "Roxbury," he prompted, "and his lovely companion. You were cut to the quick by his cruelty to yourself."

"I was?" echoed Lady Bliss, in stark disbelief.

"You were," Innis explained firmly. "You must have been, haven't you, if I say so?"

There seemed to Adorée to be some flaw in this logic, but she failed to pick it out. "I suppose. But did you think her lovely? Miss Lennox? She is not generally held to be so."

"Miss Lennox," retorted Innis, with the utmost sincerity, "is the most beatific vision I have laid eyes upon in many a long day. Could I but gain an introduction to her, Adorée, I would die a happy man. And I believe I may trust young Cristin to bring about that highly desirable state of affairs!"

Lady Bliss did not ponder the various inconsistencies inherent in her brother's speech, nor did she consider it odd that a hardened rake like Innis should wax so enthusiastic about a young woman who was generally considered thoroughly superior, amazingly indifferent to the gentlemen, and overly encumbered with virtue. "Innis!" she cried, with the utmost delight. "I do believe you have been smitten at last."

Innis did not quibble with this unflattering assessment of his condition; it was precisely what he wished his sister to believe. There was even a degree of truth in her assumption, though it was not Miss Lennox herself who had aroused his ardor, but Miss Lennox's overflowing pocketbooks. "I have," he admitted modestly.

"Oh, dear!" Adorée had fallen from the heights of excitement to the depths of despair. "Innis, I do not mean to make you unhappy, but do you think Sir Malcolm would *approve?*"

Innis knew beyond the least shadow of a doubt that Sir Malcolm would suffer an apoplexy at the mere thought of his beloved Jessamyn in connection—especially in the manner of connection Innis envisioned—with an Ashley. Innis's private opinion, however, was not to be aired to his sister, who retained a sickening and most inconvenient fondness for all her past beaux. "What care I for that?" inquired Innis, with a beautifully eloquent gesture of nonchalance. "Sir Malcolm may cast her out without a farthing, and still I would adore the girl! Ah, sister! Love has come to me late, but doubly potent for its tardiness! Only you can help me to achieve the object of my dreams."

Lady Bliss eyed her brother with astonishment. Never had she heard him speak in such a manner of any damsel; perhaps this time he *was* sincere. "If Sir Malcolm were to cast her out, how would you live?"

"It matters not." Innis had cast himself with abandon into his role. "In a little cottage in the country—if need be, I would even hire myself out as a laborer! Do you know, Adorée, I think Miss Lennox might even make an honest man of me?" His sister goggled at this unheard-of notion, and he feared he'd gone too far. "Or maybe not! But I dote to distraction on the chit, all the same."

Lady Bliss could well understand such emotion; Lady Bliss had doted to distraction on a great many gentlemen during the course of her reckless career. "Oh, Innis!" she breathed. "How very moving! And how sad that your great love should be doomed to unfulfillment! For you know as well as I that Miss Lennox is betrothed to Roxbury."

Innis refrained from reminding his sister of his heady successes with the opposite sex, and from expressing his conviction that the superior Viscount Roxbury hadn't a chance of winning any competition with himself. These opinions weren't inspired wholly by vanity, though of that vice—indeed of all vices—Innis certainly had his share: Innis Ashley had for years set feminine hearts fluttering with his dark and dashing handsomeness. "Betrothals," he said abruptly, "can be broken. You may trust me for *that*, Adorée. All I require is to make the acquaintance of Miss Lennox, and there our silly widgeon of a niece has given me the *entrée*."

It occurred to Lady Bliss, who had been wallowing in an excess of emotion, inspired by contemplation of her brother's hopeless passion for a lady quite beyond his reach, that Innis was speaking of his heart's desire in a singularly cold-blooded manner. "And," he continued, "that will leave Roxbury free to pick up where he left off with you. And don't tell me you don't want a reconciliation, Adorée! Miss Lennox don't need a fortune, having one of her own, but *we* do."

Such paradoxes as her brother presented were beyond Lady Bliss's comprehension. "How will Cristin give you the *entrée*?" she asked, in search of enlightenment.

Innis recalled, belatedly, that he had not meant to show his sister his hand. He wondered vaguely from where she'd learned her scruples, such liabilities being alien to the other members
30

of the Ashley clan. "Cristin knows of my sad plight," he explained, rather mournfully, "and sympathizes whole-heartedly. A great deal more than *you* appear to, I must say! She has written to Miss Lennox, and begged her to call on us."

"I cannot think," Lady Bliss interrupted doubtfully, "that it is at all proper for Miss Lennox to present herself at this house."

"If Miss Lennox don't mind it," snapped Innis, exacerbated beyond bearing, "why should *you?* This skimble-skamble stuff you're spouting is the outside of enough, Adorée! Can it be that you do not *wish* your little family to be happy? Do you not wish to see Cristin happily settled, or me to win my object? It seems not! It seems that you would stand between me and she who holds my heart enthralled, would prevent Cristin from enlivening her dull and dreary days with her dearest friend. Lady Bliss, they call you! Hah! *I* could tell the world that you are completely heartless."

Thus accused, and most unjustly, Adorée profusely apologized. She claimed herself more than willing to secure her little family's happiness by whatever means were necessary, and promised even to oblige her brother in the matter of the viscount. Then, exhausted, she dissolved again into tears.

Innis eyed his sodden sister with a fine blend of exasperation and contempt, and approached the brandy decanter. Women were ever-contrary creatures, he mused, as he filled a glass; and the most contrary of them all, according to rumor, was the fabulously wealthy Miss Lennox. Innis raised the liquor to the light. He did not think that even the contrary Jessamyn would long withstand the fatal charm of the Ashleys.

Chapter
Four

Nor did Lord Peverell think that Miss Lennox would benefit from acquaintance with the feckless Ashleys, though he did not phrase this foreboding so clearly, even to himself. He trailed along behind Miss Lennox, a dazzlingly beautiful young man dressed in the highest kick of fashion: light brown coat, a fifteen-guinea embroidered waistcoat from Guthrie in Cork Street, nankeen pantaloons fastened at the ankle with two brass buttons. His guinea-gold hair was cut in the fashionable Brutus crop; his physique was excellent; his eyes, if a trifle vacant in expression, were a warm shade of brown. "I wish you'd reconsider, Jynx!" he protested, as with brisk and purposeful step Miss Lennox approached a certain red brick dwelling in Portland Place. "If Shannon should find out about this, there'll be the devil to pay."

"Fiddlesticks." Jynx surveyed Lord Peverell who, having given strident voice for the past several minutes to his great disapproval of this enterprise, was sadly short of breath. "Don't tease yourself, Percy! What is Shannon to do, pray? Should he find out about this excursion, you need only explain that you accompanied me of your own accord, to protect me from the consequences of setting forth without so much as a footman in attendance, and thus clear yourself of all blame."

Lord Peverell doubted that his innocence would be so easily established. Shannon Quinn was a deuced high stickler, and this was grave indiscretion indeed. Furthermore, Shannon Quinn was of an athletic persuasion, and had a very handy bunch of fives, and a temper that was no less terrifying for its infrequent appearance. "When we were at Eton together," Percey offered, "Shannon swam the Thames with a live hare in his mouth."

So little impressed was Miss Lennox with this proof that

her fiancé was a gentleman to be reckoned with that she merely cast her friend an amused glance before setting her foot on the red brick stair.

"Damned if I don't think you're cast away!" uttered Percy, as Jynx approached the front door. She looked inquiring. "Bosky! Foxed! *You* know, in your cups! Dashed if I can think of any other reason why you should be acting in this huggermugger way. Or," and his eye lit up hopefully, "maybe it's all a hum? That's it, ain't it, Jynx? You're bent on hoaxing me! Well, you've done a deuced good job of it, and I've been properly taken in, so be a good girl, do, and come away!"

"Gammon." Miss Lennox applied herself forcefully to the door knocker, brass in the form of a lion's head. "You're a pudding-heart, Percy!"

Lord Peverell took no exception to this unflattering remark, having heard himself referred to in such wise all his life, and in addition frequently called a handsome moonling. He supposed there must have been some truth in at least the latter, or he would not have been persuaded by Lord Roxbury's betrothed to call with her upon Lord Roxbury's all-too-recent inamorata, the consequences of such action being much too dreadful to contemplate. Percy had a rather horrible vision of Lord Roxbury once more plunging into the Thames, this time to violently drown his old friend of Eton days.

Miss Lennox, meanwhile, had stepped back to study the house. "It doesn't," she remarked judiciously, "*look* like a den of iniquity."

"Little do you know!" responded Percy, in the gloomy tone of one who *did* know, and to his cost.

"No." As ever, Miss Lennox was of good cheer. "But I'll wager I'll soon find out!"

The front door swung open to reveal an impeccable individual of superior and suspicious mien. "Truly, we are neither law officers or spies!" Jynx remarked, when the butler exhibited a great reluctance to step aside. "Oh, you silly man, do let us in!"

The butler did so, due not to the young lady's insistence, but to his belated recognition of the young lady's companion. "Good day, Lord Peverell," he unbent sufficiently to say. "May I express our pleasure at seeing you again at Blissington House? The master was remarking just yesterday on your absence."

"Good day, Tomkin," Percy replied, very much aware of

Miss Lennox's interest. He was vastly relieved when she was distracted by a flurry in the upper hall.

"Who is it, Tomkin?" A lovely dark-haired lady peered over the railing, then hurried down the stair. "Ah! Not the bailiffs, then!" She grasped Jynx's hand. "My dear, you *do* have a look of your father! I can't tell you how I'm relieved."

Miss Lennox studied her hostess, whose dark hair was fastened up behind and fell in light ringlets from the top of her head to her neck. Lady Bliss wore a prodigiously low-cut gown of gray muslin which not only matched her eyes, but was so transparent that it revealed the lines of leg and thigh. "Relieved, ma'am?" inquired Jynx, in her lethargic way. Lord Peverell cast his eyes heavenwards, clearly wishing to disassociate himself from the scene.

"Oh, not that you look like your father, though I'm sure Sir Malcolm is a very presentable man—and so are you, my dear, though not a man, but very presentable all the same—but that you're not a bailiff! Not that anyone would think you *were* after they'd had a good look at you." She paused for breath and giggled. "What a pea goose you must think me! My dear, I am Adorée Blissington."

"So I perceived," Jynx replied, a trifle drily, and extricated her hand. "Forgive me for bursting in on you in this manner, Lady Blissington, but I wished——"

"I know, and it is very good of you, but I have been thinking about it very seriously, and I have decided you should not!" Lady Bliss frowned, an enchanting exercise, as she tried without success to grasp at logic. "I mean, of course you should see Cristin, for *she* at least is unexceptionable, but no matter what Innis may say I do not believe it proper that you should have come *here*. Not that I am not pleased to meet you, for naturally I am, particularly since I *wouldn't* have in the ordinary course of things—but still, you'd be much wiser to have refrained."

"There!" Lord Peverell was delighted to receive assistance from this unexpected quarter, and anxious to prevent Lady Bliss from embarking in her bird-witted manner upon the taboo topic of a certain viscount. "Told you it was a hubble-bubble notion. Deuce take it, Jynx, a gaming house!"

"Precisely." Lady Bliss had no difficulty following Lord Peverell's reasoning; his intellectual prowess was no greater than her own. She practically shoved her guests toward the door. "A privilege to make your acquaintance, Miss Lennox, but you'd better leave before further harm is done."

"Harm, Adorée?" came a masculine drawl from the staircase. Lady Bliss, Jynx noted, turned pale as parchment. "You are being very foolish, dear sister. And Peverell! You'd leave us so soon? But now I remember! Your cousin redeemed your vowels, did he not? In return, I suppose, for your promise to remain at a safe distance from the cards and the dice?" Percy, to Jynx's surprise, blushed and stammered incoherently. She turned to regard the gentleman who had roused in her companions such stricken response.

He was a very handsome man, she decided, in a very rakehelly way. His gray eyes rested on her with a brooding, knowing expression, and his dark hair tumbled in a studied manner over his brow. He was dressed for riding in a blue coat with brass buttons, breeches, and top boots, and such attire left no doubt that his physique was superb. "Miss Lennox," he said, as he approached and bent over her hand. "I am more happy than I can say to make your acquaintance. Innis Ashley, at your service, ma'am."

Innis may have been sincerely happy at this development, but he was the only member of the quartet to greet this development with the least felicity. Lady Bliss, who had taken a sudden liking to Miss Lennox, and who additionally recalled the fate of other young ladies with whom Innis had professed himself enamored, was very much afraid that this latest flight would land them all in the suds; Lord Peverell considered Viscount Roxbury's probable reaction were he to learn of this, a reaction that would doubtless involve Percy's head being severed from his neck; and Jynx wished that the dashing Mr. Ashley would not retain such firm possession of her hand. A great lot for the casual embrace, the Ashleys. Then she recalled Lady Bliss's reckless reputation, and realized the aptness of her errant thought, and smiled.

Innis congratulated himself, considering that smile inspired by his polished address. Lady Bliss, whose conclusions were similar, again frowned. Percy cleared his throat, and shuffled his feet, and suggested timidly that his horses would grow tired of standing.

"Surely," said Innis, "you cannot be serious! Miss Lennox has not yet spoken with my niece—and that was your purpose in calling, was it not, Miss Lennox? Adorée, take Peverell into the saloon while I speak with our guest." His glance at Percy was wicked. "You might pass the time with an innocent game of picquet."

Though Lady Bliss did not like the situation, especially

since Miss Lennox's appearance recalled strongly to mind Sir Malcolm and his gallant if unsuccessful courtship, she knew that to try and interfere with Innis was extremely unwise. Too, Innis claimed to be bewitched by Miss Lennox, and she could not bring herself to throw a spanner in the workings of his romance. But again, Lord Roxbury too had always been gallant. "It is very difficult," she said aloud, "this knowing what is best for everyone. Come along, Percy!"

Lord Peverell did not in the least wish to leave Miss Lennox alone in the company of a noted profligate, but Innis's mention of gaming debts had unhappily reminded him that all those debts had not yet been paid. There remained a sum of several hundred pounds which he had not dared mention to his cousin, and that sum was owed to none other than Innis Ashley. He cast an anguished glance at Jynx, as Lady Bliss led him away.

"If you will accompany me?" murmured Innis, and offered Jynx his arm. She allowed him to escort her up the stairs.

Miss Lennox, for all her phlegm, was not an unobservant soul, and Miss Lennox had decided that, in Blissington House, any number of things were afoot. Evidently Percy had fallen into careless ways, and she was unhappy about it; though to be in the clutches of moneylenders was more or less *de rigueur* for a young gentleman, Percy was a nodcock, and could not be expected to extricate himself. Then there was Lady Bliss, who was equally brainless, and who was obviously caught up in a dilemma of some sort. Jynx recalled the incoherent note she had received, and wondered if Cristin's dilemma and her aunt's dilemma were one and the same.

Innis glanced down at the silent Miss Lennox, and decided that she had been stricken speechless by his abundant charm. He found her more attractive than he had expected, in her gown of pale green muslin with waggoner's sleeves, a cottage vest of sarsenet that laced across the bosom—on which his glance lingered appreciatively—and a white gauze hat adorned with tea roses and green foliage. An expensive ensemble, reflected Innis, and perfect for a wealthy and docile young lady. It seemed that this was to be an easier conquest than he'd dreamed.

"You must not think poorly of my sister for running polite gaming rooms," he remarked as he led Miss Lennox into the drawing room. "Everyone in society gambles, after all. Even ladies of fashion succumb to the fascination of the tables."

"Staking fortunes and estates on a single throw of the dice?"

36

Jynx seated herself in the uncomfortable cane chair and prepared to divest the dashing Mr. Ashley of his delusions. "Gambling has ruined more men than drink and dissipation combined. I do not approve of it."

Innis was not so easily daunted; he merely quirked a dark brow. "In England the fashionable vices are gambling and wenching and drunkenness—not pretty vices, I'll admit, but better than elsewhere. The Turks, for example, prefer smoking opium and practicing sodomy."

Any other well-brought-up young lady would have, upon being presented with this most improper view, shrieked and swooned away. If he had hoped to shock Miss Lennox out of her languor, however, Mr. Ashley had gravely failed. "You would know about that, I suppose," she remarked absently, and had the pleasure of seeing him stare. "We have strayed a great distance from the subject of your niece. I would like to see Cristin now, if you please."

"Dammit, I *don't* please!" Innis had recourse to the brandy decanter. "It seems to me, Miss Lennox, that you have a damned poor notion of my character."

"Should I not?" inquired Jynx, with increasing ennui. "You are the companion of gamblers and demireps, sir, the leader of a set of *roués* who seem to glory in excess. You are said to entertain depraved cronies at parties too lascivious to describe; you number among your escapades an attempt to abduct an actress, whom you later treated savagely. In so doing, you have forfeited all title to anyone's esteem."

Innis looked rather as if a piece of furniture had suddenly come to life and bit him. "Who the *devil*," he inquired, in strangled tones, "told you all this?"

"My father," replied Miss Lennox, who was secretly enjoying herself. "Sir Malcolm also said that you are an arrant fortune hunter who has been dangling after a rich heiress for years, and that with the least encouragement you will take all sorts of encroaching fancies." Her gaze was bland. "I shouldn't like that at all, you see, so I thought it would save us both a great deal of bother if I warned you *not* to make a dead-set at me."

Innis was prey to a number of conflicting emotions: anger, resentment, and a queer mirth. He stared at his intended prey, who returned the look in her usual composed manner, and glee won out. Miss Lennox was treated to the sight of the reprobate Innis Ashley grasping his sides and howling with merriment like any scrubby schoolboy. "My darling girl!" he gasped, at length. "I quite see that I have underestimated you."

"You have," agreed Jynx calmly. "Much as I dislike nit-picking, I feel I must also point out that I'm not your darling anything. Now that we've settled this little matter, do you think I might be allowed to see Cristin?"

"No," retorted Innis, and seated himself on the settee. "Why in God's name did a delightful and desirable young woman like yourself enter into a betrothal with such a curst cold fish as Roxbury?"

"Nor need you," sighed Jynx, "throw the hatchet at me! I am totally immune to flattery. As for Viscount Roxbury, we shall not discuss him, sir."

"Very well." Innis regarded her in a fascinated manner. "But you must call me by my name, instead of that damnably proper 'sir.'"

"I don't see," complained Miss Lennox, "why I must call you anything. I've told you that you'll gain nothing by laying siege. You would be much wiser to amuse your leisure hours with something or someone more interesting to you."

"But I cannot," protested Innis, with warmth and a degree of sincerity. "Any other woman would in comparison seem a cold collation as opposed to a hot meal."

"More flummery." Totally unmoved by hearing herself referred to in so unique a manner, Miss Lennox reflected that her Aunt Eulalia, in those countless discourses on the evils of fortune hunters, had failed to mention the fact that to be pursued by such could be extremely diverting. "It will not serve. Try as you may, you will not, as I have already told you several times, induce me to act indiscreetly."

"I hesitate to point this out," countered Innis, without the least hesitation at all, "but you have already done so in coming here. What would Viscount Roxbury say, I wonder, if he knew the character of his intended was so very *loose?*"

"Viscount Roxbury," retorted Jynx, though with her dimpled grin, "is already familiar with all the facets of my character. And my indiscretion, as you call it, was prompted by the most worthy of sentiments—which you must admit would hardly be the case had it been inspired by yourself."

"Viscount Roxbury is a lucky man," Innis interrupted. He spoke, which was unusual, the simple truth. "Would that *I* could be! I realize I've made a botch of it already, Miss Lennox, and have insulted you greatly, as well as having given you a most unfavorable opinion of myself. Won't you forgive me all that, and allow me to begin over again?"

Miss Lennox contemplated her newest admirer, whose candid countenance was completely free of guile. "Generously said," she approved, "and the answer is no. Now! We've kept poor Percy's horses standing entirely too long, and I've grown most anxious to see Cristin. Therefore, if you please?"

Innis did not please; Innis was discovering that his quarry's disfavor added a certain zest to the pursuit; but just then Cristin herself burst into the room. "Oh, Jynx!" she wailed, and flung herself upon Miss Lennox's breast, and dissolved promptly into tears. No more than Innis did Miss Lennox appear to appreciate the tendency of the female Ashleys toward excessive sentimentality. She winced as Cristin gripped her even more firmly, and dislodged her hat, and wept all over her muslin gown.

Innis made no effort to aid Miss Lennox in her predicament, but met her speaking glance with a wicked grin. Gaining access to the Lennox fortune, he mused, was going to be a most pleasurable pastime. "Say that you forgive me," he offered, "and I will leap to your assistance, Miss Lennox!"

"Oh, very well!" agreed Jynx, who was half-smothered by her little friend's exuberance. "I forgive you."

In this case, at least, Innis proved as good as his word. Cristin's deathlock grip was broken, and she was gently reprimanded for her behavior, and at that point, as Cristin was proferring abject apologies of her own, Lord Peverell entered the drawing room.

"Jynx!" Percy was obviously in a state of great perspiration. "My horses!" And then his gaze fell upon Cristin, and his mouth dropped open, and he stared thunderstruck.

"Now I suppose I must thank you," Jynx remarked to her savior, as she straightened her abused hat. "If I did not see that it must be impossible, I would swear you contrived the whole thing."

"I might have, had I thought of it." Innis contemplated the doting fashion in which his niece was being regarded by the gullible Lord Peverell. It was a sentiment, judging from Cristin's equally besotted expression, that his niece appeared to share. Then his gaze moved to Miss Lennox, whose piquant features were, alas, totally devoid of any similar emotion. "I might be of even greater benefit to you, if only you would allow me to be."

Even a lady so unappreciative of ardor as Jynx could hardly fail to understand the veiled meaning in those words. "I do wish you'd stop carping on that subject!" she complained, and rose. "How many times must I tell you, Mr. Ashley, that you will not lead me into an affair of gallantry?"

"You may tell me as many times as you wish, and I shall listen to you with pleasure, and I will remain unconvinced." Innis took her hand once more. Jynx watched with a certain degree of bemusement as he bent his dark head and pressed his lips to the inside of her wrist. Innis raised his head, and noted her startled expression, and smiled. "Are you a coward, my darling?" he asked, so softly that had the others been listening, which they most definitely were not, they still could not have heard. "Give me only half a chance, and I will overcome your indifference."

The man was persistence itself! "And beguile me into tossing my bonnet over the windmill?" Jynx raised her lazy eyes to his reckless face.

"But you wish to speak to my niece." Innis released her, just as she parted her lips to deliver him another stinging rebuff. "I will leave you to it."

Without another word, he left them. Miss Lennox's gaze followed him, thoughtfully.

Chapter
Five

Mr. Ashley then returned to the smaller of the two saloons
which had been fitted up for gaming, where his sister was engaged in a desultory round of solitaire; and informed her that
his quarry had risen, nibbled and swallowed the bait. In no
time at all, averred Innis, Miss Lennox would be doing all
manner of imprudent things to him and with him, and most
happily. He additionally professed himself most delighted by
the prospect, which he wagered would be more stimulating
even than his recent stay with a certain crony, the object of
which had been a delirium of sensuality, and the achievement
of which had involved the participation of several maid-
servants. And he regretted that he had not made the acquaintance of Miss Lennox sooner, for she might have attended
with him the Opera Masquerade, and have supped with him
behind the scenes, in company with the ballet master, several
harlots, and a bawd. Lady Bliss listened to these disclosures,
and pondered the sorrow that would inevitably be Sir Malcolm's upon his daughter's disgrace, and sniffled dolefully.

But Lady Bliss lamented Miss Lennox's downfall a great
deal too soon, and Mr. Ashley had counted his chickens before
the eggs were even laid. So far was Miss Lennox from suc-
cumbing to Innis's rakish charm that, with his absence, all
thought of him had left her mind. She regarded her two companions, who still gazed at one another in that positively
sottish way. "Ahem!" uttered Jynx, and seated herself once
more in the cane chair.

Thus abjured, the stricken pair, still staring in a heartfelt—
and, Jynx thought, idiotic—manner into each other's eyes,
collapsed in unison upon the settee. "Percy," said Jynx, rather
ironically, "allow me to make you known to Cristin Ashley.
Cristin, meet Perceval Phelps, Lord Peverell."

"Charmed," murmured Cristin, soulfully. Stricken speechless by such enthusiasm, Percy grasped her hands and beamed.

"We shall go on a great deal more prosperously," announced Jynx, acerbically, "if the pair of you would stop making sheeps' eyes! Cristin, what was the purpose of that letter you sent me? Those melancholy and frightful disclosures you hinted at? Because, my girl, you don't appear the least afflicted to me!"

"Afflicted?" repeated Cristin, rather vaguely. "Oh no, Jynx. I'm as happy as a grig."

Miss Lennox was extremely affected by this little speech. In fact, Miss Lennox was so far roused from lethargy that she ground her teeth. "Then what the *deuce* did you mean by that note?" she inquired, in tones so severe that both Percy and Cristin gaped. "I warn you, Cristin, that I am sadly out of patience, and I expect an explanation immediately!"

"Now, now, Jynx! No need to be ripping up at the girl!" Percy patted Cristin's hand, possession of which he still retained. "Pay her no mind, Miss Ashley. Jynx is feeling a little out of sorts."

What Jynx was feeling was an unprecedented urge to strangle this crack-brained pair. "Well, Cristin?" she demanded. "I'm waiting!"

"Oh, Jynx, it's been an age since we met." Cristin's blue eyes filled with tears. "Don't be angry with me, please. I was so sure you'd understand—my poor father's untimely end, and Aunt Adorée and Uncle Innis—oh! 'Twas such a sad affair."

"*Now* see what you've done!" Percy shot a bitter glance at Miss Lennox. Encouraged by his sympathy, Cristin cast herself weeping onto his chest, to the detriment of his cravat and embroidered waistcoat, neither of which desecrations Percy seemed in the least to mind. "There, there, Miss Ashley! No need to make a fuss! Jynx don't mean half of what she says!"

"Oh!" Miss Ashley raised her pretty little face, the charm of which was not a whit diminished by tear stains. "Call me Cristin, pray!"

"Delighted!" Lord Peverell was much moved by this sign of favor. "And I'm Percy!"

"And the pair of you are addle-brained!" commented Miss Lennox, who was excessively weary of listening to loverlike absurdities. She sent up a silent prayer of thanksgiving for Viscount Roxbury, who did not fatigue her with such flummery. "Am I to understand, Cristin, that you *wish* to stay in Blissington House?"

"But, Jynx!" Cristin's wet eyes were wide. "Where else should I go? And I am very fond of Aunt Adorée, and even Uncle Innis, though they do argue a lot, and especially because Uncle Innis wants me to come into the saloons at night, and Aunt Adorée will not agree." She frowned. "I suppose she will give in eventually; Uncle Innis usually has his way. And truly I would not mind so much, except for Eleazar Hyde—indeed, I think it would be great fun to meet fine ladies and gentlemen!"

Miss Lennox refrained from pointing out that Cristin was unlikely to become acquainted with the *crème de la crème* in the Blissington gaming rooms. "Who," she ventured, "is Eleazar Hyde?"

Cristin grimaced, enchantingly. "Oh, the most dreadful old man, and I cannot but think his attentions a great deal too *particular*. But he is a friend of my Uncle Innis, and I am to be nice to him, my uncle says. So I am." She looked perplexed. "But he does say the strangest things to me."

Lord Peverell had been making the most extraordinary faces during this naive speech, and his comely, if vacant, countenance bloomed with color. "Hyde!" he ejaculated, at last. "A curst rum touch! I tell you, it won't do!"

Jynx suspected that for once Percy had made a shrewd deduction; any friend of the gay and profligate Innis Ashley was very unlikely to be fit company for his unworldly niece. She set that matter aside for later consideration, and pursued her original line of endeavor. "But if you are quite happy with your lot, why did you write *so* to me?"

"Because you're lazy, Jynx!" Cristin's giggle was very reminiscent of her aunt's. "I knew that if you saw all was well you would not visit me. But if you thought I was in trouble, you would immediately come to my rescue, like you did when we were in school, and you kept the other girls from teasing and bullying me about my father!" She looked cautiously at her friend. "And I *did* wish to speak with you, Jynx!"

Had Miss Lennox trusted herself to express an opinion of this candid confession, she might have remarked that her championship of Cristin Ashley was the sole piece of folly in an otherwise blameless career. "Why?" she inquired bluntly.

"Haven't you guessed?" Cristin clapped her little hands in

glee. "And you were always the clever one, Jynx! It is about Innis, of course! I fancy that my uncle has developed a decided partiality for you."

This ingenuous utterance roused Lord Peverell from his entranced state into a tardy realization that Innis Ashley's attentions toward Miss Lennox had been particular indeed. "Oh, God!" said he, in tones of the deepest dismay. "The Lennox fortune! I might as well give Shannon my head for washing without further ado!"

"Shannon?" queried Cristin, confused.

Miss Lennox did not offer enlightenment. Instead, she took advantage of Lord Peverell's momentary coherence. "I'll warrant you're more than slightly acquainted with that rough diamond," she remarked. "What was it about your cousin paying your debts?"

"Dash it, Jynx, you know I don't come into my estate until I'm twenty-five." Percy was glum. "Dominic and my mother keep me on a curst short string. Why my father left things so tied up I'll never understand!"

Miss Lennox *did* understand, perfectly, and even spared a commiserative thought for Lord Peverell's long-suffering family. "Were there gaming debts, Percy?" she prodded gently. "I suppose you tried to catch the smiles of fortune by risking a few pounds you could ill afford to lose?"

"Hah!" Lord Peverell retorted inelegantly. "A few pounds! I'll be all to pieces, Jynx, if I don't manage to raise the wind. And don't tell me to apply again to Dominic, because he's already told me that if I don't stop wasting the ready, he'll see that I'm obliged to knuckle down." He met her eyes, and read in them censure. "The deuce! You needn't look at me like *that!* I'm not the first to play beyond his means and find too late that he can't stay the course!"

"No," Jynx replied thoughtfully. "I don't suppose you are. But I still think you should tell your cousin that you failed to give him an accurate rendering of your accounts."

Percy snorted. "And you call *me* paper-skulled!" Miss Lennox preferred no response and he turned with relief to Cristin, and proceeded to enlighten her regarding certain games of chance. Miss Lennox listened without comment to an explanation of macao, a form of *vingt-et-un* which called for no particular skill but a steady nerve, and of E.O., a game of chance in which balls came to rest in niches in a table marked with the letters *E* and *O*; but when Percy embarked upon a discussion of the merits of various gentlemen's clubs, and extolled the virtues of White's, where one could plunge at hazard and faro, over Watier's, where macao was the game, she felt called upon to intervene.

"Oh!" Cristin clasped her hands in a worshipful attitude. "You know *so* much, Percy!"

"And *you*," replied Lord Peverell, who had never in his life been spoken to or of in such admiring terms, "are fine as five-pence, Cristin!"

"Percy!" interrupted Jynx, before she was presented with a further enactment of two hearts stricken by Cupid's arrows. "Who holds the notes that remain unpaid?" Lord Peverell opened his mouth, flushed, then clamped his lips together firmly. "I thought as much," said Jynx. "Innis Ashley! Lord, but the man's a rogue!"

Among the attributes Lord Peverell lacked was an ability to dissimulate. He stared woodenly at the floor. "What do you mean by that?" Cristin bridled, in defense of her uncle. "If Innis is holding Percy's notes, it must be for a very good reason, and I don't think it's very kind of you, Jynx, to infer that my uncle would behave shabbily! Especially when Innis has taken such a marked fancy to you!"

"I suspect," Jynx retorted wryly, "that your uncle has good reason for everything he does, and that we should be grateful we're not acquainted with it!" Cristin looked indignant. "Your uncle is a philanderer," Jynx added bluntly. "Any *tendre* he nourishes is inspired wholly by hopes of gain."

"Oh no, Jynx!" Cristin protested. "Innis said you'd feel that way, but it's not true. He even said it utterly sinks his spirits that you're rich as—as Croesus!—because he fears your wealth will ruin his chances with you."

"Balderdash!" Miss Lennox uttered rudely, and Lord Peverell was prompted to agree. "Up the garden path!" he hazarded. "Definitely in the petticoat line! Why, Innis Ashley's played fast and loose with half the females in the town!"

"How *dare* you!" In defense of her bold uncle, Cristin leapt feet-first into the fray. "Next you will say that Innis is bound for perdition, and all because he is taken with Jynx, which I'm sure is a thing no one can blame in him, even though Jynx is wanting in dash, and not at all in his style! I think you both are very cruel." And again she wept.

"There, there! No need to get up on your high ropes!" Lord

Peverell wasn't the least disturbed to discover that the lovely Miss Ashley was so credulous. "Jynx didn't mean anything by it, you know, and you mustn't think poorly of her for speaking her mind." Cristin only cried the harder, and he nobly offered up his waistcoat for further sacrifice. "Tell you what, think of pleasant things—like Almack's, and the opera, and all that sort of feminine frippery!"

Cristin drew back and stared at him. "Oh, *could* I?" she breathed. "Oh, Percy!"

Lord Peverell was accustomed to young ladies who gazed as awestruck upon him as if he held the keys of heaven in his rather awkward hands. "Don't see why not!" he stammered. "Jynx will see to it."

"No, Jynx will not!" announced that lady, in whom these continued histrionics had roused a raging headache. "Can't you just see me, Percy, introducing to Sally Jersey the niece of Lady Bliss? I swear that the pair of you have windmills in your head!"

Percy did not take kindly to this frank observation. "Dashed if you ain't the most cold-hearted female in existence!" he protested, as Cristin sobbed copiously into his handkerchief. "And a deuced addle-plot! I wouldn't have thought it of you, Jynx. I'd have said you didn't care a groat for such things."

Jynx could not help reflecting upon Lord Peverell's rather unique opinion of herself, which seemed to include a conviction that she should not cavil at ruining her own credit with the world so that Cristin might be granted a little amusement. "If Cristin wants to go to the opera," she said merely, "I'm sure her aunt will take her there. Almack's is out of the question, and you needn't mind it, Cristin, because the whole thing is very dull."

"I do mind!" wailed Cristin, with conviction. "And my aunt won't take me anywhere. She's only taken me to Hyde Park once, and she won't even do that again, because Viscount Roxbury was so rude. She says that my connection with her will do me harm, and that if I wish to contract a suitable marriage, I must play least in sight!" She subsided into hiccoughs. "And how I am to do that, when no one even sees me, I'm sure I don't know, unless I'm expected to marry that nasty old Eleazar Hyde!"

"Never!" ejaculated Lord Peverell. "You'd do much better to marry me!"

"Oh, *may* I?" Magically, Cristin's tears subsided. She gazed up rapt at her savior's face. "I should like that a great deal more."

"Don't see why we shouldn't!" responded Percy, equally taken with the idea. "Saints preserve us!" moaned Miss Lennox. Percy turned on her a most unappreciative look. "Now don't you go moralizing, Jynx! Who I marry is none of your affair."

True, and Miss Lennox sent thanks to heaven for that fact. She rubbed her throbbing temples. "No, but it is your cousin's, and what he'd say to this I can well imagine, even if you cannot. You can't marry without his permission, Percy, until you come of age."

"We could elope," offered Cristin, unwilling to see her roseate dream go so quickly up in smoke.

"No, that won't fadge," decided Percy, to Jynx's vast relief. "It ain't the thing. Beside, if I did that, likely be cut off without a farthing, which I wouldn't like."

"Oh," Cristin murmured woefully.

Miss Lennox was a good-natured creature, for all she disliked fuss; she was inspired with pity for the two downcast countenances before her; and she thought she saw a way to prohibit this extremely bird-witted pair from doing something rash. "Of course," she offered slyly, "Percy may do as he pleases when he turns twenty-five, which isn't very long distant."

"So it ain't!" Lord Peverell brightened immediately. "Only three months! That's the ticket, Cristin. All we have to do is wait till then."

"And *then* I shall go to Almack's!" Cristin's pretty little face was briefly suffused with joy. Then her lips turned downward and her blue eyes brimmed. "Unless I am made to marry someone else in the meanwhile, and I wouldn't be surprised if my Uncle Innis has something like that in mind."

"I thought you liked your uncle," intervened Miss Lennox, in waspish tones. "I'll be *damned* if I understand you, Cristin!"

"No, and I do not expect you to," the young lady replied simply. "Innis says that we Ashleys are a breed apart. And I cannot help think of Innis's hopeless passion for you, Jynx, and of my aunt's——"

"Think I should tell you!" Lord Peverell interrupted hastily. "Miss Lennox is betrothed, to Viscount Roxbury!"

"Oh, I almost forgot!" Cristin's hands flew to her mouth. "I'm sure I wish you happy in your approaching nuptials,

Jynx, and I see that it is a most eligible connection, though I don't at all understand why over my uncle you should prefer Viscount Roxbury!"

So Cristin was acquainted with Shannon? That odd fact would also merit future contemplation. "Lord, child, let's cry friends and have an end to this!" Jynx's head ached in good earnest now. "Don't go borrowing trouble. I'm sure that you misjudge your uncle. He will not force you to wed against your wishes."

"You don't know Innis." Cristin was downcast once more. "Adorée says he can get anyone to do anything."

Miss Lennox, fatigued beyond bearing by these continual alarums, sighed and pointed out that now Cristin had Lord Peverell to champion her cause. "No, she don't!" said Percy, also deep in gloom. "You forget that Innis holds my vowels. If I go against him, he'll call them, and then I'll really be in the basket."

"But your fortune," persevered Jynx, "is such as must be acceptable to him. There, *that*'s solved! Percy, I hesitate to remind you, but your horses have been standing all this while, and I think we should go!"

For someone who had approached Blissington House with the greatest resistance, Lord Peverell exhibited a large reluctance to depart. "It ain't solved," he replied, in tones that were positively dire. "Innis needs money, and he ain't likely to wait for it three months."

"I'll be married off to Eleazar Hyde!" offered Cristin, dramatically. "Percy and I will be kept apart forever. Oh, whatever are we to do?"

"Stuff and nonsense!" Jynx said, and briskly rose. "Three months is not so long! I'm sure that something may be contrived." It seemed a safe enough remark; Jynx doubted that this suddenly formed attachment would last a week. And if it did prove enduring, as Percy had pointed out, it was scarcely her concern.

In that, she erred. Two suddenly hopeful faces turned to her. "Knew you'd help us!" cried Lord Peverell as he grasped and pumped her hand. "There, Cristin, you may trust to Jynx to see all's settled tidily. She may *seem* slow, but she takes every trick."

"Oh, Jynx!" breathed Cristin, damp-eyed. "You are so *good!*"

Jynx was no such thing; Jynx was possessed of no wish to lend her doubtless strenuous assistances to this most tiresome

48

romance but, instead, of a cravenly impulse to flee. But could she, despite her patent unenthusiasm, leave these nitwits to muddle along on their own, and abandon Cristin to the loathesome-sounding Eleazar Hyde, and Percy to the tender mercies of Innis Ashley, who would doubtless see him ruined?

"Hell and the devil confound it!" uttered Miss Lennox mournfully, and she sank back down in her chair.

Chapter
Six

A gentleman so greatly sought after as Viscount Roxbury
might have enlivened his evening hours with any number of
amusing pursuits. He could have chosen among dinner parties
and balls and galas, for Viscount Roxbury was welcome in
every fashionable residence in London, including Carlton
House, a formerly modest two-story mansion which Prinny
had transformed into a palace worthy of an oriental potentate;
he could have presented himself at any of his clubs, White's or
Brooks', have dined luxuriously with the *beaux* at Watier's,
have listened to more serious discussions at the Alfred Club
at No. 23 St. James's Street.

Viscount Roxbury did none of these things. Nor did he
venture forth to the Italian opera; nor don knee breeches and
white cravat and present himself at Almack's, there to survey
this season's crop of young marriageable ladies; nor visit
Vauxhall Gardens, where among the Turkish minarets and
Arabian columned ways an adventurous gentleman might
encounter unfettered females of quite another kind. Instead
Viscount Roxbury enjoyed a solitary dinner in his own home,
which had been built by Sir Christopher Wren, then set out on
foot for nearby Lennox Square. His destination achieved, he
did not present himself at the front door, but crept about the
side of the house in the most clandestine of fashions until he
came to a small walled garden. The viscount's odd behavior
did not end then: he proceeded, in a very skillful manner, to
climb an old oak.

The garden lay before him, a charming enclosure lush with
lilac bushes and roses and noble trees. Directly below him
was a marble bench, upon which a young lady sat in an attitude of gloom. The viscount inched further along the limb,
and dropped a handful of acorns upon her bent head.

"The devil!" gasped Miss Lennox, and gazed upward.

"Shannon! *What* are you doing up there, you wretch? I suppose you had better come down."

Lord Roxbury did so, with such athletic grace that even his fiancée—whose opinion of sporting gentlemen was only slightly more favorable than her opinion of persistent suitors—was impressed. "I didn't," he explained, as he seated himself beside her on the bench, "wish to encounter your Aunt Eulalia."

"That," uttered Miss Lennox with great sincerity, "I can very well understand. It was a similar desire that brought me out here." She wrinkled her nose. "Do you know, Shannon, sometimes I think Eulalia doesn't *want* me to marry you?"

Shannon was inclined to agree. The spoilt darling of London society, he reflected, received scant preference in Lennox House. He took Jynx's hand. "Or anyone," she added, before he could speak. "Eulalia has waxed eloquent all the evening about the pitfalls of marriage, of which she seems to consider Prinny the prime example. For my own sake, I could wish that the royal domestic troubles weren't made so wretchedly public! But what must they do but allow the whole matter to reach the press, so that now Prinny is more unpopular than ever because he's forbidden his wife to see their daughter more than once a fortnight." She sighed. "And the Princess of Wales after dinner each evening makes a fat wax statue, and sticks it full of pins, and puts it to roast and melt on the fire."

"A fate," observed the viscount, "that your aunt apparently wishes me to share with Prinny. Do *you* still wish to marry me, poppet?"

"A fine thing if I didn't!" retorted Miss Lennox. "The announcement of our betrothal has already been published. A nice figure I'd look, wouldn't I, if I cried off *again?*" It was hardly a speech designed to allay a lover's anxiety. In defense of Miss Lennox, however, it must be said that she was aware neither that she had a lover, nor that the gentleman was prone to anxiety. "If you wish to break off our engagement, Shannon, *you* will have to jilt *me!*"

It grew rapidly clear to Viscount Roxbury that his fiancée was not in the best of spirits, and that her thoughts were centered elsewhere. He remedied the situation by grasping her shoulders and shaking her till her untidy hair came tumbling down. "Good God, Shannon!" said Jynx, not in terror but bewilderment; the viscount was disposing in a most ruthless manner of the remainder of her hairpins. "What ails you?"

Lord Roxbury was by no means a fool, and thus did not

attempt to explain the nature of his latest—and, he suspected, fatal—malady. "*I* don't wish to cry off," he announced rather grimly. "If you will recall, we were talking about you."

"But, Shannon!" Jynx's hazel eyes were raised to his face, and in them was not ennui but great curiosity. "Why ever should you think I've changed my mind? And why have you taken down my hair?"

"Because I like it *so.*" Lord Roxbury's fingers were tangled in the chestnut curls. "And you have not answered me."

Her betrothed, decided Miss Lennox, was in a decidedly queer mood. Her wisest course of action appeared to be to humor him. "Shannon," she soothed, "any female in her right mind would wish to marry you! You have the distinguished manners belonging to your rank, a general affability which places everyone at ease and gives a particular charm to your society; you have been endowed by nature with a superior mind, which has been highly cultivated and improved by education, and you can converse on any subject."

"Thank you!" responded Shannon, rather sarcastically. It was amazing how Jynx could simultaneously make a compliment and deliver a set-down. "You have forgotten, in this list of virtues, to mention my social position and my personal appearance—neither of which, I believe, is negligible!"

So startled was Jynx by this unusual display of temper that she drew back to stare, an act which caused the bright moonlight to fall in a most illuminating manner on the low-cut bodice of her sea-green evening gown. Lord Roxbury groaned. "Shannon, what the devil is the matter with you? Of course I'm aware of your exalted social standing and your looks— what female *isn't?* I hope you do not mean for me to present you with a catalogue of your assets daily after we are wed!"

It was not his own assets with which the viscount, at that moment, was concerned. He drew Jynx down against his shoulder and struggled to regain his self-control. "I would not ask you to so fatigue yourself, poppet. Forgive me, please."

"Don't I always?" Miss Lennox found the viscount's chest quite receptive. It occurred to her that she'd been less than generous. "Truly, you *are* handsome, Shannon—as you must very well know! A good number of the young ladies of my acquaintance are breaking their hearts over you."

"But *your* heart is inviolate, isn't it, Jynx?" A foolish question; he had always known it was. "Tell me, where were you this afternoon? I waited quite an hour."

"Oh, heaven!" moaned Jynx. "I had engaged myself to you.

Shannon, I'm sorry! I didn't mean to be gone so long, but I became—er—involved, and I forgot you. Have I sunk myself below reproach?"

"Not at all." Viscount Roxbury gazed upon the disparate elements of the face that was turned up to him, and wished that he might see the generous mouth dimple again. And then he thought, with a bit of surprise, that it would be the happiest man in existence who wakened those sleepy eyes. "It's certainly not the first time, poppet, that you've kept me kicking my heels."

Nor would it be the last, reflected Miss Lennox, who did not deem it prudent to inform her fiancé that she'd been pitchforked smack into the middle of a most exhausting imbroglio. A fine thing, when a lady who disliked above all things to bestir herself was forced to energetically take up the cudgels on another's behalf. And she anticipated precious little help from those she sought to defend. Silently Jynx heaped curses upon the head of the scatterbrained Lady Bliss and her equally imprudent retinue.

Lord Roxbury derived some consolation for his exacerbated emotions from the fact that Jynx had not withdrawn from his embrace. He did not attribute this to his personal charm, but to Jynx's patent abstraction. "Where did you go?" he inquired, rather harshly.

A plague, thought Jynx, upon Adorée Bliss and company! Not only had she been drawn into a wretched situation, but now she found herself under the disagreeable necessity of spinning Shannon a tall tale. "I'm to be married, if you will recall," she muttered, and hid her guilty face against his neck. "It is an event which involves the selection of bride clothes."

Lord Roxbury was utterly astounded that Miss Lennox should move of her own volition closer in his embrace; all the same, he was not so astounded that he did not recognize a clanker when he heard one, a perspicacity he had highly developed during his long acquaintance with Miss Lennox, who would prevaricate mightily in an effort to avoid tiresome unpleasantness. "With *Percy* in tow?" he said in bemused tones. "Doing it too brown, Jynx! And don't bother to tell me Percy wasn't with you, because the pair of you were seen."

"But Percy was invaluable, Shannon!" protested Miss Lennox, thinking rapidly, and wondering frantically just where she and Percy had been observed. "We met quite by accident, and he was most enthused. And you must admit that he has a nice eye for color."

"Color? Certainly! Green waistcoats with yellow stripes! I suppose I may expect you to appear in Hanover Square dressed as a clown—if, indeed, you do appear; and with your Aunt Eulalia making every effort in the opposite direction, I'm not certain of that." Nor was Shannon certain, in light of the companionable way in which Jynx had snuggled up against him, that he would not ruin his own chances by some audacious measure. "I don't suppose, poppet, that you'd care to bypass all the bother and elope to Gretna Green?"

It was a proposal more attractive than the viscount realized; a young lady embarked upon an elopement could hardly be expected to for other people undertake various expedients and shifts; but it unfortunately put Jynx in mind of another damsel who had professed a desire to flee. "We can't do that and you know it," she replied. "It would cause no end of fuss." But further diversion was called for, lest Shannon pursue the topic of her shopping expedition; Shannon was aware of her dislike of such pursuits, and equally aware of Percy's deficiencies in matters of sartorial elegance. "You met Percy at Eton, did you not?"

Viscount Roxbury was indeed distracted, not by Jynx's words but by the fact that, seeking a more comfortable position, she'd thrown her arm across his chest. With difficulty he removed his mind from the tantalizing prospect of getting himself an heir. "Yes," he replied, absently. "Percy was in his first year there when I was in my last. Why?"

Jynx shrugged, an act that—in light of both her ample proportions and her close proximity—very nearly dealt the death blow to Shannon's restraint. "I cannot but think," she remarked obliquely, "that many of these school friendships turn in later years to a positive liability! Percy's all to pieces again. He says he hasn't a feather to fly with. You know the family, Shannon. Why is poor Percy treated so shabbily?"

"He's not." Lord Roxbury dared run an idle finger along the line of her cheek and jaw. "His mother dotes on him, which is half of Percy's trouble; the other is his cousin Dominic, who compensates by insisting on strict discipline. It's ridiculous, but I cannot blame them. Percy is about as capable of looking after himself as a newborn chick."

Jynx wasn't particularly happy to have her own opinion confirmed. "Shannon?" she inquired dolefully. "What happens when one can't pay one's debts? If one is truly done up and there's no help for it?"

"Then one flees to the Continent." Lord Roxbury found it

extremely difficult to concentrate on the conversation. "Or else one finds oneself in the devil of a fix. Why?"

If only she had access to money of her own, she might have bailed Percy—and herself—out of the deep water in which they foundered. But Jynx did not, and she could not imagine that even so indulgent a father as Sir Malcolm would without question hand over the sum of several hundred pounds. "I suppose it must be fate," she murmured, and tried to rise. "I must go, Shannon. Eulalia will be looking for me."

"Let her! She can hardly accuse me of compromising you, since we're already betrothed." Shannon allowed Jynx to sit up, then placed his hands on her shoulders. "I want to know, poppet, precisely what your aunt's told you about marriage."

"Marriage? Very little, save that it's a highly undesirable state." Jynx studied the viscount's handsome face, and considered the warmth of his hands on her bare skin, and wondered from whence Eulalia's wisdom sprang. "Not only marriage, for that matter. Eulalia is fond of pointing out the folly of Caro Lamb, who's made such a cake of herself over Lord Byron. Have you heard the latest *on-dit*? Caro asked Byron for a lock of his hair as a memento, and he sent her one of Lady Oxford's instead. I can't imagine what Byron sees in a woman more than fifteen years older than he— although he's certainly not the first to find her alluring, as witnessed by that brood of lovely children known as Harleian Miscellany! Then again, I cannot see what any lady sees in *him*. Caro would have done better to stick to her resolutions of last year, when she burned Byron's letters and his miniature on a bonfire at Brocker Hall!"

"Byron is a coxcomb!" interrupted Lord Roxbury who, despite this noble effort, was not swayed from his course. "Back to the subject, if you please."

"The subject? Oh, marriage! Well, Eulalia says that gentlemen do not care to be subjected to unbecoming displays of feeling, and that ladies who conduct themselves in a forward manner give rise to disgust."

"Rot!" Lord Roxbury's hands moved to encircle her throat. "Forget everything that woman's told you, Jynx. It's clear she don't know a hawk from a handsaw."

"Do you mean to tell me, Shannon, that a well-brought-up young woman *shouldn't* conduct herself with maidenly reticence?" Miss Lennox looked amazed. "But you yourself said that a woman too much in love was troublesome."

"Surely not!" protested Lord Roxbury. And if he had ever

55

made such a cork-brained remark, fate saw him amply repaid. "What does Sir Malcolm say to this nonsense?"

"Sir Malcolm said that he didn't know anything about what well-brought-up young women should and should not do, and that if I wished the truth of the matter I should apply to you." It had not been the most prudent of advice suggesting that Lord Roxbury's experience with young ladies was legion, and that Sir Malcolm's experience was with females of quite another variety, and Jynx smiled at the memory. Viscount Roxbury was thus aroused from his fascination with the pulse that beat at the base of her throat to an awareness that this was the first time during all of their conversation that her dimples had appeared.

"What's troubling you, Jynx?" he asked. "Why are you so blue-deviled? Tell me and I will fix it, whatever it may be."

Miss Lennox's smile vanished. "It distresses me beyond measure to refuse you, Shannon, but I *can't* tell you. You wouldn't like it above half. But I promise you'll forgive me after the *fait accompli!*" The viscount released her. On his brow was a frown. "Now," she observed, "you look very much like Aunt Eulalia."

"Don't tell me! You should not like to marry a man who looks to you like your Aunt Eulalia!" Jynx watched with interest as Lord Roxbury delved into his pocket, extracted a small box, and placed on her finger a stunning diamond ring. "What are you doing?" she inquired faintly as he again twined his fingers in her hair.

"I am going to show you both what a gentleman expects of his affianced bride, and the difference between myself and your Aunt Eulalia!" announced Shannon, whose patience was at an end. He drew his affianced bride closer and kissed her most thoroughly, during which process he so far forgot his sworn restraint as to dishevel her considerably. "Well, poppet?" he inquired, in thickened tones, when belated prudence demanded that she be allowed to breathe. "Will you now berate me and demand apology?"

Miss Lennox stared at her fiancé in a most distracted manner and sought feebly to readjust the bodice of her gown. The viscount scowled and performed the service for her. "One grows weary," he added, "of forever behaving with decorum and affability. However, if you wish me to moderate my manner, I suppose I must try." It came to his notice that Jynx's shoulders were shaking in a most odd fashion, and that she was biting her lower lip. "Good God, Jynx, I'm sorry! There's no need to *cry* about it! I promise that I certainly haven't developed a disgust of you and—and that you aren't ruined!"

But Miss Lennox was not weeping; Miss Lennox was in the midst of a fit of hysterical merriment. "Oh, Shannon, you idiot!" she wailed, and then subsided into gasping incoherence. So encouraged was Lord Roxbury by this unexpected response that he embraced her once again.

Nonetheless, Miss Lennox was not to receive further enlightenment on the question of what well-brought-up young ladies should and should not do. Eulalia, aware of her niece's habit of taking solitary strolls in the garden after dinner, though not aware of what had initiated that habit, felt herself neglected for too long. Therefore, she entered the garden in pursuit; thus, she witnessed the lethargic Jynx engaged in a most energetic love-scene.

"Well!" ejaculated Eulalia, in the most disapproving tones. "A fine thing, I must say!"

Lord Roxbury opened one eye, observed the lady who loomed over him like an avenging nemesis, and reluctantly pushed his fiancée away. "*I* thought so," he remarked impenitently. Then, before Eulalia could say another word— and that Eulalia had a great many more words to say was obvious—he dropped a kiss on Miss Lennox's brow, stepped up onto the marble bench, and in the manner of his arrival took his leave.

Chapter
Seven

After parting company with his fiancée, Lord Roxbury proceeded to Watier's, where the going was so heavy that few could stand the pace, and there encountered the celebrated Mr. Brummell and the amiably ugly Lord Alvanley, together with Sir Henry Mildmay and Henry Pierrepoint. These gentlemen being intimate drinking companions of the viscount, with whom he had passed some joyous unprofitable evenings, and the viscount feeling that a celebration of some order was indicated, since he had roused if not her passion then Miss Lennox's mirth, he retired with his friends to the Beau's lodgings in Chapel Street, which ran from South Audley Street to Park Lane.

In the book-lined downstairs parlor next to the dining room, the gentlemen took their ease and sampled several bottles of Beauvais claret from the Beau's cellar. Lord Alvanley protested the persistence of his duns, which made such a noise every morning that he couldn't get a moment's rest, and hit upon the happy notion of ordering the knocker taken off the street door; and Mildmay shared a secret confided to him by Scrope Davis, to wit that Lord Byron's careless ringlets were achieved by the nightly application of curling papers; and Pierrepoint delivered his opinion of the poet's latest offering, *The Giaour*, a tale of oriental adventure that had required little thought from the author and less from the reader. Meanwhile, Mr. Brummell lounged in a *dégagé* attitude, with his fingers in his waistcoat pocket, and occasionally offered his quaint absurdities. One of these concerned Lord Roxbury's upcoming nuptials—the Beau offered his services, if the need arose, and professed himself a matchmaker of no small degree—and further libations were deemed necessary. Glasses were raised to the bride and to the groom, to the friends of each, and to their families—save

Eulalia Wimple whose mere name, declared Lord Alvanley, was enough to turn a healthy man bilious. The evening degenerated rapidly from that point, though the only fatality was an ormolu greyhound.

Consequently it was with aching head and fuzzy memory that Lord Roxbury the next day rose, and with a fervent wish that he had been more sparing of his libations to Bacchus. Even in such dire straits, however, Lord Roxbury was a discerning gentleman. Removed from Miss Lennox's befuddling presence, and from the Beau's clever nonsense and splendid Beauvais, Shannon's thoughts achieved a degree of coherence again.

It had not been kind of him, he mused, to abandon Miss Lennox to her aunt's wrath—but had he stayed, he would have lost his temper with Eulalia, and Shannon knew well the adverse effects of argument on pursuits so happily begun. He did not fear that the infernally interfering Eulalia would steal back the ground he'd gained; Shannon knew his Jynx, and the young lady had a mind of her own. It was enough, for now, that he'd planted in that fertile brain the suggestion that Eulalia's frequently aired opinions were so much poppycock. Let her rant and rave! Shannon grinned, then winced. Judging from the dazed expression last seen in Miss Lennox's eyes, he felt confident that she wouldn't be unsettled by her aunt's tirade, probably hadn't even heard a word of it.

But if that matter was on the way to being satisfactorily settled, others were not. Lord Roxbury recalled various enigmatic remarks that had been uttered by his betrothed and his smile vanished. Shopping with Percy? Certainly not! And what had she said about a *fait accompli*? Shannon scowled as he recalled what else Jynx had let drop. Percy and school friends and gaming debts? Shannon had an excellent grasp of the logic of mathematics, and those integers added up to only one sum: Blissington House. Wearing an expression as black as thunder, Shannon set out.

Lady Bliss was in her drawing room, nibbling at slices of cold partridge from a china plate, when she heard a carriage draw up outside. So sunk in depression was Adorée that she did not, as was her habit, rush fearfully to the window in anticipation of bailiffs, but remained stoically on the medallion-backed settee. "Take me, then!" she uttered, without glancing up, as her caller entered the room. "What with claret forty-two shillings the dozen, and coal forty-five shillings the ton, and two free suppers every night, I'm not sure that debtor's prison wouldn't be preferable!"

"Oh?" inquired the viscount. "Things are that bad? I give you joy, Adorée."

"Shannon!" Lady Bliss was magically elevated from the depths to the heights. "You do, I vow! Have you come to repent your cruel treatment, you heartless lad?"

Lord Roxbury grimaced slightly at this form of address, which was hardly appropriate for a gentleman of eight-and-twenty. Still, Lady Bliss had some justification for speaking so; she could give him seven years. "Cruel, Adorée?" he murmured, and disposed himself elegantly in a cane chair. "Have you already forgotten the sapphires?"

If so, it was little wonder, since those gems had remained in Lady Bliss's possession barely overnight. She wondered if Innis had found a buyer for the jewels, and what he had done with the money thus obtained, none of which had found its way into her empty pockets. "I'm sure it's not surprising if I have," she retorted. "You behold me, Shannon, in a perfectly morbid state."

What Lord Roxbury beheld—as Lady Bliss perfectly well knew—was a lady whose dark hair was dressed *à la Madonna*, with a center parting and flowing locks, and who had clad herself in a gown of cherry-striped silk. Since Lord Roxbury was, all told, a tactful gentleman, he did not inform his one-time flirt that she reminded him strongly of a peppermint stick. "Then I am sorry for it," he replied courteously. "I especially wish to speak with you, Adorée."

"Then come sit here beside me!" Encouraged by his sympathy, Lady Bliss patted the settee. All might still be well if the viscount could be persuaded to lend his assistance.

"*Talk*, Adorée," repeated Lord Roxbury, with a slight smile. "You know that I have not come a-courting, and why."

"I know what you say!" snapped Adorée, rendered irritable by this indication that the viscount had no further interest in frivolous pursuits. "I do *not* see why. Your marriage is to be one of convenience, and as such should permit you freedom in matters of the heart. Heavens, Shannon, everyone has an inamorata! Why should you be the exception?"

"Why should I not?" Lord Roxbury was no whit moved by such flattering overtures. "I hardly think my wife-to-be would care to have me enter marriage complete with romantic entanglements."

"Pooh! She's a good, obliging girl, and much too lazy to make a fuss." Belatedly aware of her blunder, Lady Bliss waved her hands in distress. "Or so I hear! I have not heard you say, moreover, that you've formed a lasting passion for Miss Lennox, so I don't see why you should feel obliged to break off your acquaintance with me!"

"Dipped again, Adorée?" Lord Roxbury inquired bluntly. "I told you how it would be if you allowed your brother to ride on your apron strings. Be rid of him and you'll find you've done away with your greatest expense. But I did not come to discuss your brother with you!"

Mention of the improvident Innis recalled to Lady Bliss her brother's strictures concerning the viscount. Innis, she reflected, would not be pleased with her handling of this scene. With more animation than enthusiasm, she rose from the settee, then flung herself to the floor at Lord Roxbury's feet. "Shannon, I beg you, heed me!" The tears in her gray eyes were most effective, if inspired by thought of Innis's displeasure should she fail. "I have tried to forget you, to set you firmly from my mind, but to no avail! If you only knew of the misery I have suffered since you quit me, of the jealousy I've endured, of the sleepless nights I've passed!"

"Heavy work, ma'am!" retorted Lord Roxbury, unmoved. Adorée thought of her debts, and her expensive brother, and clutched his knee.

"Ah, Shannon, you do not believe me!" she wailed. "You think I am a frivolous, flighty creature who exists for only her own pleasure. It is not so! I *do* have a heart, for all my love of adventure! Why, I could tell you——"

"I wish that you would not!" Lord Roxbury interrupted hastily. Lady Bliss possessed not only an overwhelming appetite for adventure, but an astonishing naiveté about men, and she was hardly likely to kindle his ardor by wrinkling and weeping over his excellently fitting unmentionables. "Do cease enacting me this Chentenham tragedy and get up off the floor!"

Adorée did so, having found it distinctly uncomfortable, but she had not yet abandoned hope. She perched on the arm of his chair. "Shannon, Shannon!" she murmured, into his ear. "We were so happy once. You cannot deny it! Surely you cannot have already forgotten the hours we passed together." If so, she would remind him. "Our *tête-à-têtes!* Ah, the things you said to me, the romantic gestures, the——"

"The generosity I displayed!" So little affected was Shannon by her frequent and inviting smiles that he pushed her off the arm of his chair. "I beg I may hear no more of such things! Innis put you up to this, I suppose, because it's not at all like you to make such a rowdy-do. You may tell your brother that you tried, and failed, and there's an end to it."

Sniffling, Lady Bliss resumed her seat on the settee. "I'm sure you needn't blame Innis," she said into her handkerchief. "The moneylenders are urgently pressing him for payment, and I fear their menaces will be put into execution, for Innis simply cannot satisfy their claims. I tell you, it all casts me quite into despair!"

Lord Roxbury might have been more sympathetic had not Lady Bliss teetered on the brink of disaster during the whole of his acquaintance with her. That acquaintance, despite the lady's reputation, had permitted of no greater license than casual familiarities; they had engaged in a flirtation that was both amusing and safe, requiring as it had no depth of emotion from either participant; and Shannon wondered what prompted Adorée, now, to make the devil of a fuss. In search of enlightenment, he made known his puzzlement.

Lady Bliss was in no position to offer explanations, although she might have expressed concern for her niece, and fear of the lengths to which her feckless brother might dare go, and a great curiosity of her own regarding his proposed pursuit of the wealthy Miss Lennox. "You are thinking me a greedy, grasping female, I suppose! But Shannon, I am not! I have a very large and sincere affection for you, and for you to abandon me for a dab of a girl more than ten years my junior is the outside of enough."

Shannon had been thinking, but not precisely that; he had been comparing Adorée's gray eyes to Miss Lennox's sleepy hazel orbs, and Adorée's pouting lips to Jynx's generous mouth, and had discovered in himself a large preference for haughty noses and forceful chins. "I am not the only wealthy man in London, Adorée."

"No," agreed Lady Bliss, deep in her own ruminations, "but word has gotten around about Innis, and most of the wealthy men of my acquaintance consider him a great deal too dear, and those who do not are either repulsive or common." She crumpled the handkerchief. "No matter how dire my straits, Shannon, I will not enter into an alliance with a—a sugar baker! But you are patently disinterested in my dilemma, so tell me what prompted you to part long enough from your fiancée to visit me."

"It seems to me," remarked Lord Roxbury, stretching out his long legs, "that you are suddenly very interested in my fiancée."

"Why shouldn't I be?" Lady Bliss asked bitterly. "The chit caused me to suffer a great disappointment."

"How strange." Shannon's gaze was keen. "You did not seem particularly disappointed when I first told you of my betrothal to Miss Lennox."

"Naturally not." Lady Bliss was deep in gloomy contemplation of her household accounts, in particular the sum of seventy-five pounds outstanding for candles. "I had not met her, then."

This idle observation acted on Viscount Roxbury like flame to kindling. He rose abruptly from his chair. "And when was that, Adorée?"

"When was what?" she queried absently.

"When did you make the acquaintance of Miss Lennox?" Shannon sat down beside her on the settee. "Don't try and say you *haven't* met her, Adorée, because in your usual cockle-brained way you just told me that you did."

Lady Bliss took less exception to the inference that she was a ninnyhammer than she did to the viscount's grasp of her arm. "Oh, Shannon!" she whispered, and collapsed against him. "I knew you'd change your mind!"

Lord Roxbury disabused Lady Bliss of that notion speedily. He pushed her away. "If you do not tell me the truth instantly, I shall shake it out of you!"

"Oh, I *do* appreciate a masterful man!" sighed Adorée. The viscount's dangerous expression warned her not to pursue that line of attack. Still, she had no intention of acquainting Lord Roxbury with her brother's intention of inducing Miss Lennox to make a byword of herself. "It was all quite unexceptionable, and you've no need to make such a piece of business over it! However, I understand that my life and past history are not such as you would wish in a companion of your affianced bride." Unable to master his impatience, Lord Roxbury growled. "I see what it is!" Lady Bliss added, hastily. "She doesn't know about us, Shannon, I'm sure of it!"

Not yet, amended the viscount silently. An excellent gambler with a great degree of cool caution, he'd lay no odds against Miss Lennox's eventual enlightenment. "Shannon, do not be angry with me," pleaded Lady Bliss. "I told her she shouldn't have come here."

"Jynx came *here?*" Lord Roxbury repeated, in awful tones. "The deuce you say! How *could* you allow it, Adorée?"

Lady Bliss, though she might harbor her own reservations about Miss Lennox's appearance at Blissington house, could not be expected to react kindly to similar sentiments from a gentleman who had long had the *entrée.* "You sound," she said wrathfully, "like my home is no better than the fleshpots! What causes you such alarm, Shannon? Do you fear your fiancée will fall in with raffish company? Well, even if she should, I'm sure you need not fear anyone will make off with the chit, because she's too plain for anyone to dream of it!"

Lord Roxbury, in turn, did not appreciate this frankness, and said so. How, he wondered, had he ever been so lunatic as to become embroiled with a creature so conscienceless— and short-sighted—as Adorée Blissington? That sentiment, too, he made known.

But Lady Bliss, who though frivolous, was not unkind, was already deep in remorse. "It's not true, one word of it!" she sobbed into her handkerchief. "I spoke out of pique! Miss Lennox is not at all plain. There is something about her—why, Innis even goes so far as to call her a nonpareil!"

Shannon, by this fulsome praise, was not soothed. *"Innis?"* he repeated ominously. Lady Bliss regarded his brooding expression, and the fingers that dug painfully into her arm. "Devil take it!" said she.

Extracting information from Adorée Blissington, reflected Lord Roxbury, was no less anguish-filled than the drawing of teeth. "You'll tell the truth now," he remarked, and waited. Silently, Lady Bliss contemplated her handkerchief. "I await your pleasure, Adorée!"

"If my pleasure meant anything to you," retorted Lady Bliss, who could not let this patent taradiddle pass unchallenged, "you would not be upbraiding me! I'm sure I don't know how I was to prevent her from seeing Cristin. What would you have had me do? Deny her entrance?"

"Cristin." The viscount's fingers relaxed their grim hold, and Lady Bliss sighed with relief. "Your niece?"

"At least," replied Adorée, following her own train of thought again, this time to the effect that young Lord Peverell was positively haunting her house, despite the promises made his cousin to the contrary, and in the process increasing his indebtedness to Innis, "I have managed to keep *her* out of the gaming rooms."

"The gaming rooms!" Lord Roxbury, who had grieviously misinterpreted this last remark, looked dumbfounded. "You don't mean to tell me Jynx has taken to *play?*"

Of course Lady Bliss meant to tell the viscount no such thing, and she tried to explain, but the viscount was not listening. "So *that* was what she meant!" he exclaimed, recalling his fiancée's pointed questions about unpaid debts. "Oh, my poor darling! No wonder she is so ill-at-ease and fretful! And I had attributed it all to the infernal Eulalia. Tell me, Adorée, I entreat you, is it serious?"

Lady Bliss was prey to conflicting emotions. Obviously Lord Roxbury nourished a degree of affection for his betrothed, and she did not wish to interfere with his romance. On the other hand, she could not be the means by which her brother's hopes were dashed. Yet Innis planned to deliberately wrest Miss Lennox from the arms of her unwary betrothed, and it was hardly fair that the viscount—who after all *had* been generous—should be at such disadvantage. "Damned serious," she said gloomily.

"Then I must see Jynx out of her difficulties. How great is the sum?"

Such forebearance was very nice in the viscount, decided Lady Bliss, but it posed her further difficulties. "I do not know. Innis—" And then she bit her tongue.

Shannon recalled, unhappily, the allure that Innis Ashley held for the ladies. He also recalled Miss Lennox's remark that he resembled, in disapproving moments, her Aunt Eulalia. And then he cursed the day that Miss Lennox had got caught up with Lady Bliss and her rake-helly crew.

Lady Bliss had engaged in her own cogitations, to good effect, despite her unfamiliarity with the exercise. "Shannon," she pointed out cautiously, "I do not think you should tell Miss Lennox what you've learned. She will be cruelly embarrassed, and is likely to blame it all on you."

"You're right," agreed Lord Roxbury, with no little surprise. "Not that Jynx would be embarrassed, but my interference would put her all out of patience with me." And, he added silently, as he recalled the two baronets, three earls, the royal duke and the unhappy marquess, his position was not so firm, despite the encouraging advances made the night before, that he dared hazard Miss Lennox's displeasure. "Adorée, I think I may see a way out of this, but you must help me."

"*I* help *you*?" echoed Lady Bliss. "I don't know how you think I may help you when I myself am in the suds! And don't tell me to rid myself of Innis and close the gaming rooms, because for one thing Innis wouldn't go! And if I did close the gaming rooms I would be no better off, because I can tell a Greek or a Captain Sharp, and I can deal for a faro bank, but I can do absolutely nothing else and have no other way to bring in money!"

Lord Roxbury was in no frame of mind to listen further to such woes. Nonetheless, he was a well-bred Englishman of rank, and this lady had whiled away with him some pleasant hours indeed, and furthermore he required her assistance. "Help me," he interrupted, "and I will in turn help you." She stared at him, arrested in midspeech. "I will pay off the most pressing of your creditors, Adorée. Make me up a list."

"Shannon!" So relieved was Lady Bliss to be rid of this problem that she flung herself again into his arms and wept. Lord Roxbury, who was singularly unstirred by tears that fell as easily as spring rain, waited with resignation for the storm to pass. Jynx had a penchant for the cards? he mused again. It seemed he had much to learn about Miss Lennox.

No less did Innis Ashley, and he looked forward with pleasure to educating himself. With equal pleasure he observed his silly sister sobbing in the arms of the generous viscount. "A truly moving scene," Innis drawled from the doorway.

Chapter
Eight

Lord Roxbury had been prudent indeed not to wager on his
fiancée's continued ignorance of his association with Lady
Bliss, as he had been wise in viewing Eulalia Wimple as an
adder in his path. Eulalia had a veritable bladderful of
poison, and she meant to disgorge it in such a fashion that it
could not miss its target.

This evening found the Lennox family at a musical party
held by the great Whig hostess Lady Holland. It was a small
gathering of about one thousand persons, and among them
were many illustrious members of the *haut ton*. Concerts at
Holland House were fine entertainments where only the
greatest talent in the metropolis was engaged.

Nonetheless, Miss Lennox was not enjoying herself to any
great degree. This was no fault of Catalini, who had been
lured away from the King's Theatre in the Haymarket to
enliven Lady Holland's fete, but to the insidious voice of
Eulalia Wimple in her ear. "Look at our hostess!" hissed
Eulalia, who was once more embarked upon her favorite
theme. "*She* was originally Lady Webster before she ran
off with Baron Holland—married, I believe, at sixteen. And
then there are the Duke and Duchess of Devonshire and
their 'dearest Bess.' "

"All three of whom," retorted Miss Lennox, under cover
of Catalini's rather piercing voice, "live together in the utmost
amity. What *is* the point of all this, Aunt Eulalia?"

Eulalia smoothed the velvet skirts of her gown—which was
mouse-colored, turned up with scarlet and richly embroidered
with silver, and leaned closer still. "I have confirmed certain
disgusting rumors that have recently reached me, and I do
not think you should be kept longer in ignorance."

Jynx hoped fervently that those rumors had not concerned
her own sudden interests in gambling and low life. She turned

her head to look at her aunt. Eulalia's air was nothing short of triumphant. "What rumors are these?"

"Child, I am sorry to tell you this, but you have been misled." If Eulalia harbored any such regret, it was not apparent to the eye. "I am not one to discount the advantages of a title, but there are limits to how far one should go to become a ladyship. In short, dear Jessamyn, I fear that Lord Roxbury is no better than one of the wicked, if not the greatest blackguard alive! Those who consider him an unexceptionable young man may have been gravely deceived."

Such comments might have been—in truth, *had* been—expressly designed to pierce Jynx's equanimity. Still, she did not react as Eulalia might have wished—with curiosity, or embarrassment, or dismay. Instead, Miss Lennox's haughty nose quivered with outrage. "Fudge!" said she, in tones so firm that they called to her the attention of Prince Paul Esterhazy, Austrian Ambassador to the Court of St. James, who smiled benevolently.

"Mind your tongue!" snapped Eulalia. "You may not mind making a spectacle of yourself, but I do!" Jynx refrained from commenting upon which of the pair of them was behaving outrageously, and Eulalia continued more calmly. "I see I must be frank. Very well! I do not scruple to tell you that your precious viscount—with whom you have been behaving in the most imprudent manner!—has been *most* friendly with a certain lady for years." She paused in anticipation of mortification and piqued vanity.

But Miss Lennox was totally free of the sin of vanity, and she had—owing to her most unpaternal sire's open propensities—more than a passing acquaintance with the habits of unmarried gentlemen. She remarked only that, in light of the way in which women fawned upon Lord Roxbury, it would have been a great deal more remarkable if he hadn't availed himself of such companionship.

"Lud, if you ain't a green-head!" It was Eulalia's voice that, this time, caused heads to turn. She lowered it, hastily. "I suppose you won't mind that your husband's fond of women, although tied up, and that he neglects you for high-flyers? For I must tell you, miss, that he ain't given up his little 'companion,' for all he's betrothed to you!"

"I don't see," retorted Miss Lennox, unenthusiastically, "why you must tell me anything of the sort, especially when I don't wish to hear it. Ah, here comes Percy. I am promised to go into dinner with him."

Eulalia did not concede defeat so easily. She held her niece immobile with a hand on the skirt of her gown. "Then ask Peverell," she retorted, "about Roxbury's association with Adorée Blissington! And ask him, too, how Roxbury occupied himself during the two hours he spent at Blissington House today!" That would make Jessamyn sit up and take notice! Eulalia rose and swept magnificently away.

"Lady Bliss?" Jynx echoed blankly. This novel notion explained a great many things, such as that aborted encounter in Hyde Park, and Cristin's knowledge of the viscount, and even Percy's odd behavior. But that gentleman—resplendent in evening attire, to which he'd added a waistcoat done up in a broad stripe of salmon and cramoise—had reached her side. "Dinner, Jynx," he prompted. "Deuced if you don't look knocked up! What's plaguing you?"

Miss Lennox took his arm, and in her eye there was a purposeful gleam. "Lady Bliss," she explained succinctly.

Lord Peverell might have been, as his doting family claimed, a trifle wanting in the cock-loft; but he was not so addle-pated that he failed to realize the extreme impropriety—and great danger—of a discussion of Lady Bliss. "Pooh!" he said, as he led Jynx into a separate room where had been set up a long table with the most delicate and choice refreshments of every kind. "There ain't nothing *bad* in her running a gambling den. Among ladies of fashion it used to be the thing."

"Not for thirteen years!" It must be remembered that Miss Lennox was the daughter of a magistrate. "Not since Lady Buckingham was relieved of the box containing the cash of the faro bank, despite the precautions of blunderbuss and pistols, and her croupier was charged with being proprietor of the box. I was not talking about gambling, Percy."

"Good," said Lord Peverell, morosely. "I don't mind telling you that a discussion of gambling would ruin my appetite. Damned if I see how I ever got so deep in debt!"

Miss Lennox might have explained that matter to him, so uncharitable was her mood, had not fate—in the form of their fellow guests—intervened. Dinner was served up in a buffet style by servants, uniformed in white gowns and aprons, who stood on the other side of the table; and the crush was considerable. Nor did such enforced intimacy lend itself to a discussion of private matters. Jynx listened absently to the chatter all around her, and thus learned that Lady Oxford had recovered from the blood vessel she'd burst upon learning of a meeting between Lord Byron and Caroline Lamb; and that the poet Shelley had written a work entitled *Vindication of Natural Diet* which traced man's evil impulses, and most wars, to a meat diet; and that Madame de Stael, who allegedly considered herself as free as a man to sample romance, had been denounced on the floor of the Convention for conducting a monarchist conspiracy under cover of cuckolding her husband, and had consequently been exiled by Napoleon from France.

"My accounts," remarked Lord Peverell, as he seated himself—with particular care to the lead weights sewn into the hem of his coat to insure that it hung immaculate and creaseless—at one of the small tables placed about the room for the convenience of the diners, "are of the *most* desponding cast. What do you mean to do about it, Jynx? You said you'd help us out."

"*I* said," retorted Miss Lennox, with her fork suspended in midair, "nothing of the sort, as you may recall. Give me one good reason, Percy, why I should help you."

"Well, if that don't beat all!" Lest he erupt into indignation, Lord Peverell took a very large gulp of a very potent champagne punch. "And I was relying on you! What about Cristin, eh? You'd let her uncle marry her off to that curst rum touch, Eleazar Hyde?"

Jynx, a good trencherwoman, saw nothing in this dire pronouncement to interfere with her enjoyment of her meal. "I have no influence with the Ashleys," she replied calmly. "You'd do much better to apply to Shannon. No doubt he would be willing to present your case to Lady Bliss."

Unfortunately, the champagne punch had flown straight to Percy's brain. "A precious lot of good *that* would do!" he uttered irritably. "Adorée Bliss won't fly against her brother, and Shannon has no influence *there*. The truth of the matter is that Shannon can't abide Innis Ashley."

Miss Lennox had recourse to her own punch glass. "Can he not?" she repeated thoughtfully.

"No, and I don't wonder at it! Adorée may be content with a pretty bauble now and again, but her brother won't leave off dipping into a man's moneybags. *That* affair's cost Shannon a pretty penny, I can tell—" And at this point he was rendered abruptly sober by the look in his companion's eye. "The devil fly away with you, Jynx! It'd be bellows to mend with me if Shannon knew I'd told you."

"From all accounts," Miss Lennox retorted unsympathetically, "it'll be bellows to mend with you anyway. Don't fly into alt, Percy; I'd already heard the tale. I merely wished to have the information confirmed."

"I'll tell you what you are, Jynx, and that's too clever by half!" Lord Peverell's glare was most unappreciative. "Leading a fellow up the garden path and causing him to trip over his own tongue! And if I didn't tell you, who did?"

With a fine indifference, Miss Lennox licked her spoon. "My Aunt Eulalia." Percy burst into garbled speech, in which the terms "tale pitching" and "prattle-bag" played a major role. "I understand," Jynx interrupted firmly, "that it is a friendship that has continued for a considerable time."

"You refine too much on it." Percy had a noble, if ill-founded, notion of defending his friend. "The lady is, ah, friendly with everyone! She made a dead-set at him!"

"And of course Shannon could not be expected to find it in himself to rebuff her." Jynx regarded her glass and in one swallow emptied it. "Never mind, Percy! I only wished to ascertain if the tale Eulalia told me was true."

Lord Peverell had recourse to his usual means of dealing with difficult situations; he signaled for more punch. "Well, now you have it, and I wish you hadn't, for Shannon will be convinced I'm a dashed loose-screw!"

Jynx was far too kindly to point out that not only Viscount Roxbury, but the entire world, was already convinced of that very thing. "Shannon will be convinced of nothing of the sort, because you are not going to tell him of this conversation, just as you are not going to inform him that I am aware of his fondness for Adorée Blissington. Do you understand, Percy?"

It was another of Lord Peverell's flaws of character—or virtues, if regarded from the point of view of moneylenders, and Captain Sharps, and others of that breed—that he was easily led. He would no more have attempted to argue with so determined a young lady as Miss Lennox than he would have tried to emulate Lord Roxbury's feat of transversing the Thames in company with a live hare. "If you say so," he replied doubtfully. "But I wouldn't call it a *fondness*, Jynx. It's my opinion Shannon don't care two figs for her."

Even one fig would have been too many, reflected Miss Lennox, cast into a further confusion of the spirits by this additional evidence of her fiancé's profligate tendencies. Bad enough to learn that the viscount was thick as thieves with a dashing lady like Adorée Bliss; worse still to discover that his affections were not engaged. If Lady Bliss meant so little, and Shannon yet continued to pay her court, then his affianced bride could only mean less. Jynx recalled that recent interlude in the Lennox gardens, and Lord Roxbury's warm attentions. "We will speak no more of it," she said repressively.

"Good!" Lord Peverell was making great inroads on his second glass of punch. "Then maybe we can speak of *my* affairs! Dash it, Jynx, you must help us! It's your duty! If not for you I wouldn't have gone back to Blissington House, and I wouldn't have met Cristin, and I wouldn't have run up more debts!"

Lord Peverell's efforts with his champagne punch were as nothing compared with those of Miss Lennox, who had already emptied her glass. It was, perhaps, the quality of the brew that attributed a certain justice to his sentiments. "Why *did* you gamble further?" Jynx focused on her companion with some difficulty. "I cannot imagine that Cristin encouraged you."

"No, but Innis did. He won't let me see Cristin unless I first try my luck with the cards." Percy glanced up, and over his pleasant face spread an expression of horror. "Must go now! A previous engagement! Say you'll help us, Jynx!"

Miss Lennox eyed her companion with a certain resentment. "Oh, very well, Percy." But her words fell on empty air; Lord Peverell, deeming prudence the better part of valor, had taken flight. Jynx wondered at it, briefly; surely Tom Moore, the Irish poet who functioned as a pet minstrel, and who was currently singing ballads in another room, did not exercise such powerful allure. And then she fell to pondering the recent *on-dit* that the selfsame poet had been responsible for the anonymous publication of the satirical *Intercepted Letters, or the Twopenny Post Bag,* which had included several sharp gibes at the corpulent regent and his current favorite, Lady Hertford. Eulalia had some basis for her unflattering opinion of the gentlemen, it seemed.

One such specimen was standing before her, and a fine figure of a man he was. "I do not think," Miss Lennox stated severely, "that I should wish to share my husband with anyone."

Somewhat taken aback by this pronouncement, Lord Roxbury studied his betrothed. She was looking very elegant in a high-waisted and low-bodiced gown of pale Italian crepe, ornamented around the hem with pink and silver ribbon;

and her hair, for a change, was arranged very tidily. Then he noted the two empty glasses on the table before her, and the very vague expression in her eyes. "I can understand," he offered, "why you should feel that way. Come along, poppet! Lady Holland has provided an orchestra for dancing, and you will feel a great deal better for the exercise."

Jynx doubted that anything short of retirement to a convent would elevate her spirits, but she allowed the viscount to draw her to her feet. The room tilted crazily about her, and she clutched at his arm. "I think," murmured Lord Roxbury, "that some fresh air is in order." His amusement was barely concealed.

"One hopes so," replied Miss Lennox, who maintained her balance with only the greatest difficulty. "One also feels that one should have been warned about the effects of that punch." She hiccoughed.

A great number of people remarked upon the fond manner in which Jessamyn Lennox hung onto Lord Roxbury as he led her through the room where a waltz—that dance but newly come into fashion, which was still considered by many as an obscene display—was in progress and out onto the terrace, and upon her abstraction, which was so extreme that she did not respond even to direct comments. So skilled was Viscount Roxbury, and so polite, that no one suspected the true source of Miss Lennox's remoteness. Moreover, so enchanted did the viscount appear with his Jessamyn that Lord Peverell breathed a sigh of relief, thinking that Jynx was a good sort of girl who wouldn't let a minor indiscretion on the part of her fiancé weigh unduly on her mind; and Eulalia sighed in quite a different manner, considering her niece a great deal too tolerant.

Both conclusions had a certain amount of truth in them, yet both were erroneous. Jynx indeed possessed great forebearance, and she had no intention of ripping up at the viscount; but she had been rendered acutely uncomfortable by the revelation that Lord Roxbury was a Man of the World. She gazed up at him, at the gleaming red-gold hair and fascinating features and bewitching green eyes. "One needn't marvel at it, I suppose. It is not your fault that you have a face that makes women fond and men jealous. Doubtless birds of paradise have vied for your favors ever since you came of age."

"True," murmured Shannon, with his dazzling smile. "In point of fact, I believe I came to their notice sometime

73

before. Wealth exercises great allure, poppet, as you must know."

Certainly Lord Roxbury's wealth did, as was more than amply demonstrated by the tenacious Ashley clan. Jynx wondered if the viscount would ever be able to extricate himself from their toils—if extricated he wished to be. "Shannon—" she began, then paused. One could hardly tax even so old a friend with the folly of his *amours*.

Lord Roxbury, alas, took this unfinished remark to refer to gaming debts. "I know, Jynx," he said. "Don't blame yourself for it! All of us at some point blot our copybooks. In truth, the follies of mankind are so legion that one cannot help but be amused by them."

"Providing," retorted Jynx, on whom the fresh night air was not having a salubrious effect, "that one does not sully one's reputation in scorn of the consequence. Are you a cynic also, Shannon? I would not have thought it of you!"

It occurred to the viscount that they might be talking at cross-purposes, but if Jynx did not refer to her gaming debts, he could not imagine what she might mean. "You make too much of it," he soothed, and drew her closer. "My experience with such things is a great deal broader than yours, and you may trust me when I tell you it is the merest peccadillo, nothing more."

Miss Lennox had been merely depressed by the revelation that her fiancé had formed—and apparently meant to continue—a liaison with a lady of questionable intellect and undeniable beauty; but by this indication that he considered such behavior unremarkable she was overwhelmed. "The devil!" she said, faintly.

"You are not to regard it, Jynx!" The viscount was not a little alarmed by Jynx's determination to censure herself. "Believe me, at least in this matter I know what is best for both of us. I do not wish you to be plagued by such things, poppet. All will be settled satisfactorily, I promise. You need think of it no more."

It was true that Jynx had in the most practical of manners arranged this marriage, and equally true that she had expected of her husband no romance, but by this polite indication that in the course of that marriage he intended to elsewhere find both diversion and companionship, she was entirely crushed. "What," she asked feebly, "if I *wish* to think of it? Oh, I admit that I had not expected to, but I recently learned differently, and I think it is *most* shabby of you to tell me I may not!"

"Shabby?" echoed the bewildered Lord Roxbury, who was still under the delusion that Jynx spoke of gaming debts. "I'd call it damned generous. Good God, Jynx, you can't expect me to *like* you to lower your character with such improprieties!"

Miss Lennox could not trust herself to speak, else she would have pointed out that the viscount, just recently, had appeared to like those same improper pursuits very well. She was possessed of a strong desire to slap his beguiling face. But, since violence was foreign to her nature, she rose on her tiptoes, and placed her hands on his shoulders, and kissed him instead. He did not, she noted, protest. And then, because she could clearly no longer trust herself in his presence, in her own turn she fled.

Alone on the terrace, Lord Roxbury straightened his rumpled jacket, and absently adjusted his mussed cravat, which was arranged rather ironically in the Trône d'Amour, a well-starched style with a single horizontal dent in the middle. Shannon was surprised by that queer embrace, and gratified, and he harbored a strong suspicion that Miss Lennox had gone quite mad.

Chapter Nine

Lady Bliss was once more in her drawing room, a chamber that she had come to consider alternately her place of refuge and her prison, for there she withdrew from such annoyances as the gaming gentlemen who haunted her house, and the creditors who threatened to do likewise; and there she sat and twiddled her thumbs in a voluntary incarceration brought about by the fact that she dared not set foot out-of-doors, in fear of bailiffs and other bogeymen, who no doubt lurked just around the corner in wait for her, until her bills were paid.

Adorée glanced around the room, which once she had liked very well. Now she found the damask-hung walls offensive, and the caned furniture dull. Furthermore, the cost of hock had risen to thirty shillings the dozen, and the novel she had chosen for diversion—*The Absentee* by Maria Edgeworth—was no romantic effusion but a realistic description of Irish exploitation by English landlords. She dropped the volume onto a sofa table veneered with mahogany and inlaid with bands of satinwood, its flaps supported on hinged brackets, which stood on a central pillar with a claw base. That, too, aroused Adorée's displeasure. She thought she might like to retire to the country, there to have a garden and some chickens and a cow, perhaps in time to contract an alliance of mutual benefit with some rosy-cheeked squire.

It would not serve, alas; Innis would not let her go so easily. Adorée had fallen completely out of charity with her brother, who had no notion whatsoever of conduct that befit a gentleman. She hated to think what his latest wild start might be, and knew only that it concerned their niece. Cristin was absent from Blissington House, once more in company with the loathesome Eleazar Hyde. The girl was obviously unhappy, and Adorée was sorry for it, but she didn't see what she could do to remedy the situation.

Then there was the matter of Miss Lennox. For a gentleman suffering the pangs of unrequited love, Adorée mused, Innis was being remarkably patient—and for Innis to in any situation be patient was in itself a highly suspicious circumstance. Lady Bliss wondered if she should inform Lord Roxbury that he had made various erroneous assumptions, and acquaint him with the truth, especially since he had been so kind as to take with him a rather staggering total of her overdue accounts. Of the fact that he would pay that total, as he had promised, there was no doubt; Lord Roxbury always kept his word.

Unfortunately, this reflection brought Lady Bliss no relief. Though her bills were to be paid, an event worthy of the most profound thanksgiving, she was expected in turn to present Lord Roxbury with her assistance, and an accounting of his fiancée's further excursions into depravity. How she was to do so, when Miss Lennox hadn't given any indication of being the slightest bit depraved, Adorée could not say. Meanwhile Innis, having witnessed Viscount Roxbury embracing his sister, considered them reconciled, and Adorée had dared not tell him otherwise. Nor had she informed her brother that certain of her debts were to be paid, lest he somehow divert the funds for his own use. Clearly, decided Lady Bliss, she was reaping the rewards of a misspent life. There was scant consolation in the thought that things could grow no worse.

But even that small comfort was not granted her for long. Tomkin appeared in the doorway, an apron tied over his butler's suit and a feather duster in his hand, and an expression of deep suffering on his face, all of which were occasioned by the circumstance that the housemaids had once again parted for greener pastures, their wages in sad arrears. "Lady Peverell, madam!" he announced, then departed, after an oddly commiserating glance. A diminutive creature—clad in a velvet pelisse and bonnet and kid boots, all of violet, a cashmere shawl and lace ruff, Limerick gloves and a large ermine muff—tottered into the room. "Lady Blissington?" she inquired, in fading tones.

Adorée merely nodded, and watched in fascination as her caller without invitation sank into a chair. So devoid of animation was Lady Peverell, so languidly languishing, that she might have expired momentarily. Lady Bliss hoped fervently that to her already bursting budget of woes would be added no death scene. "I am Tansy Phelps," murmured Lady Peverell. "I'll warrant the name is not unfamiliar to you."

"I believe," Adorée replied, and tugged the bell-pull, "that

I am acquainted with your son. There is a marked resemblance between you." This was no idle flattery: Tansy Phelps was a faded version of her handsome son, with the same guinea-gold hair, and the same brown eyes. In Tansy's case, however, the golden curls owed less to nature than to artifice, and the brown eyes were not vacant but brimming with an indefinable emotion.

Tomkin appeared once more, bearing a tea tray, which he placed on the table near his mistress. Her butler was an invaluable individual, mused Adorée, as that dignified individual exited the room. Among Tomkin's countless abilities were considerable culinary art and no small skill as a lady's maid. At least one person was wholeheartedly devoted to the feckless Ashleys. Thus reflecting, and wondering what possible motive had brought Tansy Phelps to Blissington House, Lady Bliss poured tea.

"Jade!" announced Lady Peverell, as she accepted a teacup. The emotion that filled her eyes was now easily defined, and it was malice. "Hussy! Jezebel! There is no point in denying it, for my son has told me all! He is forever boring on about you, and it is enough to make one wish to scream, for he speaks of you with an affectionate familiarity that is positively nauseating! Even for an unprincipled female, which even you must admit you are, your behavior leaves much to be desired, Adorée Blissington!"

Lady Bliss was thrown by these very great incivilities into a state of such extreme consternation that she almost dropped the teapot. Carefully, she set it down. "I beg your pardon?" she said, weakly. "There seems to be some mistake."

"I suppose that shoe *must* pinch!" retorted Lady Peverell, whose habitual invalidism did not prevent her from doing energetic battle in behalf of her son. "Certainly there has been a mistake, and it was yours! Tell me, Lady Bliss, why a tremendous flirt who always has admirers in tow should go out of her way to make a conquest of a scrubby schoolboy? Did you think to prepare for a rainy day by encouraging poor Percy to form a lasting passion for you? To lead him into a life of dissipation so that you might bleed him dry?"

Adorée, left breathless and bewildered by this attack, gaped at her visitor. "Did you think I wouldn't learn of it?" inquired Lady Peverell, with a ladylike sneer. "If so, you are the strangest mixture of coquette and perfect idiot that I have ever met! I have my spies, Lady Blissington—with a nodcock like Percy as a son, one needs must have one's spies! Your skillful work has been most artfully done, but you must have known that Percy would speak of you, and that his family would take steps to end the relationship. And if you did not know it, you are as want-witted as Percy is!"

Adorée saw one tiny gleam of enlightenment in this dire and confusing speech. "Percy spoke of me?"

"Fulsomely!" Lady Peverell dipped into her reticule and extracted a vinaigrette. "I'll own he had sufficient sense not to do so by name. You have, I'm told, an angelic face and lovely figure. You are additionally—Percy's vocabulary being limited—a regular Trojan and bang up to the nines. And in all things maidenly!" Her keen eye raked her hostess. "Zounds! If I didn't know before that Percy had windmills in his head, I'd know it now. Maidenly! Faith, you're thirty if you're a day."

Lady Bliss did not take kindly to this remark, even though she was rather more than thirty; just that morning she had surveyed her mirrored image, and had decided that in her simple round gown of white lawn with a long sash she looked absurdly young. Additionally, Lady Bliss was cut to the quick by these wild accusations, for she didn't number the entrapment of handsome moonlings among her various misdemeanors. "It is very ill mannered," she remarked, "to refer to a lady's age."

"You speak to *me* of manners!" Lady Peverell waved the vinaigrette indignantly. "You, who have displayed to the world the essential vulgarity of your disposition, who can only be condemned for the heartlessness of your conduct? A female elbow-shaker who has so bewitched my poor son that he thinks you a wild and delightful sort of person, and cannot see your basic infamy?" She frowned. "In truth, so befuddled is my poor Percy that he distinctly said your hair was yellow and your eyes blue. And if that's not proof of your influence over him, I don't know what is!"

Lady Bliss tugged a dark curl and blinked her gray eyes. "Blond?" she echoed, on the brink of revelation. "Blue? Oh, Lord!"

"Well you may call upon your Maker!" Lady Peverell said piously, still wielding the vinaigrette. " 'Tis said He listens to even the most unworthy of His flock, and welcomes repentant sinners back into the fold. You might consider the torments of eternal hellfire, if nothing else will sway you from your iniquity."

Lady Bliss stared once more, stunned by her guest's abrupt transformation from maternal vengeance into the means of rescuing her immortal soul. She almost explained to Tansy Phelps that it was her niece who held Percy so enthralled, and then realized she could not. The world in general was happily unaware of Cristin's presence in Blissington House, and an announcement of that fact could only mean Cristin's ruin. Adorée still hoped that, in spite of her own current difficulties and Innis's unknown but undoubtedly infamous plans, Cristin might be settled acceptably. How this was to be accomplished, Adorée did not know, unless heaven intervened in her behalf —an event that, in light of Lady Peverell's most recent remarks, seemed a great deal less than likely—but Adorée could not take a step that would seal Cristin's doom. "I don't see," she protested, somewhat absently, "what you expect me to do."

"Well, now, how very obtuse of you!" Lady Peverell, during her hostess's rumination, had caught her second wind. "I expect you to give him up, naturally! And I might also tell you that I know he's offered you marriage, a piece of sublime wrong-headedness. I suppose I must give you credit for turning down his suit—or perhaps you knew Percy cannot marry without consent until he comes of age?"

Lady Bliss did not explain that she had never had the honor of refusing Lord Peverell's hand because he had never offered it to her; instead, she wondered what had prompted Cristin to reject such a flattering offer. And then she realized that if she was unacceptable to Lord Peverell's family, her niece was not likely to be less so.

"Percy will never be allowed to contract such a *mésalliance*," added Tansy, setting the seal to Adorée's distress. "Lud! A baggage from a gaming house! And one who cannot live within her income, and changes residences frequently to avoid the bailiffs! Gad, to even think that our line might be united with the wild blood of the Ashleys!" She shuddered, dramatically.

"As you have pointed out, it is not likely to come about," Lady Bliss was induced to offer this crumb of comfort by Lady Peverell's demeanor, which strongly suggested a lady on the verge of an apoplexy. "You distress yourself without cause."

"Stuff and nonsense!" gasped Lady Peverell, who would not even if dying accept succor from a shameless hussy. "You are correct in saying it will not come about, madam; I doubt that even you are skilled enough to hold my son's devotion until he comes of age. You may be a diamond of the first water, but you're far from your first youth, and that a younger woman will eventually catch Percy's eye is clear as noonday."

Lady Bliss could not argue with this, nor could she point out that a younger woman already had. Poor Cristin! she thought. Even if the Fates smiled, and the girl was allowed to have her gullible lordling, she would gain this termagent as her mama-in-law. Then Adorée's thoughts turned to herself, who was no less deserving of pity. Here she was, a woman without protection or solace or the admiration of any gentleman, and what must this inconsiderate Lady Peverell do but harp forever on her age?

"Still," remarked Lady Peverell, who despite her words wasn't convinced that Percy would recover from his infatuation, in regard to which he exhibited a refractory behavior quite unlike his usual amiable obedience, "I am willing to parlay with you. My son's sentiments are not widely known, nor do I wish that they should be. In order that the family may avoid the shameful *éclat* which the publication of such disgusting intimacies would produce, I am prepared to offer you recompense."

Adorée, whose temper had already been sorely tried, found in this pretty speech considerable grounds for offense, chief among them Lady Peverell's opinion of the quality of her embrace. Disgusting intimacies, indeed! Had Lord Peverell truly been among her swains, he would have been in extremely illustrious company, for the admittedly lengthy list of those who had sued for—and most ardently—the favor of Adorée Blissington included the most influential gentlemen in the land, up to and including the prince regent. Not, she added silently, that Prinny was any great conquest. But there were practical matters to consider. "Recompense?" Lady Bliss repeated, warily.

"Exactly." Convinced that she had correctly judged her adversary, Lady Peverell abandoned her vinaigrette. "I am prepared to offer you ten thousand pounds."

"Ten thousand!" For that sum, Adorée could have a small mansion in the country and a whole herd of cows. Providing, of course, that Innis didn't divest her of it first.

"Not a penny more. Do you think me a flat?" Lady Peverell's vocabulary had been greatly broadened by conversation with her son. "Well, madam, what do you say? In turn all you need do is see my son no more and deny him entrance to your house."

Adorée's dreams abruptly collapsed. She took no offense at Lady Peverell's offer to buy her off, and considered it an admirable solution to a great many things; but she recollected that Percy's fondness was not for her, and realized that by barring him from Blissington House she would deny her niece any chance of happiness. But, ten thousand pounds?

"Perhaps," continued Lady Peverell, contemplating her son's new-found and rather addle-pated tenacity, "you had best first blast him with a devastating rejection, and *then* deny him your presence. That would do nicely, I think."

Lady Bliss, who had never locked her door against any admiring gentleman, and who furthermore had no greater ability to deliver a scathing rejection than she had to fly, goggled wordlessly. Lady Peverell, who had not expected such dull-mindedness from a lady who lived by her wits, made haste to point out the alternatives. "You are, I imagine," she remarked, "acquainted with criminal conversion cases? Those legal offenses in which an adulterer may be accused of assault and trespass on a person's property, which frequently bring for the plaintiff heavy damages, while the defendant, if unable to meet this bill, is sent to debtor's prison? It would be a great pity, Lady Blissington, if you were sent to gaol!"

Lady Peverell's grasp of matters legal may have been a bit shaky, but Lady Bliss's was even worse. In addition to her recurrent nightmare of the debtors' ward at King's Bench Prison, she had a horrid vision of herself blazoned throughout the civilized world as a seductress of innocent and unwary young men. Even clearer, however, was her mental image of Percy's sadness should he be forever parted from the object of his affections, and she rose to the occasion with a nobility of character that surprised even herself. "I cannot do it," she said sadly. "I cannot be the means by which that young man is plunged into grief."

Lady Peverell was not gratified by this hard-wrung admission that her son was regarded with some fondness by the notorious Lady Bliss. "You are not only an unscrupulous female," she announced, with a repetition of her sneer, "but a fool to boot! Very well, Lady Blissington, we shall play this out your way—but I warn you that the responsibility must be upon yourself! I have no recourse but to lay the entire matter before my cousin." She rose to her feet. "You would have done much better to take my offer. Dominic will make you pay for leading poor Percy to the brink of infamy, and I'll warrant his price will be dear."

"I wish," retorted Adorée, herself on the verge of a distempered freak, "that you would leave! Tomkin!" The butler appeared as if by magic in the doorway, a feat explained by his habit of eavesdropping. "Show this female the door!" With a last reproachful glance, Lady Peverell exited, trailing her shawl. In a mood of great lamentation—which included everything from her virtuous refusal of ten thousand pounds and the consequent loss of a little place in the country and the probable ruin of what remained of her good name, to the countless indiscretions of the Ashley family, to her own reckless career and the inception thereof when at the age of eight she had embarked upon a flirtation with the gardener's lad— Adorée tottered in a remarkable if unconscious imitation of her recent caller to her own bedchamber, there to console herself with a large dose of laudanum.

Chapter
Ten

It was not a great deal later that Miss Lennox, prompted by a prodigiously inconvenient conscience, approached the red brick house in Portland Place and raised an apathetic hand to the door knocker. It was true, as Lord Peverell had pointed out, that if not for her, he would not have returned to Blissington House; and Jynx meant to learn from Cristin just how serious was his case. She rapped on the door.

The portal swung open, and she stared, as did Tomkin, still in housemaid's attire. "We are at sixes and sevens today, miss," he said severely. "You would do much better to go away."

"And you," Miss Lennox retorted serenely, "are the most rag-mannered butler I have ever encountered. I begin to think you dislike me, you know. Do you mean to keep me standing on the doorstep, or will you inform Miss Ashley that I am here?"

"Oh no, miss!" Tomkin allowed her to enter and behind her barred the door. "It is just that I knew you was a lady the minute I clapped my eyes on you, and I was very wishful to keep you out of our little hobbles! But if you wish to see Miss Cristin, I'll take you to her, and no more said."

Jynx eyed this rather disgruntled-looking dignitary speculatively. One member of the Ashley household appeared to possess a smattering of common sense. "It isn't that I *wish* to see Miss Cristin," she allowed, "but that I think I must. Word has come to my ears that her affairs are in a bit of a tangle."

"You might say so." Tomkin was so delighted by the opportunity to carry on a rational conversation that he completely forgot his place. "What with her ladyship stretched out stiff as a corpse on her bed, and Master Innis raving like a lunatic because he's discovered her ladyship's bills are to be

84

paid, and Miss Cristin—well! Least said, soonest mended, I always say."

Miss Lennox did not subscribe to this maxim. "I don't understand," she murmured, as they mounted the stair. "Why should Mr. Ashley be angered by the payment of his sister's debts?"

Within Tomkin's dignified breast, prudence warred with a love of gossip, and lost. "Because Master Innis would've much rather had the money to use for himself, and the thing was fixed so he could not. I might as well tell you, miss, that the bills are to be paid by her ladyship's most particular friend, and Master Innis has no great love for that gentleman." Diligent as was Tomkin's eavesdropping, it had not acquainted him with Miss Lennox's association with her ladyship's most particular friend, and he thought it odd that with these happy tidings Miss Lennox should turn pale. "There!" he said solicitously. "I've tired you out with my prattle, and I'm sorry for it. If you'll wait in the drawing room, I'll fetch Miss Cristin."

"No!" Miss Lennox, recovered from her shock, had no wish to stem the butler's flow of confidences. She gestured to a suite of rooms. "Are these the gaming saloons? Will you show them to me? You see, Tomkin, I've no notion of how such things are carried on."

Tomkin wasn't at all reluctant to further a young lady's education, particularly when such philanthropy postponed the detested moment when he must go and deal with the mountain of dirty dishes that filled the kitchen sink. He pointed out the apartments where deep basset was played, and whist; he indicated the E.O. table, the stands for the punters' rouleaux and glasses, and explained how it was the way of E.O. banks to win. When he moved on to a discussion of piquet, and the tendency of luckless gentlemen to hope for a change each rubber, to risk all on the chance of a big coup, which too often eluded them, Miss Lennox deemed it time to interrupt.

"You are devoted to the Ashleys, I gather?" she inquired sympathetically. "I feel for you, then! It must be a wearing task, keeping them from going off the deep end."

Tomkin had long ago given up the luxury of offense at the various uncomplimentary remarks that were made about the Ashleys, most of which were true, and Miss Lennox's acumen only increased his respect for her native wit. "Needs must when the devil drives," he uttered gloomily. "I'm mortal afraid to turn my back on any one of them in case of what they may do. I don't mind admitting, miss, that they have me fretting my guts to fiddlestrings, and that's the plain truth! Just yesterday I had my teeth examined, and was told that I've been grinding them in my sleep, and have chipped their edges!"

"You poor, poor man!" Jynx's sympathy was not spurious; she suspected her own molars might suffer the same fate. "It is a shame the family is not more considerate of you."

"Considerate? An Ashley?" Tomkin so far abandoned his dignity as to snort. "Dicked in the nob, the lot of them, and these two are no more than a loose fish and a pea-goose!" He realized the extent of his imprudence, and flushed. "Not that it's my place to say so, or to be standing here jawing! If you'll wait half a minute, miss, I'll bring the young lady to you."

Miss Lennox watched the butler's exit, which was hastily accomplished, and with considerable effort restrained her mirth. It was fortunate that she did so; at the doorway, Tomkin turned back. "Since you're here, miss, which you shouldn't be, I'll give you a word of warning as shouldn't: steer clear of Eleazar Hyde!"

Jynx would have liked to ask a great many more questions, all of which concerned that last-mentioned gentleman, but Tomkin had departed. She wandered to the E.O. table, all merriment gone. Eleazar Hyde, she mused, a man of whom she had not thus far heard one good word said.

Slightly less than half a minute had elapsed when Cristin ran into the room. "Jynx!" she cried, and embraced her friend. "I am glad to see you, but my aunt is ill and I cannot stay."

Jynx held Cristin at arm's length and studied her. The girl's natural gaiety was considerably dimmed, and her blue eyes were dark-shadowed. "What's wrong with your aunt? Nothing serious, I trust? Child, you look shockingly worn!"

"Aunt Adorée? I don't know. A seizure of some sort. She keeps drumming her heels against the bed and wailing in the most distracted manner about ten thousand pounds. I can't make any sense of it." Cristin's eyes dropped. "As for myself, there's nothing you can do about it, Jynx, so you need not even try."

Though it was not designed to do so, that martyred statement had the effect of inspiring Miss Lennox to make inhuman efforts. She grasped Cristin's arm, thus aborting an attempt at flight. "Cristin," she said sternly, "who the deuce is Eleazar Hyde?"

Still, Cristin refused to meet her friend's gaze. "A friend of my Uncle Innis. Or maybe not really a *friend:* I think Mr. Hyde has some sort of hold over him." She took a deep breath. "You might as well know, Jynx, that I have told Percy we would not suit. I am to form a connection with Mr. Hyde instead."

To refuse the handsome Lord Peverell in preference of a depraved-sounding person like Eleazar Hyde was behavior incomprehensible even in an Ashley. Miss Lennox, a plain-spoken soul, said as much. The result of this bluntly expressed opinion was that Cristin flew into a rage.

"I know you think I'm a gudgeon!" declared that damsel, wrenching free of Jynx's hand. "You believe that I possess the Ashley lack of stability! Well, my understanding may not be great, but it's greater than Percy's, and if I make myself agreeable to Mr. Hyde, my uncle may be persuaded to let Percy off the hook." She met Miss Lennox's stunned gaze, and shrugged. "Mr. Hyde is heavy company, without a grain of humor, but he will not expect much of me. Besides, I am only Percy's calf-love, so what does it signify?"

"Moonshine!" exploded Miss Lennox. She was prepared to utter a great many more objections but fate, in the form of the dashing Mr. Ashley, intervened. "Cristin," he remarked, from the hallway, "your aunt is calling for you." Cristin's leave-taking was accomplished in a manner that left little doubt that she held her uncle in a great deal of awe.

Innis contemplated Miss Lennox, who was toying in a dilatory manner with the E.O. table, and watching the gyrations of the little ball, and congratulated himself on the fore-sight that had kept him from his usual daily pursuits, from a stroll up St. James's Street, a spot of exercise in the fencing rooms of Gentleman Jackson's Bond Street boxing saloon, a pleasant hour passed in examination of the latest acquisitions at Tattersall's. In truth, it had not been so much foresight that had prompted Innis to refrain from the usual pursuits of the gentlemen of fashion that he aped, but an unconquerable fury at his sister's unprecedented sleight-of-hand. However, to Innis, it was ever the end that was important, not the means.

"You are in high bloom today, Miss Lennox!" He sauntered into the room, noting with approval her simple—and ob-viously expensive—white muslin pelisse and walking dress. "A sight to brighten the eye of the most jaded gentleman."

Jynx raised her own sleepy eyes to him. If Innis expected an exchange of compliments—and well Innis might have, for he was a figure of quiet splendor in his coat of green superfine, well-starched shirt collar that brushed his earlobes and framed his chin, pale salmon marcella waistcoat, green kerseymere trousers, and tasseled Hessian boots—his hopes were doomed. "A pretty scoundrel *you* are!" Miss Lennox remarked indifferently. "If you did not run up such profuse expenses in the gratification of your caprices and luxuries and silly appetites, you would not have to go about coercing people to your will."

Innis was a trifle discomfited by this cold remark, which was clearly as much a reflection on his intelligence as on his habits; but Innis was also sublimely confident of his ability to lure the loftiest young lady down off her perch. Therefore, he adopted a disarmingly rueful expression. "Sweet torturer, I thought you had forgiven me."

"I expect that is your problem." Jynx didn't appear the least affected by either contrition or palpable charm. "People have forgiven you all your life, so you think that they are bound to do so, and therefore you are absolved of one offense only to go out and commit another." She cast him a distinctly quelling glance. "I do not think I wish to engage in conversation with a shocking rake-shame."

Innis wondered if perhaps he would not have found more congenial company in Bond Street or St. James's. But that company would not have been half so wealthy, he reminded himself, and persevered. "You wound me," he murmured, and came even closer. "If that is the way you speak to all the gentlemen who discover in themselves a distinguishing preference for you, my darling, you will soon lose all your *beaux*."

"Excellent!" retorted Jynx. "I've already told you I don't care for *beaux*. We will go on much better, you know, if you spare me your nonsensical vows and professions. I have no taste at all for Spanish coin."

Nor for him, it seemed, Innis reflected with chagrin. He wished to please Miss Lennox, and not entirely because of her wealth, but in lieu of fulsome praise he did not know what to say. Perhaps she might prefer a man of action to a man of words? He took hold of her shoulders and drew her abruptly into an embrace.

Miss Lennox, however, was no shrinking violet to be cast into confusion by an uninvited caress, nor was she unacquainted with familiarities attempted by reckless gentlemen. Innis attempted to kiss her and she averted her head, so that he found himself in close proximity to her bonnet's ostrichplumes; he sneezed and she kicked his shin. Innis swore in a most ungentlemanly manner and released her. Jynx grinned at him. "You can't say," she observed, "that you were not warned."

The situation was nothing short of deflating for a man considered on all sides dangerous. Innis scowled, then noticed how enchanting were her dimples, and then found with some amazement that he was returning her smile. "Witch!" he said, when the pain in his abused leg had subsided enough to permit him to speak. "It seems I must apologize again. I don't suppose you'd believe me if I assured you that I should pine away of a melancholy if you are not reconciled to me?"

"Don't sham it so." Jynx perched in a graceless manner on the E.O. table. "A simple expression of your regret is all that's required."

"But I *don't* regret it, only that you foiled my attempt. Nor do I promise to refrain from trying again." Innis fancied that control of the situation was again his. "Now, since you are here, would you care to try your luck at the bones? Perhaps play a rubber or two of piquet?"

But Miss Lennox, thanks to the efforts of Tomkin, was forewarned. "I do not gamble," she reproved, as her gaze traveled around the room. All the same, she wished to speak further with Innis Ashley. "There, sir, is the perfect thing. I will engage in that game with you, if you so wish."

It was a game of an altogether different nature that Innis had in mind, but his brief association with Miss Lennox had already taught him the wisdom of biding his time. He fetched the board. "You came here alone?" he asked, as he set up the game. She nodded. "And you call *me* imprudent, Miss Lennox?"

"I am supposedly matching some ribbon." Jynx pulled off her gloves in preparation for play. "There's none to say that I'm not doing that very thing, even my poor maidservant, whom I gave the slip in the Pantheon Bazaar. And now, sir, since you are a betting man and I would not wish to spoil your pleasure, I will suggest a wager of five pounds on the outcome of this game."

"You *are* my pleasure, so you can hardly destroy it." Innis had watched with no small appreciation the serious manner in which she prepared to play. "No matter how you try. Very well, five pounds it shall be."

And so the game began. Innis quickly discovered that his opponent had no small skill. She also possessed no little guile, for she distracted him at crucial moments with questions that required all his attention. For example: "I understand," remarked Miss Lennox, "that you have lured Lord Peverell further into debt. Was that an honorable act, Mr. Ashley?" Of course, Innis was forced to defend himself. And: "I also understand," observed Miss Lennox, as her fingers flew over the board with lightening speed, "that you have encouraged Cristin to turn down Percy's suit. It seems very foolish to turn aside a prospectively wealthy nephew-in-law when one is persistently in debt." To this, Innis responded in greater length. Eleazar Hyde, he explained, was a much larger catch than Lord Peverell, and additionally Percy was already deep in his debt. So stirred was Miss Lennox by this admission that she remorselessly cleared all his pieces from the board. "You have underestimated your opponent once again," she commented, with her lazy smile. "Five pounds, Mr. Ashley."

Even that small amount hurt his depleted purse, but Innis behaved like a true gentleman and promptly paid the debt. If only, he thought again, he had known of Roxbury's generous treatment of his sister in time to persuade Adorée to ask for cash. But Roxbury was a damned knowing one, and probably wouldn't have obliged. Innis glanced at Miss Lennox, who was looking very smug, and experienced a tardy astonishment that anyone should have inveigled him into something so mundane as playing checkers. In confrontations with Miss Lennox, Innis was coming out all too consistently on the losing end. "You have a positive talent for silence, my darling. I wish that you would talk more, for talking makes a woman think less."

"And you do not wish me to think about your preposterous behavior, lest I conclude that you are definitely not to be trusted, and deplorably frivolous, and that it is altogether displeasing of you to have persuaded Cristin to marry Mr. Hyde to serve your own ends." Jynx regarded his startled face. "How many times must I tell you that there are no flies on *me*, Mr. Ashley?"

"Clearly there are not." Mr. Ashley had been distracted by sight of her magnificent betrothal ring. "A pretty bauble, that. May I take a closer look?" Miss Lennox hesitated, suspicious. "Do you think I'll take it from you? I may be untrustworthy—and I admit to that!—but I'm not a pickpocket!"

Jynx was not of a temperament to willingly inflict unhappiness on any man, unless that man was a suitor who had grown too importunate; and it appeared from Innis's wounded expression that she was guilty of misjudgment. "Just who," she asked rather absently, "is Eleazar Hyde?"

"A damned fine piece," retorted Innis, with equal lack of attention. "Not Eleazar, this ring! Roxbury is very generous, as I have good cause to know. You will want for nothing as his wife, Miss Lennox."

Save her husband's affection, Miss Lennox reflected silently. "That is," added Innis, "if you prefer a husband who is distant and cold, and whose infidelities are legion—but you will tell me, rightly, that it is none of my affair." He laid his hands over hers. "Save that any man who has a fondness for you must deplore such a match. If I were so fortunate as to be in Roxbury's place, I promise I would treat you very differently."

Jynx had no doubt of this; the viscount, for all his failings, did not require that she pay his bills. Still, she did not draw her hand away. There was a vast and illuminating difference between these two men who were paying her court. Innis Ashley lost little, she thought, in comparison with a pattern card of respectability. But her poor maid was probably by this time in an absolute frenzy, wondering where her mistress had gone. "Cristin's marriage with Eleazar Hyde?" she prompted, gently.

Frowning, Innis hesitated, then decided to be honest. She'd find out the truth, anyway, soon enough. He turned over her hand and with his fingers traced the lines of her palm. "You have been deceived. It's not marriage that Eleazar offers. I trust I need not be more specific?" Jynx stared at him, horrified. "Do not look at me *so*, my darling! I'm in need of a great fortune, and Eleazar is prepared to come over handsomely. What else can the girl hope for?"

"A great deal more than that, I think!" Now Jynx did try to draw away, but Innis held her fast. "What kind of man are you, who'd sell your own niece into debauchery?"

"A weak one," retorted Innis, who was dismayed to discover that Miss Lennox possessed such high principles, and no less dismayed to discover in himself a vast reluctance to allow her to think so poorly of him, great wealth or no. "But not wicked, I swear it! I like this no better than you, but there is no help for it. It was Eleazar's decision, and I dare not say him nay."

"You need a fortune so badly?" inquired Jynx, more quietly. The depth of his emotion was unquestionable, though his sincerity remained in considerable doubt.

"I do." Innis conceived suddenly of a notion that was staggering in its simplicity. "There is only one thing that might stay me from my course, that might allow me to tear up Percy's vows and allow Cristin to have him. You know what that is, I think."

Jynx thought so, too, and her predicament appalled her. "Tell me."

Carefully, Innis set the betrothal ring on the card table. "Yourself," said he. Before she could speak, he drew her to her feet, and embraced her passionately. Too stunned by these recent disclosures to put up a defense, Jynx submitted. It was, after all, an admirable opportunity to study the differences between the honorable Lord Roxbury and the extremely dishonorable Mr. Ashley.

"I thought," Miss Lennox said, rather breathlessly, when she was at length released, "that you dared not defy your friend Eleazar."

"My darling," murmured Innis, who was no less short of breath, "for you I think I would dare anything."

"Dare me and be damned!" came a voice behind them. Jynx regarded Innis, the picture of guilt, and spun around. Before her was a stout and balding individual of advancing years and dissipated countenance. Miss Lennox had no prior acquaintance with such creatures, but she had no doubt she beheld a *roué*. "A nice enough filly," remarked the *roué*, who had observed her in turn. "She ain't exactly to my taste, but I daresay the Dragoons would like her." Innis made a choking sound.

Tomkin had, after a severe struggle with his conscience regarding the mountains of dishes that remained to be washed, succumbed to the lure of eavesdropping; and Tomkin adjudged it time to rescue Miss Lennox. "I beg pardon," he announced, from the doorway, "but the young lady's carriage is waiting."

"Thank you, Tomkin!" Miss Lennox—who found she did not appreciate being stared at as if she were plump and tasty fowl—sped in a positively energetic manner from the room. In the hallway, she regarded her unlikely savior. "I suppose you know that I do not *have* a carriage?" The butler's expression was wooden. "I am grateful to you for sparing me from being put further to the blush."

"Precisely, miss." In perfect charity with one another they proceeded down the stair. She had been well served, reflected Miss Lennox, for seeking distraction from her own problems

—which concerned her fiancé's dilatory attitude and lecherous tendencies, and her own shocking behavior on the night of Lady Holland's party—in Blissington House. Upon her arrival she'd had only to worry about whether or not she had actually dared kiss the viscount, her memory on the point being rather fuzzy. Now she was presented with the further matter of Cristin's proposed liaison with Eleazar Hyde, the mere contemplation of which made the flesh crawl on her own bones, and the question of whether it was precisely honorable to encourage Innis in an ardor that she didn't mean to return. "The devil!" Jynx said aloud.

"Quite, miss." Tomkin's prolonged sojourn in the hallway enabled him to speak with the utmost commiseration. So sunk in despondency were the both of them that neither recalled Miss Lennox's abandoned betrothal ring.

Chapter
Eleven

True to her word, Lady Peverell no sooner returned to her charming home in Clarges Street, a white-painted stucco structure with round bow windows, a low-pitched roof and fanlights over the door, than she retired to her sitting room, sat down at the delicate writing desk that stood in front of a small window, and dashed off a note to her cousin Dominic. That Lord Erland would respond promptly to her summons, she had no doubt; it was couched in such terms that the earl must surely think that Tansy had gained knowledge of a disaster second in magnitude only to imminent invasion by the French.

Restlessly, she paced the chamber, which was a lovely little room with painted paneling and gray brick fireplace and gay rococo ceiling, furnished with a profusion of gilt and mahogany, the most outstanding piece of which was a tall bookcase, its doors embellished with painted glass showing scriptural stories in black and yellow. Tansy heard the footsteps that she had awaited, and threw herself in a stricken manner upon the sofa. The footsteps came closer. She moaned.

It was a performance lacking for nothing, suggesting it did that Lady Peverell had at least one foot, and possibly a great deal more, through death's doorway; but it won no appreciative ovations from her audience of one. Dominic Devlin, Earl of Erland, was singularly unappreciative of ladies who languished and swooned. In point of fact Lord Erland, a confirmed bachelor, had scant time for ladies of any kind, which is not to say that he had not, at the age of five-and-forty, enjoyed countless successes among the fair and the frail. Definitely, Lord Erland had done so; his conquests were legion; but so far was the earl from an appreciation of genteel hearts and blue blood that he took his pleasure among the muslin company.

Unnerved by the continued silence, Lady Peverell opened

a cautious eye. Dominic stood gazing down on her, a hostile expression on his swarthy face. This did not discourage her; Dominic always looked hostile, or angry, or something of that sort. He was tall, dark, ill-tempered and, as is sometimes the case with indifferent gentlemen, completely bewitching. Tansy Phelps was not the only lady to secretly nourish a *tendre* for the earl, who had successfully avoided entanglement with parson's mousetrap for a disgustingly long number of years.

"Well, Tansy?" Lord Erland inquired, in that deep harsh voice that invariably afflicted those who heard it, particularly if they were of the female persuasion, with delightful goose-bumps. "What catastrophe has occurred this time?"

"Dominic!" Lady Peverell extended a languid hand, which the earl sidestepped adroitly. "I did not hear you enter. Tell me, what news?"

"News?" repeated Lord Erland. "Surely you didn't drag me away from a meeting of the Four-in-Hand Club just to acquaint you with the latest occurrences?" Tansy opened her eye wider, and discovered that her cousin was clad in a long and voluminous driving coat, silk-lined and of the appropriate down-the-road cut, a high-crowned beaver hat, drab trousers and top boots.

"It all seems so nonsensical," she commented, in fading tones. "All this pother simply to drive to the windmill at Salt Hill to dine. I would think, Nicky, that you might find some more *useful* way to pass your time."

Lord Erland did not ponder the injustice of this remark, as presented to a gentleman who busied himself in Parliament and on committees and with matters of state, and who was additionally a top-sawyer with four-in-hand. He wondered if equally disparaging remarks were proffered by the families of Lords Sefton and Barrymore, Colonel Berkley, the Marquess of Worcester and Sir John Lade. "I suppose I must indulge you," he remarked, as he seated himself in an armchair of graceful proportions, built of mahogany with fine details of reeding and grooving in the arms and back. "Your interest in the state of the country is commendable, for all that it comes so late."

At this unkind cut, Tansy's other eye opened, and she regarded her cousin cautiously. If she knew the signs—and none knew the signs better than she—he was in one of his hey-go-mad humors. "Nicky——"

"No, don't apologize! I am glad to oblige you. I always *do* oblige you, do I not, cousin?" Lord Erland looked nothing short of saturnine. "Let me see, where to begin? Ah, I have it! You will be interested to know that I am engaged with a society of coal owners formed to consider the problem of safety lamps. A Dr. Clanny of Sunderland has produced one, but it is too unwieldy. We plan to apply to Sir Humphrey Davy, once he returns from France, where he has gone to accept a Napoleon Prize for his discovery of sodium and potassium. The emperor himself issued Sir Humphrey a safe conduct—marvelous, is it not? With all Europe at war!—and Humphrey and his assistant Michael Faraday are engaged in travel through France and Italy, visiting various laboratories and making diverse experiments. At last report they were engaged in proving that the diamond is a form of carbon."

"Diamonds?" Lady Peverell hadn't the least interest in the world beyond the boundaries of the *haut ton*, as her cousin very well knew. "Safety lamps?"

"Definitely, safety lamps." Among Lord Erland's vices was a strong tendency to engage in sardonic humor. "I assure you, naked candles will not do, especially in the deeper pits. The lower the men work, the greater is their risk of encountering fire damp, the deadly explosive gas. You may recall the explosion last year, when over ninety men and boys either burnt to death or suffocated."

"I beg you, do not speak of such things to me!" Lady Peverell raised a hand to her pallid brow. "Recall that I am a victim of intermittent ill health, and that I must be treated carefully."

"For myself, if I must expire of an illness, I would prefer to die the martyr of excess. You must suit yourself, of course." Lord Erland, in his highly imitated left-hand-only method, opened his snuffbox. "What other news can I give you then? I attended a grand night at Mrs. Hope's recently. The regent stood for one-third of the evening in converse with Lady Elizabeth Monk, who leaned gracefully the entire time on a bronze ornament in the center of the room. And the king, it's said, has ordered his yacht to London in the belief that the city has drowned."

Lady Peverell wondered uncharitably how much of the old king's madness could be attributed to this one of his statesmen. Dominic was sufficiently provoking to inflict in even the most rational being—which George III had certainly never been—a brainstorm. "Nicky," she said again. "I wish to speak to you!"

"We *are* speaking, are we not, cousin?" Lord Erland was at

96

his most bland. "It promises to be a lively season, does it not? Madame de Staël is due to arrive in London momentarily, where she will doubtless be lionized, less on account of *De la littérature*, in which she dared compare our own age with the decadent pre-Christian Roman Empire, than because she has now been exiled for the third time from France; and Caro Lamb is now sending Byron clippings of hair from—well, I shan't tell you where from, but you may imagine."

Lady Peverell could indeed imagine, and she uttered an outraged shriek. "Nicky! How *can* you speak of such things to me? Must I remind you that you are not in the company of one of your demireps?"

"No," retorted Lord Erland, without the least repentance. "Believe me, Tansy, I am well aware of the difference. Now sit up and cease enacting me high drama and tell me what dire occurrence has led you to summon me here so peremptorily."

As usual, he had managed to put her at the disadvantage. Tansy arranged herself in a less invalidish position and regarded him. Lord Erland might be cold and stern and artful, tiresome and standoffish; he might be quite cavalier about his visits to her, and invariably made her cross as crabs; but there was an aura of distinction about him, and he was extremely clever, and the merest glimpse of his unfriendly face left her heart pounding and her throat dry. "Nicky," she said soulfully, "you must be prepared to hear very bad news."

Every time Lord Erland entered the home of his cousin, he was greeted with such, and he had harbored little hope that this visit would prove the exception. He slouched down in the chair and, without hesitation, told her so.

"Nicky, we are undone!" Tansy clasped her hands to her rather meager bosom, and assumed a look of woe. "You behold me in a perfectly morbid state."

What Dominic witnessed was a lady embarked upon histrionics of an appalling degree, and he had no more patience with such high flights than with their perpetrator. That opinion, also, he made known.

"If you aren't the most aggravating man!" Lady Peverell abandoned her swooning posture sufficiently to glare. "I suppose next you will tell me that you consider it perfectly acceptable that Percy has taken to—to philandering!"

"*Has* he?" For the first time, Lord Erland exhibited signs of interest.

"Oh, Nicky, he has!" wailed Lady Peverell. "And I don't know what to do about it! He is dancing attendance on a *most* unsuitable female, and you can well imagine the anxieties that must constantly prey on my mind. Dear cousin, you *must* help me put an end to it!"

"Must I?" Lord Erland was patently unenthusiastic. "Why? It's high time the boy made his acquaintance with the petticoat line. *Past* time, really, since he's four-and-twenty." His smile was wicked. "Why, *I* was but——"

"Never mind!" Lady Peverell said hastily. "The world knows your opinion of women, and that you grew disenchanted at an early age. But for you to encourage Percy in such behavior is both cruel and unnatural. He is so *impressionable,* and that creature will encourage him in every sort of excess!"

"You've seen her?" Lord Erland helped himself once more to snuff.

"I've not only seen her, I've spoken with the jade!" Lady Peverell's indignation lent color to her cheeks. "Nicky, you simply cannot permit Percy to persist in this folly. Heaven only knows what will come of my foolish boy if he continues along this path."

"Fustian!" remarked Lord Erland. "What do you expect *me* to do about it, Tansy? I'm no longer Percy's guardian, and he would highly resent any hints dropped by me. And so he should! It would be a great piece of impertinence for me to interfere, and if you've any sense you'll hold your own tongue. If Percy is desirous of mounting a mistress, it's none but Percy's affair."

The color that had briefly suffused Lady Peverell's cheeks faded with this blunt vulgarity. "If that were all!" she moaned. "Nicky, my bird-brained son has offered marriage to the wench!"

Lord Erland, who having settled this little matter to his own satisfaction, if not to that of his cousin, was preparing to depart, sank back down into his chair. "He *what?*"

Her son's indiscretions were almost made worthwhile, decided Tansy, by the expression on her cousin's face. Never had she seen the saturnine Lord Erland look so dumbfounded. "I *told* you it was serious! Oh, she's turned him down this time, and seems to have no other view but that of fleecing him, but I don't doubt that if he persists she'll have him in the end. In fact, I'm sure of it! What other possible reason could she have for turning down ten thousand pounds?"

"Ten *thousand?*" echoed Lord Erland, in the exact tones—though he could not know it—that had been voiced by the subject of this conversation. "I think you'd better start at the beginning, Tansy!"

Lady Peverell did so with gratification, having at last secured her cousin's full attention, which was not an easily accomplished feat. The tale she related was far from succinct, and highly dramatic, but she presented the truth as she knew it with laudable accuracy.

"One moment!" interrupted Lord Erland, at a particularly emotional point in the tale. "Do you mean to tell me that you've set *spies* on the boy?"

Actually, Lady Peverell had *not* meant to tell her cousin that, for she knew he would disapprove, but now the fat was in the fire. As was her custom, Lady Peverell promptly sought to shift the blame. "What else was I to do? *You* had abandoned poor Percy, had left him to wander unprotected through the leisures and dissipations of this town. Heavens, Nicky, have you no notions of the pitfalls that await the unwary in London?"

"I fancy," Lord Erland replied testily, "that I've a greater notion of those pitfalls than you, having in my own callow youth tumbled into every one of them. Cut line, Tansy! This maternal solicitude of yours is nothing more than a desire to keep Percy forever in leading strings."

Lady Peverell ignored this unchivalrous remark. "Surely," she said sternly, "you don't mean that Percy should follow in *your* footsteps?" Lord Erland, given the choice of allowing his cousin to continue or quarreling with her, which would doubtless result in her strangulation at his hands, fell silent. With a distinct air of triumph, Tansy continued her tale.

She had not gone far, however, before Lord Erland was once more driven to speech. "So you called on the creature and offered to buy her off. Sometimes, Tansy, I think you're as paper-skulled as Percy!"

Lady Peverell stared in outrage at her cousin, and pondered the inequities of a fate that had decreed she should harbor tender emotions for a gentleman who was so blind to her true worth, and found relief in an attack of vapors. Lord Erland regarded her without the least sympathy. Undeterred by his lack of encouragement, Tansy waved her vinaigrette. "I do not know," she gasped, "how you can be so cruel to me."

Lord Erland squelched an unchristian urge to explain. "This

is fair and far off!" he said impatiently. "Who *is* this female who's sent Percy tumbling head-over-heels?"

"Oh, Dominic!" Tansy's voice was weak. "You will understand my perturbation better when I tell you that Percy has formed an attachment for Adorée Blissington!"

"Lady Bliss?" Once more, Lord Erland looked stunned. "Good God, I didn't know the boy was so discerning!"

This remark, which might have gratified Lady Bliss no end, plunged as she had been by Lady Peverell's remarks into a premature contemplation of her own unlovely and unloved old age, had the opposite effect on Tansy. "Sense!" she screeched. "One of faro's daughters! A family of ne'er-do-well vulgarians!"

"*That* won't wash!" the earl retorted crudely. "Our own family has been notorious for centuries for savagery and violence. Come down from the boughs, Tansy! I meant only that Adorée Blissington is a deucedly pretty woman."

"So she may be!" Lady Peverell's choler, if truth be told, was inspired not so much by Lord Erland's callous attitude as by her own jealousy. *Pretty* was a word that Tansy had never before heard on the earl's lips, and she would have very much preferred, if hear it she must, that it apply to herself. "She is also twice his age!"

Lord Erland, who very well understood his cousin's sentiments, and deplored them even more, let this rank exaggeration pass. "So she turned down your offer," he mused. "I wonder why. She can't seriously mean to *marry* Percy."

"What else *can* she mean to do?" Recalling that she wished to engage her cousin's efforts in her son's behalf, and also that her cousin was quite capable of walking out on her if he became either enraged or bored, both of which states afflicted him with unnerving frequency, Tansy refrained from further demonstrations of outrage. "Even I, as Percy's mother, cannot think she has a true fondness for him. I can only suppose she has an eye to his fortune—although I will admit she didn't strike me as a *managing* sort of female!"

This remark had the effect of bringing a definite sparkle to Lord Erland's dark and wintery eye. "I think it safe to assume that," he said wryly. "From all accounts, Lady Bliss has a positive genius for *mis*management. You made a great error, Tansy, when you offered her money. God only knows, as a result, what maggot the lady will get in her head."

"Nicky!" Lady Peverell looked aghast. "You don't mean——"

"I mean you've made a rare mull of it!" Lord Erland rose and donned his elegant driving coat. "It would've been much better to let the matter take its course."

"Oh, Nicky, I am very sorry if I've made a botch of it, but I didn't know what else to do!" Tansy was the picture of woe. "I didn't wish to bother you with my little troubles! You have already done so much for Percy—and for me! Pray do not be angry."

Lord Erland liked his cousin no better in a fit of contrition than when vaporing, and whatever efforts he had taken on behalf of the Peverells had been inspired by a sense of obligation and a great disgust with Tansy's dramatic megrims. Though ill-natured and harsh-tempered, however, Lord Erland was not cruel. "I am not angry," he lied. "Do not take on so, Tansy."

Lady Peverell's pale eyelashes fluttered prettily. "You will help me, then?"

Lord Erland's expression was almost savage. "I have scant choice in the matter. As one of Percy's trustees, I am duty-bound to see what may be done." With this deflating comment, he turned on his heel, and was gone.

Tansy sighed disheartenedly, then consoled herself with the reflection that she was not the only lady to unsuccessfully bear the torch for Dominic, and that he had for none of his admirers exhibited the least preference. Indeed, he tended to avoid them like the plague, amusing himself instead with females less demanding and more reckless. It was Dominic's stated opinion—and how like the man!—that such creatures were a great deal more congenial than their so-proper counterparts.

Dashing females? Lady Bliss! Tansy sat bolt upright, stricken to the soul by the tardy realization of what she had done.

Chapter
Twelve

Lennox Square was crowded with carriages and mettlesome horses and the clatter of iron hoofs and wheels. Coachmen swore mightily at one another as they tried to force their way through the confusion. In turn, and after considerable effort, each drew up to the brightly lit residence of Sir Malcolm Lennox, and the occupants were by liveried servants assisted tenderly in disembarking. Bright streams of light shone from the mansion's windows, and the music of an orchestra drifted out into the night. Despite Eulalia Wimple's great efforts to the contrary, the betrothal between her niece and Lord Roxbury continued in effect, and Eulalia had taken what scant consolation was available to her and had harried Sir Malcolm into throwing open his home to the *ton*.

The ballroom was a splendid chamber, decorated in a fashion that only Eulalia—and perhaps the regent—could applaud. It was an oriental fantasy, lush with such unforgettable Chinese motifs as pagodas and waterfalls, strange elongated birds and dragons and icicles, japanned furniture and screens. On the walls were scenic papers designed to continue around the whole of the huge room; from the ceiling hung a vast central chandelier featuring silvered dragons and tinted lotus flowers, a misconceived fantasy which only Prinny fulsomely admired.

It was the usual assemblage of beauty, splendor, and profuse magnificence. The regent was present, as were the more distinguished and powerful and amusing of his subjects. So crowded were the premises that there was standing room on only the staircase, and at least one young lady had fallen into a faint. It was a shocking crush, all agreed; the most successful ball that this season had yet seen.

Yet not all present were gratified by the triumph, and the most notable of these exceptions was the young lady in whose honor the festivities were being held. Miss Lennox, it was noted, was not her usual lethargically cheerful self. One unkind wit went so far as to whisper that Miss Lennox looked less like a young lady soon to embark upon the pathway to marital bliss than a prisoner en route to the guillotine.

There was good and sufficient reason for Miss Lennox's distraction—a state that had induced her aunt to dose her with everything from Godbold's Vegetable Balsam (for Consumption and Asthma) to Velno's Vegetable Syrup (for All Else)—and that reason was not unrelated to her upcoming nuptuals. Miss Lennox had become aware of the loss of her betrothal ring. There had been no opportunity to slip away to Blissington House to retrieve it; Eulalia, having sniffed something in the wind, had been sticking as close as a court plaster to her niece all day. Consequently, Miss Lennox was doing her utmost to avoid her fiancé.

She looked quite lovely in the evening gown of pale pink sarcenet with tiny puff sleeves and a narrow skirt trimmed with double ribbon fluting, with which she wore a small fortune in matched pearls; and she stood out among the women in their elegant variegated dresses, enhanced by sparkling diamonds and waving plumes, like a perfect rose in a cabbage patch. Jynx did not appreciate this fact, nor the viscount's tall stature. She knew perfectly well that his brooding gaze followed her around the room.

Still, appearances must be kept up. She paused briefly by her father, who was holding forth to Lord Castlereagh on such matters as the upper class, which throve on enhanced rents and paid too small a portion of the war taxes, revenue that was raised largely by duties on consumption, and the effect of which was felt mainly by the poor; she listened to Sir Sydney Smith's revised vision of heaven and hell, the latter of which consisted of a thousand years of tough mutton, and the former *pâtés de foie gras* eaten to the sound of trumpets, and to his remarks on the regent's Royal Pavilion at Brighton which, said Sir Sydney, looked as if St. Paul's had gone to sea and had pups. Then she fell prey to Lord Alvanley, who was once more worrying about his rich uncle, a sickly gentleman who never quite managed to die, an event that Lord Alvanley had anticipated for years, so that he might settle his debts and then enthusiastically accumulate new ones. From Lord Alvanley she was rescued by the celebrated Mr. Brummel, without whose presence no party was a success. Mr. Brummel spent several moments in

103

gently satirical conversation with Miss Lennox and informed her of his inclination, should the regent continue to behave badly, to bring the old king back into fashion. Miss Lennox smiled politely at all these sallies; and responded in her usual slumbrous manner to the flattering attentions presented her; and grew increasingly more depressed.

Meanwhile, Lord Roxbury grimly watched, performed a minuet and a number of country dances in the most completely elegant style, and drank rather more of his host's excellent claret than was wise. At length, he judged that Miss Lennox had been made to suffer long enough, and made his way to her side. With so little grace was this accomplished, and with such poor success did Miss Lennox mask her strong impulse toward flight, that several persons remarked upon the fact that, since the betrothal of Lord Roxbury and Miss Lennox, the amiability of both seemed to have deteriorated rapidly.

"Shannon!" uttered Miss Lennox, rather unoriginally. Lord Roxbury grasped her arm, steered her past a flamboyant matron who was discoursing at loud length upon Turner's *Snowstorm*—in which the painter had employed Hannibal crossing the Alps as an excuse for offering a huge and violent sky—and behind a potted palm.

"Well met, poppet!" uttered the viscount, in tones that were anything but cordial. "You are looking very out-of-sorts tonight."

It elevated Jynx's spirits not at all to be thusly informed, especially after the great effort she had made to look sublimely without concern; and it appalled her even further to discover that her fiancé had, in the vulgar parlance, shot the cat. "You've been into papa's claret," she said severely. "And there's nothing wrong with me save that Eulalia's been worrying me to death all day."

"Not only Eulalia, I fancy!" Shannon discovered a certain unsteadiness in his knees and leaned against the wall. "Shall I tell you about the damned odd thing that happened to *me* today?"

Miss Lennox studied her betrothed, who was most oddly presented against a background of peach blossoms and imperial dragons and impassive mandarins; and did an unforgiveable thing. She giggled. "Shannon, you're foxed!"

It was obvious to Lord Roxbury that Miss Lennox did not adequately comprehend the gravity of the situation. "And so would you be, were you in my boots!" he announced, in such ominous tones that Jynx's amusement fled. "Just where is your betrothal ring?"

Clearly, it was the moment for confession, and Jynx thought it would be a great relief to bare her soul. Wishing only that the viscount was a trifle more sober, she opened her mouth.

"Don't bother! I am obliged to stop you in order to avoid the unpleasant necessity of convicting you of a plain lie, I see." The remark was not precisely truthful; Lord Roxbury's vision was far from clear; but the sneering manner in which he made his delivery was masterful. "Good God, Jynx, have you not *one* estimable or redeemable quality?"

Miss Lennox, the number of whose virtues was nothing short of remarkable, was not a little alarmed by this unfair attack. "Shannon, why are you so devilish out-of-humor? And tonight of all nights what possessed you to drink too much?"

Lord Roxbury did not care for this suggestion that he was in his cups. He was, of course, and he admitted it, but it was very bad of his fiancée—whose character, as had been all too amply demonstrated to him, was far from admirable—to make such a fuss over his little lapse from propriety. He told her so. "Furthermore," he added, as his sense of injustice increased, "I suppose you think you are clever to hold my devotion while ignoring my advice! I tell you, Jynx, I don't like the appearance of things at all!"

Nor did Miss Lennox, who had been struck dumb and almost lifeless by the viscount's remarks. Almost lifeless, but not quite. A spark still beat in her astonished breast, and that spark was very close to being ignited into a blazing, and unprecedented, rage. "Moderate your manner, Shannon!" she hissed. "Remember where we are. What the devil has driven you to ring such a peal over me?"

"As if you didn't know!" The viscount's left knee betrayed him and, in regaining his balance, he performed a neat little dance-step. "Don't bother to spin me a Banbury story! I already know you to be an unconscionable little liar."

"This," Miss Lennox uttered wrathfully, "is beyond everything! Devil take you, Shannon, make an end. What is it that I'm supposed to have done?"

In this manner recalled to the purpose of the conversation, Lord Roxbury fumbled for his coat pocket. He found it on the third attempt. "I was visited today by no less than Mr. Rundle—of Rundle and Brydges, the jewellers. You are acquainted with Messrs. Rundle and Brydges, Jynx? The gentlemen from whom I purchased your betrothal ring?"

"I have," Miss Lennox admitted cautiously, "heard of them. Court silversmiths, are they not?"

Lord Roxbury was not to be led into side issues, such as the most recent purchases of the regent, and the ladies upon whom those purchases had been bestowed. "Mr. Rundle," he continued inexorably, "brought me a curious tale. It seems a gentleman came to him this morning with a certain ring to sell. Mr. Rundle recognized the ring and its bearer; fortunately, he also recognized the potential scandal involved." He extracted his hand, not without difficulty, and extended it. "Well? Have you nothing to say for yourself?"

Miss Lennox did not, it seemed; Miss Lennox appeared at that moment to be turned into stone. She wondered who Mr. Rundle's caller had been.

"I thought not!" Lord Roxbury, alas, misinterpreted her silence. Considering the vast number of misapprehensions under which Lord Roxbury labored, it is not at all surprising that he should. "If you had to sully your reputation, Jynx, you could have chosen a less unscrupulous knave than Innis Ashley to do it with! As you can see, he betrayed you at the first opportunity."

With this revelation, Miss Lennox was roused to speech. "It was *Innis* who took back the ring?"

"Who else?" Lord Roxbury's brows had drawn together in a tremendous scowl. "I know the truth, so there is no need to try and prevaricate. Good God, is our betrothal of so little importance to you that you would game away your *ring*? Am I to have a wife who is forever involved in various escapades and scandals? The prospect turns me perfectly sick!"

"Game?" echoed Miss Lennox faintly. "Scandals and escapades?"

"I told you not to try and pull the wool over my eyes!" Shannon looked, she thought, as if he wished to wring her neck. "I guess I must not blame you; Innis Ashley would be irresistable to most women; but I would have thought you of all women to have more sense. But no! You go blithely off to Blissington House, which is bad enough; and you take to gambling, which is even worse; and then you compound your folly by engaging with Innis Ashley in private interviews! Don't you realize that you have been *compromised?*"

Miss Lennox, who labored under a few misapprehensions of her own, had come to realize a great many things during this tirade. Among these realizations were that Lord Roxbury's mind was of a mean and little structure, and that his great popularity had endowed him with an insuperable vanity and an appalling tendency to utter officious and disgusting sentiments, and that the situation in which she found herself was utterly insufferable. And in addition, she thought as she studied him, the wretch was as proud and as conscienceless as Lucifer.

Belatedly, the viscount suspected that he had gone too far, a suspicion born distinctly out by Miss Lennox's features: she was staring at him as if he were the fiend incarnate. "There!" he said, and placed the ring in her hand. "I have had my say, and we will think no more of it. No doubt your love of excitement carried you almost unconsciously into impropriety."

Miss Lennox positively loathed excitement, for all that it had recently come to be her lot; she was also extremely provoked by her fiancé's moralizing. "So you do not despair of me, Shannon?" She clutched the ring so tightly that the stones cut through her gloves. "You will trust me to refrain from indulgence in any more Bacchanalian scenes?"

It occurred to Lord Roxbury that he had never before witnessed the particular expression that now rested on Jynx's piquant face. If such a thing were not unheard of in a young lady of quiescent disposition, he would have thought her on the verge of a temper tantrum. "Of course I trust you," he replied cautiously. "I daresay I've been a little harsh, but you must see—"

What Jynx saw was that in addition to his previous sins the viscount was a hypocrite. She informed him of both her former and latter conclusions, in a voice that shook with unmistakable fury. "A *hypocrite?*" repeated Lord Roxbury, appalled by the manner in which his great scene of righteous denunciation had slipped beyond his control.

"A hypocrite!" Miss Lennox stamped her foot on the floor. "You berate me, yet your conduct has been worse! All *I* did was go and see Cristin—and how you came by this notion of me gambling is quite beyond my comprehension, though it is true that I spoke privately with Innis, in an effort to learn if I might extricate Cristin and Percy from his toils!" She was pleased to note his horrified stare. "The only game I ever played in Blissington House was checkers, by which I won from Innis five pounds!"

Lord Roxbury did not pause to ponder the whimsical picture of the rakish Innis so innocently engaged; Lord

Roxbury had been rendered abruptly sober by the realization of how grievously he'd erred. "Oh, Lord!" he mourned. "Jynx——"

But Miss Lennox was in the grip of temper for the first time in her life, and it would have taken an act of the Almighty to prevent her from having her say. Since the Almighty was apparently not inclined to intervene, the viscount, as well as any number of interested bystanders, were privileged to hear Miss Lennox's virgin outpourings of wrath. "It was Lady Bliss who told you, I'll warrant! Trust her to muddle the thing so completely!"

"Not Adorée," protested the viscount, but Jynx gave him no opportunity to explain that Tomkin had, from the most altruistic of motives, dropped a word of warning in his ear.

"Not?" Miss Lennox's hands were on her hips, and her hazel eyes sparked fire. "Balderdash, Shannon! I know what she is to you!"

Such an audible outburst of spleen was, alas, bound to reach any number of ears. Conversation faded; the orchestra ceased to play; all waited avidly to hear what might next issue from behind the potted palm. Even Sir Malcolm, who had made even greater inroads on the claret than Lord Roxbury, stopped halfway through a discussion about a notorious Vere Street brothel, the clientele of which included a startling number of noblemen and wealthy cits, to peer about him in an owlish manner and wonder what caused the queer behavior of his guests.

"You do?" inquired Lord Roxbury, in a bemused manner. This untimely distraction was caused by the sight of Miss Lennox's magnificent, and heaving, breast.

"I do!" Jynx proceeded to demonstrate the truth of her words. "You say our betrothal is of little significance to me, yet *you* have a light-o'-love, and mean to keep her, and even pay her bills—and *I* was prepared to accept the situation, to remain calm about your stated intention to honor her above me, quelling prospect as it seemed!"

"But, Jynx!" protested the Viscount. "I didn't——"

"Of course you did, and I recall it clearly, so you needn't try and bamboozle me!" Miss Lennox became aware of the direction of his gaze. "My God, are you incapable of resisting no woman who wants you? It seems not! And it quite decides me *not* to marry you!" She hurled the ring at him. It missed its target and went skidding across the marble floor.

108

A murmur rose from the rapt crowd. Consequently both Lord Roxbury and Miss Lennox were roused to a realization of their surroundings, a realization that made the viscount grind his teeth and Jynx flush with embarrassment. "Are you quite through?" he inquired, in a most deadly tone, as he grasped her arm.

But Miss Lennox's wrath had built up in her slowly, and no quicker would it depart. Too, she was beset by conflicting and confused emotions, among them misery that Shannon could even temporarily think the worst of her; and a great regret that she had broken off their engagement, no matter how shabby his behavior; and an even greater disappointment that she should be so lacking in pride and dignity as to weep all over her lost love.

Weep she did, to the spectators' fascination, but it was not on Lord Roxbury. Instead she drew back her hand and slapped his handsome face, and bid him go and be damned, and then picked up her skirts in a definitely vulgar manner and ran from the room.

Naturally, after the first startled moment, confusion reigned. Eulalia, viewing success beyond her wildest dreams, hid her triumph behind an elegant swoon; Sir Malcolm, unacquainted with the circumstances that had led his daughter to make such a scandalous spectacle of herself, promised the furious-looking viscount that she should be indefinitely confined to bread and water in her room. After Lord Roxbury was heard to retort that he thought such extreme measures to be a very good thing, speculation hummed like a thousand buzzing bees.

Chapter
Thirteen

At all events, Miss Lennox was not fated to suffer incarceration in her room. She entered this chamber in the conventional manner, crossed the floor, and exited through the window via a handy oak tree. Due to the method employed in her exit, none of the guests who were at length persuaded to reluctantly depart Lennox House were aware that the object of their avid conjecturings had already taken her leave. Miss Lennox considered that although the rest of her behavior may have been appalling, for this tidy feat she deserved praise.

Many would take leave to doubt this conclusion, and among them was Lady Adorée Blissington. The hour was late, and her gaming rooms were in full swing. She watched a young gentleman punt frequently against the bank, so that he lost on one side what he won on the other, and could never lay claim to any considerable sum; she overlooked a not very serious game of hazard in the smaller saloon; she tiptoed past a group of gentlemen engaged in a deadly game of whist, played for high stakes indeed. Then she entertained various of her guests with a deck of playing cards, which she opened and closed like a fan. This legerdemain was, she thought, the only legacy left by her deceased spouse.

That reflection sent her mood plummeting again. Adorée was in a sad case, alternately in tearing spirits—Lord Roxbury had proven as good as his word, and her debts had been paid—and in the sullens. The latter case was brought about by a great many things, which need not be reiterated here, and the combined result was that in one moment Lady Bliss felt herself incapable of coping with the difficulties that beset her, and in the next attributed her debility to the onset of advanced age. Deep in woe, she induced the cards to climb like a ladder up her arm. A cold hand touched her shoulder. Envisioning the grim reaper come to claim his own, Adorée shrieked and dropped the deck.

"I'm sure I beg your pardon, madam," Tomkin said hollowly. On his gaunt features was an expression that could only be interpreted as shock. "I wasn't wishful of startling you. If you would step into the hallway, my lady, there is a small matter that requires your attention."

Lady Bliss knew that tone, and it betokened catastrophe. She excused herself, and proceeded her butler into the relative privacy of the hallway. "Tomkin!" she hissed, when they were alone. "There *can't* be bailiffs in the house; my bills have been paid! Unless Innis's creditors—but Innis always manages to lay his hands on money when it's that or the River Tick, and no one ever comes dunning him!"

"Not bailiffs, madam," interrupted Tomkin, in the familiar manner of an old family retainer who was personally acquainted with his mistress's various little shortcomings, rather to his regret. "Worse."

"Worse!" Lady Bliss was uncomprehending. "Tomkin, nothing can be worse than bailiffs in the house!"

The butler snorted, skeptically. "I wouldn't lay odds on that, if I was you madam! I've put the young lady in the book room, not thinking you'd be wishful of the gentlemen getting a glimpse of her. And I've given her some refreshment, too, and lit a fire, because if she comes down with pneumonia we'll really be in the suds, and she's in a shocking condition."

Adorée suffered, during this little speech, great presentiments of doom. *"What* young lady?"

Tomkin, it appeared, could not bring himself to explain. "If I may advise you to make haste, my lady, before one of the gentlemen comes looking for you? I would not trust the young lady to stay put, the state she's in. Very put-about she is, and muttering to herself, and looking like she's wishful of breaking things." Convinced of the need for haste, Lady Bliss—though she would much rather not have—proceeded to the book-room.

This was a small chamber, sparsely furnished, in which Lady Bliss did—or as was more often the case, did *not* do—her accounts. Slowly, cautiously, she opened the door. With a great deal more haste she closed it, and herself, inside. "My dear Miss Lennox! What on earth has happened to you?"

"Well you may ask!" replied that young lady, who was

111

lounging in a careless manner on the sofa, and whose gown and elegant coiffure had not adapted well to climbing down trees and making midnight flights. "Suffice it to say that my usage in every respect has been barbarous!"

"In *every* respect?" Adorée sank to her knees by the sofa. "You poor child! Surely Innis did not—I mean, I know he is impatient, but—oh, dear!"

"Definitely, Innis!" Miss Lennox contemplated her empty glass. "Could Shannon but see me now, he would probably accuse me of having taken to brandy, on top of all else! And I'm sure it would be little wonder if I did."

"Shannon?" Bewildered, Lady Bliss sank back on her heels. "But I thought it was Innis who had ill-used you. Heavens! You cannot mean that *both* of them——"

"I mean precisely that!" Miss Lennox looked as if she might spit nails. "I cannot say whose was the original abuse, but the other certainly compounded it!"

"You cannot say?" Lady Bliss echoed faintly. "Both of them? But they don't even *like* one another! How did this horrid thing come about?"

Miss Lennox, aware of her hostess's extreme consternation, temporarily forgot her own wrath. She regarded Adorée, who wore a gown that could hardly have been more revealing, and whose dark hair was fixed atop her head in a flower-adorned Apollo knot; and recalled the reputation of the lady to whom she spoke. "Lord, not *that!* Though I am as effectively ruined as if it had been, I'll warrant. It's merely that Innis pawned my betrothal ring, and Shannon thought *I* had done so to pay gambling debts, and made the devil of a kick-up!"

Lady Bliss recalled her brother's latest windfall, one hundred guineas of which had gone to purchase a lively miss from a noted procuress, and moaned. "I cannot understand," continued Jynx, whose temper was still on the flare, "why men should be regarded as unquestionably superior beings! It seems to me that they are uniformly bacon-brained! And it is beyond bearing that Shannon should upbraid *me* for flaunting public opinion when *he* is nothing more than a—a voluptuary!"

"He is?" queried Adorée, perplexed. "Shannon? I mean, Lord Roxbury?"

"Indubitably." Miss Lennox nodded wisely. "An utterly dissolute young man. Surely you do not deny it!"

Lady Bliss could have easily done so, but she did not deem it wise. Recalling her rapidly advancing age, and the brittle

112

tendencies of old bones, she climbed stiffly to her feet. "I'm very sorry that Innis has behaved so badly," she offered, with great sincerity. "He was always the worst of us. Our elder brother was merely improvident and a reckless plunger, and I am merely improvident and feather-brained."

"While Innis is improvident and a Johnny Sharp and a scoundrel, to boot! You have spoiled him, you know. Actually, it is not Innis's part I mind so much—it is no more than one can expect of him! Shannon has a great deal more to answer for."

Lady Bliss touched her temples, which were aching with her efforts to understand. "I think we could both use further refreshment," she murmured, and touched the bell-pull. Tomkin appeared, in his usual magical manner, bearing the brandy decanter and another glass on a silver tray. "Now," said Lady Bliss, when they were private once more, "why are you so angry with Shannon—I mean, Lord Roxbury? It doesn't seem unreasonable that he should have been upset to think you'd game away his betrothal ring."

"He *shouldn't* have thought it! Shannon has known me all my life, and should consequently have known that I have no taste for such things." Miss Lennox, a fiery gleam in her eyes, drank thirstily of her brandy, choked, and drank again. "But no! I have succumbed to the lure of the tables! I am bound for perdition, says Mr. Facing-both-ways!"

"Gracious!" Lady Bliss sank down on the sofa beside her guest. Jynx moved her feet so that her hostess might have more room. "I *tried* to tell him—" And then she bit her tongue.

"Never mind," responded Miss Lennox, in a manner that was both doleful and magnanimous. "I know about all that, and I think none the less of you for it, though I do think you could do a great deal better than Shannon."

"You don't mind?" repeated Lady Bliss; then she took solace from her own brandy glass.

"An unprotected woman in any circumstance is to be pitied," said Jynx, somewhat pontifically. "I've seen enough of your brother to realize he's worse than no protection at all! Besides, it's no longer any of my affair."

Lady Bliss, who found her guest's conversation very difficult to follow, strove mightily to concentrate her mind. "But you are betrothed to Lord Roxbury. His concerns *must* be yours, Miss Lennox."

"There you're out!" Jynx grasped the decanter and filled

their glasses again. "And since we seem fated to see a great deal of one another, you might call me Jynx." She pondered her nickname, bestowed upon her by her doting papa after a childhood incident in which she had emptied an ink well on some dusty-looking papers that had turned out to be of great importance in a legal suit. "I'm not, despite appearances! As for Shannon, I need not concern myself with him at all, since we are no longer betrothed."

" 'Twas a mere misunderstanding. He's bound to come about."

"You think so?" Miss Lennox's expression was wry. "So do I not! You see, Lady Bliss, all this occurred during a ball. Shannon ripped up at me, and I grew angry in turn, and threw his ring in his face. Or I meant to throw it in his face, but I missed. So then I slapped him. *And,*" she added with gloomy satisfaction, "everybody saw."

Lady Bliss regarded her guest with utter fascination, and tried to envision the lethargic Miss Lennox in so excitable a state, and failed. "The deuce you say!"

"Exactly." Once more Jynx drained her glass. "So you understand why Lord Roxbury need no longer concern me. I have washed the dirty linen in public, and that Shannon will never forgive. So you need suffer no pangs of conscience on *my* account."

Lady Bliss wasted no time in inquiring why her conscience, which had lain dormant for time out of mind, should suddenly rouse to cause its owner anxiety on Miss Lennox's behalf. "My dear, I am very sorry for all this," she said, "but what induced you to come *here?* It is like jumping out of the frying pan into the fire. It would be a very great calamity to be known that you had entered a gaming hell. 'Twas bad enough in the daytime, but unthinkable at night!"

"I haven't made the situation clear; I already *am* in the fire! By now I must be the talk of every groom and footman in the town." Absently, and ineffectually, Jynx tried to smooth the wrinkles from the abused skirt of her gown. "I couldn't stay at home, for Papa was furious and Eulalia was having vapors, and at the best they would have made my life a misery. I cannot bear to be teased and scolded! And at the worst they would have packed me off to the country somewhere to live down my disgrace—not that I ever shall! I did not *wish* to spend the rest of my life rusticating."

Lady Bliss wished to do that very thing, but she could not expect her guest to share her views. She regarded Miss Lennox, who was by this time a trifle tipsy, and wondered what on earth she was to do with her. With Sir Malcolm's temper, Adorée was more than slightly acquainted, having more than once brought down his wrath on her own unwary head; and while his ire lasted, it was both unheeding of reason and formidable. She could hardly send Miss Lennox home, in her present sorry state, to face the consequences of paternal wrath; nor could she contact Lord Roxbury, who was doubtless still stinging from his fiancée's blow, and probably engaged—much as was Miss Lennox—in drinking himself insensible.

At that point, Miss Lennox interrupted her hostess's cogitations. "So," she said simply, "I ran away from home. I left a note, in the correct romantic style, informing my father that I would take refuge with relatives in Cornwall." She hiccoughed. "I also told him that under no circumstances would I marry an overbearing and cork-brained person like Shannon. Not that I imagine Shannon will wish to marry me after tonight!"

It was evident to Lady Bliss—whose experience in matters of the heart, after all, equipped her to be a very fair judge—that this conclusion had cast Miss Lennox plump into the dismals. "Surely you're mistaken!" she soothed. "Once Shannon's temper has cooled—I mean, once——"

"Lord Roxbury's temper has cooled!" Jynx managed a weak grin. "Don't sham it so, ma'am. Shannon's temper will *not* cool, and besides he didn't wish to marry me in the first place but I bullied him into it, because *I* wished to marry him. I always have." She sighed. "Well, I've well served for my forwardness. I've no hope of forming any eligible connection now."

"But why not?" wailed Lady Bliss, whose head was throbbing like an African drum. "Miss Lennox, I do not understand!"

"No, since I failed to inform you that Shannon accused me—also in front of witnesses—of having *tête-à-têtes* with your brother, by which I have been compromised." Jynx attempted to set her glass on a table, and missed. It shattered on the floor. She regarded it unhappily. "This is my evening for catastrophes! And after Shannon said that to me, I could not help but retaliate by taxing him with his association with

115

you. I had meant to be very philosophical about his preference for you, and to try not to mind that you are his—Well! But I *do* mind. Oh, curse the man!"

This much, at least, had come clear to Lady Bliss. She was horrified. "My dear Miss Lennox, I am *not*——"

"It does not matter!" Jynx blew her nose on the hem of her petticoat. "I shall not wear the willow for him, I vow! And now let us speak no more of Shannon, for I have not told you why I came to you, and it is very bad of me, and I'm not at all surprised that you should be confused!"

Confusion was far too mild a term for Adorée's condition of complete befuddlement. "Please do!" She took her guest's grimy hands. "I am very sorry for this dreadful hobble—though I think you make a great deal too much of it!—and I wish very much to help you, but I do not comprehend——"

"You are so good!" cried Miss Lennox, with every evidence of gratitude. "I am so very much obliged! I had not meant to come here, but I was not thinking clearly when I left home, so I did not take anything that I might pawn. I've already spent my pin money, as usual—Papa is not *mean,* and I lack for nothing, but he does not hold with females handling their own affairs. A great piece of nonsense, I've always thought, and never so more than now! Anyway, I am temporarily without funds, and I can hardly lay my case before the governors of the bank, and I thought myself at point nonplus—and then I thought of you!"

"Of me?" Not King's Bench Prison, decided Lady Bliss, but Newgate, to be charged with abducting the offspring of a peer. "But——"

"You, and Innis," persevered Miss Lennox. "It is all his fault that I made a Jack-pudding of myself. Furthermore, I'll stake my reputation—or I would if I had a shred of reputation left—that neither Papa nor Shannon will think to look for me here."

"Look for you?" Lady Bliss not only sounded like a parrot, she looked every bit as witless as that bird. "Do you think they will?"

"Probably," admitted Jynx. "I'm not sure Papa will swallow that clanker about Cornwall, because he knows I cannot abide those relatives. They are all so very *fidgety.* As for Shannon, I'm sure he will wish to find me, so that he may break my neck. I embarrassed him dreadfully, and he will wish to wreak his revenge on me."

Adorée goggled at the diabolic portrait thus drawn of a

116

gentleman whom she had always considered most amiable. "I know Shannon will call on you," Jynx hastened to add, "but he needn't tumble to my presence here, need he? If I am very stealthy and keep out of the way? It wouldn't be for so very long, merely until I decide what to do with myself." Still, Lady Bliss was speechless. "And I would be company for Cristin, and I might even think of some way to thwart your brother's plans for her, which I cannot like."

With this sentiment, at least, Adorée agreed. "My dear, neither do I! And I don't see what's to be done about it! Cristin is so unhappy, and so is that nice Lord Peverell." She recalled Lord Peverell's mother, and Tansy's dire threats. "Oh, *what* am I to do?"

"About what?" Miss Lennox inquired helpfully. "Tell me!"

Lady Bliss saw no reason to deny herself this opportunity to unbosom herself, and so she complied. Jynx was presented with a highly garbled tale in which Innis Ashley's schemes and Cristin's plight were jumbled together with references to country cottages and the specter of advancing age and, inexplicably, ten thousand pounds. "There, there!" consoled Miss Lennox. "Come out of the mopes. I daresay I can put it all to rights, for I am very good at straightening out other people's tangles."

"But, Innis!" It was Adorée's turn to sniffle; Miss Lennox had been doing so for some time.

"Pooh! I can handle Innis!" Miss Lennox was positively jubilant. "In truth, I should greatly relish putting a spoke in your brother's wheel. It was one of the reasons why I came. You must admit, Lady Bliss, that Innis deserves to be repaid for the ill turn he has served me."

This seemed, to Adorée, only fair. "It would be easy enough to keep your presence secret," she mused. "There are no servants in the house save Tomkin, and he is loyal; and Innis and Cristin can be trusted not to give you away."

Jynx doubted that Innis could be trusted in any circumstance, but she had the utmost faith in her ability to outwit him. Lest Lady Bliss be prompted at this late moment to deliver an emphatic set-down, she added, "You need not consider my reputation; I've already made a byword of myself. I think I must have crossed the Rubicon and burned my bridges behind me! And what does it signify anyway, since no one will know?" She watched the various expressions that flitted across her hostess's lovely face, and held her breath against what Lady Bliss might next say.

The delivery of set-downs, emphatic or otherwise, was demonstrably beyond the abilities of Adorée Blissington. In fact, such a feather-head was Lady Bliss that she did not even briefly contemplate the inevitable consequences to herself if the daughter of Sir Malcolm Lennox was discovered in her gaming hell. "What shall we do about your clothing?" she asked, stricken. "You've brought nothing with you, and that gown is beyond repair. We cannot order you new things without inviting suspicion, for Cristin and I are of a much different size, and there's nothing in the house that will fit you save some cast-off maid's uniforms!"

"The very thing!" Jynx replied cheerfully. "I'm sure I can be of some help to poor Tomkin, and I never meant to be a charge on you. With a little intelligence, things can *always* be arranged satisfactorily."

"My dear," Lady Bliss uttered mistily, "I begin to think you are a godsend!"

"Or almost always," Jynx amended miserably, thinking of the furious viscount. Thus it was that when Tomkin once more opened the book room door, he found the ladies weeping all over one another with the utmost camaraderie.

Chapter
Fourteen

Not without effort was Lady Bliss torn away from her newfound confidante—who promptly put her head down on the sofa pillows and, owing to the excessive amounts of brandy she'd consumed, passed out—to meet a gentleman caller whose identity Tomkin could not have revealed, even had he known it, because of lack of oppportunity.

"Infamous beyond all description is the way the girl has been treated!" said Adorée as they proceeded toward the drawing room. "She has been forced to go to ground for a while. You will tell no one, Tomkin, of her presence in the house."

The butler ventured an objection in which such words as "hornies" and "nicked" were frequently heard. Lady Bliss understood this to mean that Tomkin expected them all to be momentarily arrested by peace officers. "Pooh! I'm sure none will be the wiser, because she means to lay low." Adorée frowned. "It is our fault she is in such a pickle, anyway—though I can't imagine who told Shannon that she and Innis were having *tête-à-têtes*."

Tomkin did not have to imagine; he knew, and it was enough to cause one of his queer turns. Who would have thought that so much disaster could result from a few whispered words? He had acted only from the best of motives when he'd warned Lord Roxbury that Miss Lennox was well on the way to becoming a *habituée* of Blissington House. Which, he thought, was all too often the way with good deeds.

"Give me your word!" demanded Adorée. "We have a responsibility to Miss Lennox, as you must agree."

Certainly Tomkin agreed, but he thought that responsibility might be more readily discharged if the young lady was not on the premises. He presented this opinion. He also offered

119

the viewpoint that if the young lady remained on the premises, they would all find themselves the richer of handcuffs that closed with a snap and a spring.

Lady Bliss was in excellent spirits, however, and dismissed this grave foreboding with a smile. "Fiddlesticks! Meanwhile, Miss Lennox has promised to set all to rights." Tomkin, whose dignified countenance grew graver by the moment, expressed a strong disbelief that any mere mortal could accomplish such a feat. His mistress glowered at him. He swore silence, reluctantly.

"Good!" She patted his arm. "Now, Tomkin, tell me about this visiting gentleman."

"There's nothing *to* tell." That the butler's acquiescence had been secured against his better judgment was evident from his aggrieved tone. "He demanded to see you, and wouldn't be naysaid; and he expressed a wish to avoid the gaming rooms."

"Odd." In Lady Bliss's experience, the gentlemen preferred gambling over almost every other pursuit. Almost? She caught herself up short. There was one pursuit, as she very well knew, that held allure even greater than that of the cards and dice. She tugged at the bodice of her gown, and smoothed her hair, and experimentally fluttered her eyelashes. "I will see him. That will be all, Tomkin." All being, in this instance, the outside of enough, Tomkin retired to his pantry, there to fortify himself with a quartern of gin. Adorée took a deep breath, then glided in her most seductive manner into the drawing room.

He stood in a negligent attitude near the fireplace, a tall and dark and impatient-looking man clad in an opera dress suit of black superfine and a white marcella waistcoat. Tossed carelessly on the settee was an opera cloak of dark blue lined with scarlet serge. Adorée decided, as the gentleman glanced at her, that he looked less like a hopeful aspirant to her favor than a man in the devil of a rage.

"Can it be," she asked, a trifle wistfully, "that you are angry with me, sir?"

He straightened. "It is my curst countenance, ma'am. I look to be ill-tempered even when I'm *aux aegis*."

"Oh." Adorée doubted that so cold and stern a gentleman could be sent into transports. She eyed him curiously, as she approached the medallion-backed settee. "You have come from the opera?"

"I have." The gentleman's impatience grew even more obvious. "And so?"

If this was an admirer, Lady Bliss would eat the flowers that adorned her hair. She might not be the most clever creature in existence, she reflected, but she'd had more than ample opportunity in which to learn to size up *beaux.* "And so, nothing." Prettily, she shrugged. "It is merely that I dote on the opera. A splendid sight it is, with the great horseshoe auditorium and the tiers of boxes, the circular vestibule that is almost lined with looking glass and furnished with sofas. It is London's most fashionable center of entertainment, I believe."

"Then I see no reason," the gentleman remarked, irritably, "why you should not indulge your fancy for it. As I hear it, Lady Bliss, you are not one to practice self-restraint."

He was not unfriendly, but openly hostile toward her. Adorée shoved aside his cloak and sank down on the settee. "You have me at a disadvantage, sir. You know my name, but I do not know yours."

"So you don't." The gentleman was not only cool in manner, he was frankly presumptuous. "Why *don't* you attend the opera? It's a meeting place for others of your stamp!"

Not only did he dislike her, he held her in great disrespect, it seemed. "Others of my stamp," Adorée retorted, "may be less nice in their notions than I. Beside, what with green peas and champagne and hock—to say nothing of the cost of lamp oil and candles!—I can hardly afford to pay the subscription fee." And, she added silently, the days when her swains had done each other bodily injury for the privilege of escorting her about the town seemed to have vanished with her youth. "You have not told me, sir, who you are, or what you wish of me."

"What I *wish* can wait for later," he replied. "I am Dominic Devlin, Earl of Erland, ma'am. Cousin to a very dear acquaintance of yours. I doubt I need say more."

He was correct. "Percy!" uttered Lady Bliss despondently. "Oh dear, you *are* angry! It is such a shame. But all of a piece with my wretched luck."

"I beg your pardon?" Dominic looked quizzical. Adorée— who could hardly explain that she preferred tiresome and aloof and unfriendly gentlemen above all others, not that she held those others in poor esteem—remained silent. "I believe you had a visit from Lady Peverell recently."

"So I did," Adorée admitted. Her tone almost made Lord Erland smile.

"Poor honey, was it so very bad?" Lady Bliss was so startled by this unexpected sympathy that she stared at him. "She is a tiresome female, I admit; and I don't imagine she had the least notion of how to handle you." Lord Erland's tone left no doubt that this ignorance was not shared by himself.

Nor did Adorée doubt him. "It was," she admitted cautiously, "a bit unpleasant."

"Tell me about it!" The earl tossed aside his opera cloak and sat down beside her on the settee. At such close quarters, his magnetism was nigh overwhelming. Adorée would have happily told him her entire life history, for the pleasure of keeping him by her, but unfortunately she could not.

"There's little enough to tell." She folded her hands in her lap and steadfastly regarded them. "Lady Peverell taxed me with, er, leading her son astray; and demanded that I give him up. I refused." Briefly, she forgot to whom she spoke. "Heavens, to listen to the woman, you'd think I made it a practice to lure young gentlemen into iniquity. And she kept harping on the matter of age."

Lord Erland gave a great roar of laughter, and Adorée jumped. "I'm glad *you* find it amusing! I tell you I am afraid to look into the mirror, lest I discover that I have overnight become fubsy-faced."

"I do not think you need worry." Lord Erland grasped her chin and studied her features. "You're a deuced pretty woman, as I told my cousin, and I'll warrant you've a few good years left in you."

It must be recalled that Lady Bliss, in company with the distrait Miss Lennox, had imbibed no inconsiderable amount of brandy. So bemused was she by Lord Erland's extreme presumption, and by his deep rough voice, that she made no objection to being appraised as if she were salable merchandise. The earl's features were not handsome, she mused, but compelling in a harsh, stern way. "Thank you!" she murmured, weakly.

"What May-game are you playing?" the earl inquired. His fingers moved from her chin to her cheek. "It's plain as a pikestaff that my young jackanapes of a cousin can't mean anything to you."

Of course he couldn't, but this man could; never had Adorée felt her widowed state more keenly. Yet, she could not betray Cristin, and shatter Percy's dreams. "He's rich," she said gloomily.

"He may be, in a few months." Dominic released her. "Providing he doesn't waste it all on pretty high-flyers and gambling debts!"

"Pretty high-flyers?" Surely Percy wasn't already playing Cristin false? "Oh! You refer to me. I must take leave to tell you, sir, that Lord Peverell hasn't squandered so much as tuppence on me."

"More fool he." Lord Erland idly touched a dangling dark curl. "Diamonds would suit you best, I think: hard and cold and brilliant."

Adorée silently agreed, but could not let so arrant a misjudgment pass. "I am not," she protested, "cold!"

"I did not think you were, else how could be explained your remarkably tempestuous—and foolish!—reputation? It was the fascination of opposites to which I referred: cold, hard gems and a woman who is both soft and warm." To her horror, Adorée blushed. Lord Erland smiled. "Why *did* you turn down my cousin's offer to buy you off? Ten thousand pounds would surely be of great assistance to a lady who is forever outrunning the constables."

Lady Bliss, whose thought processes were erratic at the best of times, had the greatest difficulty in maintaining some vague semblance of order in her fevered brain. "Scruples," she said, unhappily. "You will not believe that I possess them, but I do."

"And they are both inconvenient and uncomfortable?" Lord Erland appeared to derive a perverse amusement from this upsetting interview. "Still, it was with an eye to Percy's potential wealth that you first lured him to your cozy evening parties?"

"I do not know why everyone assumes that *I* lured your cousin anywhere! You make him sound like a donkey and me a carrot—and anyway, as Lady Peverell pointed out, I am older than he."

"That rankled, did it?" Lord Erland's smile was all the more effective for that it seldom appeared. "You are speaking in a very odd way about a young man from whom you refuse to be parted. Come, admit the truth! You find Percy a dead bore."

Lady Bliss could do no such thing, true as it might be. Things had come to a pretty pass, she lamented, when she must turn aside a gentleman in whom she could easily feel the keenest of interests on behalf of a pair of young lovers who between them lacked sufficient sense to appreciate the magnitude of her sacrifice. "I don't see," she said stiffly, "what it has to do with you."

"Of course you do." The earl still toyed with her curls. "It must be apparent even to a ninnyhammer that my relationship to Percy brings me close to this affair."

"And I am a ninnyhammer, I suppose?"

"You know you are." Dominic took her hand. "Albeit a lovely one. Give up this nonsense about Percy, and admit that you were but cutting a wheedle with Lady Peverell, and that damp-eared halflings aren't to your taste."

If only she could! "You speak disparagingly of your cousin, sir!"

"And so would you, had you been responsible for him these past ten years." She did not comment. "Very well, then consider what must be the result to Percy of association with yourself! Apparently you must have *some* fondness for him or you would not persist in this wrongheadedness. Percy has a great deal more hair than sense, and he is like to be totally ruined by association with gamblers and loose-screws. There isn't an ounce of vice in the boy at present, for all his foolishness—but a month in the company that you and your brother keep will cure *that*."

"Sir!" gasped Adorée, outraged. "I think that you had better leave."

"Not until I've accomplished what I've come for." His fingers on her wrist were as inescapable as Tomkin's dread handcuffs. "You don't want Percy and you know it and you shan't convince me otherwise."

Since her heart would not be in protest, Adorée refrained. She had dreaded this moment ever since Lady Peverell's mention of her cousin Dominic, though for all the wrong reasons; and now she wished that she had never set eyes on a single member of the Peverell clan. Bad enough to have become embroiled with Cristin's ill-fated romance; infinitely worse to be forced to lie to this discerning gentleman.

"That's better," said he. "Had you pitched me any more gammon, or prattled on to me about the anguish of separation and such bosh, you would have lowered yourself inestimably in my opinion."

Adorée regarded the strong brown fingers that were clamped around her wrist. "I don't see how you can have any opinion of me at all!"

"Have I said other than the truth?" Lord Erland looked surprised. "Lord, *I* don't censure you! Your foolishness is to be laid directly at the door of your brothers and Courtenay Blissington. Too," and he smiled again, "I have a weakness for beautiful nitwits."

Never had Adorée met a man so deft at turning insult into praise, or vice versa. "You knew my husband?" she inquired, seeking respite.

"Knew him? Who did not?" Dominic's tone was absent, and his eyes were fixed on her face. "Everyone knew Courtenay, to their cost."

Adorée abandoned the struggle. "Just what," she inquired, staring up at him, "is Courtenay supposed to have done to me?"

"Married you," replied the earl. She gasped. "Introduced you into a circle where frivolity was a way of life, then told you he cared nothing for your conduct, and that you could flirt and go about with whom you pleased. As a result of which you are sitting here with me, and I am persuading you to give up my cousin, and you are wondering how, if you let Percy off the hook, you are to contrive that your bills may be paid."

Adorée had heard out this explanation with, in order, gratification at Lord Erland's understanding, pleasure in the beauty of his rough voice, and amazement at his abrupt *volte-face*. "I do not," she said sincerely, "expect Percy to pay my bills."

"You need not." Without the least evidence of compunction, Dominic attempted to steal a march on his cousin. "Give up this nonsense and *I'll* see you provided for."

"*You?*" cried Adorée. The earl wasted no further time in explanations, but drew her abruptly into his arms. Lady Bliss exhibited no dismay at this further presumption. Indeed, she returned the embrace to the best of her ability.

That ability not being inconsiderable, as neither was his, some several moments elapsed before the conversation resumed. "There is no conceivable reason," remarked Lord Erland, "why a woman of your caliber should waste herself on a handsome moonling like my cousin. Tell me, what do you know about the Irish question?"

So odd a *non sequitur* was this that it caused Lady Bliss to blink rapidly. However, not for nothing had she waded through *The Absentee* and endured the oratories of her more serious-minded swains. "Catholic emancipation," she replied, with an expression that clearly indicated her surprise. "Many fear the consequences of allowing political privileges to the Roman Catholics, either in Ireland or England."

"Hah!" uttered the Earl. "Sir Humphrey Davy?"

"A chemist knighted last year by the regent."

"And your opinion of Castlereagh?"

"Foreign secretary and leader of the House of Commons? Some say he has devoted himself intensely to the wrong side in almost every great issue. Others claim his diplomacy is brilliant, for he is holding together the European princes who have allied themselves against Napoleon." Adorée remarked his contemplative look. "Heavens! I may be a pea-brain, but I *do* know what goes on in the world!"

"So it would seem." Dominic ran a lazy finger up her arm. "We will do well together, you and I."

So they would, if only they could, which they could not. Adorée took a deep breath and thrust all thought of such unimportant things as rapture and ecstasy from her mind. "You misunderstand."

Lord Erland scowled, dreadfully. "Do I, by God?" he thundered. "You mean to say that you will *not* give up Percy?" Adorée did not trust herself to speak. Mutely, she shook her head. "I make you my compliments, madam! I have no high opinion of your sex, and had thought you might be the exception, but it seems you are no better than the others—in short, an unprincipled baggage!"

"But I am not unprincipled!" wailed Lady Bliss, as he rose. "Pray, do not be any more out of temper with me! I cannot give up your cousin, because—"She could hardly tell Lord Erland that Percy was not hers to give up. "Well, there it is. I can tell you no differently."

The earl had reached the doorway. There he turned and paused. "I've the strangest notion, little jade, that you could, but you will not. This idiocy puts me all out of patience with you."

Adorée had no difficulty in comprehending why it should, nor did she mind that he spoke to her so disrespectfully. In truth, she reflected somberly, it mattered not *how* he spoke to her, so long as speak to her he did. "I don't suppose," she ventured, "that you have a little place in the country?"

Lord Erland quirked a brow. "As a matter of fact, I do."

"It fits," Lady Bliss uttered, in tones of the utmost despondency.

"The devil! Is *that* what you hanker after? Percy can't

give it to you, you know!" He waited, but she said nothing, a feat accomplished by clamping her teeth down on her tongue. "Let me know if you change your mind. I like all that is new and rare for a moment—but little more."

Adorée thought that she wouldn't mind being the favorite of the moment only, if only favored she might be. "Goodbye, Lord Erland," she said, woefully. "I don't imagine we shall meet again."

"Rot!" retorted the unsentimental earl. "Of course we will. I have not forgotten, as it seems you have, the matter of Percy." Having fired that shot of no small caliber, which did not fail to hit its mark, he bowed and took his leave.

Tomkin emerged from his pantry at last and went in search of his mistress. He found her in the drawing room, wrapped in Lord Erland's forgotten opera cloak, staring at the doorway through which had vanished precisely the sort of gentlemen that she most preferred.

"Ten thousand pounds!" wailed Adorée, as her butler goggled. "A little place in the country! I tell you, I am tempted to put a period to my life!" And then she yanked the folds of the cloak over her head, and drummed her heels against the floor, and sobbed hysterically.

Chapter
Fifteen

In the meantime, the viscount was taken in hand by Mr. Brummell and Lord Alvanley. The trio retired once more to the Beau's quarters in Chapel Street, where Lord Alanley prescribed his own remedy of frequent bottles of champagne, which he shook vigorously in both hands before pouring. Since Mr. Brummell had no objection to this remedy—indeed, he confessed to having drunk four bottles of that brew in company with Harriette Wilson during a period of stress— and Lord Roxbury being sunk in a morbid silence, the debauch was underway. It ended some hours later, after the Beau had conducted his companions to his dressing room, and had seated himself before the mahogany-faced cheval glass with two brass candle-arms, and had demonstrated for them his particular method of dealing with the yards of white starched muslin that were with great patience and careful lowering of the chin induced into the exquisite folds of his cravat.

Lord Roxbury, despite these efforts, could not be roused from gloom. He refused an offer to Mr. Brummell's personal snuff—Martinique, from Fribourg and Freyer's; he ventured not the smallest smile when Mr. Brummell remarked that garden produce was fit only for common people, and admitted that once he had eaten a pea; he did not even laugh when Lord Alvanley mocked the Beau's profound bow, which held the duchesses of Devonshire and Rutland and York entranced, and in so doing came perilously close to shattering a fine piece of Sévres porcelain. At that point, the gentlemen gave up their efforts at diversion and allowed the viscount to drink himself under the table, and then carried him to his carriage and ordered him driven home.

Consequently, Lord Roxbury rose the next morning with the devil of a head, and an imperfect memory. A bit of effort recalled to him, in all its gruesome detail, the previous evening. He supposed he should be grateful, as he peered into a looking glass, that Miss Lennox had raised on his jaw no bruise. It made little difference, since by now the entire town must know that Lord Roxbury's fiancée had seen fit to slap his face, and to throw at him his ring.

Shannon grimaced and turned away from his reflection which, with its red-rimmed eyes and stubbled jaw, was not the loveliest of sights. He felt simultaneously indignant and contrite. Jynx's assault on himself had not been without provocation, but he still found it difficult to believe that she would act so vulgarly. Then, as if that were not sufficient offense, she had apprised the world of his association with Adorée Blissington. He groaned.

Not that the world had hitherto been in ignorance, for there had been nothing in the association that Shannon sought to hide; but Miss Lennox should have been in ignorance. It was nothing remarkable for a gentleman to have a flirt or even a lady love; to frequent fashionable courtesans was as much of the social round as race meetings and the opera in the Haymarket and the summer showing at the Royal Academy. The fact remained that Miss Lennox should not have been aware of such things. And who had led her to the erroneous conclusion that Adorée Bliss was *his* lady-love? Eulalia Wimple, of course. And Jynx had made no explanation of how Innis Ashley had come into possession of her betrothal ring. Lord Roxbury eyed that item, which rested on his dressing table. If the bauble could speak to him, he thought, an interesting tale it would have to tell.

The viscount had not yet achieved perfect sobriety. Sober gentlemen, after all, do not spend long moments in contemplation of the excesses of depravity that may have been witnessed by betrothal rings, nor compromise themselves by strongly worded vows to have the truth by whatever fell means were necessary, up to and including application of thumbscrews. Lord Roxbury's valet, who was privy to this lunatic display, appraised his master's behavior, and decided that the Viscount was not only under the weather but also sulky as a bear, and he trod warily.

After some time had elapsed, during which Lord Roxbury was bathed and shaved and garbed in the manner appropriate to a gentleman whose daily round consisted of making calls and visiting his clubs, the valet proffered for his master's perusal a note that had recently arrived. Lord Roxbury's expression, which had lightened somewhat during his valet's deft ministrations, darkened once more. The valet prudently withdrew.

Much as he would have liked to, Shannon could not ignore an order to call in Lennox Square. He wondered if Miss Lennox had been induced to offer him apology, and if he would accept it, or hurl her words back into her teeth. Thus ruminating, he set out. Nothing had power to distract him, not beadles and town criers in cocked hats and flaxen wigs; nor postmen in scarlet and red uniforms; nor even the judges in scarlet in ermine who were setting out for the country assizes, accompanied by outriders, while all the church bells tolled. In the same state of indecision as Shannon had departed his own home, he arrived in Lennox Square.

Sir Malcolm was in the dining room, seated at the table of semicircular design. With him was Eulalia. Shannon could not decide whether he was relieved or disappointed by Jynx's absence. "Roxbury!" uttered Sir Malcolm. "You took your sweet time getting here."

The viscount winced as these unfond words assaulted his abused head. Sir Malcolm, who suffered a similar malaise, grunted. "Sit down!" Shannon sat. "I think you must admit that your temper has caused everyone great misery."

"*My* temper!" echoed Shannon. According to his recollection of the appalling events of the previous evening, it was Miss Lennox's temper that had brought them to grief. He had merely presented his objections to her behavior in a cool and reasonable manner; *she* had been the one to take offense, to turn a private disagreement into a free-for-all. Granted, his objections may have been a little strongly worded, may have risen from misapprehension, but the fact remained that he had not turned the matter into a public quarrel. And so he explained.

"Be damned to your impudence!" bellowed Sir Malcolm, in tones so strident that they caused his own brow to ache. He ignored the discomfort. Sir Malcolm was mighty desirous of finding an object on which to vent his spleen. "The girl never caused me a moment's trouble until last night, and I mean to get to the bottom of it! What the devil did you do to my daughter, Roxbury?"

So all was to be on *his* head? Shannon was so enraged that he dared not speak.

"It's my opinion," offered Eulalia, whose eyes rested on Lord Roxbury with triumphant malice, "that the entire affair

130

is your fault, young man! I have always deprecated this alliance, and so I have said, and now my forebodings are proven correct."

Shannon had noted her expression, and thought it boded no good for himself. All the same, Sir Malcolm was not in the habit of humoring his sister-in-law. Shannon waited for her inevitable set-down.

He waited in vain. Never had Sir Malcolm been so in charity with Eulalia, who had considerably advanced her own case by agreeing wholeheartedly with his most ill advised remarks, chief among which to date had been a strongly expressed wish to break the viscount's blasted neck. "Well, sirrah?" snarled Sir Malcolm. "We must have this business settled. You deny that your behavior is strongly to be deprecated? I doubt that you're prepared to go into the witness box and so swear!"

"Good God!" Shannon was no little bit startled to be addressed as if he were a defendant at the bar. "Why should I? Surely you cannot doubt my word!"

"No?" Sir Malcolm was in a fractious, pompous mood. He paused, dramatically, and Eulalia was heard to murmur a comment upon the untruthful tendencies of young gentlemen who lived depraved lives. "Did you know, Roxbury, that the theft of property worth more than one shilling can be punished by death? Then what price the theft of my daughter, eh?"

As clearly as if he wore his robes of magistrate, Sir Malcolm was set on dispensing justice from the bench. Lord Roxbury, who had never expected to make an appearance at the bar of the Old Bailey, found the experience singularly unnerving. "I'm afraid I haven't the slightest notion of what you mean."

"You would do much better to confess your guilt." Eulalia's manner was as ghoulish as if a public execution was imminent.

"Oh, don't harangue the lad!" Sir Malcolm did not care for interference in his examination of the witness; and he had recognized the gleam of temper in the witness's bloodshot eye. "I imagine it's true enough that he doesn't know anything about *that*. It stands to reason. If Jynx had gone to him, he'd hardly dare show his face here."

"Jynx is *gone?*" Shannon had thought her, as Sir Malcolm had promised, confined to bread and water in her room. "Where?"

"That's precisely what *I'd* like to know!" Sir Malcolm waved a tattered piece of paper. "She says she's gone to Cornwall, but how she's to get there I can't imagine, since she left without money or clothes."

"Without clothes?" repeated Lord Roxbury. His mind boggled at the notion of Miss Lennox wandering in a state of nature through the London streets.

"Not a stitch, save what was on her back." Fortunately, Eulalia did not guess the viscount's thoughts. "Poor child, I am afraid her case must be desperate! It will be all your fault, Lord Roxbury, if our dear Jessamyn is lured into the—the fleshpots! I'm sure it's not at all surprising that after the way you played fast and loose with her that she should have run away."

"After she made a cake of herself, you mean," interrupted Sir Malcolm.

"And who," said Shannon, in a dangerous tone, "*told* Jynx that I had, as you put it, played fast and loose with her?"

"I'm sure I don't know!" Eulalia realized that she'd put her foot in it. "It's common knowledge. I mean, Lady Blissington!"

Sir Malcolm had no desire whatsoever to enter into a discussion of Adorée Bliss, not because of Lord Roxbury's pursuit of the lady, but because of his own. "There's no need to discuss *that*," he said sternly. "It's water over the dam. The question is where Jynx has got to. Well, Shannon?"

"How the devil," retorted the viscount, "am *I* supposed to know? You seem to forget that your daughter got to dagger drawing with me last night. She'd hardly acquaint *me* with her plans!"

Sir Malcolm made a violently irritated gesture, and overturned his water glass. "Yes, and I'd like to know what inspired her to engage in a public brangle with you! God in heaven, it's not like the chit to go beyond the line."

"Jessamyn's conduct was altogether displeasing," offered Eulalia, "but it may be partially excused by her discovery that she had clasped a serpent to her bosom." She glared at Lord Roxbury. "A nefarious hellhound!"

Shannon refrained from a display of temper, difficult as it was; both Sir Malcolm and Eulalia were regarding him as if he was a suspicious and desperate character. "That also is water under the bridge," he replied, in sorely goaded tones. "What *I*'d like to know is why no one attempted to prevent Jynx, in her highly overwrought condition, from leaving the house!"

Sir Malcolm dabbed ineffectually at the water that had splashed across the table to drip into his lap. "Because," he said testily, "she went out through the window of her room! I could hardly be expected to think of that accursed tree."

Lord Roxbury, who had expected to learn that his fiancée had departed Lennox House in a clandestine manner, and who had questioned Sir Malcolm about the matter only to turn the conversation from the topic of what had caused their quarrel, digested this information. Silence reigned. And then Shannon, no longer able to control his mirth at the picture thus presented of Miss Lennox, in complete evening attire, scrambling out her window and down a tree, dropped his face into his hands. His shoulders shook.

Sir Malcolm eyed the viscount with no small bewilderment. "Do you think," he said to Eulalia, "that we may've been a little hard on the lad?"

"Nonsense! There's more than ample ground for suspicion of his part in this." Eulalia, too, stared. "What an odd affair!"

It was too much for Shannon to bear. He whooped with laughter. Unfortunately, Sir Malcolm and Eulalia regarded his mirth as a most suspicious circumstance and, once Lord Roxbury had regained control of himself, a feat accomplished all the more quickly by his being the focus of two glacial glares, the inquiry was once more resumed.

Most rigid and searching were Sir Malcolm's questions, and Shannon could offer no explanations that were acceptable. He could not present Sir Malcolm with the truth, as he had realized the moment he stepped into the dining room. Such was Sir Malcolm's present temper that if he learned Innis Ashley had pawned his daughter's betrothal ring, Innis would promptly be clapped behind bars. Briefly, and wistfully, Shannon contemplated that delightful vision. Alas, he decided regretfully, it would not serve. He and Jynx had between them already caused sufficient scandal. Were Innis to be imprisoned, and all London made aware of his possession of the ring, tongues would wag mightily.

Not, reflected Shannon, that they weren't already doing so. Jynx had apprised the *ton* of her conclusions regarding his acquaintance with Adorée Blissington; and he had apprised the *ton* likewise of her *tête-à-têtes* with Innis Ashley; and he could easily imagine what was being said over chocolate this morning about this *ménage extraordinaire*. In truth, it was not as much fear of further gossip that made Shannon hold his tongue as it was dread of Jynx's reaction should Innis be jailed.

Again, Lord Roxbury mused that Miss Lennox had never

explained Innis's possession of her ring. If it had not been used in repayment of gambling debts, then how had he come by it? Surely Jynx did not nourish a *tendre* for him? Shannon rather thought among the sentiments of which Miss Lennox had so soundly delivered herself last night had been a stated preference for himself. As she had also stated a strong reluctance to engage in marriage, Shannon took little consolation from that long-awaited admission.

Meanwhile, Sir Malcolm proceeded with his interrogation, in a manner so stern that Lord Roxbury next expected to be told that Sir Malcolm held a warrant for his apprehension, and that he must consider himself held in custody. "May the accused," Shannon interrupted, "enter a plea on his own behalf?"

"Eh?" inquired Sir Malcolm, disoriented by this breach of protocol.

"Damn it all, not guilty!" Shannon uttered wrathfully. "Sir! We are no forwarder than we were when I first arrived, and though you may not share the sentiment, I am prey to a very great anxiety about Jynx!"

"So you might be," remarked Eulalia, unable to bypass an opportunity to alienate the two men. "Since the entire thing is your fault."

Lord Roxbury swore, fulsomely. "I suggest you apply to Jynx concerning *that*—if ever she's found. Which, since the pair of you seem a great deal more interested in heaping recriminations on my head than in discovering her whereabouts, seems unlikely!"

Sir Malcolm could not be expected to quietly tolerate this slur upon his parental aptitude. "Damn your eyes! I've already sent a man to Cornwall to see if she's gone there, *and* I've called in Bow Street." Belatedly, he was stricken by the impact of the viscount's words. "Do you mean to say that *Jynx* was responsible for that accursed contretemps? By god, if so, I'll disown the little twit!"

"At this point," retorted Lord Roxbury, as he rose and in a most careless manner crammed his hat onto his head, "I cannot say which of us is more offended or offended against!"

"Just where do you think you're going?" Sir Malcolm had in no wise vented the total of his spleen. "I haven't given you leave."

"This is not a courtroom, and I am not obliged to await dismissal from the bench, or endure further cautions on my conduct!" The redness of Shannon's eye was not entirely attributable to excess. "In answer to your question, however, I feel it my duty to inform you that I shall first remove to White's, where I shall seek relief from a bottle of port, in which I stand in great need after the fatigues of this long and unpleasant morning."

"Disgraceful!" uttered Eulalia. If looks could kill, and Lord Roxbury wished they might, she would have been stricken down on the spot.

"And *then*," he continued ominously, "I intend to make the most unceasing exertions to effect the return of my fiancée!" Behind him, the door slammed shut.

"Humph!" remarked Sir Malcolm into the sudden silence. "I'd no notion there was so much *spirit* in the lad." Eulalia voiced her opinion that the viscount's outburst had been most disrespectful, and as such served as further evidence of his innate depravity.

Sir Malcolm paid his sister-in-law's jabbering no need. Once more he perused his daughter's farewell note, in particular her statement that Lord Roxbury was overbearing and unbearable. Under no circumstances, Miss Lennox had written, would she marry such a brute. Nor, she had added, in almost illegible script, would he wish to do so, after the spectacle she had made. Therefore, she begged her father, whose disgust of her must be as great as Shannon's own, to think of her no more, and to allow her to pass the remainder of her days in obscure and repentant spinsterhood.

"Damned if it's not a love match!" announced Sir Malcolm gleefully.

Chapter
Sixteen

Miss Lennox immediately struck up a friendship with the guilt-laden Tomkin, who was very much impressed with her good humor and domestic accomplishments. Thus was her fund of knowledge considerably increased. She was present when Tomkin caught the chef engaged in shady dealing with the buyer of kitchen stuff, and learned with some surprise that it was not uncommon for overlords of the culinary regions to dispose of portions of excellent meat and whole loaves of bread and even, as in this case, silver candlesticks, along with the more acceptable drippings and grease, all of which were later resold in poorer areas. She was instructed also in the care of the wine cellar, and the proper decanting of wine for daily use, and shown not only how to fine, or clear, wines, but also how to detect alterations committed by unscrupulous tradesmen. A piece of chalk the size of a pea, explained Tomkin and proceeded to demonstrate, would disclose the presence of aqua fortis and oil of vitriol; and an admixture of lime water to port would reveal alum. With meats, Tomkin added solemnly, claret was offered. Tokay was fine with pudding; hock and sherry did nicely throughout the meal; but port must be relegated to wait for the cheese.

In return, Miss Lennox offered enlightenment of her own, including a description of her presentation at court, and her journey there in a sedan chair from which the top had been removed to make room for her elaborate headdress, as well as an explanation of the steeply rising cost of lamp oil and candles, due to the increasing scarcity of whale oil and Russian tallow, direct results of the Napoleonic and American wars. So gratified was Tomkin for these gems of wisdom that he followed her around the house, watched with benevolent eye as she shook carpets and mopped the water closet and dusted countless rooms, and gifted her with his family recipe for chestnut soup, a beef broth rich with puréed chestnuts, ground pigeon and veal meat and bacon, onions and carrots, pepper and herbs and mace. And then he informed her, as she was cleaning out the grate, that a servant through whose carelessness a house was set on fire was liable by law to a penalty of one hundred pounds. At this point he abandoned his pupil, his presence being required at the front door.

No sooner had Tomkin departed than Miss Lennox sat down abruptly on the hearth, and the good humor which the butler had so admired likewise fled. Jynx was exhausted both in body and in spirit, and she did not know what to do about a predicament that frightened her out of her wits. While she was pondering said predicament, with her legs crossed beneath her and her elbows on her knees, voices sounded in the hall. Jynx knew those tones, and they made her despondency complete. Unmoving, she waited for Cristin and Percy to enter the drawing room.

She did not wait long. "Cristin!" Lord Peverell threw himself to his knees in front of the girl. "I beg you, reconsider! I would be the happiest man alive if only you would say yes."

Cristin raised a dramatic hand to her pale brow. "I cannot, Percy! Do not press me! You know that my refusal is for your own sake. If only it could be—but it cannot! If you would not break my heart, you must not further torment me."

Lord Peverell did not seem to mind that his determined courtship should be spoken of in such terms. His handsome face aglow with sincerity, he clasped Cristin's hands between his own. "You noble, saintly girl!" he cried. "All the virtues are yours! To think that for my sake you would so sacrifice yourself!"

"I trust," Cristin replied, in a brave little voice that clutched Lord Peverell's heart strings, "that I know you to behave like a gentleman!" Miss Lennox, on the hearth, was stricken with a fit of giggles, the containment of which required no less nobility. "I don't mind being immolated on the altar of duty because it is for *your* sake, Percy!"

"How like you," sighed Lord Peverell, and he rained kisses on her hands. "My darling girl, you will *always* deal honorably!" Overwhelmed, Cristin dropped to her knees and embraced him.

"What larks!" remarked Jynx vulgarly.

Lord Peverell appeared a trifle discomposed at being caught out in such an awkward situation. With Cristin clinging to him in a limpetlike manner, he clambered to his feet and sought the source of the untimely interruption. He glimpsed a black-clad figure. "Oh, go away, do!" Then his attention returned to Cristin, who was trembling in his arms.

That Lord Peverell should have mistaken Miss Lennox for a menial is not remarkable; Miss Lennox wore black stockings, a black stuff gown, a cap and a neck handkerchief. Too, she squatted on the hearth in the most ungenteel manner imaginable, and her face was streaked with soot. Overtaxed muscles protested as she rose, and she winced.

Cristin and her swain were oblivious to all but one another, and neither paid the least attention as Jynx crossed the room and dropped into a chair. She regarded them. Lord Peverell, enthusiastically kissing the young lady, looked on the verge of strangulation by the excessive dimensions of his cravat. "Papa told me once," remarked Miss Lennox, "that Prinny started the fashion for those ridiculously high cravats, and all because he wished to hide swollen glands in his neck."

Percy released Cristin as abruptly as if she'd been a nest of wasps. "Jynx! Hang it, what are *you* doing here?" He took in her bizarre attire. "Dressed like *that?*"

"It's a long story." Jynx pulled off her handkerchief and applied it to her face. "And I don't want to talk about it."

"I should think not!" Percy watched with a wistful eye as Cristin settled on the settee. "From what I hear, you've made a rare mull of it!"

"Oh?" A touch of temper brightened Miss Lennox's eye. "Just what *do* you hear?"

"Depends on who's speaking!" Percy lounged against the back of the settee, from which vantage point he could gaze down in a mawkish manner upon Cristin's gleaming curls. "At last account, you'd gone after Shannon with a dessert knife, or a broken laudanum bottle, or a pair of scissors." He frowned. "No, that was Caro Lamb."

Cristin stirred. *"She* attacked Lord Roxbury? The more I hear, the less I think of him!"

"Not Roxbury, Byron. Something to do with a waltz, as I recall." In response to this explanation, Cristin remarked that she found it all very queer. "Anyway, everybody's talking about it!" added Percy. "What possessed you to run counter to conventional behavior, Jynx? In your situation, *I'*d apologize!"

Miss Lennox was heard to state, in the most unequivocal terms, that she had no intention of volunteering apologies. Furthermore, she added, Lord Peverell's affairs were not in such good train that he was qualified to remark on hers. "That's very true," observed Cristin, as Percy's face reddened with embarrassment. "Sometimes I wonder if you're bent on your own destruction. Even if we *could* marry, I wouldn't wish a husband who was addicted to play. There is already enough of *that* sort of thing in the Ashleys."

"Cristin!" Percy leapt over the back of the settee and crashed to the floor at her feet. "You are unfair! You know it is only because of your uncle that I visit the gaming rooms."

"Innis," Cristin remarked coolly, "is a curst rum touch. He reminds me very much of my father, and deep basset was *his* ruin. I wouldn't wish to see *you* in the basket, Percy. If you can't outwit Innis, I don't think you should continue to come here."

"Why, Cristin!" Jynx watched with appreciation as Lord Peverell, from his ignoble position on the carpet, sought unsuccessfully to voice the numerous emotions evoked in him by Miss Ashley's speech. "I thought you cared for Percy."

"And so I do!" retorted Cristin, woefully. "So much that I wish to see him beforehand with the world—which you must admit is not likely to come about while he is in my uncle's pocket!"

"That accursed man!" uttered Miss Lennox, with great emphasis. "Have you not noticed, Cristin, that since *I* came to Blissington House, Innis has played least in sight? And well he might, the wretch!" But both Percy and Cristin were regarding her curiously. "Never mind that. I fancy Percy may call on you with relative impunity for the nonce. And if he tries to bully you, Percy, you may send him to me!"

"Dashed if you ain't a good sort of girl, Jynx!" Percy picked himself up from the floor. "And so I told Shannon."

"Shannon?" Miss Lennox cut across Cristin's requests for enlightenment. "When?"

"This afternoon." Percy sat down beside Cristin. The horror-filled expression on his face was not due to the young lady's promixity, but to unpleasant memory. "Ran into him at White's, and damned soon wished I hadn't! He rang a regular peal over me."

"Don't get in a pucker," soothed Cristin. "You needn't worry about that nasty man."

"Not nasty, merely a trifle high in the instep!" Percy gazed rapt on Cristin's pretty face. "And in a rare pucker because Jynx made such a kick-up, for which I can't blame him. *You* wouldn't rip up at a man in public, would you, Cristin?"

"Heavens, no!" With interest, Cristin returned his gaze.

"Angel!" ejaculated Percy.

"Poppycock," remarked Miss Lennox. "If Cristin received the provocation that I did—but there's no need for the two of you to trouble yourself with *my* affairs!"

This sarcasm, which was far from gentle, completely missed its mark. "I'll allow," confessed Percy, "that I'd just as soon not. But it seems like I *should*, since you've bungled the thing so completely. Shannon's in a rare taking. I was shaking like a blancmanger, I tell you."

Miss Lennox would much rather have been told the viscount's exact remarks, and so she hinted. Subtlety made little impression, however, on Lord Peverell, who was regarding Cristin very much like a hungry man might eye a beefsteak, and she was forced to be a great deal more blunt. "Devil take you, Percy!" cried Miss Lennox. "What did Shannon *say?*"

Thus chastised, Percy wrenched his eyes away from the object of his fantasies. Those eyes, as they rested on Miss Lennox, were distinctly unfriendly. "A great many things," he retorted, "most of which you wouldn't care to hear! Dash it, Jynx, it's your own fault that everything is going as badly as possible."

"Now *that*," interrupted Cristin, whose knowledge of the events of the Fateful Night—owing to her habit of thinking of Lord Peverell during every waking moment, to the detriment of her ability to grasp explanations, and to the despair of the explainers—was very sketchy, "is extremely unfair. If Jynx doesn't want to marry Lord Roxbury, I don't think she should have to." She sniffled. "To be married to a man one doesn't love must be a wretched fate."

"My treasure!" cried Percy. "On all things, you feel just as you should." He looked bewildered. "But what does *love* have to do with it?"

"Oh, Percy!" wailed Cristin, in a heartbroken fashion. "Everything!"

"I suppose," Jynx interrupted, before the proceedings became totally out of control, "that Shannon has an unfavorable and unalterable opinion of me?"

"Lord, *I* don't know what he thinks—except that I introduced you to this house, which was a very great piece of nonsense, and so I told him! I don't see why I should take the blame, when it was you that brought me here!" Percy's tone was distracted, because of Cristin, whose golden head was resting on his shoulder. Therefore, he was considerably startled by Miss Lennox's response.

"You told him *what?*" she shrieked.

"Dash it, Jynx, you needn't screech like a fishwife. There, you've made Cristin cry! Hush, my angel, she don't mean anything." It occurred to Lord Peverell that Miss Lennox seemed to be in a very sad way. "I didn't tell him anything else. Got indignant and refused to speak further with him. A man can't be expected to tolerate being told he's queer in the attic, even by a friend. And you needn't look like you agree with him, Jynx, because he said the same thing about you."

Miss Lennox contemplated this information, and found in it nothing that could be construed hopefully. "What was the *purpose* of the conversation, Percy?"

"Hanged if I know! Shannon seemed to think you'd loped off. Said he wanted to find you so he could wring your neck." Revelation struck, albeit tardily. "Damned if you haven't! *That's* what you're doing here! You'll ruin your reputation, you know. I can't think it very smart of you to have slipped the leash!"

"Your reputation?" Cristin raised her head. "Oh, Jynx!"

"Being as a lady's reputation lies not in what she's done, but what she's *thought* to have done," growled Miss Lennox, "and being as—thanks to Shannon!—I'm *thought* to have done any number of shocking things, I do not think we need to worry about what little remains of my good name! We would do much better to consider what can be done for the pair of you."

"If you mean to help us in the way you've helped yourself, we had much better *not* consider it!" Percy uttered ungraciously. Cristin voiced protest. "Oh very well, I apologize! But with Shannon ringing peals over me, and my mother in one of her takings, and my cousin saying Cristin isn't quite the thing—well! It ain't *comfortable!*"

Miss Lennox could easily sympathize. Well she knew how it felt to be reduced to such straits. "Wait!" said she. "Your cousin knows about Cristin?"

"He must, mustn't he?" Percy's handsome cheeks were bright with recalled rage. "He said she was playing a Maygame with me. And that she was a rare high-flyer and a great deal above my touch, and any amount of skimble-skamble stuff, including that my present course is ruinous. And he asked how I expect to support a wife when my pockets are to let."

"Ruinous!" As might have been expected of her, Cristin dissolved into tears. "I'm sure I'm a very *good* manager! Any daughter of my father's had to be, or starve."

"And then," continued Percy, "he complimented me on my taste! It was the strangest thing. Nicky has the devil's own temperament, but I've never known him to go off in odd humors before."

"And I've never even *met* him!" Cristin sobbed. "Oh! It is all so unfair."

"You are not," Percy said grandly, "to regard it. I sent him off with a flea in his ear."

"One moment," uttered Jynx, before Cristin could demonstrate her appreciation of so masterful an attitude. "Your cousin said all that about *Cristin?*"

"I'm ruined!" moaned that young lady. "And my conduct has been irreproachable. Or almost irreproachable! How can fate be so unkind?"

"I don't know who else Nicky could've been talking about!" snapped Percy, as he patted Cristin's head. "There, angel, don't take on so! What Nicky thinks don't signify!"

Neither of the young ladies appeared to derive much from this patent, if well-intentioned, fib. Cristin wept the harder, while Jynx scowled thoughtfully. She wondered—"Once more, Percy, did your cousin ever refer to Cristin by name?"

"Well, he wouldn't, would he?" Lord Peverell's irate face indicated his opinion of this persistence. "Nicky may be a curst addle-plot, but no one can say he ain't tactful! He kept referring to her as my little ladybird."

"I see," murmured Miss Lennox, and she did. It took no great intelligence to equate Lady Bliss's interview with Lord Erland—of which Jynx had heard in great and incoherent detail, along with a large number of disclosures about Lady Bliss's past infatuations, none of which was at all suitable for her maidenly ears—with Lord Erland's remarks to his nephew. "Cheer up, the pair of you! Lord Erland wasn't talking about Cristin."

"Lord Erland?" Cristin blinked. "He was the gentleman——"

"He was," agreed Jynx.

"The opera cloak!" Once her mind was guided into a certain channel, Cristin could reason very well. She sought to share her enlightenment with Lord Peverell. "Innis wanted to sell it, and he and my aunt quarreled mightily."

"Oh." Percy was blankly uncomprehending.

"I think," offered Cristin," that she sleeps in it. She was wearing it at breakfast this morning, at any rate."

Lord Peverell sought to make sense of these remarks, and failed. Miss Lennox, who was having a severe struggle with her errant sense of humor, was unable to offer assistance. *"What,"* he inquired, "does my cousin's opera cloak have to do with anything? Sounds to me like your aunt has rocks in her head!" Cristin stared at him, aghast, and once more burst into tears.

"Don't fly into alt!" begged Percy. "I didn't mean it! I'm sure your aunt is a very good-hearted soul, for all she's addle-brained!" When these words of comfort failed to quiet Cristin's sobs, he cast an anguished eye at Miss Lennox. "Jynx!"

"Don't apply to me!" replied that young lady. "I don't know what she's maundering on about! It seems that your cousin, Percy, hasn't the least notion of Cristin's existence and thinks your visits here are prompted by love of Adorée." Lord Peverell looked dumbfounded, and she grinned. "A pretty pickle, isn't it? Look at it this way! Your family will probably be so relieved to find out that it's *not* Adorée you wish to marry that they'll welcome Cristin with open arms."

Percy, who knew his family a great deal better than Miss Lennox, who did not know them at all, failed to be convinced. "Curst high sticklers!" he mumbled mournfully.

"Piffle!" Miss Lennox thought this affair might be more easily settled were not the two principals both bird-brained and cow-hearted. "Then elope!"

On this callous advice, Cristin emerged from her tears. "I think," she said unkindly, "that you want to see us *all* ruined, Jynx! Have you forgotten the money that Percy owes Innis? And Eleazar Hyde? And if Percy's family dislikes my aunt, they aren't likely to approve of *me!"*

"True," uttered Lord Peverell, gloomily.

"As for Innis—" Miss Lennox fell silent, stricken by the suspicion that Innis would soon realize that she could not turn him in for theft without herself landing in the suds. Nor could she divert his attention from Percy without access to the fortune which he coveted so mightily. Were she to attempt to withdraw funds from the bank, Sir Malcolm would learn of it, and *that* didn't bear thinking of. She could hardly, reflected Jynx, provide assistance while locked in her room. Yet, without funds she could not hope to save Percy from Innis, and Cristin from Eleazar Hyde.

"Shannon did say one other thing," offered Percy. "I forgot about it until now."

Hope fluttered once more in Jynx's breast. "What?"

Percy gazed upon her intent expression, the reddened hands clasped in her lap. "Sir Malcolm's set the Runners after you."

The Runners? The bloodhounds of Bow Street? Those nondescript and relentless agents of the law who so seldom failed in the execution of their duty, who by various unmentionable means delivered their victims—who were as often innocent as guilty—up to justice? And she had taken refuge with a lady who ran a highly illegal faro bank! "God in heaven," whispered Jynx.

Chapter
Seventeen

By mutual agreement, Lady Bliss was not informed that the dread runners were likely to come sniffing on her trail. Neither Lord Peverell, nor Cristin, nor Miss Lennox imagined that Lady Bliss would calmly accept such tidings; rather, they thought, owing to Lady Bliss's recent queer behavior, that such tidings might drive her into a brainstorm. Additionally, it was Miss Lennox's opinion, voiced only to herself, that she could hardly have been gifted with two less trustworthy co-conspirators, Cristin and Percy between them possessing a great deal less than common sense, and consequently being very likely to let the cat out of the bag. Having informed Lord Peverell very graphically of the hideous retribution that awaited him if he dared betray her to Lord Roxbury, Miss Lennox went in search of Tomkin. She found him engaged once more in argument with the chef, and diverted their attention from one another's throats by an erudite discussion of *pâtés*, enormous pies made from all manner of rich meats, including *foie gras*, pheasants, truffles, veal and lamprey.

As a result of her efforts, peace reigned briefly over Blissington House. Lord Peverell took his departure, and Cristin retired tearfully to her chamber, and Adorée ventured to her book room. A stack of bills awaited her there, from her milliner and mantua-maker and various tradesmen. The respite made possible by the viscount had come to an end. Lady Bliss had a position to uphold, and how she could do so without spending money she did not know, and so the bills once more poured in.

These problems did not long distract Lady Bliss. No sooner had she seated herself than Tomkin brought to her an armful of red roses. When Lord Roxbury arrived unexpectedly, he found his hostess sniffling over the bouquet, and a note which had come with them, to the effect that she who plucks the devil's posies must not mind a few thorns.

"A new admirer, Adorée?" he asked, ironically.

"Insouciant!" Adorée clutched the roses to her breast, oblivious to thorns. *"Débauche!* And, distinctly, *formidable!"* The viscount raised a brow. "My dear fellow, I do not mean *you!"*

Politely, Shannon refrained from expressing his relief. He suggested that the roses might show to advantage in the vase which Tomkin had fetched and now patiently held. That suggestion fell on deaf ears—Adorée was clutching and cooing over the flowers as if she held a newborn babe—and Shannon pointed out that she was mutilating the blooms. Adorée relinquished them, except for one; Tomkin arranged the flowers expertly, provided his mistress with refreshment, and then vanished discreetly.

"Who is this new admirer?" inquired Lord Roxbury, as he chose a comfortable chair. "Or shouldn't I ask?"

"He is not precisely an admirer." Adorée gazed soulfully upon the rose she held. "Nor, all things considered, is he likely to be, and it is the most wretched piece of luck. But there it is! I must thank you for settling my accounts."

Lord Roxbury's knowing eye moved to the untidy stack of papers on the writing desk, but he made no comment. Her ladyship's financial affairs were of little concern to him. Of even less was the identity of the gentleman who had dealt her a *coup de foudre.* "We had a bargain, if you recall. You were to tell me what you could about Miss Lennox."

Thus recalled to reality, and to the necessity of throwing Lord Roxbury off the scent, Lady Bliss sipped her sherry. "You have done some absurd things in that quarter, I hear."

"Oh?" said the viscount, dangerously. "What have you heard, Adorée? And from whom?"

"Lud! Everybody is talking about it, and I'm sure I can't remember who said what! It is a subject that has gained no small attention in the world. Do you know, Shannon, I fear that the exaggerated praises that have been all your life bestowed on you have given you an exaggerated idea of your own worth! It argues a shocking insensibility that you should rip up at the child that way."

Lord Roxbury had grown very weary of hearing himself referred to as the villain of the piece. "I see I must acquaint you with precisely what happened. Pray reserve your judg-
146

ment, ma'am, until I am through!" He embarked upon his version of the fateful night.

Adorée, who had already heard another account of the proceeding, fixed her gray eyes on his face, assumed an expression of intense interest, and paid him not the slightest heed. Instead she contemplated a speedy departure from her London of raffish high society, of gaming and clubs and theaters and the opera, Vauxhall Gardens and prize fights— and tradesmen who were so insistent on prompt payment of one's bills. Since the idyllic country cottage was out of the question, perhaps a course of sea bathing and sea drinking at Brighton? The waters were said to be good for asthma, cancer, consumption, deafness, raptures, rheumatism, impotence and madness. Adorée was in excellent physical health, but it could not be denied that Lord Erland had touched her heart and gravely endangered her peace of mind.

The viscount had become aware that his hostess paid him very little attention. He regarded her. She wore a blue gown of raw silk, rich in texture, with a drawstring neck. Just then, she became aware of his silence. "Poor soul!" said she.

Lord Roxbury did not imagine, even briefly, that this sympathy was for him. "Good God, Adorée!" he snapped, at patience's end. "I did not mean to question her conduct, but to warn her against——"

"Innis. I know." Lady Bliss nodded. "I cannot think that you went about the thing *wisely*."

The viscount was fated, it seemed, to encounter frustration at every turn. Percy had been far from informative, had taken offense at Shannon's blunt questions, and had retired in a snit; and the Runners thus far had not been able to trace Jynx one step. "Dammit, Adorée, I must find her! At least ascertain if she is safe."

Lady Bliss, forewarned by her niece that Lord Roxbury had expressed a wish to do Miss Lennox physical harm, was not disarmed by this outburst. "You should have thought of that sooner," she remarked callously. "Your fiancée, Shannon, is not the sort of female to yield up her reputation in society for the temporary gratification of any whim, and I know of what I speak, because I *am!* As for Innis, and the association that you accused her of, that's nonsense!"

"Is it?" Shannon looked very grim. "You can't deny she met him here." Adorée opened her mouth. "Or you *could*, but I beg you won't, because I know better!"

147

Obviously he did, but how? She hadn't told him, and Innis certainly wouldn't have. "Tomkin!" Lady Bliss said wrathfully. "So *that*'s why he's been glooming around the house! I'll see him without a character for this!"

With a patience that he did not usually possess, Shannon set about calming Adorée. He pointed out Tomkin's long and faithful service; he also pointed out that without Tomkin's services, she would be in a fix, for he knew of her perennial difficulties with housemaids. "He meant it for the best, you know! Tomkin knew that Miss Lennox's visits here would bring her under the gravest censure, were they to be known."

"But they wouldn't have been known," Adorée responded unkindly, "if *you* hadn't made such a piece of work of it!" She frowned. "In fact, I don't think they *are* known, because Sir Malcolm hasn't come breathing fire at me—and he would, I'm sure. Maybe that part of your exchange wasn't overheard. For which I must be grateful! I tell you, Shannon, your tongue is as fearsome as the sword."

Lord Roxbury wished he had such a weapon, then was glad he did not, lest he have decapitated his hostess. Never had she been so unreceptive to him. Generally, in matters of the heart, Adorée could be counted on to dispense compassion and surprisingly sound advice. Or perhaps she didn't precisely understand. "I must make a confession," he said. "I know I behaved badly, but so did Jynx. But what's done is done! I *must* find her, Adorée."

Shannon was not to know that Lady Bliss had fallen fathoms deep in love with a gentleman who was prohibited by every possible circumstance from returning her sentiment, a gentleman who was obviously aware—as witnessed by the roses—of the warmth of her regard and who meant to with it make of her a cat's-paw; or that as a result she was this day feeling unkindly disposed toward all mankind. *"Find* her?" she echoed. "Do you mean to tell me that you've misplaced Miss Lennox?"

"She's run away from home, as you'd know if you'd been listening. Adorée, give me your attention, do! This is *important.*"

"Ah, and because it is important to you, all other concerns must be abandoned by the wayside! Has it never occurred to you, Shannon, that *my* concerns might be of even greater importance to me? I suppose not! You are very used to having things your own way." It occurred to Adorée that she was being a little hard on a young man with whom she had idled away many a pleasant hour. "But I will scold you no more! What did you wish to say to me?"

Shannon, however, had been in the past days so heaped with recrimination that he had begun to wonder if the things said of him might not be true. He dropped his head into his hands. "I gather she means to avoid everything that could remind her of me, and to think of me no more. Well, I won't have it! Adorée, what am I to do?"

Lady Bliss might be proof against a young man in an intractable mood, but her kind heart was far from immune to a young man in dire straits. "Shannon——"

"And *don't* tell me that I must bear with resignation my irreparable loss, or resign myself to the will of God and reap what consolation I can from the idea that Jynx is better off without me!" Lord Roxbury was stern. "She's not, and I'm not, and I refuse to listen to such fustian."

Lady Bliss stared at him. "I think that the agonies of guilt you have suffered have deranged your mind! As if *I* would spout such nonsense! Are you saying, Shannon, that you still want to marry the girl?"

"I've never wanted to marry anyone else!" The murderous expression on Lord Roxbury's face might have led a less knowledgeable lady to doubt his sincerity. "But Jynx is so damned *skittish*, and I dared not put her to the question! Then *she* put the question to me. Things were going along in the most promising way—and then popped up the matter of that curst ring." So distrait was the viscount that his red-gold curls were discovered, and his immaculate cravat askew. "At least tell me, Adorée, how Innis came to have the ring."

So moved was Lady Bliss by his obvious distress that she might have done so, if only she'd known. Fortunately—or, perhaps, unfortunately—she did not. "I've no notion," she admitted. "It does look very strange. I *do* know that Miss Lennox has a passion neither for Innis nor for game."

Shannon was far too unhappy to question her prescience. "I must be grateful for that," he said gloomily. "Was it true, Adorée, that Jynx came here only to see your niece?"

"I don't know why else she should have done so." Lady Bliss was keenly aware of the thin ice on which she trod. "You leaped to a great number of false conclusions, Shannon."

"So did Jynx." Lord Roxbury felt required to provide his own defense. "Why she should think I'd want *you* when I have her is beyond the limits of understanding!" He realized that this bald statement might cause his hostess a justifiable

149

offense. "Not that you aren't a lovely woman, because you are, Adorée! And how the deuce did Jynx find out that I'd paid your bills?"

Mention of those items reminded Lady Bliss that she was once more in an extremely hazardous position, and she sighed. The devil was in this predicament of hers; she could hardly betray her brother to the viscount. "I hope," Shannon added cautiously, "that I haven't wounded your feelings?" She looked uncomprehending. "In stating my preference for Jynx?"

"Not at all," Adorée replied cordially. It was not that she thought Miss Lennox cast her in the shade; Miss Lennox definitely did not. Lord Roxbury's preference clearly indicated that his heart, and not his head, was involved. Adorée was sincerely glad that Shannon had found a young lady whom he might cherish, and sincerely regretful that the young lady had expressed herself extremely loath to be cherished, at least by the viscount.

Despite her abstraction, Shannon persevered. "Did Jynx say anything while she was here that might give some hint as to where she has gone? It is most urgent that I find her, Adorée!"

"Good heavens!" Lady Bliss was no little bit alarmed by this innocent remark. "You can't think Miss Lennox would come *here*?" She noticed that the viscount looked more puzzled than suspicious. "I think you worry too much, Shannon— of course, you cannot *help* but worry—but Miss Lennox seemed a thoroughly amiable and good-natured young woman, and not the sort to land herself in the briars!"

Lord Roxbury almost remarked that Miss Lennox had already done just that, then refrained, lest he further confuse the issue. He watched with bewilderment as Lady Bliss paced the floor. He thought it odd that she should be rendered unhappy by the sorry state of his affairs, then decided that his sad tale had roused pity in her tender heart.

His conclusions were not far off the mark. No lady alive had a more tender, or warmer, heart than Adorée Blissington; and no one wished less to cast a stumbling block in the way of romance. Lady Bliss was tempted to confess to Lord Roxbury the whole, to inform him that his missing fiancée had last been glimpsed below-stairs, polishing the brass. Yet she dared not, and her hesitation was not prompted only by her brother's unnerving remarks about what retribution would fall on her if she allowed the pigeon to escape the coop. Of more importance to Adorée at this moment was Jynx herself. Miss Lennox still believed that Shannon's affections were centered on Lady Bliss, and was convinced that he must despise her after her outburst, and as a result was very likely not only to lose her temper but to take to her heels once more were her presence betrayed to him. Adorée well knew the dangers of the London streets. Miss Lennox's present refuge might do her reputation no good, but at least within Blissington House she was safe.

"Perhaps," offered Shannon, on whom the sight of his hostess with her face buried in the roses had a very irritating effect, possibly because prudence had decreed he stifle his impulse to shower bouquets and expensive trinkets on Jynx, "your niece might know something of importance?"

"Cristin? Impossible!" Were that young lady privileged to converse with Lord Roxbury, she'd likely present him a rare tongue-lashing. Adorée considered that her own endeavors in that line had been sufficient for one day. "All Cristin can think, or talk, about is that handsome moonling of hers. Oh, dear! I should not have told you about Percy."

"Jynx said something of the sort. So did he." Lord Roxbury was clearly indifferent. He rose. "That, at least, is no bread and butter of mine! Since you can't—or won't—help me, Adorée, I'll take up no more of your time."

"It isn't that, Shannon!" Adorée was stricken that he should think her so unfeeling. "I *wish* to help you, truly! You must know that I have always liked you very well!"

It was a rather lukewarm accolade to bestow upon a gentleman with whom one had conducted a long and amusing flirtation, but Shannon smiled. "Then you'll let me know, should you recall anything that may aid me in my search?"

Adorée thought she would not, since Lord Roxbury's temper had obviously been rubbed raw. She decided that both parties to this tangled romance should be granted a respite in which to regain their composure before a confrontation took place. Cupid's progress would not be furthered by a renewal of hostilities. "You may trust me, Shannon!" Her tone, owing to the necessity for prevarication, a thing which she abhorred, primarily because of her lack of skill, was glum.

"Now it is I who must tell you not to worry," soothed the viscount. The delay of his departure was caused by her grip on his coat. "*My* efforts may not meet with any great success, but I have every confidence in Bow Street."

This consolation had an effect on Lady Bliss that was little short of stupendous. "Bow Street!" she cried, and flung herself as if for protection against Lord Roxbury's chest. Lord Roxbury knew from experience the only way in which to distract Lady Bliss from imminent hysteria. He kissed her.

Adorée placed little significance on that salute, nor did Shannon: gentlemen always did kiss Lady Bliss, on the least provocation, and in the case of Lord Roxbury it was far from the first time.

And then disaster struck: Miss Lennox walked into the book room. She stopped dead in her tracks, uttered a startled little shriek, then exited with great speed. Lord Roxbury released Lady Bliss, who tottered to the couch. "Who the devil was that?" he inquired irritably.

"You did not see her?" Lady Bliss inquired, in cautious tones.

The viscount had not. The viscount's back, as he rudely pointed out to his hostess, had been to the door.

Adorée fanned herself vigorously with the rose that she still clutched. " 'Twas only the housemaid," said she.

Chapter
Eighteen

In point of fact, Miss Lennox was not the only black-garbed female in Blissington House. Tomkin had taken advantage of his mistress's brief prosperity and had hired a kitchen maid, a scullery maid, and parlormaids—all fresh from the country and therefore unacquainted with Lady Bliss's reputation in the labor market—as well as waiters to serve in the gaming rooms. Nor was Miss Lennox in any way expected to perform the duties of a menial, though no one attempted to prevent her from doing as she wished: Tomkin realized that a token amount of physical labor was necessary if she was to be accepted by the servants as another, superior, member of the staff; and Adorée realized the benefit to a broken heart of benumbing exhaustion.

Not that Jynx's heart was broken, though the sight of Adorée in Shannon's arms had caused her a grave pang; the unexpected spectacle was only confirmation of what she'd always known. Adorée had tried to explain otherwise, as naturally she would, being a kindly disposed lady if one a trifle too free with her favors. Jynx had interrupted that explanation halfway through, and had informed Lady Bliss that it was unnecessary, because she perfectly understood. So moved was Lady Bliss by this demonstration of Miss Lennox's intelligence that she retired straightaway, and had hysterics in her room.

Cristin, too, had secluded herself, after a firmly expressed wish to be bothered by no one, and Jynx was left at loose ends. She amused herself with *The Lady's Companion*, containing upwards of three thousand recipes in every kind of cookery, sixth edition, 1753. It was scant wonder, she reflected, that Lady Bliss's household expenses ran so high, if she employed recipes that called for a peck of flour, five pints of cream and four pounds of butter, as well as diverse other ingredients in equally large quantity.

Evening fell, and Adorée emerged at last to preside over her faro bank. Jynx, had she been prudent, would have withdrawn to her attic bedroom. She did not; she was bored; she decided to witness for herself high life at play. She whisked herself into a closet, from which vantage point she had an excellent view of the larger saloon.

The faro bank was in full swing. Adorée looked extremely lovely, if a bit wan, in a pale blue satin Empire dress veiled with Brussels net, long white French gloves trimmed with ruching around the top, and satin evening shoes. Her dark hair was gathered high on the back of her head. It occurred to Jynx that she had never seen Lady Bliss wear jewels of any sort, and she marveled. Certainly Adorée needed no gems to enhance her beauty, but that her numerous admirers had been so uniformly clutch-fisted as to present her with none was distinctly unusual.

At the other end of the room, a group of gentlemen had gathered round the E.O. table, which was being set in motion by none other than Innis Ashley. So he dared return to Blissington House when Jynx was safely above-stairs? Her lip curled. She was almost tempted to march straight into the saloon and demand an explanation of his theft of her betrothal ring. Prudence belatedly reared its head, however, and she refrained.

Jynx was surprised by the number of distinguished people that she glimpsed in the gaming rooms. Some ladies were present, none of whom she recognized. Far outnumbering them were the gentlemen, in crisp high shirt collars, faultless cravats, freshly pleated ruffles, high-collared waistcoats, tailcoats with smartly shaped collars and smooth lapels, tightly fitting unmentionables. She diverted herself by assigning a tailor to each one: Weston, as patronized by Brummell? Stulze, who claimed Wellington among his patrons? Meyer of Conduit Street or Guthrie of Cork?

That amusement quickly palled. Miss Lennox scanned the visitors, in expectation of glimpsing Lord Roxbury. She did not see him, but the arrival of Lord Alvanley caused her to draw further back into her closet and quietly close the door. She decided his presence was not remarkable; Lady Bliss, from all appearances, played hostess to the most popular gentlemen of the *haut ton*.

Had Miss Lennox but known it, Lady Bliss had not been

hitherto privileged to welcome Lord Alvanley to her home. She was honored this night only because the amiable peer was engaged on behalf of Lord Roxbury in a bit of discreet espionage, in pursuit of which he had denied himself the pleasure of accompanying his friend Brummell to the opera in the Haymarket.

Noble as was his intention, and willing as was his character, Alvanley was not cut out to be a successful spy. He entered the saloon, was immediately challenged by an acquaintance to a rubber of piquet, and did not notice Miss Lennox slip out of her closet and toward the back stairs.

Another person did. Jynx was pondering the latest episode in the saga of Lord Byron, of which she had heard while hidden—Byron had accompanied Lady Oxford to Portsmouth, the first stage of a projected trip together abroad, and the lady's husband had at last been moved to make a stand. It was the Oxfords, therefore, who departed for the Continent, while Byron had returned to London, where he had induced Caro Lamb to histrionics with the dessert knife, or broken glass, or whatever it had been. How many interesting *on-dits* one missed, mused Jynx, when in retreat. And then a heavy hand fell on her shoulder, and she bit back a scream.

It was not her father, or her fiancé, both of whom she had half-expected to confront these past several days. Her captor was Eleazar Hyde. "I'll have a word with you, missy!" said he, and shoved her into the book room. "I'll thank you to stop trying to jab a finger into my pie."

The gentleman, Jynx decided, did not improve at closer range. He was rather under average height and of much more than average girth, and he had a sinister habit of covering his mouth when he talked. His attire combined the shabby with the shabby-genteel, and was rendered further startling by a very vulgar display of jewels. Jynx noted the array of fobs and seals, the rings on his pudgy fingers, the diamond stickpin in his cravat. "Sir?" she said warily.

"I'm as knaggy a gager as you'll meet, missy." Eleazar's smile was a gruesome revelation of why he sought to hide his teeth. "And I ain't about to be outjockeyed by a chit. You've told Cristin she needn't see me—don't say you didn't! It's as plain as the nose on your face. Things were going along as nicely as a man could wish before I—ah!—was called out of town on business."

Monkey business, amended Miss Lennox to herself, but she

did not venture comment. Eleazar was both fat and short-winded, and his speech had left him gasping for breath.

"Yes." Eleazar had recovered himself. "Irons in the fire, you might say. Should you try and interfere further with any of my little schemes, things will go very badly for you, Miss Lennox. No need to look so startled; I make it my business to know all sorts of things about little ladies like you! I know too how things would go with Adorée Bliss if there was to be an information laid against her at Bow Street."

Jynx regarded the gentleman warily. "You are threatening me?"

"Well, I'm not accusing you of impertinence!" His chubby, none-too-clean fingers grasped her chin. "Stay out of my affairs and I'll stay out of yours! We begin to understand one another, I think."

So they did. Jynx nodded, since the pressure of his fingers prohibited speech. Eleazar took this as a promise of cowed cooperation, and released her. "A comfortable prose we've had together!" said he. No answer was vouchsafed; Miss Lennox was already halfway out of the room. His crude laughter followed her down the hallway.

Jynx grasped the crystal knob of a white-painted door and flung it open, then leaned heavily on the other side. This, as befit the servants' portion of the house, had a green baize cover and a plain gunmetal knob. Then she climbed the bare wooden steps to her hot attic room. It was all a far cry from what she was accustomed to, Jynx thought.

She did not mind her Spartan quarters, the gray distempered walls and bare floorboards; she did not even mind sleeping on a lumpy mattress, or looking at herself in a spotted mirror, or bathing from a chipped basin. Nor were evenings spent tucked away in that little garret room so very bad, owing to various items that had been left behind by some previous inhabitant, including a tale entitled *The Beautiful Zoa*, which outlined the adventures of a damsel cast ashore on a desert isle, and another called *The Account of the Ghost of Mrs. Veal*.

Jynx minded very much, however, being subjected to the threats of Eleazar Hyde. Furthermore, the black stuff gown itched dreadfully. She stepped into her room, then paused, dumbstruck.

The mean little chamber glowed with the light of countless candles. A huge bouquet of flowers adorned the bureau, and a table bearing a cold collation had been drawn up—chairs

156

being among the amenities lacking—beside the bed. Jynx's heart leapt up into her throat.

Innis stepped out from behind the door, and pushed it shut. "Oh." Miss Lennox was the vistim of bitter disappointment. "It's only you."

"Who else would it be?" Innis treated her to a smile of be-witching tenderness. "I have come to apologize to you."

"I should think you might!" retorted Jynx, very irritably. "You might also apologize for one Eleazar Hyde, who has been laying violent hands on me!"

Innis studied Miss Lennox, her chestnut curls and sleepy eyes and generous mouth, to say nothing of the rest of her, which was no less generous, and suffered an impulse to do the same. The hands he wished to lay on Miss Lennox, nonethe-less, had nothing to do with violence. "Don't tangle with Eleazar," he said absently, "unless you wish to be forced to knuckle down."

Miss Lennox considered this a cravenly remark, and said so, but allowed Innis to guide her to the supper table. "I have a very poor opinion of you," she concluded. "A man who would not only steal my betrothal ring, but deliver up to that aging *roué* his niece."

Innis looked wounded. "I really won't, you know, but I dare not antagonize Eleazar. I'll figure some way out of it, you'll see! As for the ring—that was like placing a glass of water before a thirsty man, my darling. You wouldn't expect me not to drink."

Jynx surveyed the array of cold meats, fruit, and a hot goose pie. "True," she said, and helped herself to wine. "I would not expect you to behave other than like the rogue that you are. And you need not spin me any more tales, because it's obvious that you haven't the least intention of interfering with Mr. Hyde." She regarded him. "I'd guess he has it in his power to bring you to a standstill."

"Not I." Innis's tones were less than convincing. "I'll make a recovery yet. But let us not waste these precious moments talking about *him!* My darling, aren't you the least little bit glad to see me?" Miss Lennox looked as if she doubted the fidelity of her ears. "Jynx, you must know you've taken my fancy to an alarming degree!"

"You chose a queer way to show it!" Miss Lennox attacked the goose pie. "Pitchforking me into this bumblebath. I beg you, offer me no more false coin, because I shall find it—and you!—a dead bore."

Innis was not accustomed to young ladies who found his ardent protestations of less interest than a hot goose pie. Still, Innis was at heart a gambler, and he was playing for high stakes, and he could but trust to the luck of the draw. "I have something for you." He held forth a pretty snuffbox, not too large for a woman, and opened the lid. An enameled bird started up, sat on the rim, and piped in a delightful tone the notes of the nightingale. "An automaton," he explained. "Isn't it the prettiest plaything you've ever seen?"

In dealing with Miss Lennox, however, Innis played against a stacked deck. "I would like it more," she responded, "if it hadn't been purchased with the proceeds of the sale of *my* betrothal ring. Anyway, I don't take snuff."

Innis was heard, distinctly, to gnash his teeth. "I didn't buy it with that money. To do such a thing would be the act of a blackguard, and a bit much even for me!"

Jynx's glance clearly indicated her opinion that nothing was too black an act for an Ashley. "Wasting the ready again?" she asked, rudely. "It strikes me as very odd that you should have money to fritter away while your sister is always under the hatches, and that one day you should be in the basket, and the next in clover. I don't suppose you'd care to explain?" Patently, Innis did not. "Nor do I understand why you should be afraid of Eleazar Hyde."

"Afraid?" Innis looked indignant. "I'm no such thing."

"Poppycock!" Miss Lennox helped herself to fruit. "Of course you are. I'd be willing to wager that the only reason you're here is that he's below-stairs right now, looking for you."

"You'd lose." Innis was relieved to bring the conversation back into more profitable channels. "I'm here because I wished the pleasure of your company."

"And I'm to count myself honored?" Miss Lennox inquired coolly. Innis expressed a devout wish that she might. He further declared a strong desire to put the unhappy past behind them and to start anew. "My *past* wasn't unhappy!" retorted the unobliging Jynx. "It's my present that makes me wish to scream. You're looking burnt to the socket, Mr. Ashley. You'd do much better to tell me all about it."

Innis was tempted. Even Miss Lennox, presented with the woeful tale of his ever-increasing tribulations, could not fail to understand how grieviously he'd been misused. "I cannot," he said, recalling that the daughter of a magistrate was not likely to look benevolently upon illegal activities, no matter how innocently his involvement had begun. "I wish I could! But I'll see my way clear, damned if I don't! And then no one will need to worry further about Eleazar Hyde."

"You can't owe him money," Jynx said shrewdly. "*That* wouldn't bother you. Nor would indiscretions, unless of an appalling nature, and no matter how feckless you may be, I can't think you *depraved*. What then, Innis?"

But Innis would not say. His guileless countenance flushed, and his manner harried, he launched forth upon an eyewitness account of a cockfight he'd attended that very day. Miss Lennox paid little heed to the ignoble defeat of the black, and the thrilling victory of the gray, and Innis's lament that he had backed the wrong bird. She worked her stolid way through a plate of trifle and thought of a gentleman who *was* depraved, namely, Lord Roxbury. Such was the perversity of human nature that the discovery of what Shannon did with his afternoons led her to wonder how he passed his nights. Perhaps he had yet another ladybird—perhaps a flock of them!—discreetly tucked away. Innis, meanwhile, continued with his tale of gore and blood. "Curses!" he concluded. "Let's have done with this! My darling, surely you do not regard me with indifference?"

Indifference? Miss Lennox ruminated. Anger, amusement, irritation—but indifference? "Well, no," said she.

"I *knew* it!" No need, then, to abandon his plans, which included the utilization of Miss Lennox, and Miss Lennox's fortune, as an escape route. A pity that the Continent was out of bounds, owing to Napoleon's quarrel with the English—but there were countless other places in the world that would prove hospitable to a well-heeled gentleman. "My darling, you have made me a very happy man."

That she had was obvious from the triumphant expression on his face. "I don't think," ventured Jynx, "that you perfectly understand."

"But I do! Sweetheart, you've no need to be coy." Innis laughed aloud. "The cream of the jest is that Adorée's scruples have served me a very good turn! I would've been content with Roxbury's fortune, you know, but she refused to draw him in."

It had looked very much to Jynx, that afternoon, like Shannon was most firmly hooked on Lady Bliss's line. "You mean——" she began.

What Innis did *not* mean was to explain. Action being clearly called for, he kicked the table out of the way and hurled himself onto the bed. Miss Lennox whoofed, the breath knocked out of her by this assault. Then she tried to extricate herself from Innis, a task made very difficult by the fact that he had landed atop her and his weight held her virtually helpless.

It was at this moment, when Innis was kissing Jynx most fervently, and Jynx was trying her best to kick him, that Adorée burst into the room. She paused, aghast, on the threshold. A mere moment's reflection, and Miss Lennox's strenuous contortions convinced her that Miss Lennox was receiving no great pleasure from Innis's embrace. Swiftly she crossed the room, grasped the vase of flowers, and smashed it over her brother's head.

Chapter
Nineteen

At the moment when Miss Lennox was suffering Innis Ashley's advances, and Innis was suffering his sister's assaults, and Lord Roxbury—contrary to the dire speculations of Miss Lennox—was suffering the barbed comments of the other four hundred and forty-nine members of the Gambling Club at Brook's, Lord Erland was enduring an unpleasant interview of another variety.

He was in the home of Lady Peverell in Clarges Street, lounging against the gray brick fireplace in Tansy's sitting room. Clad in a gown of gossamer satin, with festooned trimming and slashed sleeves, the whole lavishly adorned with rouleaux of rose-pink satin. Tansy was walking up and down the room in great agitation. "I think I know you too well to stand upon ceremony with you, Nicky!" she said, after taking a deep breath. "It is long past time that you should settle down. I beg that you will seriously consider the matter that I am about to place before you."

"Why?" Lord Erland made it a point to seldom oblige anyone. "I have an heir: Percy." He looked thoughtful. "As well, I daresay, as a number of illegitimates."

"I wish you would be serious," Lady Peverell remarked, with a frown that suggested her dislike of levity. "You are not so old that you cannot start a family of your own." Lord Erland took leave to remark that at five-and-forty, and with twice that many liaisons behind him, he saw little reason why anyone should doubt his virility.

"That is exactly what I mean!" cried Lady Peverell, with an anguished gesture. Lord Erland quirked a brow. "I mean, I don't mean *that* exactly, but that you exhibit a sad lack of stability! All those immoral women that you, er, *keep*, and your lack of regard for what is due your name."

"I thought," remarked the Earl, unmoved, "that I was following the family tradition. In my father's footsteps, one might say, Tansy."

"That old reprobate!" Lady Peverell recalled her cousin's habit, in the midst of her tantrums, of walking out of the house. She adopted a calmer manner and clasped her hands to her bosom. "But you can't be held to blame for *his* sins. You are, however, to blame for Percy's, for he is obviously set on following in *your* footsteps, which is why you must change your ways."

"Ah." Lord Erland propped a foot on an andiron. "I begin to see the gist of this."

Encouraged by his forebearance, Tansy dramatically flung out her arms. "I am a widow, Nicky, alone in the world except for my son, yet still in my prime!" Lord Erland had a look of irony on his face, but he did not comment. "Nicky, I am not a woman who *likes* to be alone. I was made for love, she romance———"

"Then rid yourself of that damned hartshorn and vinaigrette!" interrupted Dominic. "No man wants to leg-shackle himself to a female who's a constant victim of intermittent ill-health."

That Lady Peverell did not appreciate this sound advice was made evident by the thinning of her lips. "I would do anything for the gentleman who holds my affections—for my affections, Nicky, have become fixed! Even, I think, I might get well."

"Generous of you." Lord Erland yawned. "This is all well and good, and I'm sure I wish you every success, but I don't see why you must be telling this to me. You must know that I'm no advocate of romance."

Lady Peverell looked at him reproachfully. "In happier days, you were used to partake of all my sentiments! But now you hold me at arm's length, and I think it very *hard* of you. Still, I do not mean to quarrel." Lord Erland's expression suggested that he might wish to do that very thing. "Consider the advantages!" she added, subtly abandoned in her haste. "The Peverell and Erland fortunes combined—and the estates, which march together anyway! As Percy's steppapa, you could guide him much more effectively! And aside from all that, you would gain the object of your dreams."

"I would?" Lord Erland inquired skeptically. "Sometimes I think you have windmills in your head, Tansy."

Lady Peverell ignored this poor-spirited remark. "I need a stronger hand to guide me, Nicky; every woman does. We aren't *meant* to deal with such things as scheming hussies who set out to entrap our sons——"

"If that's what's bothering you," interrupted the Earl, "It needn't. I'll deal with Adorée Blissington."

"Hah!" ejaculated Lady Peverell, with a knowing and contemptuous glance. "So well are you dealing that Percy continues to haunt Blissington House and express his intention to marry that bawd!"

"Bawd?" Lord Erland laughed. "Your claws are showing, Tansy."

"Marry me," Lady Peverell snapped, "and you'll no longer have need of vulgar mistresses. I flatter myself that I'm not an antidote!"

Since not even Tansy's worst enemy could say that of her, Lord Erland offered no argument. "You seem to suffer a slight confusion as to whether Lady Bliss is Percy's *petite amie* or my own. Battley's Sedative is very useful, I understand, when one is overwrought."

Tansy's hands were clenched into fists, but she managed a smile. "Adorée Bliss could be the *petite amie* of the entire male population of London, and I shouldn't be surprised. Do you not understand what I am telling you, Nicky? I know all! There is no longer need for you to *pretend*!" Lord Erland eyed the doorway, rather wistfully. "It was my awareness of your sentiments that prompted me to speak," Tansy continued. "Since your conscience decreed that you should not. Well, Nicky, have you nothing to say to me? I did not think that by a little frank speaking *you* would be overcome!"

Lord Erland was not precisely overset, but he was distinctly taken aback. An acutely intelligent gentleman, he understood that his cousin had somehow conceived the extremely ill-founded notion that he held a longstanding *tendre* for her. Having more than a passing acquaintance with the fury of women scorned, Dominic thought it behooved him to tread warily. Therefore, he politely informed his cousin that though he might be one to go the pace, he had not yet overstepped the mark.

"Tiresome creature!" Lady Peverell smirked. "I'm sure that union with yourself is nothing to cavil at, Nicky. Will you see to the publishing of the banns?" She noted his stunned expression. "Perhaps you would wish to be more composed before we go into further detail."

There could be no question that Dominic's customary composure had deserted him, and Tansy congratulated herself that he could not preserve his usual indifference over *this* affair. Despite her claims, she knew that he had no love for her, and she didn't require that he did. She didn't even mind if Dominic had his occasional adventures with dashing females—always excluding one Adorée Blissington—so long as *she* had his name.

Have that highly coveted name, Tansy thought she would. Dominic was a gentleman, when all was said, and she had maneuvered him into a position from which he could not escape without acting like a coxcomb. "Dear Nicky," she said softly, "you are overwhelmed. You need not be! Come, you may embrace me."

Lord Erland, however, was so much the born aristocrat that he never considered whether his behavior was or was not suitable to his station and rank. He regarded his simpering cousin and answered her without the slightest hesitation. The answer was negative.

Lady Peverell's eyes opened so wide that they threatened to pop right out of her head. "Nicky! You cannot mean——"

"I mean," Lord Erland replied precisely, "that I do not mean to marry anyone. If I want a woman I can buy her; and when I'm tired of her, I can pay her off; and without weeping or recriminations or other wifely things."

This was plain speaking with a vengeance, and Tansy blanched. The Earl, correctly adjuding her intention of hanging round his neck in tears, strode toward the door. "Nicky!" she wailed. "Don't leave me like this. Where are you going, you brute?"

"To Blissington House and see what I may do for your bird-witted son." He turned and regarded her, a touch of humor in his cold eye. "I'll admit, Tansy, that I've seldom seen a more affecting scene."

Thus he referred to her blatant exposure of her deepest emotions, her placing of her tender mother's heart at—or, it seemed, beneath—his feet? It exceeded all belief. "I congratulate you," spat Lady Peverell, whom disappointment turned shrewish, "that you've found so agreeable a way of passing your time."

"And so you might," the Earl replied cordially. "Consider, Tansy, whether you'd rather see Adorée Bliss in company with myself—or with your son."

Frankly, Tansy preferred neither. Moaning, she sank down onto the couch and groped beneath a cushion for her smelling salts. With an ironic glance, Lord Erland took his departure, pausing only once to inform the butler that her ladyship, being on the verge of a spasm, was in sore need of her cordials and laudanum.

A scant time later, the earl was in another house, and in conversation with another butler. Tomkin led him up the staircase to the first floor, past the gaming saloons, and to the closed door of the book room. He indicated, with a dignified inclination of his head, that his mistress was within. Lord Erland was not a gentleman to stand on ceremony. He brushed past the butler and opened the door.

Lady Bliss sat at her writing desk, one hand propping up her brow, the other holding in a very indecisive manner her quill. She was looking far from her usual tidy self; the pale blue satin of her gown was water-splotched, and her dark hair was extremely disheveled. As the two men watched, she tugged viciously at her curls. Tomkin opened his mouth to announce the caller. Lord Erland shoved him aside and slammed the door.

So deep had been Adorée's concentration—the composition of a missive to Sir Malcolm requiring greater cleverness than she possessed—that the sudden noise made her start and drop her quill. Ink splattered on both her letter and her gown. "Oh, dear!" said she.

"I'll buy you another!" snarled Lord Erland, and threw himself down on the sofa. He regarded Lady Bliss, who despite her extremely distrait appearance remained extremely lovely. "I'll say this much for you, Adorée: you don't have a range of vision that's narrow as a needle! And you don't spout arrant nonsense to a man."

"I hope," Lady Bliss remarked, "that you haven't come to pitch straws with me. I've had more than enough problems for one day."

Lord Erland stretched out his legs and propped them on a table, an act which drew Adorée's unhappy attention to his magnificent physique, clad in evening wear. She admired his black coat, white waistcoat, black pantaloons, all of which were of excellent cut and subdued taste. Obviously, he preferred the best in everything. It was a very great pity, concluded Adorée, who numbered among her vices no false modesty, that fate denied him a lively romance with a lady of her caliber. She sighed.

Dominic, who was expert at reading female countenances, extended a hand. "Come talk to me! You may tell me your

165

woes, and I shall tell you mine, and I promise you that I shan't scold."

Adore had a severe struggle with her scruples, which demanded that Lord Erland remain unacquainted with even the most minor of her woes. The earl, whose expression was not sanguine, would hardly refrain from scolding if he learned of matters between his cousin and her niece. Adorée stood, and knocked over the pile of bills that had rested on her desk. Exasperated with her clumsiness, she knelt and stacked them once more into an untidy pile.

"Dished again?" inquired the earl, an appreciative light in his eye. This was not prompted by the idea of Lady Bliss's dire financial straits, but by the sight of Lady Bliss crawling around the floor. "I wish you'd let me help you."

Having collected the damning evidence of her spendthrift Ashley ways, Adorée dealt with it in her usual manner, and shoved the bills out of sight. "And I wish I could let you," she retorted. "However, there remains your cousin."

"Curse my cousin!" Lord Erland's foot thudded to the floor. "I have heard entirely too much about that young chub for one night. Are you going to come here or must I fetch you?"

So it was to be a truce? Adorée regarded him, a distinct gleam in her own eye. She was not adverse to the notion of being fetched, unnecessary as the action would be. Nor was she adverse to putting aside her own problems for a time. She rang for Tomkin and requested a bowl of punch. It was not until the butler returned with this noble concoction of steaming port and roasted lemon that she seated herself by the earl.

"You know exactly how to titillate the most jaded appetite, do you not?" Dominic flicked her cheek. "You are a very unusual female, Lady Bliss."

"I wouldn't know about that, though it's true that I've had a little experience with the likes and dislikes of gentlemen." Unaware of Lord Erland's reaction to this staggering understatement, Adorée sipped her punch. "Infinitely curious and interesting they have been. But that sort of thing is beyond me now, and it's a crushing blow. I suppose I must content myself with memories."

Lord Erland choked with laughter. "You have a lot of memories, I gather?"

Adorée was not surprised that the melancholy truth should rouse mirth in Lord Erland; gentlemen, for Adorée, had few surprises left in store. "Yes. My brother may say I'm touched in the upper works, but even Innis can't deny that I *remember* things. I daresay I could console myself for years," she added gloomily, "with my memories."

Had Lady Bliss observed Lord Erland's expression at that moment, she might have realized that such a vicarious existence need not be hers. However, she was steadily, and somberly, staring into her punch cup. "For almost as many years as it took to gather them," Dominic offered wickedly. "But even you must have forgotten a few conquests along the way."

Adorée did look at him, then, rather unappreciatively. "It is not kind of you," she retorted, "to belittle my accomplishments. Heaven knows I have few enough of them! I swear that every one of my, er, conquests is as distinctly in my recollection as if it had happened yesterday."

"Including my nephew?" inquired Lord Erland. She looked bewildered. "I thought not. Why did your brother say you lacked sense?"

This simple remark distracted Adorée, recalling to her as it did the circumstances which had prompted Innis to fly off the handle, and her discovery that Miss Lennox was not at all safe in Blissington House. "He has always said it," she responded absently. "This time it was because I'd just broken a vase over his head."

"I see." Dominic was fascinated by these disclosures. "Or I will, I'm sure, when you explain."

"There was nothing else *to* do! Innis was trying to seduce—" Again Adorée's tongue had almost betrayed her. "And I'm sure she didn't want him to. Innis was very angry and Miss—Well! The upshot of it all was that I forbade him the house." She looked gloomy. "Not that it will serve but it may give me time—You will think me a dreadfully temperish female, I suppose, but truly I'm *not*."

Lord Erland might have drawn several interesting conclusions from these disjointed disclosures, had he been paying them any particular heed. Instead, he was engrossed in the various expressions that crossed Lady Bliss's pretty face. "You may make yourself easy on *that* head," he retorted roughly. "I've few delusions about either you or myself, and nothing you've told me has made me think the less of you."

Adorée was not soothed. "That," she sighed, "is because you thought nothing of me to begin with. I wish I knew what I have done to deserve this abominable situation!"

Lord Erland did not think she referred to the fact that she

was seated beside him on the sofa and sharing with him a bowl of punch. He caught her face in his hands and turned it to him. "You forget," he said softly, "how many gentlemen have found you fascinating. Indeed, I am among them. Did I not find you fascinating, I would not have come here to-night."

Lady Bliss knew perfectly well what fascination, to a gentleman like Lord Erland, must entail. Considering her reputation, and her particularity for gentlemen like Lord Erland, it would have been a great deal more surprising if she had not. But she was no lightskirt, despite her countless indiscretions, and she steeled herself to offer a protest. "You left your cloak here," she said, and blinked, because those were not the words her mind had formed. "I've kept it safe for you, in my room."

"You have been," Dominic murmured softly, as he traced the outlines of her face, "put to a great deal of inconvenience on my account."

Little did he know the truth of *that*, thought Adorée. She stared rapt into Lord Erland's cool eyes and suffered a distinct giddiness. It increased to total turbulence when he bent his head and kissed her lips. "I await only your word," said he.

Adorée considered the Earl's cousin and her own niece, Miss Lennox and Lord Roxbury, Innis and Eleazar Hyde. Callously damning the lot of them to perdition, she wrenched herself out of the Earl's arms. "You'll wait a prodigiously long time," Lady Bliss retorted gloomily.

Chapter
Twenty

The next morning saw Miss Lennox making her way to the book room. She knew of Lord Erland's call; she knew also that Lady Bliss had granted the Earl a private interview, at the close of which she had stumbled in a stricken manner up the stairs and barricaded herself within her room. Miss Lennox was not surprised; Miss Lennox thought, in light of the respective reputations of Lady Bliss and Lord Erland, that Adorée should be so sharp-set was inevitable. Too, she thought that Adorée was want-witted, and in need of some stern advice.

Adorée was curled up in the most charming state of indolence on the sofa, plucking petals from the wilted roses—which she refused to have removed from the house—as if they were daisies and from them she might learn whether she was loved. The fruits of this enterprise were strewn about the floor. Lady Bliss wore a morning gown of flower-dotted muslin which strongly resembled a bed dress, and her dark hair was tucked under a large round mob cap of cambric gathered into a band and edged with a frill. It tied under her pretty chin. Save for the shadows beneath her gray eyes, she looked absurdly young.

She also looked extremely dazed, as if she had been allowed to glimpse vistas as yet unexplored, and had not yet returned entirely to reality. Jynx cleared her throat and set a cup of chocolate before her hostess. "Ah, my dear, good morning!" said Lady Bliss vaguely. "A lovely hour, is it not? I anticipate a splendid day."

"You are," Jynx replied repressively, as she sat down in a chair, "in very good spirits."

"Am I?" Adorée looked doubtful.

Miss Lennox was fascinated, and rather disheartened, to discover that Lady Bliss in love was even more scatter-brained than in her normal state. That Lady Bliss fancied herself in love was not in doubt; she had launched upon an eloquent and soulful dissertation, which was lush with such phrases as *la génie de l'amour* and *preux chevaliers* and *chemin de velours.* The primrose path, indeed! Miss Lennox opened her mouth.

"Oh!" wailed Adorée. "I should not speak so to you, but I cannot help myself. How frustrating it is. You will not wish to hear about my conversation with Nicky—but indeed I have lost my heart! I do not always say that," added Adorée, "though you might think I do. I may be impractical and impetuous, my dear, but I don't hand out false coin. Why should I? I'm not in my dotage *yet!*"

"You seem," Miss Lennox ventured, "to be quite taken with Lord Erland."

"Taken with him? *À la folie!* I always develop decided partialities for gentlemen who sweep me off my feet." Adorée did not appear especially delighted by the fact. "And so Nicky would have done, but I did not let him, and I wish very much that I did *not* have scruples, because life would be much pleasanter. Oh! I should not have said that, either! It is all so *difficult!*"

In truth, it was, but Jynx had not yet been driven to despair. She assured her hostess that her maidenly sensibilities were in no danger of being wounded. "Did you," she asked, before Lady Bliss could once more embark upon a discussion of romance, love, and the world well lost, "speak to Lord Erland about Percy?"

"Percy?" Adorée looked blank, then utterly appalled. "We didn't discuss it. Actually, my dear Miss Lennox, I didn't even think of him."

Clearly it was midsummer moon with Adorée, reflected Jynx. Lady Bliss was reckless and tempestuous and beautiful, and in addition she possessed not an ounce of common sense. The lady was engaged in speech once more. One moment she announced that Lord Erland was a deferent and amusing companion, who was supremely self-possessed; the next she averred that he was a great deal *too* sure of himself. "And well he might be!" she concluded, and for emphasis pounded the table with the decapitated rose-stem that she still held. "Which only proves that one should not trust to one's luck, for fortune has brought me Nicky."

Miss Lennox was reluctant to interrupt these intriguing, if inexplicable, confidences; but if anything coherent was to be heard from Lady Bliss, interruption there must be. "What," she inquired hesitantly, "about Lord Roxbury?"

"Shannon? What about him? You will not understand, perhaps, but I never cared a button for Shannon, nor he for me." Adorée realized the oddity of that remark, and blushed. "I mean I *cared* for him, as I care for *all* my gentlemen, but I didn't love him."

Jynx had been sidetracked. "*All* of them?" she echoed, with scantily disguised disbelief.

"*All.*" Adorée's glance was reproving. "I hope I am not so lost to propriety as to flirt with gentlemen whom I do not like!" Miss Lennox attempted to equate propriety with Lady Bliss, and remained silent. "As for Shannon, I have tried to tell you before that he has offered me not even the tiniest compliment for some time. I will not insult you, my dear, by claiming that he never did—not that it ever signified!—but to the best of my knowledge, Shannon has been since the announcement of your betrothal as loyal as a nun."

"But I saw him kissing you!" Jynx was stricken by this intimation that the viscount might not be a profligate. "He paid off your debts!"

"Pooh! The first was a mere bagatelle. All the gentlemen kiss me, Jynx. Too, I had just learned that your father had sent the Runners out after you, and I was disturbed!" An untimely awareness that those dauntless individuals were still seeking Miss Lennox struck her, and she pushed it aside. "And Shannon only paid my bills in return for a service that I undertook for him."

Miss Lennox's suspicions were not so easily allayed. She expressed a firm intention of knowing precisely what those services entailed. Lady Bliss regarded her stubborn house guest, and silently damned that house guests's determination to interfere with her ruminations, and complied. "So you see," she concluded, "that it was nothing exceptionable. Shannon has always meant well by you."

"Oh?" Jynx's anger gave her a demented look. "It is unexceptionable that he set you to spying on me? I tell you, I am quite out of charity with the—the fiend!"

"You are making," Lady Bliss said sternly, "a mountain out of a molehill. Shannon has always acted in your best interests, and he has a sincere fondness for you. You would do much better to go on home, and tell him you are sorry, and be done with all this." She gazed upon Miss Lennox, whose cheeks were flushed. "Don't fly into a passion! You

171

must admit that I have some experience in these little matters. When dealing with the gentlemen it is their *motivation* you must consider, and not the means they employ to achieve their ends."

Miss Lennox was willing to concede Lady Bliss's experience; she did not, however, admire Adorée's logic, in which she glimpsed any number of fallacies. "I do not wish to go home," she retorted, most belligerently. "Nor do I want to be a charge on you, or to cause you problems, and if I am or have I will go elsewhere!"

"Heavens, child! Don't think of it." Adorée achieved a degree of sincerity, though she wished that her entire plaguesome retinue would take itself elsewhere. "You are welcome, but I still think it unwise. What would the world think if it knew you had taken up residence with——"

"With Lady Bliss and company," concluded Jynx. "I neither know nor care."

Once more, Adorée tried. "Shannon sincerely wishes to marry you," she said slyly. Miss Lennox, alas, gave no indication of wishing to rush out and find the viscount and hurl herself into his arms. In an attempt to divert the young lady, Adorée proffered discourse on the foibles and indiscretions of the gay and polite. In so doing, she distracted not Miss Lennox but herself, and was soon heard to remark, plaintively and inexplicably, that she wished that she might be the favorite of rather more than a moment—to be precise, several hours.

"Yes," said Jynx, who was growing very weary of hearing Lord Erland's praises sung, "and you would be done a great disservice thereby. Don't you smell a rat, Adorée?"

"Rats!" shrieked Lady Bliss, and peered in a timid fashion about the room. "Not in Blissington House!" It was some little time before she could be persuaded that Miss Lennox referred not to rodents, but to gentlemen in rodent form. "Have you taken leave of your senses? You gave me a nasty turn!"

"Not I," Jynx retorted bluntly, "but you! Consider, Adorée! Erland thinks that his cousin is infatuated with you. How can you possibly condone his conduct? In effect, he would steal you right out from under Percy's nose."

Adorée wished to consider no such thing, and said so, amid a chorus of grumbling. She considered Miss Lennox's suggestions monstrous and that, too, she made known.

"Piffle!" Jynx was encouraged by Lady Bliss's return, although reluctant, to reality. "Lord Erland seeks to dupe you, and he may very well succeed. Not only would you walk into his trap, you would rise, nibble, and swallow the bait! I think it is a very great shame."

So did Adorée, who had no difficulty taking Miss Lennox's meaning, despite Miss Lennox's scrambled metaphors. "I don't believe it," she said flatly. "Why should Nicky wish to behave so cruelly?"

Jynx fingered her coarse gown and thought that, if ever she escaped this hobble, she would never wear black again. "I don't know, but I can hazard a guess! Percy's family has already tried to buy you off, and failed; perhaps Lord Erland thinks to remove Percy from your clutches by attracting your affection to himself."

If so, he had succeeded, as was evidenced by Adorée's pale face. She looked as if she had just received her death blow. "But Nicky didn't even discuss Percy with me!" she protested faintly. "He refused to speak of him."

"Well, he wouldn't, would he?" Jynx pointed out. "He couldn't very well make you forget about Percy if you were discussing him! Trust me, Adorée. "I think *I* have more than a passing acquaintance with gentlemen's *duplicity!*"

Had Lady Bliss stopped to ponder this remark, she might have realized that Miss Lennox's experience was extremely limited. Instead, she recalled her moonstruck behavior of the previous night, as a result of which Lord Erland must think her shockingly unscrupulous, and disgustingly lax in her notions of nicety, and as bold as a brass-faced monkey. She flung the rose stalk onto the floor and burst into violent tears.

Miss Lennox had a large fondness for Lady Bliss, in spite of all the reasons why she should not, and she was appalled. She had not meant to reduce Adorée to such misery, merely to bring her down from cloud-cuckoo-land before further unhappy developments ensued. She rushed to the sofa and took Adorée into her arms.

"I should not have said such things to you!" cried Jynx, herself close to weeping. "It was most improper in me, and perhaps I was wrong. You would know more about Lord Erland's motives than I. I'm sorry, Adorée! Please don't cry."

Adorée was beyond heeding this request. "Brief though splendid!" she sobbed, against Jynx's breast. "Surely I am the most unfortunate of beings, and I should have suspected this was the case, for if ever anyone was trained in a school of sorrow, it is I! Lady Peverell was right, when she said I

173

was over the hill—and so were you, because in that case no gentleman would trifle with me unless he had something to gain!"

Miss Lennox was stricken by these revelations with an unholy impulse to giggle. "Stuff and nonsense!" she said, in a voice that was only slightly strained. "If Lady Peverell said that, it was out of jealousy. Percy told me his mother's been dangling after Lord Erland for years." Lady Bliss revealed a curious eye. "And," Jynx added, "he'll have nothing to do with her. Just think how livid Lady Peverell would be if she knew he'd displayed an interest in you."

It did not occur to Adorée that a great number of people would be not only livid but thoroughly scandalized by Miss Lennox's knowledge of that event. So cheered was she by contemplation of Lady Peverell's chagrin that she sat up, rubbed the red mark left on her cheek by the rough fabric of Miss Lennox's gown, and emptied Miss Lennox's cup of cold chocolate. "You're sure of that?"

"Positive!" So relieved was Jynx by Adorée's recovery that she perjured herself without a qualm. "I know it for a fact."

"You, young lady," Lady Bliss remarked acerbically, "are too knowing by half! Still, I suppose it is all for the best—though why people say things always *are* I do not know, because I see very little evidence of it! And there is no denying that all this has been a terrible blow to my *pride*."

Jynx, who understood that feeling perfectly, sympathized. Her hostess cut her short. Denied her castles in the air, Adorée had turned, rather astonishingly, practical. "Very well!" she said briskly. "I am restored to myself. Now, my dear, since you are so needle-witted, you may tell me how to extricate myself from this fix!"

So oddly did this weighty matter sit on Adorée that Jynx grinned. "I'd be glad to, if only I could. You might recall that I've made rather a botch of my own affairs. And don't tell me again that I may apologize to Shannon and make all well! There are between Shannon and myself serious differences."

"The deuce!" lamented Lady Bliss. "I thought you would know how to take us all in hand. Which reminds me, I must apologize to you on Innis's behalf. Never did I think he would behave so abominably! If Shannon knew of *that*, he'd call Innis out and probably skewer him."

"But Shannon *won't* know about it!" Jynx said hastily. Adorée looked distinctly damp around the eyes. "I won't tell him and neither will you. Lord, a pretty uproar *that* would make! This is profitless speculation, anyway. We would do much better to consider why your brother is so eager to placate Eleazar Hyde."

"I don't know." Lady Bliss was the picture of gloom. "Innis told me once that Eleazar had threatened to see him in gaol. And then Innis threatened me within an inch of my life if I breathed a word of what he'd said. None of this makes sense to me. Poor Cristin! The worst thing of all," she moaned, "is that I am being dunned again! I'm sure I should be used to it, since it has happened all my life, but I vow it grows ever more tedious. Nicky even offered to pay my debts for me, and I had to refuse."

Jynx regarded the delicate writing desk, in which post-obit bills were stuffed out of sight. So did Lady Bliss, with as much distaste as if it had been a guillotine. "Why refuse?" inquired Miss Lennox. "Let him pay them! Better yet, let him buy you off. After all, he wishes to make a monkey of you, so it is no more than he deserves."

Lady Bliss might be a trifle reckless in her dealings with the opposite sex, and so she frankly admitted; but she was neither unscrupulous nor scheming, and so she also said. "My dear Miss Lennox," she concluded, with a quelling glance, "I do not think you know very much about *love!*"

Obviously she did not, decided Jynx, or she would not be in her present dreadful situation. "I don't imagine," she offered, "that you'd consider applying to Shannon?" Lady Bliss stated emphatically that she would not. "Then I don't know *what* to suggest!" sighed Miss Lennox. "If only Innis had not taken that pretty snuffbox away with him—which is just like the man!—you might have sold that. I cannot draw on my own funds without my father—and the Runners—learning that I'm here, so unfortunately that's out."

Adorée, thus reminded of Sir Malcolm, sat suddenly upright. There was an expression of such intense concentration on her lovely face that Jynx stared. "You've thought of something! What?"

"I? Nothing at all!" Lady Bliss successfully hid her guilty expression by yanking her mobcap down over her face and off her head. Then she rose to her feet.

"Adorée!" Jynx was not deceived. "What are you up to?"

"What *could* I be up to?" With an almost successful look of wounded innocence, Adorée moved toward the door. "I have been dealt a grave wound, my dear, and my spirits must be raised." Miss Lennox looked doubtful that this miracle might be accomplished, and Lady Bliss further explained that it was her habit, when disappointed in romance, and she seemed destined to be disappointed in romance, to seek consolation among the various stalls and shops at the Pantheon Bazaar. Before Jynx could point out that, for a lady already deeply in debt, such an undertaking was most unwise, Adorée had whisked herself out the door.

She had not precisely lied, Lady Bliss consoled herself, as she ran to don a bonnet and pelisse. As far as she had spoken, she had spoken truth. Too, Jynx's spirits were already depressed. It was far kinder *not* to tell her that her hostess meant to make a slight detour by way of Lennox Square.

Chapter
Twenty-one

Evening had come, and the gaming rooms in Blissington House were once more in full swing. Tomkin, stationed near the front door, opened the portal to a latecomer. He stared, and grimaced in the most extraordinary manner, and looked very much as if he wished to faint but could not. Then he stepped aside and in quavering tones bade the gentleman enter.

Lord Roxbury did so. With an ironic glance at the distrait butler, he strode toward the stairway that led to the first floor.

Lady Bliss, clad in a romantic and revealing peasant costume, presided there. The more astute of her guests remarked that she did not seem to be in her usual lively spirits, and the less kind of them vowed she moved about in a fit of ambulatory somnambulism as effective as that of Mrs. Siddons's final enactment of Lady MacBeth the previous year at Convent Garden, which had so stirred her audience that they preferred to applaud her through the rest of the evening rather than let the play go on.

Shannon watched as Lady Bliss manipulated a deck of cards into a great curving fan in front of her. She lifted the first card with her finger, and the other cards, one after another in a pretty ripple, lay face upward on the green baize cloth. She touched a card on the other end, and the cards rippled again, and lay face down. The gentlemen applauded and Adorée bowed. Then she glanced up, and caught Shannon's eye, and turned ashen.

He said nothing to her, but continued to make his circuit of the rooms. Lord Roxbury was a gentleman who attracted attention everywhere he went, despite his adherence to his friend Brummel's aphorism that the severest mortification a gentleman could incur was to attract observation by his outward appearance. It was not the viscount's raiment that drew all eyes to him; the viscount's raiment was elegant in cut, and so understated as to seem, to the uninitiated eye, dull. Not the least unremarkable, however, was the viscount himself. Ladies wistfully eyed his handsome physique and red-gold hair, his sensual features and ascetic green eyes. Gentlemen regarded him also, with less appreciation but as great a curiosity; and all speculated upon the countless *on-dits* heard about Lord Roxbury, and Miss Lennox, and Adorée Blissington.

Not by so much as an eyelid's flicker did Shannon betray his awareness that a great deal of the conversation that buzzed about Blissington House that night was concerned with him, or the distaste that the situation caused him. He strolled idly through the rooms, spent a half hour at the E.O. table, punting carelessly on the spin; he engaged in a game of whist, won two rubbers and two Monkeys; he paused by the crowded ecárté table and admired its cover of black velvet embroidered with gold. Those who watched the viscount closely admitted that, for a man so plagued by rumor, he was extremely unconcerned.

Shannon was far from unconcerned, but he well knew the importance of appearances in his world. Thus he listened to a raddled dowager's comments upon the poet Byron's relationship with his half-sister Augusta Leigh, who had come to London in search of aid in her financial difficulties, and remarked that the hint of incest was not only a bit beyond the line, even for a figure of romance such as Byron styled himself, but also libelous; and he admitted to a foppish fellow that he had been present at the Dandy Ball in the Argyle Rooms, and had seen the regent cut Brummell dead, and had heard the Beau inquire blandly of Lord Alvanley the identity of his fat friend. Conversation then turned to Madame de Stael, lately arrived in England from Stockholm with her daughter, son and young lover. The fop declared his opinion that the lady was large, coarse and homely, with a total lack of beauty and grace. Lord Roxbury, who had a newly developed horror of malicious gossip, announced a prior engagement and took his leave.

In point of fact Shannon left the gaming room, but he did not depart the house. En route to the attics, where he meant to if necessary gag and bind Miss Lennox so that she had no choice but to listen to him, he passed the book room. The door stood ajar, and an altercation was underway within.

"Furthermore," said Miss Lennox wrathfully, "I do not

know what you can be doing here when your sister has forbidden you the house."

"Never have I seen so stiff-necked and stubborn a girl!" For emphasis, Innis brandished the brandy decanter that he held. "It's my home as much as hers. I live here, don't I? Anyway, everyone knows that my sister's heart is soft as mush."

Jynx had endured a very trying day, and her efforts to think of a resolution to her hostess's mountainous debts had left her with a raging headache. "You are a curst humbug!" she said rudely. "Do go away."

"A humbug, am I?" Innis was additionally three sheets to the wind, having imbibed a vast quantity of various sorts of alcohol, including a potent concoction known as a dog's nose—warm porter, moist sugar, gin and nutmeg—before starting in on the brandy. "Damned if I know why you must be so devilish disagreeable!"

Miss Lennox sank down on the sofa and dropped her head into her hands. "God in heaven!" she moaned.

Innis still nurtured hope for the success of his grand plan. He dropped to his knees on the floor in front of her, carefully set down the brandy decanter, and grasped her hands. Jynx tried unsuccessfully to free herself. Innis then launched into a dissertation upon her wit and beauty, and offered protestations of loyalty unto death. "My darling," he concluded, "fly with me! Once the knot is tied, no one can ever part us again."

"Nothing," remarked Jynx, "can be more revolting than this persistence of yours! How many times must I tell you that I am perfectly aware of your deceit and duplicity?"

Innis was not deterred by her unappreciative tone, or the jaundiced expression with which she regarded him. "Even a man of notoriously bad character," he offered, and kissed her hand, "can by affection be reformed."

Miss Lennox snorted and yanked her hand away. "You are the most impudent rascal that ever existed! First you steal my betrothal ring, and then the other night——"

"I am more sorry for that than I can say!" interrupted Innis. "You must understand, my darling, how a man may be driven to——"

"I understand nothing!" Jynx said impatiently. "Except that your behavior is strongly to be deprecated! I do not love you; I do not even think that I *like* you, and that you should take it upon yourself to bully and badger me is too much to be borne! I will not fly with you, I would not even walk to the street corner with you. Now be done with this nonsense!"

Even then, Innis did not despair of rousing a tender emotion in Miss Lennox's chaste and fluttering breast. She might refuse him in the most emphatic manner, she might state unequivocally that she wished to hear no more on this subject, but she had forgotten the aces that he had up his sleeve. He proceeded to remind her of them. "What of Cristin?" he inquired slyly. "And Lord Peverell, and my sister? Recall that you may condemn them all to woe, or grant them happiness." Miss Lennox stared at him, stunned. "Come, my darling, admit that alliance with myself is not all that hideous a fate. I am not, I hope, a *cruel* man."

"What you are is a candidate for Bedlam!" A muscle twitched in Jynx's cheek. "So I am expected to sacrifice myself on the altar of the Ashley intemperance? To give myself—and my fortune!—over into your hands so that Cristin and your sister may be spared the consequences of their own follies? That is the most idiotic notion I have ever heard, and I've heard a great many idiotic notions since I came to this house." Innis, who was trying to regain possession of her hands, did not look convinced. "It is utterly out of the question!"

For the first time, Innis realized that he might fail. Lest this opportunity totally escape him, as it appeared she might, he determined on a more direct approach. Miss Lennox would sing a different tune were she truly compromised. He swore at her and lunged.

Jynx was prepared for exactly such an attack. She boxed his ears vigorously, shoved him over backward, ran across the room and grasped the fireplace poker. Innis was no little bit startled to see the phlegmatic Miss Lennox transformed into a snarling virago.

Not so Lord Roxbury, who several times had been tempted to interrupt this shocking scene. Lord Roxbury, during several of the preceding moments, had experienced the novel sensation of feeling his blood boil in his veins. In the interest of enlightenment, however, and an enlightenment of which he stood sorely in need, he had refrained from interference. Shannon congratulated himself for it. Had he rushed to defend Miss Lennox, he would not have been privileged to witness her shatter forever the myth of the weaker sex.

Shannon stood erect, for he had leaned against the wall for support. His sides ached with suppressed mirth. With an air of leisured unconcern, and only the slightest of smiles, he strolled into the room. Innis turned, gasped, and fled.

Miss Lennox's reaction was a great deal more complex. She did not blanch, or start, or gasp; she did not even appear especially surprised. Instead, she carefully replaced the poker. "I gather," she said without expression, "that Adorée spilled the beans."

Lord Roxbury had no objection to a slight inelegance of speech. He moved further into the room. "She did."

"I thought she would eventually. To request silence of Lady Bliss is as futile as to ask a babbling brook to be dumb." Still Jynx remained impassive. "What did she tell you?"

"Me? Nothing." The viscount thought, erratically, that he would prefer to see Miss Lennox animated by a very bad spirit instead of so lifeless and spent. "It was to Sir Malcolm that she made her confession, and Sir Malcolm did not confide to me the details of it."

Miss Lennox was seen to wince. "I suppose he is very angry."

"Extremely. He blames you for his present onset of gout—though it's my opinion that a turkey stuffed with chestnuts is the true culprit." Shannon was stirred to compassion by that still figure and shuttered face. "You need not fear Sir Malcolm's wrath, poppet. He has promised he will neither scold or punish you, if only you will come home." Jynx's expression indicated doubt of this paternal magnanimity. "All of us have been very worried about you."

This politely phrased reminder of the extent of her transgressions caused Miss Lennox to raise her eyes at last to the viscount. Perhaps because she had not seen him for what seemed a very long time, she was stricken anew by his figure and appearance. He was looking at her not with anger, as she had expected; his face wore only the smallest of frowns. Jynx did not consider this an indication of concern, but of indifference. "You are looking," she said hollowly, "very fine."

Lord Roxbury regarded her face, pale against the hideous black gown, and her untidy chestnut hair. "Well, you're *not!*" he retorted. "Good God, what the devil possessed you, Jynx? Our difficulties might have been settled easily enough had you not seen fit to publish them to the world."

If Shannon had expected to continue their argument, and Shannon apparently did, he was doomed to disappointment. Miss Lennox cast him a very odd glance, then turned her back on him and stared into the fireplace. Shannon glared at her stiff spine. "And then," he said grimly, "to come of all places here, and allow all of us to think you had been kidnaped—or worse! And apropos of worse, just what *did* Innis Ashley do to you the other night?"

Jynx had no intention of offering detail. "It was nothing so very bad," she murmured. "He only kissed me."

"Only!" uttered the viscount angrily, and in three strides was across the room. He grasped Miss Lennox by the shoulder, spun her around, and kissed her himself. "Since you are on the way to becoming expert in such matters, how does *that* compare?"

Jynx stared at him, then touched her fingers to her bruised lips. "It doesn't," she said faintly. Lord Roxbury cursed viciously and turned away, fast in a paroxysm of rage. "Perhaps I should leave you here, after all!" he growled, at which point Miss Lennox displayed the good sense for which she was celebrated, and which had been demonstrably absent these past many days. She sniffled, choked, then gave vent to heart-rending sobs.

"Jynx!" Lord Roxbury was apalled. "My God, Jynx!" These soothing remarks failed to have any appreciable effect, so he took her once more into his arms. "But, Jynx, you never cry!"

"I've learned it from Adorée!" wailed Miss Lennox, who had thrown her arms around the viscount's lean waist and was hugging him so tightly that he could barely draw breath. "And what I meant was that I didn't like *Innis's* embraces, not yours!"

It took Shannon a few moments to make sense of this utterance, and when he finally did his face was thunderstruck. "What about that accursed ring?"

"It's *not* accursed!" sobbed Jynx, to the grave detriment of his satin waistcoat. "It's a lovely ring, and I'm sure anyone would be happy to wear it! Innis asked to see it, so I had taken it off—I had just beat him at checkers, you see—and then that dreadful man came in, and Tomkin came to my rescue, and I *forgot*. And by the time I'd realized, it was too late, and you accused me of *gambling!*"

"Good God!" Shannon was quite oblivious to the discomfort of Miss Lennox's grip on him, and his own lack of breath.

"And I'm very sorry," continued Jynx, who was determined that her confession should overlook no detail, "if I accused you unjustly, and I doubt I'd have believed just Eulalia, or

ust Innis, but they both told me the same thing." She hiccoughed. "And I *like* Adorée, so I thought it perfectly reasonable that *you* should!"

Lord Roxbury, perhaps owing to his lack of oxygen, was
feeling dizzy. "Goose!" he said. Miss Lennox seemed to consider this encouraging; she loosened her death grip, stepped
back, and looked at him. The viscount responded as any
right-thinking gentleman must: he kissed her again.

Some time later, they were established companionably on
the couch. "I still don't understand," Miss Lennox remarked,
"why you should think I'd taken to gambling—and *tête-à-
têtes* with Innis."

"I'm not sure myself." No longer bedeviled by frustration,
Shannon was in a most amiable mood. "I think it had something to do with Percy, but I don't distinctly recall. What
does it matter, poppet? It's all behind us, and there's no use
in crying over spilt milk. So let's forget the Ashleys."

Thus recalled to her responsibilities, Miss Lennox removed
her head from Shannon's shoulder, where it had been resting
comfortably, and looked at him. "I'd be very pleased to," she
said, with a certain trepidation, "if I could, but I cannot!
The Ashleys are conspicuously crazy—I would be the last to
deny it—but I cannot abandon them. Oh, not Innis!" she
added quickly, lest the viscount fly once more into the boughs.
"*He* can go to the devil in a handcart, and I will wave him
goodbye. But you would not wish to see Percy in the basket!"

Lord Roxbury was at a loss to understand what Percy had
to do with the feckless Ashleys. Jynx folded her arms beneath her bosom—an act which did not escape the viscount's
appreciative attention—and proceeded to explain. Shannon
was gifted with an exact account of Miss Lennox's sojourn at
Blissington House, the discoveries she had made, and the remarkable occurrences she had witnessed. As a result he roared
with laughter. His merriment was infectious. Lady Bliss found
them clutching one another in a mutual fit of giggles when
she cautiously stepped into the room.

"You're not angry with me, then!" Beaming upon their
flushed faces, Adorée advanced. She bore a bottle of champagne and three glasses on a silver tray.

"Oh, no!" gasped Jynx, and wiped her damp eyes against
the sleeve of her ugly gown.

"Tell me, Adorée," said Lord Roxbury, in strangled tones,
"*did* you give Erland back his opera cloak?"

"Well," Lady Bliss looked extremely guilty, "no." She might

183

have explained that she had quite forgotten the cloak, as apparently had the earl, had not her reply sent both Lord Roxbury and Miss Lennox into fresh outbursts of mirth. She regarded them tolerantly.

"Ah, Adorée!" gasped Shannon, when he had recovered partially. "Give me an accounting; *I'll* pay your bills!"

"You'll do no such thing!" Lady Bliss looked faintly scandalized. "You're not my—ah! You have no reason to be held responsible for my debts, and to allow you to be so would be very bad of me." She eyed Miss Lennox warily, but that very insensitive young lady was still giggling. "Anyway, there seems little point in it, since no sooner are the wretched things paid off than I am plagued with more! They are the most insidious things, I swear! If they do not multiply like rabbits—or is it guppies?—of their own record, I do not know how they are to be accounted for!" Lord Roxbury and Miss Lennox seemed to be stricken mutually hysterical by these observations, and Adorée thought it time the subject was changed. "We shall not talk about such disagreeable things, if you please! I wish to drink a toast to your reconciliation—you *are* reconciled? Good!—and to your continued felicity and good health!"

"And in turn to yours, Adorée!" Jynx raised her glass. "I owe you a great debt."

"We will not," reproved Lady Bliss, grimacing, "speak of debts. Or my health, which is always very good, though with the way things are going I'm sure I should be prostrate." She regarded Miss Lennox, who had choked on her champagne. Lord Roxbury, with great effort, had kept a straight face. Obviously, they were in perfect charity with one another, and lovers in perfect charity were famed for queer behavior, so Adorée wasted no concern on their combined eccentricities.

"People may say what they wish about me," she remarked, "and that they talk about me I'm aware, not that I regard it! I may be so improvident that I am dragged off to debtors' prison, and I may be so foolish as to suffer an unrequited passion, but," her tone was triumphant, "*no* one knows more about romance."

"Shannon!" gasped Jynx, who was laughing so hard she could not draw breath.

"Oh no, child!" cried Lady Bliss, horrified. "*Not* Shannon!" It was the final straw; Lord Roxbury clutched Miss Lennox to his chest and went off in whoops.

Reassured that her efforts toward the reunion of this pair were not to be set to naught by a chance remark, Lady Bliss helped herself to more champagne. A pretty picture they made, Lord Roxbury sprawled on the sofa, his immaculate jacket rumpled and his pristine cravat askew; and Miss Lennox, in an equally crumpled condition, sprawled across his chest. A very nice chest it was, reflected Lady Bliss, though she prudently refrained from voicing that opinion. Miss Lennox hiccoughed weakly and the viscount, shoulders shaking, buried his face in her disheveled hair. "Ah, love!" sighed Adorée.

Chapter
Twenty-two

Miss Lennox, after passing a blissfully restful night in her very own goosefeather bed, donned a pale green muslin frock, which fastened behind with hooks of flattened copper, and made her way to the dining room. So restored was she by a good night's sleep that she felt she could deal successfully with any dragon that appeared in her pathway.

And appear a dragon did, if not precisely in her path; Eulalia Wimple was already seated at the semicircular dining table. Eulalia may not have breathed fire—though Miss Lennox had a distinct notion that wisps of smoke hovered in the far corner of the room—but there was an unmistakable hint of brimstone about her this morning, and she made no effort to hide her fangs. From the moment of Jynx's appearance, Eulalia was off on a venemous discussion of her niece's myriad sins.

In her usual stolid manner, Jynx embarked upon her meal. That she made no effort to defend herself—in truth, seemed not even to hear her aunt's strictures—increased Eulalia's rage. Miss Lennox was a graceless, thankless chit, Eulalia made known; respectable young ladies did not disgrace themselves and their families by making public scenes, or steal away from their homes in clandestine manners, or indulge in vulgar behavior that gave rise to just the sort of scandal-broth that must be most abhorred. Eulalia's spirits, she announced, were utterly sunk by Miss Lennox's misdeeds. Miss Lennox, Eulalia was convinced, had by her actions placed herself beyond the pale of society. And then, with a certain grim satisfaction, she elaborated upon the sort of thing that Miss Lennox had once been privileged to enjoy and now, due to her folly, would know no more. She rhapsodized about breakfast parties and masked balls and musicales; elegant suppers catered by Gunter's, the famed confectioner; water parties in carpeted boats with bands playing under delicately colored awnings. Still, Miss Lennox failed to react in a manner befitting one so recently ruined. Eulalia watched with disapproval as her niece nibbled daintily at a sausage. "You unnatural girl! You've frittered away your chances *now*. Have you nothing to say for yourself?"

"I don't think it is as bad as all that." Jynx turned her attention to her chocolate cup. "If Shannon has forgiven me— and I him!—the rest of the world can hardly do less."

"Shannon!" Eulalia had not been witness to her niece's return to Lennox Square, and thus had not previously been gifted with this highly unwelcome intelligence. *"Forgiven?* How *could* you, Jessamyn?"

"As it turned out," replied Miss Lennox, with a reminiscent smile, "quite easily. Shannon goes this morning to an archbishop of his acquaintance, so that we may have the marriage performed immediately, without the usual posting of the banns."

These happy tidings filled Eulalia with woe. "Marry in haste, repent at leisure," she uttered hollowly. "Already I can imagine the torments you will suffer when the details of your divorce are published in the *Times*." Behind his copy of this morning's edition of that newspaper, Sir Malcolm was heard to snort. Jynx simply continued to smile.

Eulalia did not care for the quality of that grin, which hinted at some highly gratifying knowledge that she was not fortunate enough to possess. "And I'd like to know, miss, just where you went when you ran away! It wasn't Cornwall; that much we do know."

Sir Malcolm emerged from behind his newspaper to grant his sister-in-law the look he gave any servant who'd made a rude remark. "You have," he said irritably, "an irrepressible nosiness! *I* am acquainted with the whole story, and that is enough." He eyed his daughter. "Damned if I thought you'd turn out to be such a mettlesome filly!"

Since Jynx wasn't certain if this was indicative of praise or displeasure, she remained silent. Eulalia was less prudent; Eulalia expressed a stern intention of getting to the bottom of what she considered an extremely hugger-mugger affair.

"I don't know what business it is of yours if my daughter chose to take refuge with—with friends!" Sir Malcolm retorted unfairly. "I'm sure I don't blame her for it! When I think of your eternal moralizing, I'm tempted to do something of the sort myself."

"Well!" Eulalia's bosom swelled with indignation. "How unspeakably odious!"

"Then *don't* speak of it! If Jynx created a scandal, you are a great deal to blame." Having with this Parthian shot silenced Eulalia, and caused her to turn a queer shade of mottled purple, he regarded Jynx. "See anything queer while you were there?"

"Queer?" Jynx crumbled a biscuit. "Not unless you consider——"

"Hah!" uttered Sir Malcolm. "Drinking hard and plunging deep, I hear."

"I'm sure I don't know *how*," commented Jynx. "I understand his accounts to be of the most despondent cast, though he always seems to have money readily at hand. Nor do I understand *that*, since drunk or sober he has not the least appearance of being a clever man." Eulalia was prompted at this point to inquire, in fading tones, under what circumstances her sheltered niece had encountered an inebriated gentleman.

"I've encountered any number of them!" replied Jynx, with some surprise. "Shannon was foxed on the night of the ball, and papa——"

"Never mind that!" Sir Malcolm interrupted. "Back to the subject of——"

"Yes," said Jynx. "I think this conversation would go on a great deal more easily, Papa, if we referred to them as Madame X and Monsieur Y." Sir Malcolm expressed admiration of this brilliant notion, and she regarded him with the hint of a frown. "I thought you'd be angry with me for having gone to her."

Sir Malcolm toyed with his fork and steadfastly studied his plate. "You could've done worse. She has a good heart, when all's said. I suppose the worst that can be attributed to her is that she's so strongly under her—Monsieur Y's influence." Aware of his daughter's keen, and amused, attention, Sir Malcolm flushed. "Anyway, I've gone to her myself! And if Shannon don't mind, I don't see why *I* should kick up a fuss."

"I rather thought," Miss Lennox said blandly, "that you were not unacquainted with Madame X."

"Every gentleman in London," replied Sir Malcolm, in self-defense, "has at some point been acquainted with Madame X!"

Eulalia, who had followed this extremely odd conversation with increasing bewilderment, expressed a desire to learn the identities of Madame X and Monsieur Y. She did not think it proper, despite her niece's comments on the subject, that Jessamyn should be familiar with inebriated gentlemen.

"Oh, do hush, Eulalia. I daresay that Jynx wasn't *familiar* with him." He lifted his eyes from his plate to his daughter. "Were you, Jynx?"

"Well," murmured Jynx, who didn't like to lie, "I didn't *wish* to be! But Monsieur Y wanted to be familiar with my pocketbook, so it was very difficult. You must not mind, you know! That was why Madame X, er, blew the gaff on me."

"I cannot think," said Sir Malcolm, while his sister-in-law voiced her opinion of vulgar expressions from the lips of well-brought-up young women, "that you have benefited from your association with the lady!"

Jynx eyed her most unnatural parent, and grinned. "I'll warrant that *you* did, Papa! A charming addle-brain, isn't she? I perfectly understand why Shannon—but I will not speak of that."

"I should hope not!" Sir Malcolm looked to be on the edge of an apoplexy. "Jynx, you aren't supposed to know about such things."

"Then people should not tell me about them!" Miss Lennox cast a shrewd glance at her puzzled aunt. "None of this would have come about if certain individuals had not wished to make trouble, and therefore talked too much. Still, I do not regret it, because if they had kept silent I would not have become closely acquainted with Madame X, and I should have hated to miss that." Sir Malcolm was heard to splutter. "Oh, climb down off your high horse, Papa! I came to no grief."

"No, but you've set the cat among the pigeons, the cat being Bow Street. Or *I* did, on your behalf." Recalling his promise to refrain from chastising his surprisingly wayward daughter, Sir Malcolm took a deep breath. "The Runners couldn't trace you, but they did trace some other very interesting things, and the upshot is that matters draw very fast to a crisis. They found a trail, you see, and though it wasn't yours, it led them straight to—Well! That place."

With a sinking sensation, Jynx recalled Innis's broad hints. "Am I to conclude that you refer to Monsieur Y's unexplained resources?"

"I am," Sir Malcolm replied obliquely, "being plagued by a rash of thefts. The Runners are very poorly paid, and must eke out their existence by the rewards paid for the recovery of stolen things."

Carefully, Jynx set down her chocolate cup. "And the Runners are very skillful at following suspects without being seen. Papa, are you *certain?*"

"No," said Sir Malcolm, in most unjudicial tones. "Thank God! Still, Monsieur Y has very extravagant tastes, and Madame X has lived like a duck being hunted by a spaniel for years."

"Of course she has! One has to cut one's garment to fit one's cloth, and Madame X wields the most awkward pair of scissors I've ever seen. Papa, you cannot possibly suspect her! You must know she wouldn't be involved in such a thing—at least, not willingly. After all, you once wished——"

"I know," Sir Malcolm interrupted sternly, "that she's a peagoose! I also know that I've a job of work to do."

"*What* a damnable dilemma!" Jynx said, gloomily.

"The cursedest dilemma possible!" amended Sir Malcolm, ignoring Eulalia's request for enlightenment on various obscure points. "The ultimate discomfort of both is merely a matter of time."

Jynx was not deceived by her father's choice of words: discomfort, for those convicted of theft, was of a degree that encompassed imprisonment, or transportation, or being hanged. "what is to become of Madame X? She *must* be innocent."

"Must she? There's no telling what length Monsieur Y may have drawn her into."

"You didn't answer my question, Papa. Surely you must have *some* concern for the lady's future!"

"There isn't much future in having one's neck stretched!" Sir Malcolm eyed his daughter who, on this blunt comment, had turned pale. "Which is why I want you to drop a word of warning where it will do the most good. Perhaps the threat of recrimination may put an end to this cursed work."

In a somber manner, Jynx studied her newly restored betrothal ring. Lord Roxbury had promised to do what he could for Percy and Cristin and Adorée; and she had promised in turn to leave the matter to him. She had not exactly sworn to go no more to Blissington House, but she knew perfectly well that Shannon assumed she would not go next or nigh it again. Now, however, her father asked the exact opposite of her. Jynx began to greatly sympathize with Lady Bliss's dream of a peaceful cottage in the country.

"You keep your head in a crisis," remarked the unpaternal Sir Malcolm, "or I wouldn't ask it. Tread warily, all the same, lest you want to suffer the indignity of being brought to court as a witness."

Jynx wondered if her father would be equally generous if he knew that proof of Innis Ashley's villainy reposed in his own dining room, in the shape of his daughter's betrothal ring. Evidently Lady Bliss's confession had been highly expurgated. "I don't imagine you'd want to deal with it yourself, Papa?"

"I?" Sir Malcolm looked stern. "May I remind you, miss, that I am a man of law?"

And a lazy one, thought Jynx. She sighed.

"I cannot like this!" announced Eulalia. "It definitely sounds *not* to be the thing."

"*You,*" Sir Malcolm said wrathfully, "do not like a great number of things, including my future son-in-law! I am perfectly aware of what your curst meddling did there, Eulalia, and I think very poorly of it. *Very* poorly! *So* poorly that if you just once more try to stir coals, I'll see you in the street!"

This altogether displeasing notion caused Eulalia to choke on several sentences. She could not, alas, doubt Sir Malcolm's sincerity. Feebly, she sought to exonerate herself.

It did not serve; neither Sir Malcolm nor his daughter paid her the least heed. "Papa," said Jynx, as she juggled the jam pot, "I've a question for you. If a man is heir to a large fortune, but has not reached the necessary age to receive it, can his family prevent him from doing so?"

"Why," he inquired judiciously, "should they want to?"

The jam pot had lacked a lid. Jynx licked her sticky fingers. "Because," she said indistinctly, "the family doesn't like the lady of his choice. It's a great piece of nonsense, and fraught with misunderstandings, and it seems the only way he may have her is if they flee to Gretna Green. But she will not do so, because she fears he'd be cut off without a farthing, and she doesn't wish to be responsible."

"Good-hearted girl," approved Sir Malcolm. "It would depend on whether the estate's entailed. If it *is* entailed on him, then his family can't do a thing. Outside of raising a dreadful uproar."

"Now that," mused Miss Lennox, "is most interesting. I shall have to ascertain——"

"Elopements!" shrieked Eulalia, who assumed Jynx had been speaking of herself. "Hasn't this family seen enough scandal? I thought you said Lord Roxbury had gone after a special license! And what is all this about an entail?"

191

"Heavens!" Jynx looked startled. "Not, Shannon, Aunt Eulalia, but *Percy!*"

Sir Malcolm labored under none of his sister-in-law's misapprehensions, having been presented by Lady Bliss with at least that part of the tale. He deemed it time the conversation was turned into less dangerous channels but was prevented from doing so by a commotion in the hallway.

A very distraught Lord Peverell appeared in the doorway. "Beg pardon!" he gasped. "Jynx, I must see you immediately! Beg that you will come with me to—to Astley's!"

"Astley's?" Miss Lennox echoed blankly. She could not imagine why Percy should wish her to accompany him to Astley's Equestrian Exhibition at the Amphitheatre of Arts on the south side of the Thames. "Why?"

"A matter of life and death!" Percy rolled an anxious, speaking eye. "Tell you about it on the way!" Still Miss Lennox hesitated, and he hastened across the room and threw himself to his knees beside her chair. "That curst Hyde will be put off no longer!" he hissed. "Your presence is required."

Ruefully, Jynx reflected that her newfound freedom from worry had lasted one mere night. She wished that she might refuse Percy, and Sir Malcolm, and lock herself away with a nicely unexciting book. But she could not. Shannon was elsewhere, tracking down his archbishop, and the various predicaments of the Ashley clan had from all appearances taken on a grave immediacy. She could only hope that Shannon would forgive her for again defying him.

It was also apparent from Percy's contorted features that he was perilously close to the Ashley habit of tears. "Do get up!" she said crossly. "I'll come with you." Percy rose, and grabbed her arm, and practically dragged her from the room.

"What on earth," Eulalia inquired faintly, staring at the door, "was that about?"

"Astley's," said Sir Malcolm helpfully. He had a very good notion of what his daughter's proposed destination actually was, and he was grateful to Lord Peverell for forcing her to cooperate. Sir Malcolm was not oblivious to the impropriety of the expedition, but Sir Malcolm was determined that Lady Bliss should be warned. It did not occur to him that, in saving his own honor and incidentally a great deal of effort for himself, his daughter might be further compromised. "You know, founded by ex–Sergeant Major Philip Astley as a riding school and the first Royal Circus in 1768. Equestrian displays!" He raised the *Times* and withdrew.

What Eulalia knew was that she'd despaired too soon. Jessamyn preferred Lord Peverell to Lord Roxbury? So, frankly, did she. Percy would be easily persuaded to take his wife's doting aunt into his home, whereas Shannon would not have been. Indeed, Eulalia thought smugly, Percy could be easily persuaded to do anything. All that remained was to inform Lord Roxbury that his betrothal was at an end.

Chapter Twenty-three

Miss Lennox donned an elegant bonnet, and a muslin pelisse with long full sleeves, and set out in company with Lord Peverell. As Sir Malcolm had anticipated, their destination was not Astley's pleasure dome in Lambeth, but a certain red brick house in Portland Place. Lord Peverell's utterances, during this short journey, were both ominous and incoherent, and neither relieved nor enlightened his companion.

Nor did the scene that greeted her in Blissington House. Lady Bliss and her niece were in the drawing room, and both were weeping lustily. Even Tomkin, who was puttering quite unnecessarily about the room, possessed a suspicious dampness of eye. "Oh, miss!" he said, when that orb alit on Jynx. "I'm mighty glad you've come."

Thus made aware that callers had arrived, Lady Bliss emerged from behind her sodden handkerchief. "Miss Lennox! Has Percy brought you? Then he has caused you a fool's errand, and you had better go away!"

Miss Lennox blinked. "I thought you wished my help, Adorée? I do not scruple to tell you that you look to be in sore need of *someone's* assistance. What is going on here?"

"Oh, my dear! We are undone. You should not further involve yourself in our affairs." Nonetheless, Lady Bliss grasped Jynx and pulled her down on the settee. "I do not wish it to be laid at *my* door if Shannon gets up on his high ropes again."

"Pooh! Why should he, pray?" Rather helplessly, Miss Lennox patted her hostess's hand, which clutched her wrist so tightly that the bones had begun to ache.

Briefly diverted, Adorée cast her a shrewd glance. "You can't deny that Shannon wouldn't like your being here. The future Lady Roxbury shouldn't be lowering her character by such improprieties."

"The future Lady Roxbury is a sad case, I fear," retorted

Jynx. "She doesn't give a fig for propriety! And you may leave Shannon to me."

"I shall!" Adorée looked dismayed. "A man with a young wife is hardly what I would—oh! Now I understand! Do you know, my dear Miss Lennox, I never suspected that you would prove to be so much of a little *minx?*" Sternly she gazed upon her guest, whose lips had begun to twitch. "Jynx, if you start to *giggle* again, I'll box your ears! There is absolutely nothing in this dreadful situation about which one may laugh."

"I wouldn't dream of doing such a thing!" Jynx's voice was strained. "Do you think you might explain the situation to me? You might as well, since I am already here."

Cristin had become belatedly aware of that fact. She tore herself away from Percy, who had been murmuring vague but encouraging promises in her ear, and hurled herself at Miss Lennox. "Oh, Jynx, you *must* help me! I know I said I would go through with it for Percy's sake, but now I have found that I cannot! It is *infamous!* What are we to do?"

Miss Lennox straightened her bonnet, which Cristin's assault had knocked forward onto her nose, and voiced a faint request that Cristin would cease to manhandle her. Sniffling, Cristin removed her arms from around Jynx's neck. "You refer to Eleazar Hyde?"

"Do not even speak his name!" Cristin looked distinctly nauseous, and Adorée moved hastily out of the way. Cristin immediately appropriated her aunt's place on the settee. "He says he will no longer be put off by missishness, and I am to go away with him as soon as he returns to town."

"Never!" ejaculated Percy, who'd come to perch on the arm of the settee, in which position he looked—and was—extremely uncomfortable.

"When is that to be?" inquired Jynx. "His return? And where does the man go on these jaunts? He seems to be very often out of town."

"I'm sure *I* don't know!" Cristin retorted pettishly. "I only wish he might stay there. And I don't care *what* threats he may have made my uncle, I don't wish to sacrifice myself for Innis! It is too much to ask entirely."

With this sentiment, Lord Peverell energetically agreed. Lady Bliss remarked—from the writing desk where she sat shuffling in a despondent manner through a stack of bills—that she wished to hear no more against her brother. Even though Innis was the greatest scoundrel in nature, Adorée explained, he was still an Ashley. "And the Ashley blood is thicker than most," she added solemnly. "Considering our lack of credit with the world, it has to be! Anyway, Innis said he'd fix it up all right and tight, so I don't know why Percy saw fit to drag you into this, Jynx! He knows we are in anxious expectation of more news."

"Innis—" Jynx began, then stopped as she noted the intractable expression on Adorée's lovely face. "No one has told me when Eleazar Hyde is to return."

"In a couple of days," offered Percy, since this question had reduced Cristin once more to tears. "We don't know exactly. Don't go saying Cristin should go off with him like—like a lamb to the slaughter!—because I won't have it, Jynx!"

Miss Lennox, who had never suggested anything of the sort, bit back several sharp replies. "Percy, is your inheritance entailed?"

"Dash it, Jynx, what has my inheritance to do with anything?" On Percy's handsome, and rather vacant, countenance sat an expression of extreme indignation. "Of course it's entailed! Not that it matters! Now do try and concentrate on what's to be done."

Miss Lennox had an unprecedented impulse to tear at her hair. "I am!" she snapped. "Which is a great deal more than can be said for any of you! Don't you see, Percy? Your family can't do anything if you elope with Cristin!"

Lord Peverell's indignation was replaced by a dazzling smile. "You *are* a good sort of girl, Jynx! I always said you was! Did you hear, Cristin? We can fly to Gretna Green!"

"Oh, I wish I could!" Cristin wrung her hands. "But if I did, think what would happen to my aunt! Eleazar would be very angry, and I do not think he would let us go unpunished. You owe a great deal of money to Innis, and there's no telling what Eleazar would make you do."

"You need not," Adorée announced woefully, "concern yourself with me. I'm already in such deep water that a few more bucketfuls would merely ensure that I drowned, which is of all things what I would prefer. And Eleazar can do nothing to me that hasn't already been done, so you might as well be on your way."

Percy was, despite his lack of native wit, very much a gentleman; and so he demonstrated. "Can't do that!" he protested, albeit unenthusiastically. "Cow-hearted! Tell you what, I'll pay your debts."

Miss Lennox regarded Lord Peverell's triumphant expression, and Lady Bliss's hopeful one, and reluctantly intervened. "Percy, you cannot even discharge your *own* debts! You couldn't possibly raise a sum large enough to cover Adorée's as well without approaching your trustees." Three uniformly unappreciative faces turned to her. "Has anyone considered applying to Lord Erland?"

"It is Lord Erland," Adorée responded dramatically, "who has brought us to a standstill! I should have believed Percy's mama when she said I was at my last prayers—but no! I had to wear my heart upon my sleeve, even though I knew as soon as I clapped eyes on Nicky that he was a *downy* one, up to all the rigs! I have been sadly taken in, Miss Lennox—bamboozled! I can perfectly understand *why* he did it, of course, but it was cruel in the greatest degree that he should set all of us on our ear." She frowned. "I do not think I shall even forgive him for it, not that I suppose he cares."

Miss Lennox gazed with no little apprehension upon her hostess, who wore a dress made from an Indian shawl, its wide border forming the hem; and begged to be told the extent of Lord Erland's perfidy. Lady Bliss clutched her bosom, swore she suffered palpitations, and announced faintly that her beloved Nicky was a stiff-necked whopstraw. Cristin being by Percy's proximity rendered equally unintelligible, it was left to Lord Peverell to explain.

"Nicky has a winning gambler's temperament," he said, with a hint of admiration. "The coolest nerve I've ever seen. And his calculation of the odds is wonderful to see. I've watched him go down very heavily without even turning a hair."

"But he didn't go down last night!" Adorée, who still sat at her writing desk, was in a most nervous and prostrate state. "He won! And I'm sure he *meant* to, because all along he has been playing the concave suit."

Miss Lennox reflected that few gentlemen sat down to gamble with the intention of taking a loss, but she did not confuse her hostess with this side issue. "Lord Erland came here last night," she prompted. "Then what?"

"It was very late," said Adorée, looking most forlorn, "and you had already gone. I refused to speak to him—remembering, my dear Jynx, what you had said about *motives*. Well! Nicky retired promptly to the faro table, and broke the bank for five thousand pounds."

"Five thousand!" Jynx repeated, stunned.

"It has put me," Adorée remarked with awesome understatement, "very much out of frame! You must not blame yourself, Jynx; *I* do not blame you. Even though if you hadn't pointed out his duplicity, I would not have refused to speak to him; and if I hadn't refused to speak to him, he wouldn't have gone to the faro table, and I wouldn't now be on the edge of *ruin!*"

This example of Ashley logic caused Miss Lennox to suffer palpitations of her own. "Oh, God!" she said weakly.

"There! I knew you'd be upset, which is why I expressly told Percy *not* to inform you of it." Lady Bliss studied that young man, who had assumed an extremely contorted position so that Cristin might rest her head against his shoulder. "I should have known he would immediately do the opposite. You meant it for the best, Jynx, and it was your concern for me that prompted you to speak—and even though I could wish you had been *less* concerned, I do not hold it against you!"

So overwhelmed was Miss Lennox by her suddenly assumed role as the harbinger of the Ashley doom that she rose abruptly to her feet. Lord Peverell immediately assumed her place on the settee. "You think Lord Erland *didn't* deliberately set out to alienate you from Percy? But then——"

"Is it so wonderful," Adorée asked awfully, "that a gentleman should be attracted to myself? I have thought a great deal about it, and though I may not be terribly intelligent, I have a certain *instinct* about such things!"

Briefly, Percy roused himself from his preoccupation with Cristin. "Can't imagine why I asked you to help us, Jynx. Now that I consider it, you've made a sorry mess of things!"

"Nonsense!" Moved by Miss Lennox's stricken expression, Lady Bliss took her hand. "I'm sure we are not *entirely* without blame. Dear Jynx, do not distress yourself. Innis has promised to set all to rights."

Miss Lennox doubted Innis Ashley's ability to amend any situation, but she hesitated to say so. "How?"

"I didn't ask." Adorée frowned. "Should I have? It is so very hard to be logical when so many things are plaguesome! And I cannot but think you should leave, dear Jynx—though I am very happy to see you again, in spite of all my little worries!—because I do not wish that you should fall from grace again! Your papa was very angry when I told him where you were; he made some very unpleasant comments about the path I tread and accused me of always *stumbling;* but fortunately I knew just how to handle him." Doubtfully, she regarded Jynx. "Forgive me, my dear, but I don't think *you* do."

Much as Jynx hated to add to Adorée's budget of woes, the deed must be done. "You do not understand, Adorée; Sir Malcolm wished that I should come to you."

"He did?" Lady Bliss's eye brightened. "My plea in your behalf was more effective than I imagined, then!" But then remembering her difficult if not impossible position she was more disconsolate. "I wish," she said unhappily, "that I might go into the country on a repairing lease. So I would, if one did not need a certain amount of money even for ruralizing!"

Jynx glanced cautiously at Cristin and Percy, who were so absorbed in one another that they would have been deaf to the trumpet of doom. All the same, she deemed it wise that they be removed from earshot. After several attempts, she gave them to understand that the garden offered both salubrious air and a great deal more privacy. They departed, arm in arm, in which posture they encountered a passing difficulty with the doorway.

Miss Lennox turned back to her hostess. "It is about Innis that Sir Malcolm wished me to speak to you."

"Innis!" Lady Bliss looked shocked. "My dear, you didn't tell him——"

"No, no! Heavens, Adorée, I'm not such a goose-cap!" Jynx caught Lady Bliss's skeptical expression. "I don't suppose you'd consider telling Lord Erland that you misjudged him?"

Charitably, Lady Bliss refrained from pointing out that she was not the one guilty of misjudgment. "Certainly!" she responded scathingly. "When pigs can fly! No, my dear, the breech will not be healed. Our paths lead in different directions, Lord Erland and I." Stricken by her own nobility of character, and the grievous misuse she'd received, she allowed a few tears to fall. "Should I ever set eyes on the wretch again, I vow I'll strangle him!"

This was all very interesting, but it got them nowhere. "About Innis," Jynx began, then paused. Adorée's sentiments toward her brother were at best ambiguous. Perhaps this warning would best be delivered with subtlety. "Bow Street is exceptionally busy just now."

Subtlety had no place in Lady Bliss's scheme of things. "That's nice, my dear," she said absently.

"Adorée, you must listen!" Miss Lennox was privy to an

unchristian wish that she'd never so much as heard of the provoking Ashleys. "The theft of property worth no more than one shilling may be punishable by death! I know all about it, as does my father, and it is a *very* serious thing!"

Lady Bliss did not share this knowledge, as she speedily made clear. "Theft!" said she. "I may have led a reckless life, but I have never *stolen* anything, except perhaps a few hearts." She looked contemplative. "Oh, let us be honest, a lot of them! But one cannot place a monetary value on human hearts, and you may tell Sir Malcolm so for me. Or I suppose one *could*, but my heart is not for sale, even if someone wished to pay *all* my debts, and you may tell Sir Malcolm that also! I would not have thought him so mercenary. Which just proves that one *does* learn something every day, and most of it one would much rather not know!"

"You have it wrong," protested Miss Lennox, and sought support from the writing desk. "Not you, but Innis!"

"Sir Malcolm and *Innis?*" Adorée was dumbfounded. "Now this *does* beat everything!"

"*Not* Sir Malcolm, but theft!" wailed Jynx, who was herself on the verge of tears. Torn between frustration and amusement, she could only persevere. "Remember that Innis pawned my ring."

"You told your father that? Why, you ungrateful girl!" Never one to long hold a grudge, Adorée relented immediately. "Not ungrateful, but misguided, which isn't surprising in one so young and inexperienced! But *why* did you tell Sir Malcolm that Innis filched your ring? It makes no sense to me!"

Jynx sought desperately to set this deranged conversation back on course. "I didn't! Sir Malcolm told me that Innis is behind the thefts that have been plaguing Bow Street."

"Innis?" Adorée was equally relieved to have the confusion cleared. "How very enterprising of him!" Miss Lennox choked. "My dear, you must admit that it is very clever of Innis to have contrived so well."

Miss Lennox was incapable of admitting any such thing; Miss Lennox was possessed of an overwhelming impulse to weep hysterically and drum her heels against the floor. That she did not was due to Tomkin, who appeared in the doorway. "Lord Erland," he announced, in tones of doom. Dominic walked into the room.

Lady Bliss could hardly, no matter how strongly expressed her wish, strangle the earl. Her pretty hands lacked suffi-

cient strength to choke the life out of a man; and Miss
Lennox was not the sort of young lady to keep quiet if she
witnessed such a thing. Denied the satisfaction of seeing Lord
Erland's swarthy face turn purple and his wicked lips gasp
futily for breath, Adorée did the next best thing: she swooned.

Chapter
Twenty-four

Miss Lennox returned home to learn that her aunt had during her absence embarked upon a shopping expedition. She found no ground for suspicion in her aunt's enterprise, though Eulalia was parsimonious by nature, and not one to derive particular pleasure from the establishments of linen drapers, silk mercers, milliners and dressmakers. Jynx might have been a great deal more concerned had she realized her aunt's destination lay not in Oxford Street or Mayfair, but was an elegant gentleman's home, built by Sir Christopher Wren.

However, Jynx was spared that knowledge, and the inevitable speculations upon just what had prompted Eulalia to seek out Shannon Quinn. She divested herself of her bonnet and pelisse, then proceeded to her father's study, a comfortable wood-paneled chamber. The walls were lined with shelves that held countless heavy legal tomes, most of which would have greatly benefited from an encounter with Tomkin's feather duster. Sir Malcolm's desk was in equally disgraceful condition, and piled high with papers and more dull-looking books. Miss Lennox fished a deck of playing cards out of a desk drawer.

Many years before, her nanny had showed her how to read her fortune from the cards; and Miss Lennox was in sore need of learning what her future might hold. Time and again she laid out the cards, and read from them doom and destruction, betrayal and heartbreak. Jynx considered the ominous nature of these portents, and fervently hoped that she hadn't got the knack of the thing. When a footman appeared to announce a gentleman caller, Jynx was consequently relieved. She assumed the gentleman was Shannon, and said that she would see him.

Not Lord Roxbury but Lord Erland was ushered into the room. Miss Lennox scrambled to her feet with alacrity.

"You left so quickly that I had no chance to speak with you." Dominic's face was set in extremely ill-tempered lines. "Forgive me for this intrusion, Miss Lennox, but you appear to possess a modicum of sense, and I wish that someone would tell me what the devil is going on!"

"I suppose," Jynx replied gloomily, "that Adorée told you who I am."

"She did." Lord Erland looked even more grim. "Since that's the only thing she told me that was at all coherent, I remain scarcely enlightened. I am the vilest wretch this world was ever cursed with, I am given to understand; and additionally I have deprived her of the only happiness left her to enjoy upon this earthly world. And *then* she looked penetrated with grief and said not another word."

A great many people, reflected Miss Lennox, did not share her aunt's scruples about what was fit for a young lady of breeding to hear. "Percy was right; I have made a rare mull of it. You had better sit lown."

"That bad, eh?" Lord Erland sat. "You know my cousin, Miss Lennox? Lord, of course you do! You must be Percy's Jynx. I must tell you that my cousin thinks you are——"

"A very good sort of girl!" concluded Miss Lennox, in long-suffering tones. "So he has told me. May I offer you refreshments, sir?"

"No. I will be content if you tell me what has reduced Adorée Blissington to blithering idiocy." An ironic gleam appeared in his eye. "She has given me to understand that you Know All."

"Good God! Not all, I hope—though not because Adorée was stinting of detail. She remembered just in time—several times!—my maidenly sensibilities." Jynx studied Lord Erland, an elegant figure in buckskins and top boots, a blue coat and buff waistcoat. "*Did* you ever reclaim your opera cloak, sir?"

"What has my cloak to do with anything?" Dominic quirked a brow. "Adorée seems to have confided a great deal more to you than she should. In truth, that you are even acquainted with her is dashed irregular, Miss Lennox."

Tall, dark and short-tempered, reflected Jynx, who was assessing the Earl's points very much as if he were a horse; not handsome but compelling in a rough way; with a deep harsh voice that had probably sent shivers along many a lady's spine. "If you mean to scold me," she said plaintively, "I wish you would not. I am very well aware that Adorée Blissington would be considered a highly questionable associate for a delicately nurtured damsel like myself. Still, I like her very much. And I am not so callous that I can abandon her in her present dire straits—though what I am to do about them, I don't know."

It occurred to Lord Erland that Miss Lennox was on the way to acquiring the Ashley lack of intelligibility. "I'd be very presumptuous to scold you, wouldn't I? Though I am old enough to be your father, we have just met. The circumstances of that meeting do not concern me, Miss Lennox, and I have no especial curiosity about what you were doing in Blissington House. On the other hand, I have a very great curiosity about why everything is at sixes and sevens there."

Jynx decided, abruptly, that she approved of Dominic. "I suppose you deserve to know the truth." Or, she amended silently, a portion thereof. "You will be greatly out of humor with me—not that it signifies! Everyone is out of humor wih me these days. I fear that Adorée's upset is very much my fault. I led her to think that you, er, sought her out merely to alienate her from Percy."

"What the devil has Percy to do with anything?" Lord Erland inquired irritably. "You disappoint me, Miss Lennox; I'd begun to think you a level-headed young woman."

"I was, once, but I've gone off into the oddest humors of late. I fancy it's the influence of the Ashleys." Lord Erland uttered a crack of laughter, and Jynx looked at him. "As for yourself, what else *could* I think? Lady Peverell had already offered to buy Adorée off! Then you appeared and immediately lay siege. I am devoted to Lady Bliss, but not even her most doting admirer can deny that she's a nitwit! I could not simply sit by and watch you lead her up the garden path."

"*Watch*, Miss Lennox? Dominic inquired wickedly.

"You know what I meant." Jynx did not so much as blush. "I will admit that I misjudged you, but how was I to know? As Adorée reminded me this morning, my experience with gentlemen is not great."

Lord Erland discovered, rather to his surprise, that he was enjoying this interview. As a result, he smiled. That smile was of such bewitching quality that even Miss Lennox noted it. "Adorée thought all along that I was mistaken," she added. "But she is not one to stand firm, you know." The earl observed that he had heard something of the sort, and Miss Lennox frowned. "We will not advance with any speed if you keep throwing me innuendoes. And if we do not advance, we will be interrupted by my Aunt Eulalia, and I will not be able

204

to assist you. Eulalia is an expert on propriety, and she would not in the least approve of you."

"You're not missish, at any rate." From Lord Erland, this was patently a compliment. "Very well, I shall tease you no more. I hope you won't take offense, Miss Lennox, but thus far I can make neither head nor tail of your account."

"I don't wonder at it! There is something about the Ashleys that sets coherence at naught." Jynx sighed. "Anyway, I said what I did to Adorée, and then you broke her faro bank, which somehow not only convinced her that I had been wrong about you but also that she was at her last prayers."

"If you mean to tell me that I'm solely responsible for the chaos in that house," Lord Erland interrupted, "I must tell you in turn that you're out! There's more to this than a paltry five thousand pounds."

"Palry!" echoed Jynx. "If you are *that* wealthy, you should give Adorée her cottage in the country immediately! There could be no better resolution for a great number of things."

"Such as?" Dominic looked intent. "You forget that I am the greatest rascal unhung, Miss Lennox. The lady is not likely to accept any offers of assistance from such a rogue."

Jynx did not remark that the lady had a great weakness for rogues. "Someone must look after her; I certainly cannot! *Think*, sir! Adorée Blissington has been a much-courted lady, and she has been surrounded by spendthrift idle gentlemen who are hell-bent on living high without regard of the consequence, such as her brother. She hasn't the least notion of economy, or the least restraint, and as a result she has gone on headlong to disaster. I truly think it would be in the best interests of you both were you to *rescue* her."

Lord Erland, well-acquainted as he was with ladies of every station in life, regarded Miss Lennox with something akin to awe. So far removed was the phlegmatic Jynx from all common notions of maidenly rectitude that he half-expected her to point out that Lady Bliss's stubborn retention of his opera cloak argued a strong passion for himself. "There's something you're not telling me."

A vast number of things, Jynx amended, but she kept that reflection to herself. "It may be an odd thing to say, but I have no other view but that of amending the damage I have wrought. You could do nothing better than to remove Lady Bliss from her brother's influence."

"You are also acquainted with Innis Ashley, Miss Lennox? I begin to be grateful that I am *not* your father! I would be driven distracted by trying to keep you from these highly improper goings-on."

Jynx regarded her caller in an unfriendly manner, and recalled Percy's remark that his cousin was a very disagreeable man. "As you have tried to do with Percy? I *shall* be presumptuous, Lord Erland, and point out that if Percy wasn't half afraid of you he wouldn't be in his current predicament."

"Afraid of me?" Dominic looked taken aback. "*What* predicament?"

Miss Lennox wondered if she should play the prattle-box and betray Percy, or be loyal and stay dumb. Since she could not, after judicious rumination, see that virtue brought with it any reward, she chose the former course. "Gambling debts," she said succinctly. "Innis Ashley threatens him with them. He has not told you because he fears your temper. It is rather hypocritical of you, sir, to scold Percy for gambling when you yourself just broke Adorée's faro bank!"

"I've nothing against gambling," Dominic replied absently. "Percy's sin is that he never wins. But this still doesn't hang together! Percy told me he doesn't care for gambling."

"I don't suppose he does." On thin ice, Jynx trod cautiously. "There was another reason why Percy went to Blissington House. Innis was aware of that reason, and in return for his cooperation demanded that Percy continue to play. There you have it! You would be best advised to buy up Percy's vowels and use them to prevent the possibility of such a thing happening again."

Lord Erland stared entranced at this young lady who not only knew a great deal more than she should about a great many improper matters, but now urged him to subject his cork-brained cousin to gentle blackmail. Furthermore, he realized, it might serve very well. "Have you never wondered, sir," inquired Jynx, who had no notion that she was fast gaining a reputation for complete urbanity, "just what *did* take Percy to Blissington House?"

"Initially," Again, Dominic smiled. "Alas, I allowed myself to be distracted."

Miss Lennox ignored this intriguing sidelight. "Then, think about it now! You may recall that he expressed a wish to wed?"

"Hold!" Lord Erland raised his hand. "Let us dispense with one topic before we embark upon another. You had not finished telling me what I must do about Adorée."

Jynx was not unaware of his sarcastic undertones. "You

seem to be a relatively reasonable man, and therefore you must admit that you were not making too much progress on your own. Or you *were* until I interfered, for which I apologize."

"I'll forgive you," interrupted the earl, "if only you will come to the point!"

Jynx regarded his swarthy countenance. "I perfectly understand why Percy is reluctant to cross swords with you, sir! I can only assume that with Adorée you have not been so formidable, or you would be constantly drying her tears." At this Lord Erland laughed, and she did flush. "I think that, were you to allow Adorée a few hours in which to recover from her expressed intention of strangling you, you might expect to be treated with, er, kindness. You think that I have acted other than I should, which is a trifle poor-spirited, since *you* were the one who—"

"—broke the faro bank! Peace, Miss Lennox! I am an ungrateful brute, and I will provoke you no more. You said earlier that you know Innis Ashley. What is your opinion of him?" She eyed him warily. "Your opinion is to be valued, Miss Lennox, unconventional as it is. My interest is sincere."

"Innis," Jynx replied promptly, "is unbearably tedious! There is a nothingness in him that is to the last degree fatiguing, and I do not *like* to be fatigued. I am a lazy creature, sir, and I find the Ashleys ennervating, and I wish to see their affairs tidied up so that I may once more be comfortable. Now may we return to the subject of Percy?"

"Certainly." Lord Erland was perfectly aware that his question had gone skillfully unanswered. Rarely had he been so thoroughly entertained. "Percy has expressed a desire to wed. If not Adorée—and that it is not Adorée I have known since our first meeting; frankly, my cousin's not up to her weight!—then who? Clearly, someone whom Adorée wishes to shield from me."

"And scant wonder." Miss Lennox was relieved that Lord Erland did not share his cousin's lack of wit. "Percy has painted you as a positive ogre. It is very like him to exaggerate, but I did not think of that. Truly, I did not think of a great number of things." Visibly, she shook herself. "I digress! To continue: Percy has conceived a fondness for a young lady who he fears his family will find unacceptable, and has been meeting her in Blissington House. Adorée could not tell you this without betraying Percy and the young lady, which she refused to do."

"Admirable!" remarked the earl. "She told me she had scruples, but I didn't believe it. Do go on, Miss Lennox. Who is this young lady who makes free of Blissington House—and why should Percy not wish me to know of her?"

"I don't think," Jynx said doubtfully, "that it's my place to tell you her name. As for the other, Percy took the notion you could disinherit him if you didn't approve the match. Which is all nonsense, as I pointed out! Firstly, he can't be disinherited; secondly, the young lady is perfectly acceptable—or should be! Beside, he merely needs to hold out until he's of age, when he may do as he pleases. Or he could if not for Innis Ashley."

Lord Erland shrugged. "I'll deal with Innis. Do you really think that this attachment of my cousin's will survive the test of time?"

"Sir," said Jynx, "you can have no notion of what it already *has* endured. And she has a sincere affection that has nothing to do with his wealth. Not that she won't appreciate it, because anyone must, but I've a very strong idea that she won't be squandering it. Nor does she approve of gambling."

"Then you have my blessing!" Lord Erland announced. "Damned if I see the need for all this subterfuge. Percy must have a secret craving for romance. It's all Byron's fault, with his prattling on about Sin's long labyrinth and Roman orgies and bosoms surcharged with past guilts. Still, no harm's been done, and I assure you that you are perfectly acceptable to Percy's family."

"I am?" Jynx uttered faintly.

"Of course." Lord Erland rose, crossed the room, and drew her to her feet. "I can't imagine how Percy thought you wouldn't be. It's my fault, you'll tell me, and perhaps you're correct. In the future I'll be much easier on the boy."

Jynx hadn't the least idea of how to amend the ghastly misunderstanding which had so suddenly sprung up. Even if she had, Lord Erland gave her scant time.

"You'll know just how to handle him," said Dominic, in tones that were distinctly relieved. "I don't know why an intelligent young woman should wish to ally herself with my nodcock cousin, but I am very glad of it. Welcome to the family, Miss Lennox!" In celebration of the event, he kissed her. It was as Jynx was suffering this chaste salute on her forehead, and wondering how she managed to land herself so consistently in the suds, that Shannon walked into the room.

Chapter
Twenty-five

Shannon, too, had enjoyed a brief interval of peace, during which he had with an untroubled mind gone about his usual gentlemanly pursuits. From Lennox Square he had gone to Watier's, where Mr. Brummell awaited, and had been privy to the Beau's complaints that the constant scorching of his valet Robinson's curling tongs had thinned out his hair. From there they emerged to stroll, arm in arm, to White's, where Mr. Brummell recalled with gentle irony the days when he was an officer in the prince's own regiment, the 10th Hussars, a commission he had resigned when the Hussars were ordered to Manchester to suppress a riot in the cotton mills because he couldn't tolerate the idea of being exiled to a provincial town. After White's came Brook's, and the Beau reminisced about the time when he had fallen off his horse and broken his nose. In this manner the evening grew late, and the gentlemen at last parted, mutually pleased. Mr. Brummell was an amiable and whimsical soul unless annoyed by antisocial behavior. This evening the world had been given to understand that the Beau chose to overlook the disgraceful scene enacted by Lord Roxbury and his fiancée. There was not the slightest doubt that the Beau's world would follow suit.

The viscount rose the following day in an excellent frame of mind. He tracked down his archbishop without difficulty, procured his special license, and returned home prior to attending Mr. Brummell's daily *levée* in his dressing room. Lord Roxbury was not this day to hear the Beau's witty animadversions on matters sartorial, or to gaze with awed reverence upon the pig's bristle brush with which the Beau scrubbed himself daily for two hours. As Shannon was on the point of setting out for Clarges Street, Eulalia Wimple arrived on his doorstep, big with news. When she had delivered herself of that information, Lord Roxbury set out post-haste for Lennox Square. Since he was a familiar caller there, and one who seldom bothered to have himself announced, and since Miss Lennox was always at home to the viscount, the butler unhesitantly directed him to the study.

Shannon stepped across the threshold and wished that he had adhered more closely to protocol this day. Miss Lennox flushed and stammered an introduction. Lord Erland smiled, bowed, and took a polite leave. Shannon folded his arms, and waited. Jynx practically fell into a chair.

"I know!" she said dolefully. "First *tête-à-têtes* with Innis Ashley, and now Lord Erland. You must think me the most abandoned creature alive. I suppose you wish to break off our betrothal again?"

"I didn't break if off the first time; you did." Shannon's glance was forbidding. "Your aunt has been to see me. I thought she was all about in her head, for she said not only that you meant to elope with Percy, but that the two of you had an assignation at Astley's! And so I told her. But if Erland welcomes you into his family, there must be some truth in it. Jynx, what in blazes are you up to?"

Miss Lennox propped her wary brow against her palm. "I do not expect you to believe this, but I am wholly innocent! Eulalia took that stupid notion because I asked Papa if Percy's inheritance would be forfeit if he eloped; and Lord Erland misunderstood when I explained that Percy didn't go to Blissington House to see Adorée. Erland saw me there this morning, because Percy took me to Blissington House instead of Astley's. Shannon, do try and understand! I knew you would not like it, but papa wished me to go, and the way things stand I could not refuse."

"Sir Malcolm *wished* you to go?" Lord Roxbury had not gleaned a great deal of enlightenment from Jynx's speech. "Why, poppet?"

By this familiar endearment, Miss Lennox was almost unmanned. "The fat is truly in the fire now!" she uttered somberly. "Innis is due to be arrested, Cristin is due to be carried off by Eleazar Hyde, and Adorée is due to fall victim of both a brain fever and her creditors." Shannon appeared confused. "Lord Erland broke the faro bank for five thousand pounds, and I did not know where to send you word, so *I* went with Percy."

Such was the impact of all this intelligence that Lord Roxbury felt an urge to sit down. In a room filled with countless comfortable receptacles, it was only natural that he should choose to sit on the arm of Jynx's chair. "I take it," he said cautiously, "that you *don't* mean to marry Percy?"

"Percy!" wailed Jynx. "I vow I'd murder him within a sennight. I would wish Lady Bliss and her entire company to perdition, were not this coil partially of my making—but as for marriage, I have never wished to marry anyone but you. And I should not blame you for crying off, but this is *not* the way I mean to go on!"

Of course Lord Roxbury was stricken by these words with both relief and sympathy; and of course he expressed these emotions as would any proper young gentleman. It was some time before Miss Lennox spoke again, and by then Shannon had possession of the chair, and she was seated on his lap. "I did not know," said Jynx, "that cuddling could be so comfortable!"

Lord Roxbury squelched a very strong urge to proceed with this most pleasant of pursuits, and applied his mind to practical matters instead. "I have the special license," he murmured. "Once the knot is tied, you may, er, 'cuddle' to your heart's content."

"But I can't!" Jynx drew away from him. "Not yet."

"Jynx!" The viscount's countenance was wrathful. "You just said you didn't *wish* to marry Percy."

"I promise you I do not! But I must see Adorée free of this because it is my fault that she and Lord Erland are at odds." Jynx studied Shannon's face. "It is not impossible, you know! Lord Erland would not admit it but she kept his cloak, which is a very good indication that she doesn't truly want to strangle him."

Lord Roxbury placed his hands on his fiancée's shoulders and shook her, none too gently. "Start at the beginning, if you will!"

"You aren't," Miss Lennox said gloomily, "going to like it."

"I shall like it a great deal less," bellowed the viscount, "if you do not explain!"

Jynx was an intelligent and obedient girl, and she perfectly appreciated the logic of Lord Roxbury's remarks. Therefore, she settled herself against his shoulder, and concentrated her attention on the presentation of a concise and straightforward account. She told him of her conversation with her father and of Percy's arrival in the house; she recounted her interview with Adorée Blissington and Lord Erland's remarks.

211

"That's the whole of it," she sighed. "I've no doubt that Innis is involved in the thefts; it's just the sort of crack-brained thing that he would do. But if only I can persuade Lord Erland to take Adorée away, at least *she* may be saved embarrassment."

Lord Roxbury, owing to the fact that his arms and lap were filled with a superb example of fair and fragrant femininity, had not concentrated his attention as fully as had Jynx. Still, he felt compelled to protest. "If Adorée is involved—and you might recall that she's every bit as crack-brained as her brother—Erland won't be able to take her far enough. Jynx, this is the very devil of a mess!"

"Isn't it?" Miss Lennox sat up, looking remarkably cheerful. "I was sure you wouldn't mind, once you understood. Oh, and Adorée said Innis was going to fix everything up right and tight, and God knows what *that* means! More trouble, I've little doubt."

Neither did Shannon. "Whoever would have thought," he mused, as he regarded Jynx's roguish face, "that this wretched imbroglio would result just because I said I'd marry you."

"Shannon!" She was stricken. "I wasn't thinking of it that way, but it's true that I'm responsible for a great deal of this. If I had never met Cristin, if I had not gone to Blissington House and taken Percy along—I must in all conscience see it cleared up, but you need not be involved. It is not fair to expect it of you."

Lord Roxbury was equally stricken by this selfless attitude. He pointed out diffidently that he was not entirely uninvolved, since Adorée Blissington had been his—He paused.

"Your particular friend," concluded Miss Lennox. "That won't fadge, Shannon; if all of Adorée's particular friends were to be held responsible, half of London would be involved in this contretemps. And don't start laughing again!"

The viscount tried very hard, but did not entirely succeed. "Oh, poppet!" he gasped. "If I can somehow clear up this wretched mess, then will you *immediately* marry me?"

"Certainly." Jynx eyed him with considerable doubt. "If you're positive that you do not wish a more *restful* wife."

Lord Roxbury *was* positive, and so he proceeded to demonstrate. Miss Lennox was more than willing to be convinced. "Hah!" said Sir Malcolm as he walked into the room. The guilty pair sprang apart and sought to extricate themselves from the chair. "Don't fret! You might as well be cozy while you can, for I've an errand for the both of you."

212

"Oh?" said Jynx, unenthusiastically. Sir Malcolm, an imposing figure in magisterial robes and powdered wig, seated himself at the cluttered desk. "I must tell you, Papa, that I delivered your warning to Adorée—not that it did very much good."

Sir Malcolm was indeed the most unnatural of parents, a fact upon which Lord Roxbury felt obliged to comment. "You sent your daughter to Blissington House, knowing not only that Adorée runs gambling rooms but that Innis is involved in theft? After the things you said to me about the Ashleys when you sent me to bring Jynx home? How could you, sir!"

Sir Malcolm had the grace to look flustered. "What else would you have me do?" he replied testily. "Go there myself? I couldn't let Adorée be blindly arrested, not after—Hah! *You* of all people should understand that a man feels a certain responsibility!" Since Shannon had been apparently rendered mute by this frank explanation, he turned to his daughter, who was grinning. "Well, Jynx? What did Adorée say?"

Miss Lennox's good humor deserted her. "She said that she thought it very *clever* of Innis to have contrived so well. Papa, what are we to do?"

"Not we," responded Sir Malcolm, *"you!* Not only am I a magistrate, I am *the* magistrate who just issued a warrant for the apprehension of Innis Ashley on suspicion of involvement in theft and fraud. It was the best I could do, though I will admit to you that the evidence against him is staggering."

"Poor Adorée!" said Jynx. "Must she be involved, Papa?"

"Not if you get her out of town on the *qui-vive!"* Sir Malcolm was impressed by his daughter's perspicacity. "Consciously or not, she is involved in the passing of stolen goods, because we have proof positive that Innis conducted his operations from Blissington House. Adorée's credit with the world is not such that she can emerge unscathed. All three of us know that she has *scruples,* but it's not a thing a jury would believe."

This was certain; about those scruples even Lord Erland had been in doubt. "*Does* Lord Erland have a little place in the country?" Jynx inquired thoughtfully.

"Several of them, I should think!" Sir Malcolm looked confused. "What does *he* have to do with it? Which reminds

213

me, your aunt has taken it into her head that you mean to elope with Peverell."

"Jynx," said Shannon sternly, "is going to elope with *me* as soon as this curst business is settled. With your permission, sir?"

"Given." Sir Malcolm waved a paternal hand. "In fact, I was going to suggest that the two of you would be wise to be elsewhere when this scandal breaks." He shot his daughter a keen glance. "Since neither of you are unacquainted with Blissington House and Innis Ashley."

"I must," Miss Lennox murmured serenely, "direct a note to Lord Erland."

Sir Malcolm expressed a strong desire to know why his daughter, on the eve of contracting an alliance that from all appearances she had desired for years, should be writing letters to other men. He then expressed his opinion that if his daughter was not desirous of contracting said alliance, she should not be sitting on her prospective bridegroom's lap. "Never mind, sir!" Lord Roxbury said hastily. "It would take too long to explain. A warrant has been issued for Innis Ashley's arrest?"

Successfully distracted, Sir Malcolm frowned. "It has, and I expect at any moment to be informed that he's been taken into custody. Damned if I can approve of this hole and corner affair. I don't like it above half."

Neither, suspected Jynx, would the Ashley clan. "Should Innis be arrested, then what, Papa?"

Never had a magistrate looked less happy at contemplating the apprehension of a desperate criminal. "He'll be examined by the magistrates, on which day *I* will be mysteriously ill. Damned if I can stomach interrogating the brother of a woman who—" Sir Malcolm broke off to wonder briefly if his fellow men of law would feel similarly. He decided they would not. "If the victims of the thefts fail to identify him, he will be discharged and paid for his expenses and inconvenience. But I've little hope that he'll not be identified."

Jynx recalled the brazen manner in which Innis had appropriated her betrothal ring. If that was the style in which he customarily set about stealing things, she could not but agree. "Devil take it!" cried Sir Malcolm, so stridently that she jumped. "Innis hasn't the wit to set up such an operation! I vow I'd let him go free if only I knew who set him up to this."

214

"You would, Papa?" Miss Lennox inquired contemplatively.

"No!" uttered the viscount.

"I would." Sir Malcolm's brows beetled. "You understand that I can do nothing *after* he's arrested, which is why you must go immediately to Adorée and discover where Innis is. Then you must find him, and learn from him the identity of the mastermind, and tell Innis to leave the country at once."

"And Adorée?" inquired Jynx, as Lord Roxbury opened his mouth to voice even more strenuous protest.

Sir Malcolm drummed his fingers on his desk. "Get her out of Blissington House. Where you take her is your business, but for God's sake don't bring her *here*. Stealth and secrecy, that's the ticket. None of you must be recognized.

"The deuce!" ejaculated Shannon. "I'm surprised you don't tell us to bring in the mastermind!"

"That would be very nice," Sir Malcolm replied thoughtfully, "but I do not expect miracles. And I would not want Jynx involved in something dangerous. Now stop dawdling, or the Runners will get to Blissington House before you do!"

Lord Roxbury could not find words sufficiently venomous to express his disapproval of this scheme. It was as he sought them that Miss Lennox suffered an enlightenment so staggering that she clutched at him. Roused from annoyance to ardor, the viscount clutched her in turn. "Shannon! she cried, as Sir Malcolm stated his grave displeasure with this untimely amorous scene. "Blissington House! Adorée and Innis and Percy and *Cristin!*"

Thusly prompted, Shannon achieved revelation of his own. "God in heaven!" he uttered, and released his fiancée so abruptly that she tumbled off his lap. "Eleazar Hyde."

"Yes," breathed Jynx, as she picked herself up off the floor. "Oh, Shannon, *please?*"

Lord Roxbury gazed upon her pleading face, and could not find it in himself to refuse. "Oh, very well. But you must not get in the way!"

"Bravo!" Sir Malcolm did not explain whether this praise was for the viscount's decision or for his daughter's feminine guile. "Now we come to the matter of disguise."

"Disguise?" the viscount echoed fearfully.

"What fun!" said Jynx.

Chapter
Twenty-six

Their disguises complete, Lord Roxbury and Miss Lennox ventured through the servants' entrance into the London streets. Jynx once more wore the black stuff gown that had been given her by Lady Bliss, and her hair was tucked under a concealing and most disreputable straw bonnet, which according to the viscount was much better suited to adorn a tinker's horse than his fiancée. Shannon was clad in tradesman's garb, baggy breeches and a loose, coarse homespun smock. He also wore a false moustache and wig, the possession of which Sir Malcolm had not been inclined to explain, which led his daughter to suspect of him the worst.

Without arousing particular notice, the servile pair made their way to Portland Place. It was a trek enlivened by Lord Roxbury's unappreciative remarks on the perfidious practices indulged in by magistrates in general, and Sir Malcolm in particular; and Miss Lennox's comments to the effect that though her parent's methods were a trifle unorthodox, his motives were pure; and Lord Roxbury's rebuttal of this charitable point of view. They came at last to Blissington House, to find carts drawn up to the front door, and their owners divesting the house of its furnishings. An altercation was underway as to who was entitled to what, and why.

"Dear Lord!" breathed Jynx.

"An execution, I fancy," said Shannon. "Come, poppet, around back!" Miss Lennox nobly refused to reflect upon Lord Roxbury's familiarity with the various entrances to Blissington House. She followed him.

A burly individual was posted at the back entrance, but— aside from a few pungent remarks concerning employers who gave short shrift in lieu of wages, and ladies who were as lunatic as they were lovely—did not attempt to prevent their

216

entrance. Tomkin, discovered in the kitchens, waving burnt feathers under the nose of the prostrate chef, was a great deal less accommodating.

"Cast your winkers over me, cull!" he said, among a great many other unrepeatable things, and assumed the posture of one prepared to engage in a round of fisticuffs. "If I get my dabbers onto you I'll draw your cork! Unless you're wishful of being planted a facer, you'll leave this house! There's no killing to be made *here*, what with my lady in a pelter and the curst Jews carrying off everything in the house—and if you've money owed you I'm sorry for it, but those are the breaks of the game!"

Miss Lennox dealt effectively with this slightly hysterical outburst. She drew off her ugly bonnet. Tomkin, having progressed to carrion crows who plucked the last shred of flesh off a corpse before it was dead, broke off in midspeech. "Miss!" he gasped. "You shouldn't be here."

"That much," growled Lord Roxbury, "is apparent! Now, you long-winded mugwump, where is your mistress?"

Tomkin knew that voice, and he also knew that tone, though he would never have associated the immaculate Lord Roxbury with this none-too-cleanly-looking lout. Perhaps Lord Roxbury and Miss Lennox were en route to some masquerade? Or bent on cutting a lark? He let it be known that this was no time to be indulging in such frivolity. Lord Roxbury in turn let it be known that he was in a rare taking and was not at all adverse to breaking a few butlerish bones. The chef, who had propped himself up on an elbow to observe these proceedings, moaned and suffered a relapse. A tradesman appeared in the doorway and demanded to know the whereabouts of the silver plate.

"Barricaded in the book room," said Tomkin, with wildly rolling eye. "She's in one of her takings; I doubt she'll let you in." Miss Lennox and Lord Roxbury quickly departed the kitchens, leaving a distraught Tomkin to try and explain that barricaded in the book room was not silver plate but Lady Bliss. The plate, swore Tomkin, had been popped many months past.

Shannon tapped on the book room door. "Go away!" Adorée's voice came faintly from within. "There is nothing here for you, and I vow that if you do not cease to plague me I shall swallow this entire bottle of laudanum! And then you shall have not only stripped from me all that I own, but

217

will have my death on your consciences, and I shouldn't be at all surprised if you were haunted by my ghost. Which would serve you right, for you are all heartless grave robbers!"

"Adorée!" Lord Roxbury rattled the knob. "If you do not let us in, I will break this damned door down."

"Who," her voice came closer, "is us?"

"Jynx and Shannon," said Miss Lennox. "Do let us in!"

The door opened a crack to reveal one damp gray eye. "Jynx, certainly, but I know what Shannon looks like very well, and that is not him! It is very bad of you, my dear Miss Lennox, to try and cut a wheedle at a time like this! Because you must know what Shannon looks like almost as well as I, since you are going to marry him!"

"Adorée," said the viscount, in very irate tones, "who else *would* I be?"

"Well," Adorée replied doubtfully, "I don't know, but Jynx is not without admirers among the gentlemen. Look at my brother! Or rather you *can't* look at him since he isn't here, and I'm sure I shan't care a hoot if I never set eyes on him again." Lord Roxbury swore and the gray eye blinked. "You *do* sound like Shannon, however, and I dare not leave this door unlocked unless those miserable tradesmen try and carry *me* off, so I suppose you had better come in."

They did so, and Lady Bliss bolted and barricaded the door behind them. She then regarded Miss Lennox. "My dear, you are looking positively feverish! Are you unwell?" She lowered her voice. "I hope you will not take it amiss if I drop you some advice. If you wish to marry Shannon, you should not be wandering about with other men!" Unforgiveably, Jynx giggled. "After all," Adorée said huffily, "I must be admitted to know *something* about romance."

Lord Roxbury was not as amused as his fiancée, owing to a niggling suspicion that the lot of them would be momentarily dragged off to Bow Street. "Dammit, Adorée!" He pulled off his wig. *"Will* you listen?"

Lady Bliss regarded him thoughtfully. "I rather," she said at length, "like that moustache."

Jynx forced herself to remain calm. She wrenched her gaze away from the couch, across which was tenderly draped an opera cloak. "Adorée, you must be prepared to hear very bad news. Unless we can find him first, Innis will at any moment be taken into custody for a number of crimes."

To the surprise of her audience, Lady Bliss exhibited no

dismay. "They say," she uttered gloomily, "that debtors' prisons are hotbeds of vice, run by gaolers who torture their victims at will. It had to come, I suppose! And I cannot even escape abroad."

"Why not?" inquired Miss Lennox sympathetically.

"Never mind that!" Lord Roxbury crammed his wig back onto his head. "You have to leave this house immediately, Adorée! Unless you wish to at the very least take your place in the witness box, and at the worst endure long meditation in a prison cell." She was looking stubborn. "It would be a serious business if a lady in your position was to be placed in so degraded a situation."

"What with bailiffs sleeping overnight in the house," Adorée retorted indignantly, "and executions on the premises, things are *already* in a very bad way! All that remains to me is to join the ladies who ply a shameful trade by Covent Garden— or to end my own life!"

"Adorée!" Jynx was horrified.

"My dear, you must pay me no heed!" Lady Bliss hastened to offer reassurance. "I am merely in a fit of the blue devils. Since I am also sadly lacking in courage, I will not put an end to my existence—though I am sure it would be a very good thing if I did! It is all Innis's fault, for he has not only sold all my jewels but run me deeper into debt—but when *he* is plump in the pocket and *I* must raise the wind, he says he has other fish to fry! And if it's true that I must put in an appearance at the bar of the Old Bailey, I shall not say a word in his defense." She regarded her callers, mistily. "My friends! I have not thanked you for coming to succor me in my hour of need."

Lord Roxbury, pacing the floor irritably, espied his reflection in a mirror and winced. Sir Malcolm had outfitted his future son-in- aw with definite malice aforethought. "It is very likely," he said sternly, "to be more serious than that."

"Fiddlesticks!" Adorée sank down on the settee beside the opera cloak. "Things simply couldn't be in a worse case."

"No? Not even if you and Innis are both tried at the sessions at the Old Bailey upon an indictment for conspiring together to commit theft?" Lord Roxbury was stern. "His illegal activities were conducted from this house, Adorée."

"Moonshine!" uttered Lady Bliss. "I can't imagine where you came by such a hubble-bubble notion! Innis explained the whole to me, and he expressed himself in the most subdued and penitent manner." It occurred to her that such behavior was most unlike her brother. "In short, he spun me a tissue of falsehoods from beginning to end and I believed him! Was there *ever* such a cabbage-head?"

Lord Roxbury and Miss Lennox were unanimously agreed that never had there been, but so great was Adorée's nervous agitation that their opinion went unaired. "He said it was the most trifling of misdeeds!" she wailed, into the rich folds of the opera cloak. "And that he would never have stooped to anything truly bad! Worse yet, I took it all in. Oh, to go to prison is no more than I deserve!"

It occurred to Jynx that this reaction was, even for the volatile Adorée Bliss, rather extreme. "You've seen Innis recently?"

"This morning!" sobbed Adorée. "Then he went away, because he said he could not bear the ignominy of having bailiffs in the house. But he is to return and meet Cristin and Percy, and then I will *strangle* him!"

Briefly, Jynx comtemplated Lady Bliss's newfound bloodthirst. "When he returns, he is likely to walk smack into the waiting arms of Bow Street." Suspicion struck her with a thrill of horror. "Cristin and Percy!"

"I don't know why I allowed it," Adorée moaned. "In the agitation of the moment it seemed the only thing! They were to be allowed to elope as a reward, and I was to go to a peaceable and retired village—but now I see that it is impossible that any of us should be reprieved!"

"I think," Lord Roxbury said wearily, "that if you could calm yourself, we might be able to learn just what is going on. Take a deep breath—take several! Now tell us what Innis said to you, and where Cristin and Percy have gone."

As was her habit when addressed by a personable gentleman, even a personable gentleman in hideous disguise, Adorée obeyed. So pathetic did she look that Jynx sat down beside her and clasped her cold hands.

"Innis told me he had stolen a few little things, but nothing from anyone who could not bear the loss! He said he could not bear to see me reduced to such dire straits—which when I consider it is pure poppycock, since it is very much his fault that I am in these straits! But Innis can be very convincing." She applied to Miss Lennox. "*You* know that, my dear!"

Miss Lennox glanced at her fiancé, who looked increasingly irate. "Certainly! Do go on, Adorée."

"Had not my mind been overheated by debts and earls and green peas, I should not have listened," Lady Bliss said sorrowfully. "Or perhaps I should have! I generally *do* listen to Innis, though I should not, as Courtenay used to tell me. Do you know, even though people say Courtenay was a scoundrel, things went on a great deal better before he died? There were debts; there always are; but Courtenay knew just how to go about giving one's creditors the slip." She glanced up and noted the long-suffering expressions of her audience. "I suppose you do not want to hear about Courtenay."

"Just now," apologized Miss Lennox, "we are a great deal more interested in Innis."

"Are you?" Adorée looked surprised. "I was sure you weren't! He is sadly lacking in principle and wildly extravagant, and that he would steal your betrothal ring argues in him an unhappy insensibility. If you'll take my advice, you'll have Shannon. *He*'s not a clodpole!" Doubtfully, she studied the viscount. "Even though he does look like one just now. Shannon, whatever possessed you to make of yourself such a figure of fun?"

"Bow Street." Since Miss Lennox had collapsed against the back of the settee, Lord Roxbury took over the interrogator's role. "Stop trying to throw dust in our eyes, Adorée! Where are your niece and Percy?"

"Oh, very well!" Adorée's shoulders slumped. "If I did not have to, I would not tell you, but I suppose it must come out! Innis knows the law is after him, so he sent Cristin and Percy to dispose of his latest, er, windfall." Miss Lennox was heard to moan. "My dear, you *are* unwell! Shannon, you must take better care of this child." The viscount uttered a growl. "They will be safe enough, Innis said, because they look so very *respectable!* No one will suspect that they are carrying about the proceeds of theft—and when they return with the profits, we will all go safely away. Or so Innis *said*."

"Good God!" Shannon uttered faintly. "And you believed him?"

"He *is* my brother!" protested Adorée. "And it *sounded* logical! And surely even Innis would not ask Cristin and Percy to do something that would be dangerous. Or so I thought, until the two of you appeared! Almost I wish you had *not* appeared, though I understand that you meant it for the best. Why is it, Miss Lennox, that what you mean for the best always turns out for the worst?" Miss Lennox, who clutched

221

at the opera cloak as if it might provide her a lifeline, said she did not know. "Don't fret, my dear! Things may yet resolve themselves happily."

Lord Roxbury, in a few short words, dispelled this faint gleam of hope. He informed Lady Bliss that since Bow Street was on the alert, that Cristin and Percy were very likely to tumble into the net that was being held for Innis. "Oh, no!" Adorée had recourse to her laudanum bottle. "But they are innocent! There is only one thing for it, you must go and find them, and bring them home!"

"Not home, I think," said the viscount. "I might as well take them to Bow Street as here. And how the devil am I to find them when I don't know where they've gone?"

"But I do know!" Adorée was delighted to contribute something of value. "Innis told them where to go and I have a very good memory for addresses." In proof of which she rattled off a list of destinations that made Shannon's head swim. "You must set out immediately."

Lord Roxbury frowned. "You must come with us. We cannot leave you here."

"No." Adorée's voice was unusually firm. "I have been very foolish, so it is only fair that I must take my punishment. Beside, if I can't have my place in the country, I'd as lief be in Newgate. Even a prison cell is preferable to going on the streets!"

"Don't despair!" Miss Lennox said cheerfully, and rose. "You may have your place in the country yet, if you do exactly as I say."

"You are very kind." Adorée looked confused. "But I never meant to live in the country *alone*."

"And so you shan't!" Jynx ignored Shannon's impatient gestures. "Lord Erland will be arriving very soon, and if you are a little bit conciliating, I think you may have what you please of him."

"Nicky!" Adorée clutched the opera cloak. "Coming *here*! What shall I *say* to him?"

"Whatever you please, but as little as possible!" advised Miss Lennox, as Lord Roxbury grabbed her arm and dragged her out the door. "Convince him that you are in need of rescuing!"

Lady Bliss again bolted the door, then sank back down upon the settee, and took Lord Erland's cloak in her hands. That her lovely face was contemplative was only reasonable after the events of this dreadful day. However, Adorée was not thinking of how shocking it was of the gently reared Miss Lennox to advise her to throw her bonnet over the windmill; nor was she dreading the imminent apprehension of a large number of her family and friends by Bow Street. Instead she considered her promised confrontation with Lord Erland, and wondered what a lady desirous of abduction should most effectively wear.

Chapter
Twenty-seven

After considerable difficulty, contingent upon their unprosperous modes of dress, Lord Roxbury and Miss Lennox hired the services of a hackney coach. The coachman first demanded to see the color of Lord Roxbury's money, and secondly expressed a strong reluctance to venture into the sections of the city where Lord Roxbury wished to go; and the horses exhibited an equally strong desire to kick themselves free of the carriage; and Miss Lennox stated stern displeasure with the carriage's interior, which was littered with straw and redolent of strong odors, among which the least offensive was fish; but at length they were underway.

"Poor Shannon!" Miss Lennox displayed her dimpled grin. "You were such a marvel of discretion, once. Will you ever forgive me for bringing you so low?"

"Of course." Lord Roxbury's tone was absent, owing to an erratic and most untimely recollection of the occasion upon which he had heard the Condemned Sermon preached at Newgate Prison. A coffin draped with black had stood on the enclosure called the dock, and grouped around the dock had been the prisoners condemned to die. The public was admitted to this edifying spectacle, for a slight fee. "I imagine I always shall."

Miss Lennox was greatly moved by this declaration. "I do not intend," she said thoughtfully, "that in the future you'll have anything to forgive me *for*. Once we are free of this abominable fix—if we are ever free of it!—I intend to be an absolute model of propriety." She frowned. "Except that I would not wish to snub Cristin or Adorée."

This casual remark roused the viscount from his memories, and he instead contemplated the reaction of the Upper Ten Thousand were his wife to hobnob publicly with his one-time *inamorata.* It staggered the imagination. "Even if they are in Newgate?" he asked, hopefully.

"Especially if they are in Newgate." Jynx replied. "Since a great deal of this is my fault, I can hardly abandon them." She noted his expression. "Shannon, you don't mind?"

Lord Roxbury in turn studied his fiancée's face, which was both smudged and wan, and callously condemned himself to an existence no less notorious than the Devonshire *ménage à trois.* "Why should I mind?" he said, a trifle ironically. "You must do as you think fit."

"Well, I don't know that I *do* think it fit. Certainly Eulalia would not! Papa does not seem to mind, but one can hardly look to papa as a model in such things." Thought of Sir Malcolm recalled to Jynx the purpose of this jaunt. "Shannon, how *does* one go about retrieving stolen goods?"

Lord Roxbury's tone was rather testy, owing to the fact that he was embarked upon an expedition quite contrary to what he would have preferred. "One ideally calls in Bow Street! Good God, Jynx, how should *I* know?"

"You are angry with me," Jynx said gloomily. "I perfectly understand it, but I wish you would not be. It makes me very unhappy."

If there was anything the viscount did not wish, it was that his fiancée should be in the dumps. He told her so.

"I've given you a disgust of me," mourned Jynx, in patent disbelief. "Once I thought you would mind that I was so wanting in dash, and now I'm sure you must be dismayed that my blood is every bit as wild as that of the Ashleys. All this is an illuminating example of the infinite follies of mankind, as enacted by myself! It is not *comfortable* to be the plaything of fate, Shannon, believe me!"

Lord Roxbury had been put in a remarkably cheerful frame of mind by these absurdities. "And *never,*" continued Miss Lennox, in an excess of dolor, "has anyone been caught in so many compromising situations! I am surprised that you have not long since thought the worst of me."

Shannon had quite forgotten the purpose of this trip. He pointed out that the aforementioned situations were not so compromising as Miss Lennox seemed to think, since she had not given any indication of wishing to return any gentleman's embrace.

Jynx did not deem it prudent to remind the viscount that it was he who had first accused her of being compromised.

"No," she said, with devastating honesty, "but I will not deny that I was *curious*." Shannon looked stunned. "In truth, I have been curious ever since the marquess."

"Who was a great deal too ardent," supplied Lord Roxbury. "What are you getting at, Jynx? I thought you didn't like ardent courtships."

"I didn't." Miss Lennox stared fixedly at her lap. "But that was because the wrong gentlemen were ardent and I thought that *you* would not wish to be ardent with *me*."

So bizarre a misapprehension was this that the viscount stared. "My word, Jynx!" Shyly, she glanced up at him. Shannon cast aside all attempts at rational conversation and, with his fiancée's willing cooperation, proceeded to be as ardent as any young lady could have wished. They were interrupted some time later by the coachman, who demanded rather acerbically to know if they were desirous of entering their stated destination, or if he should simply drive them around while they billed and cooed.

Recalled to the present, Lord Roxbury straightened his wig, ascertained that his moustache was firmly attached, and disembarked. Since Miss Lennox refused to be left behind, she accompanied him into the jeweller's shop, where she occupied herself with gazing at gold seals, chains and brooches and rings, while Shannon bartered with the shop's proprietor for the items that a young lady and gentleman had recently exchanged.

This was not concluded speedily. The proprietor harbored doubts both about the apparent tradesman's intention and ability to pay for the goods. There was good reason for his apprehension; a man in his profession was always haunted by Bow Street. The law did not deal easily with those charged with receiving stolen goods. Finally, however, the transaction was completed, and the shopkeeper's profit was so handsome that he was privately convinced that this queer pair were not only flats, but dicked in the nob to boot.

It was an opinion with which Shannon would have agreed. That he did not do so, did not even consider the matter, was because no sooner had they reentered the carriage than Miss Lennox snuggled in a positively brazen manner against his side. "What the *devil*," he inquired hoarsely, "are you doing, Jynx?"

"Cuddling." Miss Lennox's tone was hollow. "I do not think we will have much opportunity in Newgate for such things."

In this manner did they set about their self-appointed mis-sion of mercy, and the day steadily progressed. Over cobbled streets the carriage rattled, past inns and derelict houses and decrepit old watchmen leaning on their poles. Miss Lennox was roused sufficiently from her depression to gaze with interest upon peddlers and pedestrians, scarlet-coated porters and hawkers with bandboxes on poles. She saw small chimney sweeps laden with their brushes, slaveys in mobcaps who called insults from upper-story windows, cits in high hats and neat broadcloth; and, unbeknownst to her, beggars and mudlarks, footpads and thieves. She also saw ramshackle tenements and dark alleyways, and a hospital for the insane, and the College of Surgeons, which stood unnervingly near to the Old Bailey, where the bodies of executed felons were taken for dissection.

Still, it was spring, and Miss Lennox was in love, and had spent many hours in the company of her affianced husband. Granted, their purpose might be grim, but their spirits were not. It was as Jynx was restoring her energy with a potato roasted in its jacket that Shannon had purchased for her at a street stall, and watching with interest an enterprising youth with a dung cart, and discussing with Lord Roxbury their approaching nuptials, that disaster struck.

It was not immediately recognizable as such. Shannon glanced out the carriage window, cautiously, because they traveled through a part of London where well-dressed gentlemen dared not venture even in daylight, and in comparison with the inhabitants of these narrow, filthy streets Shannon, even in laborer's attire, was extremely well-dressed. "Look, Jynx!" be exclaimed. "There's Percy's carriage."

Jynx, too, peered at Lord Peverell's eye-catching ring, which was painted the brightest of blues and liberally touched with gold. "Who but Percy," she said scathingly, "would go about this business in something so easily recognized?"

Shannon, engaged in argument with the coachman, did not reply. The carriage rumbled to a halt, despite its owner's strongly expressed conviction that to do so was to risk both life and limb; and its passengers once more alit. "There seems to be some altercation underway in that alley," Jynx offered with great reluctance. "I suppose that we had better see what it is."

With no greater enthusiasm, Shannon agreed. Fervently, he wished that Sir Malcolm had provided him with a pistol. Cautiously, they approached the narrow alleyway's entrance. The coachman's ill temper had progressed apace with the waning day. In his opinion—shared unknowingly with a certain shopkeeper—these two were crazy as a pair of loons. Additionally, they were also very likely to soon be dead as doornails, and he did not care to become involved with a pair of soon-to-be-corpses discovered in a St. Giles alleyway. Callously, despite the large fare owed him, he abandoned them to their fate.

Lord Peverell and Cristin were indeed in the narrow stinking alleyway, and with them was a rotund little gentleman. This worthy proved better equipped with foresight than Lord Roxbury; in his chubby little hand was a wicked-looking gun. "What the deuce!" ejaculated the viscount, under the impression that Percy was in the process of being robbed.

"Glad to see you!" uttered Lord Peverell, whose handsome brow was beaded with sweat. "In a very nasty predicament!'

"Aye, so you are, cully!" remarked the rotund little man, as he turned on the newcomers a bright eye. "Caught with the goods, no less, and by no other than William Brown." He flourished an identity card in the general direction of Lord Roxbury. "For so I am, and the best of them all when it comes to running desperate criminals to ground."

"Desperate criminals?" echoed Miss Lennox, since the viscount appeared to once more have been stricken by paralysis of the tongue. "Come now, my man!"

Mr. Brown took no offense from this stark incredulity. "Don't look it, do they?" he inquired jovially. "There it is, all the same! This dandy gent is no less than Innis Ashley, and he'll be examined by the magistrates and committed for trial in less than a pig's whisper. Theft, you see, ma'am."

This complication was too mind-boggling even to contemplate. Jynx dared not imagine the to-do if Lord Peverell was brought to trial for Innis Ashley's crimes. "You are a Bow Street Runner, then?"

"I am." Mr. Brown's smile was beautiful to see; it lit up his plump little face like a morning sun. "Here in discharge of the law."

Cristin, who had been softly weeping all this time, emerged from behind her handkerchief. "Oh, Jynx! Tell him it isn't true."

"Now, now, missy, none of that!" The Runner frowned. "This miscreant has been taken for a criminal offense and you yourself have been caught compounding a felony, for which there is a government reward of forty pounds. If not for that, I might let you go, being as you're such a pretty little thing, but a man has to live somehow."

"Very well!" Cristin saw that she'd have precious little help from Lord Roxbury or Miss Lennox, both of whom were gazing with expressions of unconquerable horror upon the scene. "If he is Innis Ashley, then who am I?"

"I'm sure I can't say, miss." Mr. Brown did not seem to particularly care. "But it don't signify. You'll see the paved courtyard of the Old Bailey soon enough, whoever you may be!"

That dire prediction brought Jynx to her friend's rescue. "There is a misunderstanding here, sir," said she. "That gentleman is *not* Innis Ashley."

"Oho!" The Runner's bright eyes fixed with an unnerving intensity on Jynx's dirty face. "So you know this pretty pair, do you?"

"Yes," responded Miss Lennox, a great deal more courageously than she felt. "I also know Innis Ashley, and this gentleman is not he."

Mr. Brown looked contemplative, so much so that Lord Roxbury was compelled to intervene. "It is true," he said with marked reluctance. "I——"

"*Now* we have it!" Mr. Brown's pistol trained itself on the viscount's smock-covered midriff. "*You're* Innis Ashley! The same Innis Ashley who sent this silly widgeon to Tattersall's with a forged authority from a certain lord to collect his winnings, and then later sent those winnings round to the moneylenders to hold them off awhile. That was a very foolish business, sirrah!"

Foolish indeed, thought Miss Lennox, even for an Ashley. "*Did* he?" she breathed, while Percy sputtered and Cristin sobbed. Lord Roxbury, on the other hand, stood positively motionless, his gaze fixed on the Runner's gun.

"He did," said Mr. Brown, with that chilling amiability. "Lord but this is a good day's work, for I've captured a whole bevy of villains who'll be the better of a good hang! 'Tis plain as a pikestaff that all of you are in this together—ample ground for suspicion, forsooth!" He adopted an expression that put Jynx forcibly in mind of a sad-faced basset hound. "More than ample ground, *if* I choose to use it."

The nimble-witted Miss Lennox was quick to seize upon this thinly veiled hint. "*Choose*, Mr. Brown?"

The Runner had not been slow to note that this batch of criminals was not among the more clever of the thieving brotherhood. Therefore he awarded the persipacious Miss Lennox an approving nod. "Exactly so, miss. I figure I could stash this case—refrain from giving evidence, that is—and let you all escape me for a sum of—oh, two hundred pounds."

Cristin emerged once more from behind her handkerchief. *"That,"* she said sternly, "sounds very much like bribery!"

"So it does," Mr. Brown replied with unabated good cheer. "Like I said, missy, a man has to live. Or I can clap the darbies on the lot of you, and take you away."

Lord Roxbury roused from his stunned stupor to discover that four pairs of eyes were fixed on him hopefully. He looked bewildered. "Money," prompted Miss Lennox. "This nice man will let us all go if you give him two hundred pounds."

Shannon would have liked very much to do so, but he had anticipated no great financial crisis that morning when he'd so blithely left his house, and his purse had been sorely depleted by the outlays made from it during the course of the day. He further realized that the purchases made with those outlays were hidden beneath the seat of the hackney coach that had so hastily left them stranded. "I don't suppose," he said, with little hope, "that you'd accept my note for that sum."

The Runner snorted. "I'm a fair man, I am, but *that's* trying it on much too rare and thick! Accept a note-of-hand from Innis Ashley!" He sighed. "Well, there it is, and I tried my best, but it seems I'll have to run you in. But first you must be searched."

"Searched!" cried Cristin, outraged. Lord Roxbury said nothing at all, and Jynx backed away a pace, while Percy looked anxiously heavenward, as if he anticipated that some means of rescue would be presented by that unlikely source.

"Aye," said Mr. Brown. "In cases of felony, your miscreant is always searched when first apprehended—stilettos and pocket pistols and that sort of thing! But we must do this by the book!" He drew himself up smartly. "Innis Ashley, I take you in charge and notify you that you will be taken into the safe-keeping of—"

He never finished the statement. Lord Roxbury had become belatedly aware that the valiant, if eminently corruptible, Mr. Brown was outnumbered one to four. Lord Roxbury was also a notable proponent of the noble art of self-defense, and with one well-aimed blow to the jaw knocked Mr. Brown unconscious. "Zounds!" said Percy. Cristin peered out from behind her handkerchief and uttered a little squeal.

Oblivious to the congratulations that were offered him on all sides, Shannon knelt and bound the Runner's hands and feet with strips torn from Miss Lennox's petticoats. Then he placed Mr. Brown's pistol near him on the ground, and shepherded his companions toward Percy's carriage.

"What now?" inquired Miss Lennox, as they set out at a smart pace. "I must confess, Shannon, that I feel I have never before properly *appreciated* you."

"Thank you, poppet!" Lord Roxbury, oddly exhilarated by his adventure, would have greatly liked to further explore this topic, but Cristin was weeping all over him. Cristin, it was at length learned, was distressed beyond measure to think of poor Mr. Brown left tied up in a St. Giles alleyway.

"Well, I like that!" uttered Percy from the driver's seat, where he was in a most harrowing and inexpert manner wielding the reins. "After he threatened to do for all of us! I don't mind telling you that I was shaking like a blancmanger the whole time."

So, currently, were the rest of them, and Shannon took over the reins. "Mr. Brown will free himself readily enough," he remarked, before Cristin could raise a further outcry. "But hopefully not before all four of us have removed ourselves from town."

"Oh?" Percy looked curious. "Are we going somewhere?"

"Yes." Lord Roxbury's tone was very firm. "You and Cristin are going to Gretna Green, once you rid yourselves of this damnably conspicuous carriage. Hire yourselves a coach, and proceed by stages, and for God's sake don't use your own names!"

For a couple so set on marriage, Lord Peverell and Cristin voiced considerable protest. Cristin's, being far more emotional, had to be dealt with first. "Percy's family," she sobbed, "will be broken-hearted at the disgrace!"

Miss Lennox felt obliged to intervene, lest Lord Roxbury lose his temper, and that he should lose his temper appeared imminent. "Percy's family would be a great deal more broken-hearted," she remarked, "if you did *not* elope! I think even Lady Peverell would consider Gretna Green preferable to Newgate. If you stay in London, you are bound to be identified as passers of stolen merchandise, what with Cristin being Innis's niece, and Percy having practically shouted his name to the world via this coach." She glanced at Shannon. "For that matter, so will we!"

"Exactly," said Shannon. "Which is why——"

Percy cleared his throat. "Don't mean to throw a spanner in the works," he muttered apologetically, "but I haven't a feather to fly with. Don't see how a man can elope when his pockets are to let." Lord Roxbury sighed and remarked in exacerbated tones that he would finance the expedition from his own strongbox.

"No," interrupted Cristin, with surprising firmness, "you will not. Percy is already too greatly indebted. I am not wealthy, but I have more than enough money to pay for our journey and to tide us over until we can straighten out Percy's accounts."

This statement caused her companions to stare, even Shannon, to the extreme hazard of an unwary pedestrian. "*You* have money?" echoed Jynx.

"Of course I do, and I do not see why everyone must be gawking at me! Mama left me some money, which my father did not know about, and I've been hoarding the rest for years. Some of it has been invested, and though I have made no great killing, the returns have not been inconsiderable." Cristin looked irritable. "I know you are thinking that it is queer for an Ashley to be so thrifty, but mama told me a long time ago that I must allow myself to be guided by my father's *mistakes.*"

"Good God!" uttered Lord Roxbury, and returned his attention to Percy's horses and the narrow streets.

"But, Cristin!" Jynx said faintly. "You could have paid off the Runner, and Percy's gambling debts!"

"The *first* lesson I learned from my father," Cristin said severely, "was *not* to foolishly throw money away!" Miss Lennox might have been dumbfounded by this extreme example of Ashley logic, but Lord Peverell was not. He expressed himself delighted that his darling Cristin should possess so rational a point of view. Cristin was in turn delighted to be so well understood, and fell into his arms. Jynx regarded them with an expression that came perilously close to loathing, then gathered up her skirts and joined Lord Roxbury on the driver's seat.

Chapter
Twenty-eight

While Miss Lennox and Lord Roxbury were engaged in circumventing the law, Lady Bliss was barricaded in her book room, listening to the sounds of the house being torn down around her, and waiting without a great deal of hope for her knight in shining armor to come to her rescue. Since the brandy decanter was fortuitously barricaded in the book room with her, her vigil saw her grow increasingly tipsy. And then the noises of desecration and strife ceased abruptly, and an ominous silence settled upon Blissington House.

Into that deathly lull came the sounds of a man's footsteps on the stair. Adorée cast an anxious glance at her looking glass, then trod slowly to the door. The doorsteps halted; she flung it open. "Oh, Nicky!" she breathed. "What must you think of me!"

There was no censure on Lord Erland's swarthy and ill-tempered face, even though he was fully alert to the significance of the carts drawn up at the front door and the startling absence of furniture in the house. He regarded Lady Bliss who, wishful of being abducted, had clad herself as she deemed most appropriate—to wit, in precious little, and that a clinging violet silk. There was a distinct gleam of appreciation in the earl's wintry eye. "I've already told you what I think. Do stand aside, Adorée, and let me come in!"

She did so feebly, for his tone had been anything but that of a man prepared to venture all for romance. "It is very quiet. I suppose the sordid bloodsuckers are even now discussing how they may further humiliate me. Oh, but the situation is insufferable! Never did I think to be brought to a standstill."

"You haven't been." Lord Erland seated himself on the settee, beside his opera cloak. "I paid them off and sent them away. If you wish to keep this house, however, I fear you'll need new furnishings."

"Keep this house?" echoed Adorée. Her eye fell on the decanter, and she brought her guest a glass. "I have never wished to keep this house, but Innis insisted—it occurs to me that all my life Innis has been insisting on things, with the result that *I* am always miserable! Courtenay's family is welcome to the place; they've been trying to force me to move out for years. And I wish them joy of it, because I have been very wretched here!"

Lord Erland regarded his brandy glass. "What are your plans, Adorée?"

Lady Bliss considered her own glass, then drank it dry. "God knows," she said hollowly. "I must do something, I suppose, but I cannot think what! This horrid business has left my spirits entirely crushed. At least I will no longer be encumbered with Innis, the wretch. But you will not wish to hear of that!" She blinked in a charming manner that was reminiscent of a gently inebriated owl. "Tell me, Nicky, why have you come here?"

Dominic did not scold Lady Bliss for this belaborment of the obvious, owing to the fact that he was deriving considerable entertainment from the scene. Nor did this fact surprise him, though it was much more common for Lord Erland to be bored than entertained; he had already discovered that it was impossible to pass more than a moment in the company of Adorée Blissington without becoming both enchanted and amused. "Miss Lennox," he replied. "That singular young lady informed me very frankly that I have misused you. Why didn't you tell me that she was the object of Percy's rather sottish adoration? I've no objection to that, Adorée."

"Percy!" Lady Bliss stared. "And *Jynx?* Oh, no! I was so sure she'd have Shannon, and it would have been a perfect match. But Jynx and Percy—no and no and no!"

Dominic's dark brows had drawn into his familiar scowl. "Roxbury? He arrived at the house as I was leaving, but I didn't think—" He recalled the viscount's expression on that meeting, when Miss Lennox had been gifted with his salute on her brow. He also recalled Miss Lennox's singular lack of enthusiasm upon being welcomed into the family. His lips twitched. "Apparently I have erred. But if not Miss Lennox, who?"

"I do wish you would try and not confuse me so!" complained Adorée. "I have gone to a great deal of trouble to reunite Shannon and Jynx, and it would be very sad if it was for nothing—Innis pawned her betrothal ring, you see, and

234

Shannon thought she had lost it gambling, and she thought that he meant to keep on with me even after they were married, so she threw the ring at him, and made a dreadful scene, and ran away to me." It occurred to Lady Bliss that she had said more than she should. "And he came after her and they made it up, but you must promise me to tell no one of this, because for Jynx to have stayed here with me would be considered very shocking."

"I see," said Lord Erland blandly, and with superhuman self-control, "that Miss Lennox and Lord Roxbury were meant for one another. But if not Miss Lennox and not yourself—and do not try and convince me again that it is yourself! —then who in the name of God does Percy nourish this absurd passion for?"

"Passion," reproved Lady Bliss, as she refilled her glass, "may be ill-founded, and it may have very unfortunate circumstances, but it is *never* absurd! I should certainly know, for I have very strong passions and I have indulged them with great latitude." She sighed heavily. "Or I did once, but of course I am no longer in my first youth, so I suppose I should no longer think of such things."

"You will be thinking of such things," Dominic replied bluntly, "until you are in the grave, Adorée. We will not speak of *that* until you have explained Percy's passion to me."

It occurred to Lady Bliss that Lord Erland's last remark might be considered a promising omen. This thought did not cheer her; Lord Erland would doubtless wash his hands of her once he learned the extent of her deceit. "Oh, very well! Percy is in love with my niece Cristin. Innis brought her here when our brother died—against my wishes, but what was I to do? At least I managed to keep Cristin out of the gaming rooms and to keep the world from knowing her presence in my house. She is a very good girl, but I will not expect you to believe that."

"Why not?" The earl quirked a brow. "You might very reasonably expect me to withhold judgment until I've seen the chit. How did Percy meet your niece, if she was kept so closely under wraps?"

"That was entirely Jynx's fault—oh, not *fault*, because Percy and Cristin are sincerely devoted to one another, but if they had never met I would have been spared a great deal of fuss, and would not have been reduced to a state of constant alarm and occasional fainting fits!" Lady Bliss remembered, then, precisely who and what she was. "*Not*, of course, that I

235

am one to stand in the way of true love! Cristin and Miss Lennox were at school together, you see."

"Ah!" Lord Erland was gratified. "I begin to, at any rate."

"I guess you should know the rest of it." What mattered it now, since he must already consider her the most feckless female to ever embark upon a disorderly life, if he knew the exact extent of her culpability. Adorée explained to Dominic the entire unhappy saga of Cristin and Percy—save for the latest development, their involvement in Innis's misdeeds. "There it is! I fling myself upon your mercy, I am prostrate at your feet!"

"I'm gratified," replied the earl, who had listened to her moving tale with an expression of unholy glee, "but I don't see why you should be. You've done nothing for which you may be either censured or condemned."

"I haven't?" Adorée looked very confused. "Your cousin's all to pieces, and I'm in the basket myself, and you think I have behaved *properly?*"

"I didn't say that." Dominic treated her to his rare smile. "It is a great deal of your charm that you've no idea of *how* to behave properly! But in this instance, you've no reason to blame yourself. It's not like you set out to lure my nodcock cousin into some sort of trap."

"No," Lady Bliss replied gloomily, "but Innis did. I will not trust myself to express my opinion of that! Nicky, you do not mind about Cristin and Percy?"

Lord Erland shrugged. "He could have looked higher, but who Percy marries is Percy's affair. If anything, the durability of this affection of his makes me think the more of him."

"But," wailed Lady Bliss, aghast that the earl should not realize the enormity of her sins, "an *Ashley!*"

"If *I* don't regard it, why should *you?*" Lord Erland set aside his glass. "It sounds very much to me like Percy will marry her one way or another, even if he must wait until he comes of age, which is now only a matter of weeks. So the logical thing is to give in with good grace. His mother will have a spasm, I expect. Better yet, she'll probably never again speak to me."

Lady Bliss grew increasingly befuddled, both by the brandy and by Dominic's attitude. It seemed very much as if he was happy at the notion that Lady Peverell would never forgive his part in this affair. Plaintively, Adorée said that she did not understand.

"Simple!" Lord Erland rose. "She wishes to marry me."

"Oh!" Lady Bliss said faintly. "Well, that is not remarkable, you know. Indeed, a great many females probably wish to marry you, which seems to me very foolish—not because you are not an attractive gentleman; you must know that you *are;* but because it's as plain as the nose on your face that you don't *wish* to marry. Not that I blame you for it! Some people seem to like it very well, but matrimony, in my experience at least, has a very definite tendency to take the *spice* out of things."

"I thought," remarked the earl with a perfectly straight face, "that you were devoted to Courtenay."

"I can hardly inform the world otherwise, can I?" Adorée inquired irritably. "My reputation is already in tatters, without adding a positive detestation of my husband to my sins! And it is my practice to put a good face on things." She reached once more for the brandy decanter, but Lord Erland deftly whisked it beyond her reach. She looked reproachfully at him. "I talk a great deal of nonsense, and you will not want to listen to me. Furthermore, I am expensive and extravagant, and careless about paying my bills; I exist in a perennial financial crisis, and it accomplishes me absolutely nothing to try and be good!"

"Why try?" Dominic grasped her hands and pulled her to her feet. "I would much rather have you wicked. Since I am without doubt one of the warmest men in England, I think I can bear the expense."

"But, Nicky!" Lady Bliss's scruples once more reared their ugly heads. "You cannot wish to be bothered with my various little indiscretions! Think of your position in the world."

Lord Erland expressed his opinion of the world in a few vulgar words. He then explained that since the government was openly and admittedly corrupt—the House of Commons, for example, was effectively controlled by lottery tickets, bonds, contracts and jobs—his position was very likely to be strengthened by a scatter-brained, expensive and charming *petite amie.* And moreover, he concluded, he didn't mind in the least if she was indiscreet from Italy to the Holy Land and back, so long as her indiscretions were limited to himself.

"Naturally they would be!" Adorée grimaced with offense. "I may be imprudent but no one can call me *loose!* And if you don't mind the scandal-broth, I'm sure *I* shouldn't mind a temporary reprieve from these continual expedients and shifts! But why, if you are desirous of—of *that,* did you break my faro bank?"

"That was very badly done of me." Lord Erland's hands moved to her shoulders, and his voice was bemused. "I thought if I forced you to close Blissington House, you would have no choice but to put yourself in my keeping. I wanted to broach the matter earlier, but you had so many things on your mind that you could not properly listen to me." His eyes moved slowly over her face. "My poor little jade, you have had a very bad time of it, have you not? Never mind! I will see to it that you need trouble yourself about nothing, ever again."

Adorée could not tear her eyes away from his, not that she tried to do so. She had the strangest sensation of waking from a horrid dream. "Never?"

"Never. You shall have your place in the country, and one in town as well, and I will see to it that you are always provided for."

Now it seemed not wakening from a dream, but plunging into nightmare. "You are very generous," murmured Adorée, close to tears. "And it sounds very pleasant, but it also sounds very much like a business arrangement, and I do not think I wish to be a kept woman, not even yours! So you had better go before I exhibit a most unbecoming violence of feeling and really *do* try to strangle you."

Lord Erland looked very much surprised, as well he might; Lady Bliss, despite her selfless renunciation, clung to him as tightly as if she would never let him go. "You don't want those things?"

Adorée tried without success—and, to tell truth, without much conviction—to free herself from his grasp. "How can you talk such arrant fustian?" she cried. "Of course I do! But I want even more that you should love me, for without that anything else would be meaningless." She sniffled. "Oh! I must be positively detested by the gods, else I would not have formed a decided partiality for a man who holds me in such low esteem!"

"Why on earth," inquired the earl, who looked more amused than chagrined by this outburst, "do you think I hold you in low esteem?"

"How can you not?" stormed Adorée. "And what else am I to think when you keep calling me a *jade?*"

"Ah!" A decisive gentleman, Dominic swept her up into his arms and carried her to the settee. "Such words as 'darling' and 'sweetheart' are so grossly abused, and I would not insult you with such lukewarm and unoriginal mawkishness. I suppose, however, that since you do not like to be called a jade, I could call you my little love. It would have the advantage of being the truth."

He was, by this time, seated on the settee, and Lady Bliss was clasped firmly in his arms. She craned her neck to look at his swarthy face. "It would?" she inquired doubtfully.

"It would," said he. "I have indeed spouted nonsense—oh, not in what I offered you, but when I spoke of favorites of the moment only. You see, my—er, my love, I have at the ridiculously advanced age of five-and-forty, and in spite of my resolutions to never do such a foolish thing, formed what very much appears to be a lasting passion for you. No," he added, as her lips parted, "let me finish! I expect that I shall be senile and gout-ridden—if not in the tomb!—before your moment ends. And I have begun to doubt that it will even end then."

"Nicky! Adorée simply could not remain silent. "I have always wanted to grow old with someone!"

Lord Erland's smile was crooked. "And I hadn't meant to keep you tucked away out of the sight of the world, though that's how it must have sounded. I meant only that I should not, if you did not wish it, inflict my presence on you, or disturb your privacy."

"Inflict?" repeated Adorée. "Privacy? Nicky, you are an idiot!"

"I am," announced the earl, who was intent on baring his own soul, "a devilish disagreeable man with a very surly disposition."

"Pooh!" With her gray eyes half-closed, and her long lashes dark against her cheek, Lady Bliss looked impossibly coy. "Since you don't mind that I am a goose-cap, for *me* to mind that *you* are a trifle truculent would be shockingly ungrateful! And whatever may be said of me, no one can claim that I behave ungratefully! Or they may *claim* so, but it would be untrue!" The earl gave a great crack of laughter. "Beside, I love you with utter abandonment, Nicky!" And then she proceeded to demonstrate, in the most delightful way possible, that she did.

"Well!" said the earl gruffly, some time later. "*That* is settled, then. I confess I am relieved—"

But Lord Erland was not, at that particular moment, to confess the reason for his relief. Adorée, in sitting up, espied the opera cloak; and the opera cloak recalled to her the imminent arrests of Innis and Percy and Cristin, and her own inescapable involvement with Bow Street. Again her scruples rose to taunt her, demanding that she acquaint Lord Erland with that part of the tale, even if it resulted in the eternal ruination of her own happiness. Scruples could ask too much of a woman, she decided, and she bludgeoned them to death.

Lord Erland had watched the expressions that flitted across her lovely face. "What is it, Adorée?"

"This house! I must leave it at once! Oh, Nicky, please humor me."

The earl professed himself quite willing to humor her in all things, but pointed out that since he had already dealt with the bailiffs, she had no need for such haste. He also pointed out that he was quite comfortable.

As was Lady Bliss, and she admitted as much when she emerged again for breath. "But I cannot be happy here!" she pleaded. "Think, Nicky, how romantic it would be to flee. I have always wished to do so, and never have. You will say there is no need for it, but there *is*, and I beg that you will not ask me to explain!"

And so it came about that Lord Erland, that august and ill-tempered member of Parliament, set out on a midnight jaunt with the scandalous Adorée Blissington.

240

Chapter
Twenty-nine

Miss Lennox was deposited by her sorely beset fiancé in Lennox Square, where she acquainted her equally beset father with the details of their expedition, though not of the small matter of a Bow Street Runner left trussed up like a chicken in a St. Giles alleyway. Sir Malcolm was neither pleased with his daughter's initiative nor impressed with her abilities; in fact, he said, it was his opinion that she'd only contributed further to the mess. First it had been only the Ashleys that were involved, though that was bad enough; now to the list of persons who could not except by an act of divine intervention escape suspicion of complicity in the crimes were added Lord Peverell, Lord Roxbury and herself. In addition, did Lord Erland present himself as Jynx had suggested at Blissington House, he would be drawn into the thing, which would result in scandal of an awesome degree.

Jynx interrupted, at this point, to inquire why, if Blissington House was known to be the center of illegal activities, Bow Street had thus far refrained from storming its walls. Sir Malcolm explained that this restraint was the brilliant brainchild of one William Brown, the very clever Runner who was assigned to the Ashley case. William Brown waited for the return of Innis Ashley, and then he would close the net. Blissington House was under very sharp surveillance indeed.

"Yet you send us there?" Miss Lennox's eye held a distinctly feral gleam. "Sometimes, Papa, I think that *you* are addle-brained! It would serve you right if your part in this was revealed!"

Horrified, Sir Malcolm begged his daughter to refrain from even thinking of such a catastrophe. He then proferred his learned opinion that she could best serve the interests of justice by tracking down a certain hackney coach that carried a cargo no less dangerous than the plague. Succinctly, Jynx refused to have anything more to do with stolen merchandise. She was, she said, with or without her father's consent, going to leave town. This uncompromising attitude won her no praise. Sir Malcolm was muttering wrathfully about thankless offspring, and enlarging upon his own selfless behavior, when she left the study.

All the same, thought Jynx, as she wearily mounted the stair, she had done the best she could for all concerned. Hopefully, Percy and Cristin would set out without mishap for Gretna Green—and who could be sufficiently dead to romance to suspect a couple set on elopement of complicity in theft! Especially a pair as bird-witted as those two? Adorée, if fortune smiled on her, would be safe enough with Lord Erland, unless Bow Street stormed Blissington House and took them both into custody. That was very unlikely, Jynx decided. Not only was William Brown currently incapable of organizing such a raid, she doubted that even that bold little man would dare implicate so powerful a figure as Lord Erland in this tawdry little charade.

And tawdry it was, she decided, as she opened her bedroom door. The whole proceeding had been poorly planned, and ramshackly executed, and exhausting to a most distasteful degree. Miss Lennox concluded that she had no taste for adventuring. Or, she added, as she thought of Innis, for adventurers. Still, she wondered where he was, and how he could possibly avoid the numerous traps that had been set for him. It was difficult to imagine the insouciant Innis in captivity.

Jynx had, in her cogitations, allowed one player in this farce to escape her mind. That omission, as she glanced blankly around her room, was speedily repaired. She looked upon the elegant corner basin stand, which had a pleasing serpentine front with a tambour shutter, and a small cistern with a tap, and wished that she might splash some of the dirt from her hands and cheeks; she gazed upon her bed, which appeared like a sofa with a fixed canopy over it, the curtains looped back prettily, and pillows tossed carelessly about, and wished even more fervently that she might have a few hours' sleep. She could do neither; she was not alone in the room. "I should have expected it, I guess," Jynx said wearily. "From all appearances, you must have climbed the tree."

"So I did." Eleazar Hyde was distinctly the worse for

wear, his clothing torn and grass-stained. "I told you once before that you shouldn't try and poke your fingers in my pie."

Miss Lennox regarded those digits, which were extremely grubby, and thought irrelevantly that any pastry thus abused must be condemned as unfit. "What do you want of me?"

Eleazar studied her. Her chestnut hair was in a dreadful tangle; her hazel eyes were huge in her pale drawn face. Even in this sorry state, Miss Lennox had an unmistakable air of quality. Eleazar had a great need of a young lady with an unmistakable air of quality, and so he explained. "You may blame yourself for this, you know! I had definite plans for Cristin, but Cristin has loped off and I make no doubt that you're at fault. There's nothing for it but a last-minute substitution, and to hope that those who are in a position to mind don't!"

Jynx was bedraggled and exhausted and weary of the world, but this careless use of a plural pronoun caused a distinct *frisson* along her spine. "Are you mad?" she said. "You cannot seriously mean to kidnap the daughter of a magistrate!"

"I'll admit that it's not what I like, but a man can't hang twice, and Bow Street is getting much too close on my heels." Eleazar contemplated the deadly pistol that he held. "As to that, I don't aim to get my neck cricked at all! Nor do I aim to be nicked and lodged in the Newgate Prison. Come now, Miss Lennox, we must have this little business settled. Out the window, if you please."

But Jynx did *not* please, and so she said. She crossed her arms beneath her bosom, and jutted out her forceful chin, and further explained that he might as well shoot her on the spot, because rather than endure the depraved fate that he planned for her, she preferred to be dead.

Eleazar Hyde was not accustomed to young ladies who regarded his pistol with as little concern as if it were a bouquet of posies, and he was temporarily at a loss. "That's a very proper sentiment, but you don't mean it. I'll allow it won't be what you're accustomed to, but it must be a great deal better than being dead."

Miss Lennox, after due consideration, could not agree. "Do your worst!" she invited. "I do not intend to budge from this chair. And you might as well put that silly gun away, because you know as well as I do that you have no intention of shooting me."

Clearly, this chit had no notion of the dangerous nature of the man to whom she spoke. Eleazar proceeded to enlighten her. He was, he said, a very desperate criminal, one who had committed such atrocities as must make any young lady, gently reared or otherwise, swoon. It had been a bad day for Miss Lennox, he let Miss Lennox know, when she had come into the orbit of Eleazar Hyde. Had she let well enough alone, as he had advised her, she might have escaped his wrath. But she had not. She had taken it upon herself to act the part of a spy, and in so doing had sealed her own doom.

"Pish, tush!" remarked Miss Lennox, whose lack of terror was not due to bravery, but to an exhaustion so complete that she was incapable of feeling anything. "You have only your own stupidity to blame for the fix you're in; *I* didn't snitch on you. And if Innis didn't frighten me, you can hardly expect that you will; Innis is a great deal more dangerous than you."

Naturally, Eleazar did not care for this comparison. "That shows all *you* know!" said he. "What if I was to tell you that Innis Ashley is small fry in comparison with myself? That I duped him very successfully?"

In Jynx's lazy eye was a faint spark of interest. "So you're a deeper one than I suspected?" she mused. "It's possible. Definitely, it's possible. I never did understand how Innis could be sufficiently clever to play *any* successful crime. You did it all, I conjecture, and cleverly fixed things so that suspicion would fall on Innis and Adorée. I suppose you must have somehow involved Innis, to insure his complicity. Very crafty, Mr. Hyde."

Praise at last! With singularly unnerving effect, Eleazar smiled. "And," added Miss Lennox, before he could speak, "a very unchristian thing to do! No one with a single ounce of proper feeling would take such shocking advantage of two unfortunates like Innis and Adorée. The Ashleys may be blessed with beauty, but they *are* not blessed with intelligence, and only the greatest of blackguards would consider using them as cat's-paws."

Eleazar glared. To enter upon an explanation of the criminal mind was not at all what he had intended when he entered, after strenuous effort, this room. "Damn your eyes!" he snarled. "You think if you delay me long enough, someone will come to your rescue. That won't fadge! If you don't come with me instantly, I'll expose the lot of you in a way that won't be palatable to your feelings. Would you like to see your father in the dock, Miss Lennox? Along with your fine and handsome viscount?"

Jynx did not relish the picture thus conjured, though she suspected it might come into being even without Eleazar's assistance. "Do your worst," she said indifferently. "I have told you I do not mean to budge an inch."

Eleazar had not reckoned on Miss Lennox's calling his bluff, or remaining so unmoved by his threats that she looked very likely to fall asleep momentarily. He swore, and trod heavily across the room and yanked her from the chair. Jynx kicked him, then uttered a blood-curdling scream. Eleazar tried to silence her, and she bit his hand. He howled and dropped the gun. A fracas ensued.

For all her determination not to be removed, Jynx was inferior in strength. Eleazar had dragged her halfway to the window when the door flew open and a gentleman ran into the room. He took in the situation at a glance, then stopped and retrieved the gun. "Damn you, Ashley!" shouted Eleazar. "*You* won't take me!" He flung Jynx aside, and lunged. Miss Lennox closed her eyes and covered her ears.

It was an exceedingly short struggle; Innis shot Eleazar in midstride. He then clasped Miss Lennox in his arms. "I don't suppose," he murmured, "that you would reconsider? I do have a very great regard for you, my darling, no matter how it may seem."

"Piffle!" retorted Jynx. "You are incorrigible."

"What the *devil?*" inquired Sir Malcolm, from the doorway. A mad dash up the stairs had left him short of breath. "Unhand my daughter, Ashley!"

"You must not scold Innis, Papa," protested Jynx. "This wretched man was either going to abduct me or make of us all a *cause célèbre*, he hadn't quite decided which, when Innis saved the day."

Sir Malcolm cast an unappreciative eye upon the corpse that bled profusely over the Aubusson rug. The eye narrowed, then widened, and with a muffled exclamation he bent for a closer look. "Too," Jynx added serenely, "he confessed to me that he was solely responsible for the thefts, as well as the forged note sent round to Tattersall's."

"Hah!" Sir Malcolm was in a judicious manner going through the pockets of the dead man. "I'd like to know how you learned about *that*."

"Still," murmured Innis, into Jynx's ear, "it was a damned

good try. Consider my dreadful forlorn position, my darling, and come away with me!"

"God in heaven!" Sir Malcolm rocked back on his heels. "Ashley, do you realize what you've done?"

"I rather thought," responded Innis, with a raised brow, "that I'd shot Eleazar Hyde."

"That may be what *you* called him; we knew him by several other names. Damned if fate isn't an ironic thing; you've been instrumental in the apprehension of a very notorious criminal." Sir Malcolm studied Innis. "I have to congratulate you, much as it goes against the grain. And I thought I told you to release my daughter!"

"Then," said Jynx, along with Innis ignoring this request, "since this man, whoever he was, is your culprit, Innis may go free."

"I wish I might let him." Sir Malcolm looked very unhappy. "But the best Ashley can do now is surrender himself up as king's evidence. I *told* you my hands would be tied once he was arrested." With a stern expression, he regarded his daughter. "And speaking of hands being tied—"

But Jynx had realized what Innis's presence in Lennox Square must portend, and who must be responsible. She swooned delicately into Innis's arms. "My darling!" he cried.

"No!" uttered Shannon, who at that moment walked into the room. "*My* darling! And I'll thank you to remember it, Ashley!"

"I told him to unhand her," remarked Sir Malcolm, who was regarding the open window thoughtfully. Then he looked at Innis in a very speaking way. "Bring her over here, to the bed. I trust, Shannon, that you did not enter my study?"

"No. Eulalia was in the oddest manner barricading the door." Shannon bent over his fiancée. "Jynx, speak to me!" Sir Malcolm, in an unprecedented excess of paternal solicitude, bent over her also, and added his own pleas.

"And do it quickly!" he added, when she showed no signs of renewed life. "I know perfectly well you're shamming it, and Innis has gone."

Lord Roxbury glanced over his shoulder at the empty room and open window, and swore. "You see that I cannot, Papa," remarked Miss Lennox, her eyes still tightly closed. "Shannon is going to scold."

"No, he won't!" declared Sir Malcolm, despite strong evidence to the contrary. "Not when he realizes that you were very nearly abducted and that there is a very irate Bow Street Runner downstairs."

"Jynx's eyes flew open. "*Not* William Brown?" the viscount groaned.

"One and the same." Sir Malcolm looked harassed. "How I am to explain all this I do not know; he already thinks I'm queer in the attic! And if he lays eyes on you in that rig, child, we'll all end up in gaol. Therefore, if I may suggest—"

Lord Roxbury and Miss Lennox were already at the window. Chivalrously, the viscount allowed her to go first. "May a father inquire," said Sir Malcolm, watching with a very unpaternal eye as his daughter hitched up her skirts, "where you mean to go?"

Jynx cast an inquiring glance at Shannon, whose appreciative gaze was fixed on her shapely legs. "To find a minister, I think." She grinned and exited.

"With your permission, sir?" Lord Roxbury extended his hand.

Sir Malcolm shook it vigorously. "Definitely! I would suggest a very long honeymoon. We still may brush through this well enough, if Innis can manage to bribe his way out of the country."

"I think we may all count on that." Jynx's voice came softly and irritably through the window. "The wretch took my betrothal ring again!"

Chapter Thirty

Without mishap, Lord Roxbury and Miss Lennox gained the safety of the viscount's traveling coach, and were safely underway. The berlin was a large and comfortable conveyance, which could seat six passengers easily; its interior was lined with red cloth, and fitted out luxuriously; its exterior was both elegant and thoroughly inconspicuous, which admirably suited it to flight from the law.

A peaceful silence reigned within. Miss Lennox assured herself that Lord Roxbury was not angered by her part in the escape of Innis Ashley, that Lord Roxbury was not angered even by the loss of her betrothal ring; and Lord Roxbury assured himself that Miss Lennox did not regret embarking upon her bridal journey without attendants, or a trousseau, or even a nightdress. Miss Lennox was heard to say that she wouldn't mind marrying the viscount without a stitch of clothing to her name, in response to which the viscount promised her any number of betrothal rings. With a sigh of pure contentment, Miss Lennox tucked her feet beneath her, rested her head on Lord Roxbury's shoulder, and fell fast asleep.

So they proceeded out of London, at a spanking pace. Shannon's coachman was a first-class whip, who could spring his horses and gallop them along in a way that would have upset the coach if guided by less steady and talented hands. Shannon had no fear that such catastrophe might occur; he chose his servants with an eye to their ability, and Watkins was up to all sorts of horses, even the nervous chestnuts, and additionally possessed a great deal of courage. Lord Roxbury rested his chin on Miss Lennox's touseled curls, and contemplated the bizarre occurrences of the past few days. He, too, was almost asleep when the coach drew to a halt, and his valet—who had ridden behind the coach as might befit a

248

lowly footman, and whose sensibilities were consequently offended grievously—appeared at the door.

"I beg your pardon, but there seems to be some trouble ahead." From March's gloomy tone, he might have expected as much, and might have been pleased to have his expectations fulfilled. "A collision of some sort, and bodies strewn all over the road."

Thusly roused from rosy visions of matrimonial delights, Shannon swore. "What is it?" Jynx inquired sleepily, and blinked. So charming did she look in her newly wakened, still-dazed state that Shannon would have taken her in his arms without preamble, had not March been regarding them with such glum disapproval. Midnight flits, in March's opinion, were not at all the thing. "Shannon!" Jynx was fast achieving full possession of her senses. "Listen!"

Lord Roxbury obeyed. "Dashed if it's *my* fault," came a familiar voice, "if I don't know the way! I've never *been* to Gretna Green! And I don't see why I must be blamed if your carriage got in my way!" "That is very true," came another voice, "and it is not kind of you to rip up at Percy!" And, "Oh, dear!" came a third. Just then, a fourth and less familiar voice broke in, with strident laments over damages incurred, and an even more strident request to be paid.

"Shannon!" Jynx's eyes were wide. "Isn't that—" But Shannon was already out of the berlin. Jynx followed, and was in time to see the viscount grasp the shoulder of the hackney driver—the same hackney driver who had left them stranded in St. Giles—and deliver to that astonished individual a masterful blow on the chin. The man crumpled to the ground.

"Excellently done!"cried Jynx and clapped her hands. By so doing, she brought herself to the attention of the small group of people who were clustered, arguing, in the road.

Cristin was there, and Percy; as well as Lord Erland and Adorée. Nearby stood Tomkin, a large bundle clasped to his chest. Jynx cast him an inquiring glance. "The silver plate, miss," he explained, "as was buried in the garden to preserve it from the ghouls!"

"Very prudent," said Miss Lennox, as Lady Bliss rushed forward and enfolded her in a fragrant embrace. "But *you* are not, my dear!" said Adorée. "Whatever are you about with Shannon at this late hour? It looks decidedly queer! And it is not a good idea for a young lady of your station to make free of her favors until *after* the knot is tied. You will forgive me for speaking so frankly, I know—well, you always have! —but after all the trouble I have had on your behalf, it would be very ungrateful of you to queer my plans!"

"Enough, Adorée!" interrupted Shannon, as his coachman and valet gawked. "I promise you we will be wed. As to the hour, that was brought about by an earnest desire *not* to be taken up as accomplices to a crime."

"What crime?" inquired Lord Erland.

"You didn't tell him, Adorée?" Shannon looked slightly scandalized.

"No and that is a perfect example of why you and I dealt together in only a lukewarm way! You must always have everything aboveboard. Beside, Jynx told me to tell Nicky as little as possible, and she was obviously right, for here we are! I hope you realize, Shannon, that you are marrying a girl with a great deal of sense, and value her accordingly!"

These words, which had rendered Jynx inarticulate, and Shannon incensed, roused Lord Erland to an awareness of Jynx's presence. "Miss Lennox!" he said, and came to take her hand. "You look the most complete romp! I must apologize to you for misunderstanding the situation; Adorée tells me that Percy is not to marry you, but her niece. But I will *not* apologize for stealing from you a kiss."

Lord Erland's cool remarks fanned sparks in several breasts. "Marry Jynx!" cried Cristin. "Marry *me?*" gasped Percy. "You kissed *Jynx!*" demanded Adorée. "Nicky, how could you?"

"Pooh!" said Miss Lennox. "It was nothing. Don't make a piece of work of it, Adorée! Shannon didn't mind."

"He didn't?" It was clear from Lady Bliss's expression that she did not consider this forebearance an encouraging sign.

"Good God, Adorée!" uttered the irritated viscount. "Have you any idea how many men have been kissing Jynx lately? If I minded, I'd probably have gone off in an apoplexy! Now, may I point out that things are in a bit of a tangle here? And may I suggest that we straighten matters out so that we may proceed?"

With the invaluable assistance of Lord Erland, straighten things out Shannon did. The hackney driver, when he regained consciousness, was instructed to deliver the merchandise that still rested beneath the coach's seat to Sir Malcolm Lennox, and promised for his efforts a handsome reward. Since the hackney coach had suffered the least damage of the two—perhaps because, as Cristin unkindly suggested, it had been capable of movement in the first place due to nothing short of a miracle—and since the driver was eager to remove himself as speedily as possible from this group of lunatics, he was first to depart the scene. Lord Erland's carriage, which was in far worse condition, was dragged off the road, and his horses unharnessed, and the matter of its restoration was left in the capable hands of Tomkin, and the far less willing hands of March. The small party then arranged themselves in Lord Roxbury's berlin, and were once more underway.

"I say," said Percy, "this is a first-rate turnout!" He pointed out to Cristin the chandelier that hung from the ceiling, the seats that could be used for sleeping, the portable stove and wine cellar, the table with drawers and clock. "We'll have one, shall we? You'd like that!"

"No, I wouldn't," replied Cristin. "Because I daresay it cost a great deal of money, and I mean for us to be before-hand with the world."

"That's the dandy!" Percy was of unabated good cheer. "You must keep reminding me, because I'm sure to forget."

"I don't believe it!" remarked Lord Erland. "That from an Ashley! No, no, Percy, don't fly into alt. You have my blessing. Furthermore, when my carriage is fixed—*if* my carriage is fixed; you should never be allowed to drive anything larger than a pony cart, Percy! How did you persuade that man to let you take the reins, by-the-bye?—you and Cristin will go to my mother, who will see to it that you're married with all due ceremony and as little fuss as possible. There! Aren't I generous?"

For a gentleman of legendarily choleric temper he was very generous indeed, proof of which caused Lady Bliss to burst into tears. "Oh, Nicky, I have misled you grievously, and I am very sorry for it! I shall never forgive myself if you are taken up by Bow Street!"

"Bow Street?" The earl cast an inquiring eye at Shannon, the only other sensible member of the party—Miss Lennox had propped her feet up on the silver plate and once more fallen asleep. Shannon explained it all—the thefts, their own involvement, the death of Eleazar Hyde and Innis's escape. Lord Erland's expression changed from disbelief to astonishment to frank amusement. "This surpasses all belief!" said he.

"Then we are safe!" cried Lady Bliss. "Dead men tell no

tales, and Innis is free! Why, we could even turn right around and go back to London if we pleased."

Shannon disagreed. "You forget that I assaulted a representative of the law, and one who can not only identify Jynx and myself, but Cristin and Percy. Prudence dictates that all of us, er, lay low awhile. Beside, I have other plans— to be precise, a marriage ceremony."

Lady Bliss was not one to interfere with romance, but she thought this belated hour an odd one at which to be wed. Shannon pointed out the brightness of the moon, which made the roads as easily distinguished as if in midday, and assured his companions that wed he would be, even if he had to drag the vicar out of bed.

That matter was settled. Adorée returned her attention to the earl. "I wish you will forgive me, but I fear that is past praying for! I can only assure you that I meant it for the best—which I should have known would not serve, because look at Jynx! She has always meant everything for the best, and look what has transpired!"

"We'll wrap it up in clean linen; don't fret yourself!" said Dominic, as Shannon stated rather belligerently that Miss Lennox had greatly bestirred herself on behalf of the Ashleys, and that he would not hear another word against his exhausted darling.

"Darling!" echoed Lady Bliss. "You *do* love her, Shannon!" The viscount said, acerbically, that it must be apparent as the nose on his face that he did. "And does *she* love you?"

Thus applied to, Jynx stirred sleepily. "Ever since I was five years old and he beheaded my favorite doll. Didn't you know, Adorée?"

Naturally, Lady Bliss had known; there was precious little Lady Bliss didn't know about matters of the heart. Her only doubt had been whether Lord Roxbury and Miss Lennox were aware of where their true affections lay. "Because if you *did* know," she concluded sternly, "you have both behaved with a great deal of foolishness, and so I take leave to tell you, even if I am generally held to be bacon-brained!"

Miss Lennox had embarked upon an incoherent explanation about the difficulty of learning what lay within someone else's heart when the coach once more rumbled to a standstill, before a sleeping vicarage. It did not remain quiet long. Lights sprang up the dark windows, and a dazed gentleman appeared to see who caused the unholy commotion at his front door.

Lord Roxbury brandished his special license and explained his purpose in a few terse words.

Things still might have gone awry—the vicar was disinclined to perform a wedding ceremony so late at night—had not Lady Bliss dragged her bemused eyes from the earl's swarthy face to observe the cause of the delay. "Why, if it isn't Peterkin!" she exclaimed, with every evidence of delight. "I have not seen him since he was at Oxford! And quite a rip he was! I must tell you——"

"Please!" The vicar did not seem at all delighted to encounter this old friend. "You had better come in."

"But, Peterkin!" Adorée swept into the vicarage. "You may trust these people; they are my friends. I vow, they would be highly fascinated by your——"

"Never mind! I'll perform the ceremony." The vicar's cheeks were pink. His gaze then fell upon Miss Lennox who, looking her worst, was leaning langorously on the viscount's arm. It was not surprising that the vicar assumed he viewed a shocking prospective mesalliance, since Shannon had taken time to change his clothing, and Miss Lennox had not. "My lord, if I might have a word with you?"

Shannon was feeling a trifle benumbed, now that the long-awaited event loomed so near. He gave Miss Lennox over into Adorée's tender keeping, and let the vicar lead him aside. "My lord," murmured the vicar, in confidential tones, "I fear you are about to make a grave mistake. A gentleman of your station in life doesn't need to *marry* such a tatterdemalion wench." He chuckled. Lord Roxbury looked blank. "Man to man, I tell you it's not necessary! Though I may be a man of the cloth, my lord, I also possess a fair knowledge of the world, and I tell you it won't *do*. But I see how it is; the wench is holding out for a ceremony. Well, for a small fee I can provide for you a ceremony that will be a great deal less binding than marriage—in fact, not binding in the least!"

Unfortunately, as the vicar's image of himself as a gentleman of the world had grown, so had his tone increased. As a result his words had been heard by all—save Percy and Cristin, who were lost in one another, and Jynx who, leaning against Lord Erland, had once more fallen asleep. Lord Roxbury, so incensed by this vulgar proposition as to very nearly suffer a fatal seizure, opened his mouth to utter a scathing retort. By Lady Bliss, he was forestalled.

"Illegal ceremonies!" she shrieked. "Peterkin, you wouldn't! You couldn't! You *didn't!*"

"Now, now, Adorée!" The vicar's brow was beaded with sweat. "It wasn't that way at all. On my word, it wasn't! Courtenay never knew! I needed the money, you see."

Lady Bliss stomped her pretty little foot, and her gray eyes flashed. "If it wasn't just like Courtenay to hire a cut-rate minister! Peterson, if you tell me my marriage was invalid, I think I shall scream."

"Don't do that!" protested the vicar, who now was pale. "My wife, you know! We wouldn't want her to know about this—and I repented, truly I did, and I never did it again. Beside, what difference does it make, since no one ever knew?"

"It makes a very great deal of difference to *me!*" wailed Adorée. "I may be misguided, but I am not wicked, and now you tell me that I really am a soiled dove and that I should not *mind!*" She sniffled. "And here I am surrounded by love-birds, and they shall all be respectable, while *I* am placed beyond the pale. Oh, it is all so terrible! For married women can do all sorts of things that unmarried women cannot!"

This outburst had roused Cristin and Percy from their mutually esteemed trance. Bewildered, they stared. Lord Roxbury also stared, though an acute observer might have noted a certain tendency of his lips to twitch. The curate, too, goggled, and looked very much as if he wished to sink through the floor. Only Miss Lennox slept on, and from time to time gave vent to a gentle snore.

As the focus of attention, Lady Bliss was magnificent. In her clinging violet gown, with the earl's opera cloak flung about her shoulders and trailing on the floor, her pretty cheeks flushed and her gray eyes bright with tears, she made a breathtaking tragedy queen. "I didn't think much of Courtenay," she sobbed, "but at least I had been married, and I have always thought every woman should be married at least once, even if she didn't like it very much! Otherwise, how is she to *know?*"

"Never mind, my—er, love!" hastily interposed the earl. "If that is what you wish, then married you will be. And I promise you will like it very well indeed!"

Adorée looked very much as if she wished to swoon. Since Dominic's arms were currently filled with Miss Lennox, and since no other arms would do, she refrained. "Nicky! What *can* you be thinking of?"

254

"Tansy!" The earl smiled.

"By Jove!" uttered Percy. "And I thought you were the highest of sticklers, Nicky! Dashed if you aren't in a reckless humor—or three parts disguised!"

"*I*," Cristin interrupted sternly, "think it's a very good idea. Now we will all be respectable!"

Percy could not fail to appreciate this eminently logical point of view. For the haste with which he'd spoken, he apologized handsomely. "Dashed if Jynx didn't bring it all about! Fixed up right as a trivet! You know, Cristin, she's a very good sort of girl!"

Lord Erland paid no attention to his cousin's queer notion that he was incapable of managing his own *affaires de coeur*. Steadily, he regarded Adorée. "It is not," she said faintly, "*necessary* that you should marry me."

"If it was," retorted the pragmatic earl, "I wouldn't!"

"Oh!" Lady Bliss's scruples, having previously been bludgeoned to death, did not rise to plague her now. "In that case, Nicky, you may call me anything you please!"

"Generous!" uttered the viscount, in scathing tones. "*Now* may we get on with the business at hand?"

Lord Erland looked down at Miss Lennox, snoozing quite contentedly in his arms. "Certainly! It is very bad of us to interfere with your wedding night. First, however, I think you might wake your bride."

At last, Lord Roxbury and Miss Lennox were wed. Their union was witnessed by Lord Erland and Lady Bliss, Lord Peverell and Miss Cristin Ashley. It was a moving ceremony, all agreed, even though the vicar was so nervous that he dropped his prayer book several times. Miss Lennox made a lovely bride, in spite of the black stuff gown, and the fact that she yawned throughout the ceremony. Afterwards, the party adjourned to a nearby inn, named most appropriately The Angel with One Wing, and soothed the landlord's suspicions regarding the circumstance that of them all only Lord Roxbury had any luggage, and finally—if not entirely properly—sought their beds.

Life settled down to a much more peaceful pattern then. Eulalia Wimple continued to reside with Sir Malcolm Lennox, who discovered he could not be comfortable without her nagging him; Innis Ashley was occasionally heard of, indeed came to be of considerable value to England, since his further follies were confined to France. Cristin proved so good a manager that her mama-in-law became quite reconciled to her, though not to Lord Erland, who for the remainder of her long life she blamed for everything.

Adorée became a noted political hostess, and so exemplary a wife that her past indiscretions would have been forgotten save for her tendency to enlarge upon them at whim. The Viscount and Viscountess Roxbury devoted themselves to a serenely placid existence and the presentation to the world of a large number of charmingly lethargic offspring. And when the viscountess was stricken by an intermittent yearning for excitement—directly attributable, she claimed, to her adventures with the Ashleys—she arranged a reunion of Lady Bliss and company, and invited a certain Bow Street Runner to tea.